See It Through

Merie Vision Publishing
Merievisionpublishing@gmail.com

Copyright © 2024 by David "The Duke" Allen &
Marcellus "Bishop" Allen
Royal Bloodline Publishing

ISBN(paperback): 978-1-961213-35-7

Library of Congress control number on record

Formatting, Editing, and Design by
Merie Vision Publishing, LLC

Editing by Gloria Palmer
Printed in the United States of America

Royal Bloodline

The Duke & Bishop Story Part 1

David "The Duke" Allen

Marcellus "Bishop" Allen

From The Duke:

This book is dedicated to my angel whom I lost too quickly, Terrye Ann Allen. I love you, baby. You are the inspiration behind everything I do. Watch what your son does next!!!

To my children Yazminah, Neefah, Nasheed, and Shiquill I love every one of you to the core of me. This book is the start of something great to come. Also, to my grandchildren, Papa loves ya'll to death. I want to also send thanks out to both of the mothers of my children Shavonne and Kameelah, thank you for the blessings of these children I call my own.

Also, thanks to the only man who showed me how to be the man that I am today...my big brother, Bishop. You're the best, bro. To my Nieces and Nephews, ya'll are the next generation. Uncle loves every last one of you. Hands down!

I would like to also send thanks out to Ms. Krystal Carter and MeMe because there have been a lot of days when the chips were down. Thank you for giving me the strength to pick 'em up. Ms. Flo Jenkins and her family as well. The love and support from both parties have made my days in prison so much better. Again, thank you for everything.

Then there's my family...my Aunt Brenda who I love with all my heart. Her family means the world to me. RIP GR, LEE, STINK, and so many others I've lost over the years of being away. My love to their children and those who love and have loved them. A big shout-out goes to my Avon and Goldsmith family because without ya'll, I couldn't be the best of myself.

Tutt, Reek, Budda, Little Boob, Chic, Wali.

To my guys in Yonkers, Bloody, Mac, and my guy Nut.

To my West VA guys, RA, and family.

My Detroit family, SC, NC (Hell Boy), VA, Minnesota family (Sarrah Red).

The entire New Jersey family. OB, Boob (Johnsons).

The Richardsons, Sanders, Blaklies, K-Mack, RaBoo, Bubba Hass, Pay Lay, Mass, Omar, and a host of others.

Shout out to Avalanche, BBU Global.com, Killa Reek, and the entire Beven family.

I

Hell Boy, the realist white GD I know and have had the honor to meet. Also, my guys Reckless from the BX, Santanna-BX, Platinum-BX, JUG-SC, Saweddoff-Newark, Weezy LI-Cash-BX, LowLow-PA, D Boy, Cali-Finesse 2 times-NC, Killa-SI, Chi Chi-Kanas City, D-Rilla-Rochester-NY, J-bird-Newark, and Travis Rattray-Newark

To my West Coast family, too.

To my Attorney, John McMahon, my private investigator, and second mother, Ms. Maria Palumbo.

To everyone I met throughout my struggles being incarcerated, thank you from the bottom of my heart. Ya'll support means the world to me, and for those of you I haven't mentioned, I gotchu in the next book.

Oh yeah, to my Denver homeboy, Little Maine, and KB Much love niggas. As well as others that held me down. Good looking to my FL guys...I'm on my way. Hold a spot at the table for me.

Much love to my Homeboy Mat. Thank you for your support, my guy. Big thanks go out to my creator...GOD, who let me know every day that I am destined for greatness... Still, I Rise!...#FreeTheDuke!

Oh yeah, a special thanks go out to the haters because without ya'll my motivation and creativity wouldn't be shit! I owe all my success to ya'll. So keep up with the hate. I will not LOSE! Real talk.

I want to thank everybody who started with me from the beginning to the bitter end, and still going. For those of you who fell short...Eat a DICK! This is the year of THE DUKE!

Letter From Bishop:

First, I love to thank Allah for the blessing of Terrye Allen and her deliverance of two dynamic black men. Allowing Duke to start something that has always been trapped in my mind—writing— and for allowing me to finish our first project. I'd like to thank our supporters for the roles you've all played in assisting us complete this first wave of a new career.

To the real mothers of my children and all my children, thank you for being exactly who you are. Kisha Steele for all the connections that led to this. Ms. Gloria Palmer for being my first editor/mom. I loved our late-night talks about real life. Mrs. CiCi Merie, for taking such a load off my shoulders... wooo-weeee...Thank you.

Special shoutout to my younger and older brothers, MAN's LAW homies IYKYK, my NoirKSS Family, my Regulators, 793G's. To my people in the political game, you already know. All my family and friends who held me down out of Jersey. Hey Barbara James, aka BJ, you once asked me, "How do you balance everything?" Well, now you know. It's because of great people like you. To whomever I may have forgotten, blame my mind not my heart. I thank you all.

I can't explain how much of a journey this has been when transitioning to your true purpose, but it is worth it in the end. ALHAMDULILLAH!!!

OH YEA...STAY TUNED.

Chapter One:
Catching Up To God Quicker

"Sharelle, please call Bishop," the weakening voice of the young man said.

The woman had become severely frantic with no idea what to do first. Should she call Bishop, as requested, or dial 9-1-1 for help? She was hesitant, but quickly decided to go with her first instinct and dialed 9-1-1. It made more sense, because the district she would reach was only a small distance away. Sirens were heard wailing in the distance, heading in their direction.

"Duke! Duke!" the crackling voice cried out.

"Baby, hold on, please! Don't die on me! Please, baby, don't die!"

These were the words that crawled from her tongue as she cried and held on tightly to her man for dear life.

"Hold on, baby. Help is on the way!" she continued, trying not to squeeze the life out of Duke herself.

The sound of her voice gave Duke comfort. Despite what they were going through, at that moment he knew it was her voice that kept him clinging to life. His shirt was red and there was blood everywhere. Duke felt a little too relaxed as he started fading in and out of consciousness, but he was trying very hard to honor her wishes and hold on. He had shit to do in life. He had a great sense of recollection and was fully aware of what had just happened to him. He knew Sharelle had just saved his life; an incomparable gesture that was going to keep them bonded for the rest of their lives if he made it. He silently sent a prayer to the Creator to spare him.

As help arrived, Duke lay still in a pool of his own blood. He was still trying to hold onto his conscious mind, wondering if he was to become the next statistic, the next chalk line, then the next rider to the city morgue. Flashes of some white man cutting him open to find the cause of death went through his mind. The donor sticker on his identification made him wonder who would get his heart, his kidneys, or any part of his remains.

"Come on, Duke, you're stronger than this," he said silently to himself.

He was hearing the cries of his woman and thought he felt one of her tears land on his chin. The world was starting to go black. Now he heard the whisper of the crowd—nosy bystanders just getting an eyeful so they would have something to talk about. Of all the things going on, he heard 2Pac playing in the background:

Now, can your mind picture a thug nigga drinkin' hard liquor? This ghetto life has got me catching up to God quicker!

That was his dude, Pac was the man, but unfortunately for him, Shakur's gritty lyrics were the last words Duke comprehended before he completely passed out.

The ambulance finally arrived after what seemed like an eternity of waiting, and the EMT crew moved fast, sprinting into action. They ripped Duke out of his truck and attempted to revive him, to no avail. His woman watched while the head EMT placed the EKG pads on his chest.

"GO!" he yelled.

"I need more power! We're losing him!" he yelled as he begged God to spare the life of the complete stranger he was working on.

Duke had slipped into a coma. Sharelle began to talk to the medics after getting in the back of the ambulance. They continued to work on Duke, putting an IV in his arm to make sure he didn't get dehydrated. The whole crew was fighting desperately to maintain his life as they raced to the hospital. He had lost an insurmountable amount of blood. The medics were giving their best efforts to keep Duke alive, knowing a blood transfusion was needed as quickly as possible. Sharelle was still in tears, but she commended the medics for doing an excellent job.

"If we get him there in time, ma'am, he might be okay," the man who was working the EKG said to her.

If she had nothing else, she had something her mother had always taught her: to have more faith than a mustard seed. Sharelle thanked the man through her sobs. The mobile hospital pulled into the Emergency lot roundabout, rushing Duke's gurney through the doors. The medics were relaying to the ER doctor on duty Duke's stats, and he rushed Duke ahead of the waiting crowd to an operating room. Sharelle had to wait in a nearby visiting room.

The doctors performed multiple surgeries and a few random tests to make sure there was no extensive damage to his body. The blood transfusion and a ton of stitches had done the trick. Duke was still drowsy from the morphine, but he understood the words coming out of the doctors' mouths. After all the procedures were completed, they moved Duke into his own room and explained he would need to be monitored for the next 48 hours.

As he lay there in his own world, not aware of what was going on around him, Duke's mind started reflecting on how his life had unfolded before this unfortunate day.

_____

Duke Reflects On His Life...

"Come on, boys. Time to get up and get ready for school."

"I don't feel good, Mommy," the youngest of the two boys murmured.

"Duke, I don't wanna hear it today. It's the same with you every morning. Not today! I have to get ready for work. Get up!"

"Okay, Mom. I'm getting up."

Duke rose with a mad look on his face. He turned his attention to this older brother and asked, "What you lookin' at?"

"You, lil' nigga! Yo, it's always the same shit with you," Bishop finished.

"So what? I hate school! I'd rather run the streets than go to school!" Duke spat back.

"Lil nigga, you sound stupid. Get ya ass up like Mommy said and get ready for school!" Bishop demanded, playing the big brother role.

Duke, not able to do much, mumbled under his breath, "I'm not a lil' nigga," still doing what he had been told to do by his big brother: getting his ass up and ready for school.

Thoughts of shouts and rough times growing up in the mean streets of Newark, New Jersey, filled Duke's head as he lay in the hospital bed in Pennsylvania in a deep coma.

At the age of fourteen, Duke was coming of age, and many felt he was before his time—a kid who was destined to step off the porch and become a man, without having the opportunity to enjoy his childhood. Bishop, on the other hand, wasn't eager to embrace street life. However, with Duke as his little brother, he really didn't stand a chance, especially since the hood was all they knew and had seen growing up.

Their hood, like many hoods in their city, was infested and governed by gangs, drugs, poverty, rundown, dilapidated homes, disease-riddled people, and no-good police. They lived in a predominately African American community that suffered from gentrification. They stayed with the high hopes that one day things would change for the better. For now, it was what it was!

"Do y'all have all y'all's stuff together before y'all leave this house?" Ms. Evans asked her two sons.

"Yes, Momma, we have everything," Bishop replied.

"I know you have everything, baby. I was actually talking to Duke. Do you have everything, boy?"

"Yes Mom, I got everything," Duke said with a little force.

"Don't get smart, boy!" their mother replied with a little more force than Duke, making her tone count for something.

The boys, ready for school, rushed to get out of the building where they lived. They left the house with their mom but went in the opposite direction. She had to catch a bus, but the boys were only a few blocks away from school. Before parting ways with their mother, the boys gave her a big hug and kiss and said their goodbyes.

"Be good in school, boys," she said before turning and walking toward Clinton Avenue to catch her bus.

"Okay, we will, Mom," they replied as they started their journey toward Avon Avenue.

As the boys walked to school, the two engaged in a little small talk and did a little horseplaying.

"I just saved your life," Bishop said, pulling Duke from in front of a moving car.

"Stop playing before I tell Mommy on you," Duke responded.

"Fuck you!"

"Oooooo, I'm telling! You cussing at me," Duke said, running off.

Bishop started chasing behind Duke, trying to catch up with his fast-paced trot.

The two playing around went through the morning and well into after school.

"How was school?" Bishop asked, showing concern for his little brother's education, not to mention his day.

"It was cool, same shit different day; nothing new, as usual."

They talked as they made their way home, taking the shortcuts they were familiar with.

"Tag, you're it," Duke yelled, hitting Bishop as he took off running for the second time.

"I'ma get you, lil' nigga," Bishop replied as he gave chase to his little brother, this time catching up with him faster than he had that morning.

They started play fighting on the side of a row house, which was considered low-income housing. While the two of them played and joked around, Bishop stumbled over a gun lying in the dirt alongside a bunch of trash. What he wasn't ready for was what he saw next. There was a dead body lying right there as well, a dead man who looked like he'd been dead for some days before they found him.

Instead of getting scared, the two looked at the body for a second before Bishop picked up the gun. When they heard police sirens approaching in the distance, they took off running home. Although the police sirens they heard weren't coming for them or in their direction, the boys took no chances, getting the fuck out of there and making it home safely. Both of them were out of breath and breathing hard when reality set in-- they had just seen a dead body and found a gun. Making their way into the hallway of their building, they felt safe.

"Ooohhh shit! You saw that shit, bro?" Bishop asked, waving the gun in the air around the hallway, aiming it in different directions, and looking at it in amazement.

"Yeah, bruh. We can't tell Mommy or Dad what we found today," Duke said with excitement.

"Okay, okay. Calm down. When we get in the house, I'ma go straight to our room and hide the gun in the closet, and I want you to walk into the kitchen and distract Mommy so she doesn't peep shit out," Bishop said, laying down the plan.

Duke was ready to follow his instructions. "Okay, I gotchu, bro."

When the two entered the apartment, everything went exactly as Bishop had planned. After putting up the gun, Bishop went into the kitchen to join Duke and their mother.

"How was school, baby?" she asked Bishop, smiling and wiping her hands on her cooking apron.

"It was good, Ma. I learned a little algebra today."

"How did you like it?"

"It was a little complicated, but I'm going to get it. I always do."

"Stick with it, baby," she said, kissing him on the side of his face.

"One thing in life is you have to know math to know how to count money, which I know in my heart you're going to be something special when you get older."

"Ma, why do you always say that to me?"

"Because I expect great things from my boys, especially since you are the oldest of the two. Plus, if you don't learn math, you won't be able to count all the money I know you will one day possess. Nor will you know how to invest your money, especially since we live in a society where everyone is trying to get over. Do you understand me, Son?"

"Yes Mom, I understand."

Duke, who was listening to their conversation, felt left out.

"What about me, Mommy? I'm going to be counting a lot of money too. I want a lot of money too," Duke said, not wanting to be left out because he was young.

"Boy, shut ya mouth. The only money you'll be counting is the money I give you. Now get out the cake, boy, with your greedy self! Wait until dinner before you start eating junk food. You're going to eat everything before your father gets home from work, and he will be home soon."

"Shoot, I'm going to have my own money too!" Duke replied, licking the icing off his fingers from the cake knife.

"Whatever, boy! Take out the garbage. Can I count on you to do that?"

Frowning his face up, Duke did what his mother demanded of him. It wasn't but minutes after taking out the garbage and Duke walking back into their apartment that he heard their father enter the front door.

"Daddy!" Duke said and ran to give him a big hug.

"What's up, Pop?" Bishop added with a, "not-so-happy-to-see-you," look on his face.

His father had the, "life-is-so-fucking-hard," look on his face. Work was exhausting, but he had to provide for his family. It made him want to tell his boys, "That's why you two had better make all the right decisions." He would always make sure they understood that the wrong choice could cost them a lifetime of headaches. Shit was rough for their father, and he showed it every chance he got. The boys took the bags their father was carrying when he came in, then went to wash their hands to get ready for dinner.

"Hey, Dear."

"What's good, Baby?" their mother replied, walking into her man's arms. They embraced and sat down as a family to eat dinner.

After they were done eating, their father pulled out from his pocket his favorite drink, Night Train, which was cheap liquor. He started drinking a little earlier than normal this evening. He knew his wife hated his drinking, and the last time he'd drank during dinner, he'd made everything awkward at the dinner table. She hadn't liked it one bit, and an exchange of words had gone back and forth between the adults.

"Can you at least wait until the boys are away from the table before you start drinking?" she tried to ask in a polite manner.

"It shouldn't matter. It isn't like they don't already know their old man drinks. If you had to work as hard as I do, you would be tipping a bottle too," he replied, holding up the bottle to see how much was left in it.

"I'm just saying. You know how you get when you drink, and they don't need to hear us arguing."

"Aye, yo! Why are you always instigating shit between us? Starting fights and shit, like I don't deserve to relax?"

"See, this is what I be talking about. Here we go again," said their mother with wrinkled lines building on her forehead.

"Boys, go to your room!" their father demanded as he got up from the kitchen table and slammed down his bottle.

Their father stepped outside the apartment to sit on his stoop and finish a smoke before going back in. This was always the time when the devil's poison got the best of him and things got ugly. He had been out there for about thirty minutes, and he figured it was time to head back in and show her who the man of the house was.

When he started shouting, their mother wasn't just going to sit there without expressing herself.

"Shut the fuck up, bitch!" he blurted out and started marching toward her.

"Who the fuck you calling a bitch?!" she exclaimed, grabbing the knife closest to her.

Furious at his choice of words, she launched at him. Their father wasn't as athletic as he once was, but he was still quick enough to dodge the sharp knife she was looking to gut him with, quick enough to snatch it with his bare hands. When he saw the blood squirt from his palm, he lost it and unleashed vicious blows to her face, like she was a stranger on the streets.

After about the sixth blow, she collapsed to the floor. Her eyes had closed, there was a blood trickle from her nose, and she was unconscious. Their father grabbed a cold towel and wiped her face down, bringing her back to consciousness. They smiled at each other like that shit was normal. When he'd finally regained his own composure, he kneeled and scooped her up off the floor, carrying her into their bedroom for makeup sex.

The entire time this debacle was taking place, the boys were in their room listening, in fear that, one day, they were going to kill each other. Duke dove into his bed, burying himself under the covers, terrified, tears streaming down his face from a pain he so desperately wanted to leave him alone.

As these memories raced through Duke's mind back at the hospital, Duke's reality was he was still in a coma. Sharelle noticed a tear roll out of his eye. The heart monitor was now beeping rapidly.

BEEP-BEEP-BEEP...

Sharelle trembled at the thought of something being wrong. She hollered for the nurse with a tenacious urgency for her to hurry up. The nurse entered the room and commenced her series of checks, scanning monitors, then returning to Duke's weakening body.

The nurse was puzzled at the lack of scientific explanation for what had just occurred. Simultaneously, the monitor returned to its regular pace.

BEEP-BEEP-BEEP...

The nurse and Sharelle breathed a sigh of relief as Duke returned to his previous experiences that were flashing in his mind like a movie.

He recalled waking up the next morning after the violent night, his young mind unable to fully grasp the emotions he was feeling about it. These episodes were nothing new for him and his brother to witness. Their father frequently came home from work and fed the demons inside him. The liquor the demons craved called for a thirst quencher. When Bishop woke up and they got ready for school, Duke recited the events that had transpired the night before. Bishop hung onto every word his little brother spoke with anger and disgust as they walked to school.

"Why didn't you wake me up so I could help our mother?!" Bishop shouted at his younger brother.

"I don't know. Seems like you should've known how the shit was going to go," Duke responded timidly with his head down.

"I thought they were gonna stop arguing," Bishop replied, still worried.

"You know he never stops, especially when he's drunk and high. Remember when he wrapped that belt buckle around his hand and punched me in the head?" he asked, reminding Duke of what his father's wrath was capable of by showing him the scar he'd left on his head.

"Yeah, that's why I ain't wake you up, Bishop. I knew you would try to help Mommy. You know you ain't got no wins with him. I was just scared, man. He might have killed you this time," Duke replied.

"That's what's up. I'm going to call home and check on Mommy."

They stopped at the first phone booth they saw. Bishop dialed the number and it began to ring.

"Hello? Mommy?"

"Yes, baby, it's me. Why aren't y'all in school?" she asked, puzzled.

"We're almost there. I just wanted to check on you. I fell asleep last night, but Duke just told me what happened."

"I hate that you and your brother had to hear that last night. The things that go on between me and your father ain't right, but I'm okay, thank God. So please, son, I don't want or need the two of you worrying. Your father just had a bad day at work, that's all."

"He's always having a bad day at work," Bishop expressed with sarcasm.

"I know, baby. Everything is going to get better. I love you boys."

"And we love you more."

"I'll see you guys after school. You and your brother be safe and get to school."

"Okay, Ma," he responded and hung up the phone.

Bishop focused his attention back on Duke and said, "She's gonna always make excuses for Dad. It ain't right!"

"I know," Duke replied.

"C'mon; the bell just rang. We gotta get to class."

Bishop directed Duke to go ahead so they could get their lesson on. Duke always tried to listen to Bishop. He left Bishop behind to speak with a few of their friends, Gooch and Malik.

As Duke was sitting motionless in the classroom, reflecting on what had happened to his mom the previous night in his coma, Sharelle sat by his bedside in the real world watching in agony. She was watching over him to make sure he made it out of his current situation, contemplating how and when she felt would be the right time to inform Bishop that his little brother had been shot up! She knew those were the words no big brother wanted to hear. She knew right from wrong, and it would be wrong to make Bishop wait or to hear it in the streets. So, Sharelle decided the time was now, but was terrified to do so, not knowing what his reaction would be.

"Here goes," she said silently to herself, nervous as hell.

She dialed Bishop's cell and rang until it went to voicemail. She was about to dial him right back, but her phone vibrated in her hand before she could get the redial function to work. Looking at the caller display, she saw it was Bishop returning her call.

"Hey, Sharelle; what's cracking?" he said, sounding cheery. She hated to kill his mood.

"It's all bad," she replied, pausing.

When her brain caught up to her heart rate, she quickly told him everything. Sharelle could hear that Bishop was highly upset. It took a few minutes, but he seemed to have calmed down a little, and they actually got through the entire conversation.

"What were these fools driving?" Bishop asked.

"Looked like a Cadillac Escalade," Sharelle replied, trying to get the make right, "but I'm really not quite sure since it happened so damn fast. They had on black ski masks, so I couldn't tell who they were," she continued, wiping the tears from her eyes.

Duke had always pressed her about not slipping and being aware of her surroundings. She felt like she had failed him.

"You mentioned something about him chopping it up with a couple of dudes from the bar. Did they resemble them? I know you said they were masked, but think about height and weight, and maybe what they were wearing?"

"I couldn't really tell because it all happened so fast, like I said, Bishop, and I was scared for my own life. Plus, I've never been involved in anything like this before. I'm sorry, Bishop; I'm really, truly sorry."

She started crying, feeling like she had failed her guy and his brother. She began hurting even worse because she could not provide Bishop with the information he needed when asking certain questions. Bishop noticed how emotional Sharelle was becoming, so he decided to abruptly end their call. It wasn't her fault, and he did not want to make her feel any more guilty than she was feeling already.

"Okay, baby girl. We'll talk again soon. You've told me enough. I'm on my way there."

"Okay. Call me when you get here."

The phone call was disconnected without any further word.

Bishop jumped in his Camaro, heading straight to the highway, rushing to see his brother. He weaved between the fast-paced traffic, trying to hurry. His mind was racing like the Camaro's engine, trying to figure out who in the world would want to kill his little brother. Honestly speaking, he knew he had a long ass list of suspects to sift through, especially since Duke had stayed in so much shit when he was trapped behind those steel curtains of the State Penitentiary. But who would want him dead in Pennsylvania?

Bishop was feeling highly enraged at the moment. He knew he was now about to set out on a rampage to find out who was responsible for Duke being in a hospital fighting for his life. Bishop reached for his cellphone and spoke clearly into it, "Call Boss Hogg," and the smartphone automatically dialed Hogg's number. He figured if anyone knew anything, it would be Boss Hogg, and if he didn't know, he would be sure to find out, especially considering the fact that this was his city. Within minutes of speaking to Boss Hogg and informing him of what had happened to his brother, Bishop was at the hospital checking on Duke.

Duke was still in the ICU, and Sharelle was right there by his side. He hugged her and told her everything was going to be all right real soon. While he sat there patiently hoping for the best possible outcome for his little brother's survival, he watched intently as Duke remained in a comatose state. A tear wet the wells of Bishop's eyes as he wondered what Duke was thinking about.

Chapter Two:
Hannibal Lector

Bishop returned to school.

"What took you so long to get out of school?" he asked Duke.

"I was talking to my teacher about a few things concerning my work—if you must know."

"Yeah, I'm your big brother. I wanna know everything when it comes to you or about you, smart mouth. With that being said, let's stop at the store on our way home."

"Okay," Duke replied.

The two stopped at the local store and loaded up on all types of snacks and goodies, sodas, and sandwiches. Bishop even bought a few girls he knew something to eat—fries, cakes, etc. Duke noticed the large amount of money Bishop was spending and got curious, questioning him about the money as they walked home.

"Thank you for the stuff, bro. I can barely carry it all. And I like how you looked out for them girls too. Where did you get all that money from?"

"None of your business. You talk too damn much."

Duke sucked his teeth without really responding, then asked Bishop, "Why do you always keep secrets from me? Maybe I can help you sometimes, you know."

"Listen, I don't need or want you gettin' hurt behind anything I do out here in these trenches. Nor do I need you tellin' Mommy anything about me either... Momma's Boy." he replied seriously.

"I wouldn't tell Mommy anything, especially nothing like where you get ya money from. And I'm not a momma's boy either!"

"Whatever, lil' nigga."

"Stop calling me that. I'm not a lil' nigga!"

"Shut up and come on," Bishop responded.

As the brothers approached their block, getting closer to their building, a red sedan creeps as it busts the corner; then it hits top speed and speeds past them quickly. As it passed by them, someone in the car noticed the brothers with a handful of stuff, signaled, and gestured. It looked to Bishop like they were telling the driver to back up. The car's reverse lights started shining before it revved in reverse, backing up to where the boys were. Being from where they were from, this only meant one thing: stick-up time!

Duke froze as he carefully surveyed the car's momentum. He turned and asked Bishop, "Why is this car backing up?"

The car grew in size as it got closer and the passengers became clear to the boys. There were three gruff-looking guys riding inside. The vehicle finally came to a screeching halt as Bishop and Duke stood on the sidewalk with their hearts racing. Bishop noticed the back door fling open. He gripped his little brother by the shoulder and pulled him closer to his side.

"Get over here!" Bishop demanded of his brother. "Watch out!" he yelled as he whipped out the big .44 caliber Bulldog he had tucked on his hip.

He aimed the vehicle, firing two shots in the direction of the four-door sedan.

BLAM! BLAM!

One shot hit the tree on the other side of the street and the other slug burned a hole through the trunk of the car, exiting through the opposite side of the car. He saw the men inside duck in their seats, their adrenaline pumping from the gunfire as they sped off with the back door still open. The sound of screeching tires rang through the streets, and all that remained was the foul stench of burning rubber. Seeing the sedan was out of sight, the brothers took off running. They hightailed it straight home, heading to the back of their building to discuss what had just transpired, as well as bending over to catch their breath.

"Calm down, bro," Bishop blurted out, seeing how Duke was acting.

"I'm calm. I told you I ain't no lil' nigga," Duke replied, wanting to show Bishop he had no fear in his heart.

"Damn, you see how that car left us alone once the loudness of this heater went live? Once I started busting at them assholes, they knew I meant business. I bet their punk asses never expected their lick to go bad."

"What kind of gun is that?" Duke curiously asked.

"Don't worry about the small things," Bishop replied, feeling his waist for the warm gun. "That was crazy! Bro, that's all people in the hood respect and understand."

"What do you mean?" Duke asked.

"Whoever possesses the biggest gun or the most money is in power. All that type shit runs these streets!" Bishop reiterated, holding the gun into the air as if he'd just won a championship trophy. "Damn, Duke, this is power right here in the palm of my hand!"

"Let me see it." Duke wanted to get a sniff of the power for himself.

"They know now when they see us not to fuck with us."

"Here, lil' nigga, and don't squeeze the trigger," Bishop instructed his brother, still addressing him as lil' nigga. He felt like a father figure sometimes when it came to Duke. It should have been their pops teaching both of them about shit like this, instead of him handing Duke his first taste of power.

"It's still hot, so be careful."

Duke grabbed hold of the gun with excitement and amazement plastered all over his small face. He had no idea what was happening to him. It was like putting life in a person's hands who had no idea what to do with it next. As he held onto the gun for a few seconds, he started pointing it toward Bishop, who then snatched it away from his little brother's grip.

"Give it to me! This ain't a fuckin' toy," he told Duke as he replaced his heat back into his waistline.

"My bad, bro. I got too excited."

Their moment was cut short because their mother could hear her boys talking in the backyard and called to them. "Bishop, is that you and Duke down there?"

"Yes, Mom, it's us," Bishop responded.

"Come upstairs and do your homework."

"Okay; here we come."

Bishop removed the heat again, giving Duke a simple direction. "Take the gun and put it in your bag. I'ma go in the house first, then give you the cue to go to the room after I see where Mommy is. Okay?"

"Okay; I got this," Duke replied, overconfident.

Bishop entered the house first, as they had just discussed. He did what he'd said he would do, hearing his mother say, "There're snacks on the table. Y'all can have some after you finish your homework, and not a moment sooner."

Even though they had already had snacks on their walk home, Bishop and Duke responded at the same time, "Okay, Mom."

Bishop then signaled for Duke to go into their room, since their mother was in her bedroom getting dressed. When she emerged, she told the boys their father would be home early today.

"I have a doctor's appointment this evening and I will see the both of you when I get back home," she continued, rushing out and slamming the door behind her.

Duke watched his mother walk down the street and away from their building from the window.

"That was a close call," Bishop said as he sighed with relief.

"Good thing she was leaving out as we were coming in," Duke said as he went to put the gun up in their closet.

"Let's go do our homework before she comes back home and gets mad at us."

Duke, making it a defiant moment for them both, said, "Let me see the gun again first or I ain't doing my homework," as he walked back toward the closet.

Bishop, not liking the tone of his little brother's voice, snatched him up aggressively and walked him to the table with his book bag.

"Listen! Forget the gun and focus on your schoolwork."

"C'mon, Bish, I just want to hear that thundering sound again," Duke replied as if nothing was wrong with his request.

Realizing there weren't going to be any more loud noises being made that evening, the brothers made their way to the table to do their homework. About an hour later, it was behind them and their father had come home. They gave each other a weird look as they heard the front door open and close. Their father came in and walked straight toward his bedroom, noticing the boys were at the kitchen table doing homework and realizing his wife was nowhere in sight.

"Where's your mother? She knew I was coming home early today," he stated in an evil tone.

"She went to a doctor's appointment," Bishop replied, not liking the tone of his father's voice.

"She left about an hour ago," Duke added.

His eyes seemed to get instantly bloodshot red as the boys saw his anger growing.

"Is that what she told you, boys? That bitch didn't go to a fuckin' doctor's appointment! She's probably somewhere being a fuckin' hoe!" he snapped in a jealous rage.

Bishop was feeling some type of way about his father accusing their mother of being a liar and a whore.

"That isn't what she's doing. She went to see her doctor like she said she was going to do."

Recognizing how Bishop was defending his mother's honor, their father directed his anger at his older son.

"What the fuck you call yourself doing, taking up for her? Did she tell you to say that bullshit to me?"

The two went back and forth as Duke sat quietly at the table. Their father was talking with so much anger that the fear of what might happen next kicked into play. The tone of his voice said it all. Duke quietly interjected, hoping to help ease the tension, "Nooooo, Dad!"

Their father was so enraged, it was as if he did not hear anything the boys were trying to tell him. His mind was already made up about what his wife was doing. He felt he knew her patterns better than either kid.

"Shut the fuck up! Your mother isn't to be trusted! She's out there giving up my pussy to someone!" he said as he turned and walked toward Bishop, balling up his fist. Duke knew he was ready to plant it upon Bishop's face with lethal force.

"Keeping it real, that's how you got here. You ain't my fuckin' son you fuckin' bastard!"

In a split second, he smashed Bishop's face with such force that his head went straight into the wall, knocking him completely out cold instantly.

Duke ran to his brother, who lay there out cold, and screamed, "Dad, stop it! Stop this crazy shit! Leave my brother alone!"

It was the first time Duke had cursed in front of either of his parents. Their father stormed off in the direction of his bedroom. He looked back over his shoulder before he entered his room, then slammed the door behind him.

The boys were in the kitchen, dealing with the aftermath of their father's wrath. Duke helped his brother to his feet and guided him to their bedroom. He was trembling with fear as tears poured down both sides of his face. Duke made a mad dash to the bathroom to get a towel out of the cabinet and soaked it with cold water. He rushed back out of the bathroom, without fully turning the faucet off. He looked with sad eyes as he pressed the cold, wet towel against the face of his only brother. Tears were still falling from his eyes as the bathroom faucet dripped.

That part of his memory caused his body to quiver, even in his unconscious state. Bishop caught the movement out of the corner of his eye as if it were part of some strange choreography. Bishop's phone started ringing, and he looked at the caller display, knowing the number was Boss Hogg's cell.

"Hello. What's good, famo?" Bishop greeted him like he always did.

"Oh, I'll tell you what the fuck is up. I have some news for you."

"I'm at the hospital with my brother. Come through so we can holla," Bishop replied, knowing cellphones were never safe to speak on.

"I'm on my way," Boss Hogg replied. The call was quickly disconnected.

Bishop felt, that if progress was going to be made in locating those responsible for his brother's near-death experience, Boss Hogg was that dude; he had major connections who knew everything. What he had not counted on was the progress of the detective, Detective Burcheck, who ultimately was making rapid progress of his own on the investigation of the brothers. Detective Burcheck had been gathering evidence pertaining to the brothers ever since the time he'd followed Bishop to Pennsylvania while doing surveillance. Bishop had been none the wiser; he'd had no idea he was being followed or even investigated for that matter. Those thoughts had to be put on the back burner. The only thing currently holding his mind captive were thoughts of murder and torture, a slow and painful death for the people who thought he or his family could ever be a target.

Boss Hogg called Bishop's phone again, just in the nick of time to free Bishop's mind from his evil thoughts, if only for a second.

"Outside," Boss Hogg uttered and ended the call.

Chapter Three:
...It Is What It Is...

Bishop left his brother's hospital room, took the elevator down to the lobby, and exited the building to the visitors' parking lot. He looked around for Boss Hogg's truck, and once he'd spotted it, he made his way to the black-on-black Escalade, sitting high on 26-inch rims.

"I have some news for you, fam," Boss Hogg said, turning down his music.

These words played in Bishop's head as he entered the truck and sank back into the plush leather. The two men gave each other dap before Boss started relaying what he knew as he pulled off. Boss Hogg told him the two guys Duke had encountered at the bar that night had never made it home. Bishop was thinking when Sharelle was talking that it had to have something to do with them.

"So, you got them fools already?" Bishop questioned.

"Yeah; we have them niggas tied up in our stash spot, quiet place too. That's where we're headed right now. Soon as I get the word, everyone who's supposed to be there will be there."

Bishop's eagerness and anger started eating him alive. Revenge was what he wanted. He was bloodthirsty, and the only satisfaction he felt would be adequate was the blood of these two ignorant men. They had to be two fools who'd had no idea who they'd tried to kill that night. Bishop's mind was clouded, driven by rage, and before the truck came to a complete stop, he jumped out the passenger side and marched straight to the basement, full of a killer's enthusiasm.

Bishop stormed into the basement, anxious now to see what these fools looked like. He wanted to know who'd had the audacity to fuck with someone in his family. It was cold down there; the walls were made of solid concrete, as well as the floors. To his left, he immediately saw two vicious Rottweilers who looked ready to eat anything resembling meat.

"How in the hell are these dogs that big? What does Boss Hogg feed these animals? Must be people or something," he thought as he noticed the wetness coming from each of their mouths.

The dogs continued barking in their cages and snapping at the metal that enclosed them, keeping them from getting to their prey. Bishop had never been to this particular spot of Boss Hogg's. He took a good look at the rest of the area, checking out his surroundings like he knew to do. The area was large, with several rooms with locked doors, and a full-size bar, stocked with the best liquor. There were a couple of Boss Hogg's soldiers on duty, strapped with semi-automatic weapons. The putrid smell of dog feces, urine, and human blood filled the air.

"Over here, Bishop," one of the soldiers said, waving Bishop over.

Hogg's men pulled back a black sheet, finally giving Bishop a look at his grand prize. Lo and behold, there they were.

"Look what the fuck is behind door number one!" he said with an unfriendly smile.

His victims were dangling from the ceiling, their heads about eight inches from the floor. One of Hogg's men must have had military training. He had restrained them using a brown tweed rope, tying their hands and connecting them to the ankles. He had them upside down like a slab of meat in a butcher's freezer. It was hard to believe the metal ring drilled into the ceiling was strong enough to support them. Bishop figured it must have been some sort of torture room Boss Hogg used for these types of situations. He couldn't help snickering with a devious smirk. Boss Hogg was really his type of guy.

The perps' clothes were ripped up, shredded badly, and barely clinging to their scarred bodies. Blood was seeping out of every part of their bodies like they had been captured in a war and made collateral damage. The one on the left was of a light complexion, making the bruises and cuts on his face and torso easy to distinguish. They were in great pain, and it gave Bishop great pleasure to see them hurting. To see their pain clearly through their bloodshot eyes added fuel to the fire. The other one was darker, so the bruises were less noticeable, but the blood was just as easy to see as he looked black and blue and near death.

Both men were panting and moaning in severe anguish. The lighter one was talking, but his words were unintelligible due to the heavy duct tape covering his big lips. Their eyes were full of fear, wide open, and begging for the mercy they hadn't given Duke—and mercy they would never receive from Bishop. From the looks of their faces, bodies, and torn clothing, Hogg's men had begun what Bishop had come to finish. Bishop knew they had been beaten for at least a couple of hours from what Hogg had said. He examined the men's condition and didn't feel an ounce of sympathy for either of them. Their mothers could be tied up with them for all he cared. As far as he was concerned, nothing could compare to the trauma they were about to endure. What Bishop was about to inflict was what he called "child's play".

"WAKE-THE-FUCK UP, YOU CRAB-ASS NIGGAS!" screamed Bishop as he noticed their eyes were beginning to close. "THIS ISN'T THE-FUCKIN'-LA QUINTA INN! AIN'T NO TIME FOR SHUT EYES!"

It seemed like the men were trying to go out, so Bishop extended his arm all the way behind his body as if he were doing some type of intense yoga stretch, only to slingshot it back around in front of him and unleash a violent smack on the light-skinned one. He repeated this brutal attack multiple times, again and again on both of them, causing their bodies to jerk with each blow. The men yelled and groaned as the muffled sounds fell on deaf ears. Bishop really wanted to hear them speak, cry, and beg him to go easy. He ripped the tape off their faces. No one was going to hear them but him and Hogg's men.

"Please, man, we didn't do nothing," one pleaded.

They were talking over each other, trying to salvage what little of their lives remained.

"Who sent you-niggas to-fuck-over my little brother?!" Bishop demanded.

He asked this same question over and over again, hoping they would reveal their source. When they had no answer, he commenced unleashing more of his powerful blows to their swollen faces and bodies.

"I'm going to ask again. This time, I might not stop fuckin' you up if I don't get answers. Who sent you motherfuckers?!"

"Nobody sent us. Duke told us to bounce and we did!" the darker one cried out loudly.

"I don't believe you, motherfucker! I want answers and I want them now!"

It was even clearer to Bishop that this was getting him nowhere as their answers remained the same. He rubbed his chin, thinking he had to change his strategy to get them to talk. He searched for something to raise the temperature from hot to cold in the basement. He spotted a chainsaw sticking out of a box of tools in a nearby corner and figured the sound of the small-cycle engine should do the trick. This-nigga Boss Hogg really knew what he was doing. He yanked the cord a couple of times and the chainsaw came roaring to life. He brought the machine dangerously close to each of them before touching their flesh with the jagged blade that he knew would tear through them like an alligator.

"Have you heard of *The Texas Chainsaw Massacre*?" Bishop asked, brandishing that same menacing smile he'd had when he entered the basement.

They screamed for him to stop and begged for their lives, hollering in fear of what was going to happen next.

"Who wants to feel my pain first?" Bishop asked, not really looking for a response.

They continued to maintain their innocence and denied any involvement in what had happened to Duke, but to Bishop, it meant nothing. He knew one of them, if not both, knew something.

A few more hours passed with the two men. He had instilled punishment like the mafia, and Bishop was now convinced they were telling the truth. They really did not know anything. It was impossible for a man not to give in under the pressure he had been applying. It was not them; it could not have been. After hours of torture and facing death, they were not the ones behind the assassination attempt on Duke's life.

'I need answers and I need them now!' Bishop thought.

He left the basement with an increased vengeance that he had thought could not grow any stronger. His friend was outside, sitting in his truck and talking on his cell. He ended the call when he saw Bishop emerge from his spot.

"Boss Hogg, they didn't know shit!"

"You sure, my man?"

"I cut off an arm and a leg. If they knew something, they would have spit that shit out. I'm headed back to Jersey. I gotta change my clothes and get some rest," Bishop said, looking at the blood that had recolored his white jersey.

"If you hear anything new, make sure you hit my line. I'll be close by," Bishop told his homie in a tone that almost sounded like he was defeated.

"Okay; I got you, Bish. You'll be the first one to know."

"A'ight, I'm out, and if we've got to tie up every crab-nigga in the city to get to the bottom of this, I'm down. There can be a lot of legless niggas around this town as far as I'm concerned," Bishop replied.

As he was exiting Hogg's truck, Hogg called his name, stopping him.

"Don't worry! We *are* going to get the muthafuckas responsible for this shit," he assured Bishop.

"I won't rest until we do," Bishop replied, getting out.

———————————————————————

Once Bishop was gone, Boss Hogg sent two guys down to the basement to release what he expected to be two half-dead-niggas from their nightmare. He knew how Bishop felt about his family and could only imagine what he had done to them. As Boss Hogg's men walked into the basement, they were horrified at the sight they were seeing. They were not sure if the man who had just left was Bishop Evans or Hannibal Lecter.

First and foremost, the smell was absolutely foul, but the sight was even worse. One of them jumped back and the other one threw up on the spot when he saw an eyeball rolling around underneath the hanging bodies. There was blood everywhere, covering the floor. It was like someone had come in there and thrown buckets of blood all over the place. It was a fact that the two hanging lambs had been silenced.

The two men were battered and beaten so badly they barely resembled human beings. It was inhuman what had been done. It was so bad that even Hannibal probably could not have stomached what Bishop had done. He had punished them with his fists, a bat, and the grand finale: the chainsaw. Most of their bones were clearly broken, some of them thrusting out of the skin that originally had concealed them. There were bite marks all over the men, leaving Hogg's men to believe Bishop had intended to make them into dog food.

The way Bishop had walked out of the spot, you would have thought those two men were still alive in the basement. He was so calm, so smooth as he headed out the back door. He was completely unbothered by the things he had just done.

"Damn, that nigga is crazy!" one of the men said to the other.

"Yeah, this shit is unreal! I'm glad we're on his side."

"Damn! Let's clean this shit up and get the hell out of Dodge before I lose the rest of the Chinese food in my gut."

Detective Burcheck continued his heavy surveillance on Bishop. He watched through his binoculars, making sure he did not miss one thing. Bishop and Boss Hogg had been talking in Hogg's truck for quite some time now, and Burcheck wished he had a listening device planted. He really wanted to know what the conversation the two men were having was about.

There were a few other men he was unfamiliar with making some movements on the side of the house. They were carrying something he could not make out. He figured it probably was drugs, but without a warrant, he was not going to intervene just yet, for fear of blowing his case. He watched all of them as they parted ways, leaving what he believed to be the man Bishop was talking to at the stash house.

Curious to know why Bishop was so far away from home, Burcheck stayed behind to investigate. If it was a stash house, it would be empty now, and he could collect evidence to obtain a legal search warrant. Maybe he could follow Bishop next time he came back and catch him in the act. This would surely get him talking about the gun and help Burcheck close a cold case.

When total darkness set in, Detective Burcheck went around to the back of the suspected stash house without anyone noticing him. He crept into the house through an unlocked window almost better than any criminal he had ever busted. Once inside, Burcheck smelled heavy bleach, which was odd. For it to be a stash house, it was awfully clean inside, which Burcheck thought was also odd. He did a thorough search of the empty house, from the top floor to the basement, making sure he missed nothing. He wanted nothing more than to find some incriminating evidence that would tie the brothers to the botched robbery the .44 Bulldog was involved in.

He was upset when he came up empty-handed. There wasn't even a sign that drugs were being sold at the property.

While Bishop was in the real world, making headway in the streets, Duke was still in his drug-induced coma, preparing to make a few waves—mentally that is.

The brothers were going through constant physical, emotional, and mental torment. Their father was their worst enemy. How could the man who had given them life be the same man who seemed to want to bring them death? It was a cold world they lived in. There seemed to be no end to their suffering.

It was a cold winter day, about nine below, which was typical Jersey weather for that time of the year. Both Duke and Bishop were in school. Duke was feeling sick, so he was allowed to leave school early. The school contacted his mother to verify it was okay for them to send Duke home.

"Hello, is this Mrs. Evans?" the school nurse asked.

"Yes, this is she," answered Mrs. Evans in her professional manner.

"This is Nurse Steele at your son's school. I'm calling about Duke."

"Is he all right?"

"I'm afraid he's not feeling very well, and we think he should be sent home. We need to know if you can come get him, or do you want us to just send him home by bus?"

"Send him home, please. I'm not able to pick him up right now," Mrs. Evans replied.

"Okay; will do," the nurse said and ended the call.

"Duke, your mom said it is okay to just send you home. Do you think you're okay to make it alone?" the nurse asked with some concern.

"Yes, Nurse Steele; I'll be fine," Duke replied.

"Okay; be careful walking home, sweetie, and make sure your mom calls me when you make it," she told Duke with a worried look on her face.

Nurse Steele was old school. She never had liked sending kids home on their own when they were sick. She could not understand how a parent felt comfortable doing that, but she had to follow protocol.

"No problem; she'll call," Duke said, heading to gather his stuff.

He went to his locker, put his backpack on, zipped up his jacket, pulled his beanie over his head, and made his way out of the building. Duke felt the crisp, cold air stinging his face as Jack Frost was on full blast today. He would have to get home quickly if he wanted to get away from this cold. The worst part about it was his body was weak and he wasn't able to move very fast, let alone in this weather. He made his sluggish journey a bit faster by taking a few of the shortcuts he would take when Bishop was with him.

Duke approached their building and walked through the front door, passing the mailboxes that lined the walls on both sides. Since he was not expecting a check, there was no reason for him to check the mail. Instead, he stopped at the vending machine to his left and pulled out a crisp dollar bill. He pushed the A and the 3 keys on the machine, which made the hot Cheetos, his favorite snack, fall into the pickup slot. Duke then strolled through the second door into the foyer area of their building. He slowly walked through the hallway and made his way to the stairwell. As he opened the bag and started munching on his Cheetos, he heard a loud, piercing scream that rattled his core. He immediately recognized it as his mother's voice.

"Someone help me. Please! Help! Please, someone!" Mrs. Evans cried out loudly.

"MOM, MOM! I'M COMING, MOM!" Duke yelled out, scared to death he would be too late for whatever was going on.

He yelled, "MOM I'M COMING!" the whole time he was running to their apartment. Sprinting as fast as he could, Duke was desperate to get to his mom and find out what was wrong. He had an idea; in fact, he knew what it was. The only thing, or person, that ever brought this kind of terror out of his mom was his father and his bad rage.

Duke burst in and entered the apartment, continuing to let his mom know he was en route to her. The noise was extremely loud in the place, all coming from their parents' bedroom. Duke ran straight to his room and went to the closet, knowing the savior was hidden there. Panting and sweating, he maneuvered to the exact spot where he knew Bishop's .44 was awaiting his embrace. Still feeling a little weak and under the weather, he grabbed it quickly. He could barely hold the heavy object, but the adrenaline pumping through his veins gave him an inhumane strength to keep going. His only objective was to save his mother from his father's torment, a situation no child should ever have to fathom, let alone endure.

Duke hurried, racing toward his parents' bedroom, bursting in with no hesitation. His heart was beating so hard that he thought it had jumped out of his chest and left him there to face this tragedy alone. The first thing his vision caught was his mother sprawled on the floor with a look of fear in her eyes. It was the same look he had seen so many times before. His father was standing over his mother, hitting her continuously, like his intentions were to make this their last fight.

"Dad!" Duke yelled out.

As his father turned around, Duke could see he was in a terrifying rage.

"What?!"

"STOP, SON, DON'T GET INVOLVED!" his mother screamed, fearing what her husband might do to her youngest child for interfering.

However, it was too late. There was no way Duke was going to stand there and watch the lady who had given him life lose hers. Duke had already raised the gun, and the next thing he realized, he had pulled the trigger multiple times, unleashing five thundering roars of pure kill.

Blam-Blam-Blam-Blam-Blam...

Duke's aim was not perfect, but he had lucked up and struck his father in the leg, stomach, and head, killing him instantly and sending him home to meet his Maker. His father's lifeless body made a loud thud as his sinewy frame connected with the bedroom floor. Things were happening so fast that it left them without enough time to think clearly. Duke and his mother were both completely in shock seeing the blood pouring from his body. His mother lay there for a second, bewildered at what was happening in her home. She had no idea what to do or what Duke might do next.

As Duke stood over his mother with the smoking gun in hand, his mother looked over at her now-deceased husband, who was stretched out on their bedroom floor. He was motionless and void of a single breath. Blood was everywhere as it had poured from the holes the .44 had made.

Bishop had just made it home, entering the front door. He was shocked because he heard crying as he raced through the house, scared and confused by what he'd heard gunshots. The noise had been so loud that he'd heard it as he was coming into the building. He searched the apartment, running straight to his parents' bedroom, only to see Duke standing over their mother and dead father. Duke was still holding tightly to the .44 caliber and shaking in fear.

"Duke! Duke! What the fuck?!" Bishop called to get his brother's attention.

Duke was sweating like he had a faucet attached to him, not moving, just standing there like a statue. Bishop knew it was due to the shock that Duke's mouth was stuck shut; he was so gone that he did not respond. Instead, he just stood there, motionless like their dead father; it was as if he had just seen a ghost.

The next thing Bishop did was walk toward Duke so he could look him directly in his eyes. He searched Duke for blood, yanking the gun away from his tight grip, making sure his little brother was not hurt. Then he grabbed Duke's head and hand, pulling him close to his own chest for comfort. The family of three was trying very hard to process the scene, which looked like a Western flick was being filmed. Since Bishop was the oldest, he knew he had to figure out what to do.

"Listen, I have the gun now. Get Mommy, and the two of you get away from Daddy. I've got to figure this shit out."

Duke nodded and did exactly what he was ordered to do. He and his mother moved to the other side of the bedroom. Their mother was a wreck. She was bleeding from the nose and the corner of her mouth. Her eyes told the story: she was scared shitless. Bishop informed them that there were people outside when he was coming into the building, and they probably had heard the gunshots too.

"So, listen to what I'm saying, because that means nine times out of ten, the police will be arriving soon, but don't worry," he kept explaining. "Duke, tell me what happened, so I'll know how to spin this situation."

As Duke told his brother what had happened, Bishop looked down at him and smirked at the news of how his father had gone out. He felt relieved, to be honest. 'No more abuse,' was all he could think, especially as it concerned his mother.

Minutes after getting an understanding of what had happened, police sirens could be heard wailing in the distance. The sirens got louder as they got closer and closer to their building. Bishop, Duke, and their mother looked at each other as if to say, "What we are going to do?" Any second now, they knew the police would be in their apartment, crawling all over the place and investigating what they would deem to be a homicide. Trying to get a handle on the whole ordeal, Bishop told Duke and their mother not to say a word to anyone, no matter what questions they asked.

"Do y'all hear me? Is it clear what I'm telling y'all to do?"

Both Duke and their mother nodded their heads, letting him know they understood everything he had just said to them.

The next thing they knew, the police had come through their door with a loud noise. Boom! They had kicked in their front door with force and rushed into their apartment like madmen. The officers quickly saw Bishop, Duke, and their mother toward the back of the apartment and ordered everyone to freeze.

"Drop the gun before I put your face on the wall," one of them demanded.

Bishop, who now had the gun in his possession, obeyed the cop's order by putting the gun down. They all followed Bishop and lay down, retreating to the floor as directed. Duke and their mother were scared out of their minds, and they had no idea what was going to come from this situation. In seconds, they were all handcuffed, read their rights, and lifted off the bloody floor.

Before leaving the bedroom, Bishop asked the officer, "Excuse me, sir, we want to have a lawyer present when we get to the police station. Isn't that our right?"

Bishop remembered seeing it was their right on an episode of *Law & Order*. The same officer who had told Bishop to drop the gun looked at him like Bishop was trying to be a smart-aleck delinquent.

"Yes, you can speak with an attorney once you are at the station. Until then, boy, you done fucked up, and you have the right to remain silent. Anything you say can and will be used against you in a court of law."

"I think we know our rights, sir," Bishop replied.

"You think you're a real smart ass. We will just see about that when we get you down to the station." The cop smiled, making a note on his pad.

As they started getting things situated around the apartment to start their investigation, a few officers were left behind as others transported the family of three to the Robbery and Homicide Division. Bishop saw the yellow crime scene tape as they were leaving and lowered his head.

When they arrived at the precinct, the three were separated and taken to individual interrogation rooms. Bishop knew this was a tactic the police used to confirm stories when there was more than one suspect involved.

"This should be open and shut. The gun was in his hand when we got there, so let's get this party started," one cop was overheard saying to what appeared to be his partner.

The other cop replied, smiling and adjusting his tie, "Okay; I guess it's show time."

Bishop and his family were waiting to hear their fate and wondering what the charge was going to be. A few seconds later, the two Homicide detectives placed on the case began questioning them, one by one. One of the detectives was a tall, built, and well-dressed man. He had white hair and smelly breath. It seemed like he thought the Altoids he chewed at a rapid rate would hide the smell of coffee and Benson & Hedges cigarettes. It wasn't working. He smelled like he'd smoked cigarettes his entire life, back-to-back, pack after pack. The other detective was a heavy-built black guy, whose attitude seemed as if he lived a life of pure misery. He wore a gold wedding band, and it was obvious his obsession with jelly donuts meant more to him than his wife. Combined with the other one, they were pieces-of-shit detectives.

While the family of three was separated and placed into their rooms to be questioned, the rest of the officers were still back at their house collecting evidence in the case. The three sat patiently, reflecting on everything that had unfolded. While they waited to be questioned, they were saddened by the fact they could not be together. Suddenly, while they were sifting through their memories, a very well-dressed man walked into the station. He was a tall, built, black man with wavy black hair, smooth walking, and well-spoken, and his Armani suit looked like he knew his business well.

"Someone requested a lawyer?" he asked the first officer he encountered.

"Yes; there is a kid in room number 3 being questioned for a homicide," the officer replied.

"Let's hope the questioning didn't begin yet, or there is going to be some constitutional violation motions drawn up," the lawyer said in a meaningful tone.

The officer just gave him a piercing look.

Bishop overheard the conversation between the lawyer and officer that was happening outside his interrogation room, and he figured he at least had the right man for the job. The lawyer was accompanied by one of the officers as they entered the room without knocking. Bishop looked the lawyer right in the eye as he greeted him.

"Hey; what's going on, son? My name is Peter McMahon. Can I be of some assistance to you?"

Bishop quickly answered, "Yes. I need your legal advice and assistance."

The lawyer asked that he and his client be left alone, so they could have some time to speak to one another. The officer complied, knowing it was the law, but the officer did not want the lawyer to be able to change Bishop's mind in any way. He just wanted a conviction. Case closed. He did not want to give the lawyer a chance to invoke client-attorney privilege. The white hair detective looked at his fat partner and nodded toward the door, meaning it was time for them to vacate the room.

Bishop and his lawyer started discussing the matter at hand. All Bishop was thinking about was saving his family as he confessed that he had killed his father, and how his mother and brother were just victims of an unfortunate circumstance, letting the lawyer know they had had no involvement in harming their father/his mother's husband. He took full responsibility for his actions. The lawyer thanked Bishop for his honesty and sincerity.

"How old did you say you were, young man?" the lawyer asked as he scribbled notes on his yellow legal pad.

"I'm seventeen-and-a-half, sir."

"Damn! You seem so much older than you actually are," the lawyer replied, sounding impressed by the young man's intelligence.

Bishop's lawyer was really impressed, thinking the kid had conducted himself better than some adults he had defended.

"Listen, I get it. I am going to make sure your family is okay, and you get treated fairly by the system, okay?"

"Yes, that will be okay," Bishop responded with a sense of gratitude. "Thank you, Mr. McMahon, for everything."

"Son, you're welcome, but don't thank me just yet. You can thank me once this is all over and done with."

Without any further conversation, Mr. McMahon got up from his seat and shook Bishop's hand. Bishop watched his new mouthpiece exit room 3 and immediately summon the lead detective on the case. He wanted them to know it was okay to take Bishop's confession. He was going to work hard and hope for the best possible outcome for his client. Something told him there was more to Bishop's story, but protecting a man's family was something a real man was supposed to do. It was the right thing.

When Mr. McMahon asked to speak to the lead detective on the case, Detective Burcheck and super-cop Fletcher Davis were summoned back to the station. They were both bothered the kid had had enough sense to lawyer up before speaking. The detectives shared their opinions, knowing it was not going to be as cut and dry as they had expected.

"Man, we've been here for hours," Fletcher said to his partner.

"It's a homicide investigation, and you know the job better than anyone," Burcheck replied, wanting to nail the case.

"I'm just sick of all this interviewing and collecting all this fucking evidence and statements. Are you ready to leave or do you want to stick around?" Fletcher replied as he stared at the gun in the evidence bag.

"Man, I'm just curious to know where these kids are getting weapons this size from. This type of artillery should be unobtainable by a child, especially one as young as these boys are," Fletcher said, breaking into Burcheck's thoughts, who was busy focusing on whether or not they had a possible gunrunner in their city.

"I'm not sure where they're getting them from, partner, but here's your opportunity to find out. The kid's lawyer, Mr. Mc Mahon, is waiting for us with the kid's confession. The older brother of the two confessed to killing the father."

"What?! The kid already has a lawyer. What's next? Let's go!"

Burcheck sounded agitated about the way things were transpiring in their case. To hear about the kid's confession and already having a lawyer really pissed him off. The two partners hopped in their unmarked and rushed back to the station, furious about the news. They could not wait to address their concerns to whoever would hear them out. When the two detectives arrived back at the station, they were greeted by Mr. McMahon. The attorney said his client was ready with his handwritten confession for the killing of Mr. Evans. They went to the interrogation room, and Bishop lowered his head for a second, knowing he was ready to be taken into custody and charged. After signing his truth of the matter on paper, Bishop's bargain with the devil was to confess to the crime in exchange for his mother and brother's release.

His mother and brother had had a chance to speak with Mr. McMahon. They did not need to speak to the detectives since Bishop had already confessed. Back in the apartment, they had not had a long time to get their stories together before the cops had shown up. Bishop had known that, and he had told them before being taken down to the police station not to say a word under any circumstances. He had wanted it that way because he felt he had it under control. His mother loved the fact that her oldest son was more of a man than the one she had chosen to marry and wear his last name. There were a lot of things in her life she regretted, but the one thing she had always cherished was her sons.

The lawyer reassured Duke and his mother that everything would be alright and Bishop would be in contact with them as soon as he could get a phone call in. The mother was in tears as the lawyer put a hand on her shoulder and told her she had a strong son.

Duke and Mrs. Evans finally left the precinct, sulking because they had had to leave Bishop behind. He was going to get processed into the system for homicide. This was a bittersweet feeling for both of them. Yes, they had regained their freedom, but at the cost of Bishop's freedom, which numbed their euphoria. Duke's innocent brother was being locked up for something he had done. That really did not sit well with him. Mrs. Evans understood that Bishop was stepping up as a man for his little brother, giving him a chance at life. Maybe one day Duke would fully understand what Bishop's intentions were. For now, all Duke felt was anger and hatred toward the law that had taken his brother away from him.

Duke and his mother stood in front of the precinct, awaiting their cab in silence, her arm around his shoulder. He moved away from her hold, and Mrs. Evans gave Duke his space to allow him to grieve in his own way. She lowered her head just as Bishop had done before heading to Booking. Their mother knew firsthand that the most difficult task for a woman is attempting to raise men. They said it took a village, but in her mind, it just took two good parents, which her boys were not fortunate to have.

Duke was wondering what was taking the cab so long. His mind was flooded with all the things he would do to those two detectives, Burcheck and Fletcher, for the shit they were putting his family through.

Chapter Four:
Bishop's Predicament

For some odd reason, Detective Burcheck was taking this particular case personally. He stayed on the phone, made calls, and kept running back and forth to the city morgue, where one of his old college partners was the head forensic pathologist. Actually, he was one of the highest-ranked pathologists in the nation. Burcheck was desperately hoping to uncover some new information through the Forensics lab. He finally got the call he was waiting for from his friend a day or two later. When his friend told him to come down, that he had something to show him, Burcheck left his lunch sitting on the dinner table and did seventy miles an hour to get there.

His buddy, Amhurst Brown, was a little chubby in the gut and wide around the neck with a wide, bulbous nose. None of that mattered, because what he lacked in looks, he made up for in brilliance. He worked day and night in his lab to solve cases on the state and federal levels, and that was what had gotten him the rep where he was referred to as the black Quincy, the title character played by Jack Klugman on the old television show. Amhurst smiled wryly as he escorted Burcheck to his office, motioning and asking him to take a seat in front of his desk.

"You ready for this, Bur?" the pathologist asked. He liked calling Burcheck Bur.

"Shit can't get any thicker than shit already is, buddy, so just lay it on," Burcheck replied, hoping everything was okay.

"We fired this gun for testing several times, and I can assure you this particular gun has a unique discharge, leaving very distinguishable markings that we found to be interesting."

"Okay... Well, from what I learned in the academy twenty years ago, all guns do that, right?" Burcheck asked.

"Yes, you're correct in a sense, they do. But with new scientific breakthroughs, we can now match these markings to previously unsolved cases—even if a perp has altered the barrel, trying to make it difficult."

"I've heard that as well," Burcheck sarcastically responded.

"Well, my friend, we found the same markings on shell casings from a different crime scene," he said, looking at his watch and causing Burcheck to raise a brow.

Amhurst would not go any further into detail because it was his break time, and he did not miss break time for anyone or anything. He could taste the chicken noodle soup his wife had packed for him dancing on his pallet. Burcheck was getting annoyed, but he knew how Amhurst worked, so he knew he would have to come back after lunch if he wanted to get the information out of him.

"Go ahead and enjoy your lunch, buddy. I will see you in about an hour or so," Burcheck reluctantly quipped, looking at his cheap watch.

He left the guy alone to add calories to his already out-of-shape frame. He figured it was time to chase down Duke and his mother for some extensive questioning. As he made his way out of the city morgue, his thoughts were filled with all the tactics he had already tried on young Duke. He was just a kid, and Burcheck was confident he would get some information out of him somehow.

He trotted up the stairs leading to the front door where his outdated squad car was parked. He looked left and right, irritated mostly at himself for not getting the kid to talk in the first place. Duke and his mother were free and most likely back at their torn-up apartment. Burcheck checked his emotions, took a deep breath, and smiled his devilish grin. His phone rang in his inside pocket. When he retrieved it and looked at the caller display, he saw it was his boss.

"Burcheck, let me warn you now because I know your hot-headed ass will mess this up!" his superior officer said.

"Boss, what are you talking about now?" Burcheck asked, knowing his boss knew him better than anyone else.

"If I had to guess, you're down at the city morgue with your fat friend, trying to round up evidence on the Evans case, and as soon as you leave there, your plan is to head back to the crime scene and question the kid and his mother."

Burcheck did not for the life of him understand how the man knew him so well, but he was on point with everything he had said.

"Actually, boss, I'm heading home for a minute. I've got some blood on my shoes," he lied.

"Yeah, yeah, Burcheck. We got a confession, the oldest boy said he did it, and you know his lawyer will be all over this, trying to protect this kid's constitutional rights. So, you heard my orders, Burcheck. Don't make me regret covering for you with IAB on your last botched case. I said last time was the last time, and I mean that as sure as shit stinks."

His boss ended the call without saying goodbye. Burcheck was a hothead and everyone knew it, but most of the other detectives were jealous of him because he either got results or got away with being dirty and getting no results. He knew one thing though: he had to watch himself with this one. It was only a matter of time before the oldest brother went to trial. He would get his chance to question the boys and get to the bottom of this whole shebang.

―――――――――――――――――――――――――

Forty-eight hours had passed and Bishop was now scheduled to appear in court for his arraignment and to set a pretrial date. Bishop was bound over for pre-trial and his second appearance was set for two weeks after that. He was waiting to hear back from his attorney with any reasonable deal he could muster up with the district attorney. Either way, it did not matter to Bishop; he would have done all day to protect his brother and his mother.

Duke and their mother made sure they were at every court appearance, supporting him. This was also their only opportunity to see and speak to Bishop before they took him back to jail.

"Son, are you okay in there?" his mother asked.

He just nodded his head.

"Boy, you know I love you."

She had tears in her eyes, knowing her son was more of a man than any other man she ever had known.

"Yeah, Mom. Don't worry about me. I've got this under control," Bishop responded with his chest out to assure his mother that she had nothing to stress about.

Duke interrupted. "You don't gotta worry about us, bruh. I'm going to look after Mommy," Duke told his brother, mimicking his actions and demeanor.

"Okay, I'll see y'all at court," Bishop responded with a sly grin as he looked at the bailiff.

He was feeling mixed emotions because he was quite impressed with his little brother's maturity. At the same time, he was disappointed in himself by the fact that his kid brother even had to think this way.

'Life's a bitch,' *he thought.*

"Okay, bruh?" Duke asked, without a clue of the thoughts his older brother was experiencing. All Duke wanted to do was handle this adversity like a man. As strong as he was acting, he had no clue what that even meant.

Before Duke and his mother could even savor the little bit of time they had spent with their beloved Bishop, here came the devil in the flesh. Burcheck was dressed in an all-black suit he had probably gotten from the local Goodwill, with shiny black shoes as if he were going to a funeral. His appearance actually resembled that of a low-budget Grim Reaper. But Detective Burcheck left empty-handed again. He had planned on exchanging words with Duke and his mother, but to no avail. As he was walking in, they were walking out.

In the hearing, Bishop's lawyer, Mr. McMahon, discussed the pros and cons regarding Bishop. The only thing good about Bishop's predicament was the family had documented the history of abuse and neglect by their father. The police had been out to the apartment several times for domestic reports and even had taken the father down one time for an overnight lesson. This provided Bishop's defense with a reasonable motive for self-defense for the killing of his father. Ultimately, having this evidence on record played a major role in Bishop's case and his lawyer's defense tactics. The judge admired the fact that the defendant had chosen the speedy law process and not to drag it out, costing the taxpayer's money. It was enough for the court's ears and an essential reason why he was only given seven years, instead of the suggested 25 to life.

The family was ecstatic Bishop would not be sent away for such a long period of time. Their mother had spent many nights scared to death, thinking about the 25 years the district attorney was pushing for in the beginning. Even with an early release for good behavior, that much time would have taken too many precious years from her son's future. Every man she had ever known who had done that type of time had come home different from before they went in. She did not want that for her son, especially knowing he was a victim, just like she and her baby boy. They were all victims of the man who was supposed to have been the king of the castle.

Duke made a vow. He vowed to be his brother's keeper and his mother's keeper while Bishop was away. He knew wholeheartedly he had to step up his game since it was obvious he would be the man of the house now.

After sentencing, Detective Burcheck approached Bishop's lawyer. He asked Mr. McMahon if he could ask Bishop a few questions.

"He has been found guilty, so what more is there for you to question him about?" the attorney asked, feeling a little irritated with Burcheck.

"It's about the gun that was used in the death of his father," Burcheck calmly stated, as if it was nothing serious.

"There's no double jeopardy, and the kid has already been through enough. Let the kid go on with his life, man. He's already losing seven years of his life for protecting his family from a fucking monster, something any one of us would have done if we were put in that same situation. Can't you just let the kid breathe? He has a lot of soul-searching to do, for God's sake!" Mr. McMahon spewed aggressively and sincerely.

Mr. Mc Mahon was in full defense mode, past the professional sense. He had grown a liking for Bishop and felt he needed to protect Bishop like a real father protects his son.

Detective Burcheck stood there dumbfounded at the lawyer's response. He had no idea how this guy could be so animated over a murderous criminal, let alone a now-convicted killer. It was obvious they were not on the same side of the law. Detective Burcheck never embraced confrontation, so he tucked his tail and fell back like he normally would do. As he made his way out of the courtroom, he made an oath to himself: Someone was going to answer the questions he had for the boys. It was now his personal business more than ever. He would keep investigating, despite what his boss had said and despite McMahon's disposition. He had shit he needed answers for. Burcheck was going to make it his mission to put the brothers in jail—under the jail if he could.

Chapter Five:
Parallels

Bishop knew, with him being gone for seven years, things would be rough for Duke and their mother, especially without the financial help of their father. As bad as their situation with their father's behavior had been, he had still contributed to their well-being. At the same time, Bishop knew Duke was going to need constant guidance. Duke had always listened to his big brother, no matter what.

Time started to take its course, and throughout Bishop's incarceration for the first year or two, Duke and his relationship grew stronger with each passing day. The brothers became well-meshed on all levels—mentally, physically, and emotionally. It was as if they were evolving as one and the same person in their own way. Bishop's strength started forming in his mind and body. His ability to read people's agendas was becoming accurate to the point he knew things about people just from the first few sentences that came out of their mouths. He had become sharper than even he had expected. He could also tell what a person was up to just by the shake of a hand.

Bishop prided himself because he had also obtained spiritual growth as well. The system had driven him to start reading articles on law and law books. He knew case law like an attorney and could even recite some of the federal statutes. Bishop was set on reading everything in the law library and the regular library. He was relentless in gaining knowledge on things that had something to do with history, politics, and self-awareness. Reading was it for him. It was a great step to learning and keeping himself occupied during his unwanted vacation.

It was mandatory that everything he fed or digested into his mind had substance. Bishop was stern about who he wanted to be around on the inside. That was why he only attracted certain types of inmates, those who had a bright future like himself. For the rest of the knuckleheads, they stayed out of his way.

His bond was established quickly with those whom he took a liking to and vice versa. For the ones he did not fuck with, it was apparent Bishop was becoming a problem to them in every sense of the word. His reputation quickly preceded him, and a few inmates found out he was not to be played with like they treated the new fish who came to serve their time. There were guys who were never going to leave there, some who would die there from old age, but most of the death-row inmates met their Maker before their health went bad. The prison was full of those who were called "the walking dead". Some of the lifers started turning to Bishop for advice, even though he was still a young man. When he asked them why they had picked him for information, they all replied with the same answer: He had read so many books and they found that impressive.

Bishop started having altercations, and he was beating ass as if he had something to prove. He knew for a fact that no one in his age group or a little older could fuck with him with the hands, especially after years of he and his friend, 6'2, sparring. Although Bishop had lost every fight they had had, it had prepared him for life, making it very hard for someone his age or a little older to understand his ambition to win. They were not ready for what he had to offer, and it was not anything nice.

Duke, on the other hand, was the total opposite of Bishop. They were what the old folks called night and day. Duke could be considered night, pure darkness. The beast in him had been created from his life's experiences. He was definitely what the old folks would also call a product of his environment. He had been very well-groomed for the streets: smart, witty, and highly advanced. Duke was more advanced than the average kid his age or even a few years older, and he was much more reckless than anyone who actually wanted problems or beef with him.

Duke made motion pictures out of any situation he placed himself in. He was a pro at making examples of anyone who tried him or wanted drama. A person had better seriously know what beef was if they planned to come at him. Duke was the kind of person who always took things way too far. If he was beefing with you on the block, then it was not just about that person. It was about the whole block in his eyes. Even those who had nothing to do with the beef still had to fear what was next. He was all about making statements, which he did viciously.

Even though the brothers were different in many ways, they were also the same in many ways. Bishop had accepted responsibility for the death of their father, knowing he was mentally the strongest between him and Duke. It seemed like the right thing for him to do. The streets had always felt it was Duke's doing, that he was actually responsible for the killing of their father. The rumors were that Duke had shot and killed their father, then laughed as he watched him fade into death. Those were the whispers in the streets, but no one ever confronted him directly. Therefore, with Bishop being in prison, Duke threw himself into the streets without blinders. He got with a few childhood friends he knew were trustworthy and loyal to roll with him, friends he knew he could trust with his life. He did exactly that—put his life into their hands.

Chapter Six:
The Duke Boys

Duke put together a crew, aligning himself with four guys and a boss-bitch. His first choice was a well-known bully who went by the name of Gooch. They had grown up together and Duke felt he could trust Gooch. Gooch was a big, black-motherfucker, six feet tall, weighing roughly two hundred thirty-five pounds. He was more muscle than brains, but exactly what Duke needed. Gooch was so big, Crusher was what they should have called him in the hood, because growing up, Duke had seen him crush motherfuckers who got in his way. When Gooch went in on you, he did it fast and with ease. He was someone a person did not want to run into in a dark alley.

His second choice was a homie by the name of Malik. He was the playboy in the crew. Malik really believed he was God's gift to all women. He loved the females and they loved him. Malik had no problem getting any woman he wanted. He was not really a killer, but he killed when necessary. Duke ultimately liked him for other reasons though. They were best friends, so Duke had to bring Malik along because he also trusted Malik like he trusted Gooch. The only problem he had with Malik was his halitosis and terrible gambling habit. Other than that, Malik played his part to a tee. Duke loved having him around.

Then there was Face Hound, a fairly built young kid whose loyalty could never be questioned. Face was the type of nigga who did little-to-no talking, especially to strangers. He listened more than he spoke. He was originally from New York, the Bronx. He had moved to Newark, New Jersey, as a preteen, at around twelve or thirteen years of age. It was just Face and his mother who had relocated to Newark. Face and Duke had originally crossed paths in school. They were in the sixth grade together and sat next to each other. During that time, Duke noticed how much heart Face possessed. He had seen Face square up with young men twice his age and never back down, as some of the other boys would have. He thought that was gangster of him since Face was not from Jersey and yet he still stood ten toes down and was ready for whatever came his way—something Duke admired about Face. He had always said to himself, "This kid is built Ford tough."

There was now Gooch, Face, and Malik, and Duke needed to find the last piece of his puzzle. He knew the missing piece was a stone-cold female who could help hold it down. That is where Sheedah came into the picture. Standing at five-five and about one hundred fifty-five pounds, her weight was in all the right places, making her thick and fine. She had a banging body with curves women had to work out to obtain. For her, it had come naturally; she was the creation of a mythical goddess. With her measurements shining—36D-25in-39in—Duke had to have her.

Sheedah was a good girl who just got caught up with a bad boy, Duke, and she was smart when it came to danger. She was a Catholic girl who had been raised with good family ethics. Although she and Duke had messed around early in their relationship, they were better off as friends than lovers, and she still would do any and everything Duke asked of her. Fuck the other niggas in their crew! Sheedah's love and loyalty were strictly for Duke, and he felt the same about her high-yellow ass. No matter how many bitches she witnessed him dealing with or fucking with, she stayed true to the game. She knew, that if she wanted Duke, she could have him any time, any place, or in any position she chose to set it out in. The dick was hers for the taking if she desired, but her sole focus was money and the thrill that came along with getting it.

Sheedah's role in the crew was simple. She was the set-up queen for the weak niggas with paper. Duke knew most men's downfall was a pretty bitch with a big ass, so it was easy for Sheedah to bring the ballers out for the guys to rob or kill them. Whatever the situation brought upon the night or day would control the results and fate for those niggas. From the way she looked and how her body was built, trapping a nigga was way too easy for her. It had become second nature for her, making the licks too easy for the crew. Duke, Gooch, Malik, Face Hound, and Sheedah—that was the crew and the main threat to the streets of Newark— The Duke Boys.

Over the next couple of years, the "The Duke Boys" would become a household name that was very familiar to those running the streets. Duke and his crew ran through the city as if everyone in it owed them something. They seemed to always be faced with a life-or-death dilemma. They stayed in some shit and welcomed the consequences if there were going to be any.

———————————————————————————————

It was an unusual day, and Duke and the crew had gathered in their small apartment they called the clubhouse. It was located on Chadwick and Avon, not too far away from Avon Avenue School. It was a spot where they hung out every day and planned their illegal activities. On this particular day, they were getting ready for a stick-up robbery, and Sheedah received a call from an unknown number on her iPhone.

"Hello," she said.

A male voice responded, "Can I speak to Sheedah?" he said, even though he figured it was her since it was her cell number.

"Yeah, you can," she said, motioning to Duke that this was the call she and her girls had been waiting on. They had planned to party tonight. "This is she. What's good?"

"Are we still on for our little get-together tonight? I'm in town until Sunday evening and I wanna see your fine, thick ass."

"Of course, babe. For sure, I'm trying to see you too. Let's meet up around ten," she replied in a seductive tone, grabbing the man's attention even more than she already had it.

He replied, "Say no more. I'm checked into the Holiday Inn on First and Ninth, room 107."

He expressed that he wasn't alone and asked if she would bring a few of her girlfriends, letting her know he also was trying to show his guys a good time while they were in New Jersey.

"Okay, babe, around ten, room 107, Holiday Inn on First and Ninth. Got it. Me and my girlfriends will be there. See you then," she said, letting him know she had all the information he had given her correctly.

"Okay, sounds good," he said before the phone went dead.

After Sheedah got off the phone, a hush covered the room in the small clubhouse as everyone waited for Duke's words to break the silence.

"Who was that?" Duke asked her with concern.

"My friend. Why?" she responded with a little cockiness.

"I asked because you know we have things to do tonight, and being as you're making other plans, I need to know what's good," Duke continued with an attitude, especially with him knowing how smart ass Sheedah was trying to be with her response.

"Duke, I have a life outside of what we do, so I don't need you questioning everything I do or who you hear me talking to. Plus, I know what we have to do tonight. What we have planned won't interfere with anything we have going on. I won't be long anyway. I'll be ready in time. DANG!"

The love between the two was very noticeable; even in the wake of their frustration, anyone could sense the feelings that still existed between the pair. It was not a mistake and it was very undeniable. Duke was so heated by how Sheedah was expressing herself to him that he wanted to snap. He hit her with a cold stare as if to say without moving his lips, "BITCH! Who the fuck are you talking to like that?!"

Instead, he took the high road and simply said to her, "You're right. Just be back in time. That's it," and gave her a sly smile.

Duke made his way to another room in the apartment, leaving Sheedah speechless as he usually did. Duke always had a way with his words that fascinated Sheedah. Even the smallest exchange or the slightest utterance could say a million things. She marveled at the way he always had a swift comeback that never failed. This time he had shut her down, leaving her to walk out the house to handle whatever business she had to handle. She gave her exit some flair by slamming the door.

———————————————————

As time passed, Sheedah's mind was still stuck on their exchange. She shook off her emotions as best she knew how, which was to act as if they did not exist, so she went along with her night as if the only thing that was worth thinking about was meeting up with her male friend. She had met up with a few of her girls just as the trick had requested, and all Sheedah wanted to do was blow off a little steam. In her mind, what better way to do that than to get lit and fuck the night up.

Duke, Gooch, Malik, and Face Hound got into Duke's truck and took to the road. Duke was still feeling some type of way from the earlier exchange with Sheedah. He did not like how Sheedah had come at him earlier that day, getting him out of character when it came to her. He knew better than to allow her to get away with the bullshit she tried with him. He knew a lesson is like water, and it can take multiple forms and continue to flow if there is no shutoff valve. So, in order to get her to drink, he would have to serve that bitch a glass of action on the rocks, knowing if he let her get away with it once, she would get used to doing it again and again—something he refused to let happen on his watch. He drove listlessly, hitting corners as he continued to ponder exactly how he would get his point delivered.

Sheedah was on the other side of town with five of her fine-ass girlfriends, and all she wanted to do was have a good time. The group of women pulled into the underground parking lot of the Holiday Inn in their mini-skirts and tightly fitted dresses that clung to their properly proportioned bodies. They all took their time in the whip, making sure they looked good and smelled even better. Once they were all satisfied, they stepped out onto the pavement and walked over to the hotel elevator. They all crowded into the elevator, talking shit and laughing at each other's preparations for the evening.

"Room 107, girl," Sheedah said to one of her girls.

"Where is room 107, bitch? You act like I work here or something," the clueless chick replied.

"The first floor. That's why the number says one zero seven, goofy broad," Sheedah responded, laughing as she pressed the correct button on the elevator for her friend.

They were all ready to get turned up and make some bread. The elevator ascended one floor and they stepped out, following the sign with arrows on the wall that said, Rooms 103-112. The group smoothly sashayed down the hallway as if it was a Tyra Banks' runway and they were being considered for the Next Top Model show. All these bitches really wanted was some attention and some top-shelf liquor. They were prepared to let their hair down and twerk their night away. Finally, they halted at the door to room 107.

Knock. Knock. Sheedah tapped lightly on the door.

"Who is it?" a husky voice called out from the other side.

The girls looked at each other, making faces, like whoever that was sounded fine as hell.

"It's me, Sheedah, babe. I've got a few friends with me too just like you asked," she replied, knowing exactly whose voice it was.

The music coming from the room was blasting from behind the door. When the door finally opened, nothing but smiles and lustful eyes greeted the women.

"Come on in, baby. I've been waiting for you."

"Oh yeah?" Sheedah replied.

"For sure, lil' momma. What y'all drinking?" the well-built man asked Sheedah and the rest of the group, licking his lips.

Sheedah saw her opportunity to do her thing and put on a show. She stared him right into his eyes and gave a devious smile. She walked right up to him and the other girls went past her into the room where his boys were. Sheedah pulled the man close so she could whisper in his ear. She told him her plans for the night. Whatever she said must have aroused the man, as she noticed a bulge growing between his legs. Wearing the latest Tiffany scent, Sheedah smelled sweet enough to taste. Sheedah knew exactly what she was doing because she was a pro at this shit. She was feeling herself so much that she nibbled on his ear and rubbed on his dick since it was obviously ready.

"I drink Henny straight, Daddy," Sheedah practically moaned to the man.

He immediately made his way to the built-in kitchen to fix her a drink. Any wish she had was now his command. She could have told the dude to bring her a bottle of water fresh from the Rocky Mountains, and he would have run at a full sprint and bottled the water himself. She knew it too. She was on top of the world tonight. Nothing could stop her shine, not even Duke.

"Aye, let's turn this bitch up!" one of the guys yelled, looking at the rest of the menu for the evening.

"Get room service on the line, and y'all get whatever food y'all want. Lil bro's 'bout to hit the liquor store and grab some more bottles. I'm in my zone tonight. Watch me flex," hollered the man who had invited Sheedah and her gang over.

Twenty minutes passed and everybody started feeling the vibe. Bitches were shaking their asses that were popping out of their outfits. The niggas were throwing a little money in the air, flexing for the hoes. One of the more ratchet broads was already acting like she was drunk like she usually did. One of the guys was walking her toward the bathroom. Lord knew they were not going back there to piss together. Everyone else was in the front room, smoking blunts, sipping liquor, and enjoying the music. There was a knock on the door and at first, no one heard it. Then, there were a few more loud bangs.

"One of y'all niggas get the door. This pussy ain't going nowhere," someone called out.

"Yeah, motherfuckers, I know y'all hear that. It might be room service," a guy on the couch shouted as he was getting his dick sucked.

The dude in the kitchen stumbled to the door. "Who is it?" he asked, licking his lips and thinking about the wings they had ordered.

"Room service; your order, sir," someone replied on the other side of the door.

The guy unlocked the door, putting his hand on the door handle. He looked over his shoulder, yelling out that the food was there. Perfect timing, because everybody was hungry and starting to get tipsy from the Hennessey. He opened the door, ready to let the room service guy in with the tray of hot wings and jumbo shrimp. What he got was nowhere near that. He was definitely still about to get served. Duke and his three-member crew were standing there, ready to shake shit up. The guy who opened the door could not do anything besides stand there dumbfounded, frozen in place.

'Man, why the fuck did I come to this stupid ass party?' he thought, staring down the barrel of Duke's chunky .357.

Duke had one finger over his lips, gesturing to the man to keep his mouth shut. He smiled that same devious smile his crew knew was the signal that it was time to get busy. Face Hound was to the left of Duke with his Glock pressed against the head of the room service guy. The dude had tears streaming down his white face and was five seconds from pissing his uniform pants. Face looked down disgusted at the white boy. His pants now were soaked from him pissing on himself out of fear. Everybody was masked up and set to follow protocol. The Duke Boys were ready for action.

Duke whispered to the guy at the door to move slowly. He told the man to move toward him, one step at a time. Once Duke had him in his grasp, he and his crew eased into the room unnoticed. They left the first two victims face down on the floor under Malik's watchful eye. Face, Gooch, and Duke bum rushed the rest of the room.

"Everybody, get the fuck down and shut the fuck up! If you move or make a sound, I'ma shoot yo' stupid ass!" Face demanded, shouting what he wanted them to do.

The bitches screamed anyway, but quickly got quiet after Face Hound pistol-whipped the dude on the couch, who was still getting himself some bomb head. They ordered everybody to get on the floor and shut the fuck up. Duke was full of adrenaline and ready to show out behind the bullshit he and Sheedah had gone through earlier. He followed Face's lead and smashed the butt of his gun into another nigga's face, causing blood to shoot from his right eye socket. Duke had to put on a performance, so he hit the dude about ten times until he was unconscious. It scared the shit out of the rest of the hostages. They all thought they had just witnessed a homicide.

"Turn that muthafuckin' music up. This is my fuckin' shit!" Duke shouted, wiping the blood off his gun, and he started dancing.

"Ooooo weeee, nigga, somebody needs to get me a drink. I like top-shelf shit too," he said as he hit his smooth two-step.

Everyone was looking at Duke like he was a fucking lunatic. The music got louder to ensure that every scream and cry would be smothered. Even gunshots would be difficult to notice. Fucking with these four savages, there was no telling what was liable to happen.

Sheedah was lying face down on her belly. She couldn't believe this bullshit was happening right now. All she had wanted was to live it up a little bit tonight and get her mind off Duke. As she lay there, she began to focus on the voice that was talking.

"Everyone, stay the fuck down and y'all gonna make it outta here alive!" the voice declared.

"No, it can't be," Sheedah thought.

A couple more words and she was convinced: It was Duke's crazy ass. She couldn't believe he was doing this to her, but quickly understood it was because of how she'd spoken to him in front of the guys. She looked up at him. They locked eyes and shared that moment. He then told Gooch to check everyone's pockets and take their jewelry. Sheedah and Duke's eyes were still locked. Sheedah broke the gaze by rolling her eyes.

"Listen, muthafuckas. Anyone of you niggas do anything other than what the fuck I say to do and there's gonna be dying consequences. When I speak, you muthafuckas listen. This is my first and only warning!" he continued, emphasizing his words with a tone of authority.

The words were so aggressive and forceful that they sent chills down everyone's spine. For the very first time in her life, Sheedah was afraid of Duke and what he might do. She knew him really well and understood the extent his wrath could reach. They had shared many nights on the same pillow talking, and she knew just how crazy Duke could get.

When he had finished gathering everyone's personal belongings—money, watches, and even their phones—seeing everyone tied up and afraid gave him nothing but pure satisfaction. He smiled and said, "Thank you, nice gentlemen and pretty whores, for y'all's time. Y'all sure have some beautiful women in here. We got to bounce, but y'all have fun now, ya hear?"

Duke and the crew eased out the door the same way they had come in.

It took Sheedah and her friends hours to finally get untied. The only reason help arrived was because the hotel staff noticed the room service guy hadn't returned from room 107. Sheedah was upset and hurt Duke would play her like that. It was not the first time they had not seen eye-to-eye. It was the first time he had ever pulled a stunt like this though, and she was gonna make sure Duke knew about himself.

The next day, she did exactly that, but in a more respectful tone this time. Duke thought it was hysterical when she told him how things had gone after they had left. She also confided in him how turned on she had been too. Watching him from the victim's point of view had made her pussy as wet as an ocean. She broke down how she understood why he had reacted the way he had and apologized to him for being disrespectful. Then she asked for her cut of the money and jewelry they had taken from the guys. She also told him she needed her shit back. All Duke could do was laugh. He gave her back her personal belongings, but not a cut of the heist—it was part of the lesson. She understood wholeheartedly.

"Let's go get something to eat," he told her, and they bounced.

Chapter Seven:
Valentine's Day: Part 1

It had been several days since he had been shot, and Duke was still lodged in his comatose state. Sharelle continued to make her visits, hoping and praying he would pull through. Sharelle was always at the hospital bright and early, and today was no different. When she showed up, she expected to see the same thing – a tight-eyed hunk of a man with his eyes closed and in a world only he knew.

This morning was a little different though. Noticing the tears and smiles forming on Duke's face, she wondered what was going on with her man and shed a few tears of her own seeing him endure the pain she figured he was experiencing at that moment. With concern and curiosity, she watched, as his condition was not changing.

While Sharelle remained at Duke's bedside, Bishop was still on a mission of his own. He was relentless in his hunt for answers to who was behind what had happened to his little brother. His mind worked in mysterious ways, making him place blame on everyone he who crossed his mind. It was sad to say, but Sharelle was his prime target. With nothing to really go on—only that Duke was with her when he had been hit up and she had not caught a hot one—it just did not sit right in the pit of his stomach. Pac had been killed in a car and Suge had not caught one, but that shit was rare. Duke was his life, and for that reason alone, his little brother's situation had him looking at everyone as suspect.

Bishop was going to stop at nothing until he figured out what had happened to his brother. He was almost out of leads, so placing blame on Sharelle was the only logical conclusion for him. Bishop was never one to trust any man, and *especially* not a woman; that was something that was just unthinkable to him. So now that he was dealing with trust issues, he had no choice but to place the blame on Sharelle. He wanted to be sure he was not barking up the wrong tree, since he had already fucked up two people whom he had later figured were innocent. Bishop thought the best thing for him to do was to confront her and do his own interrogation of her. He said silently to himself, "Let's see if she keeps it one hundred," and he called her phone.

"Hello; how are you doing?" he asked with ill intentions.

"I'm all right. How are you doing, under the circumstances?" Sharelle answered, not knowing Bishop's true intentions.

'She sounds concerned,' he thought, but it was time for him to shoot his shot to see where her head was.

"Listen, Sharelle, I know my brother cares a lot about you, therefore, there's no need to beat around the bush about what I have on my mind and has been on my mind. I just wanna know what happened to my little brother. That's it."

He paused, giving her a chance to speak and come clean if she needed to come clean about anything.

Sharelle was at a loss for words. She thought she and Bishop had already gotten past this. She was filled with frustration and anger behind Bishop's question, but instead of showing her emotions to him, being the woman she was, Sharelle kept her composure and simply reiterated to him what she had already told him the first time.

"Like I told you after everything transpired, our night started off nice. Duke seemed to be in a good mood. We hung out, and he had a conversation with a couple of dudes. After that, we left and all hell broke loose out of nowhere," she replied, telling her story exactly the same as she had told him the first time.

"I don't know if I told you that he did take a call from a person while we were together; it was a guy. Duke never said the guy's name, but I did see his facial expressions change during their conversation."

"No, you didn't mention that before. Are you sure he didn't mention a name? Did the voice sound familiar to you?"

"No; he doesn't tell me everything, and I don't know who he was because I never asked him," she said, sounding like she was telling the truth.

"Hmmm..." Bishop said, wondering who in the hell Duke had talked to.

"Your brother was his normal sweet self. We had a conversation on the phone, with me not knowing he was on his way to pick me up, and everything was going smoothly. You know how he is," she said.

"Did he make the plans where y'all were going or did you pick the spot?"

"I had no idea what was on his agenda. When he got here, I was just going along for the ride. He liked surprising me, so I wasn't going to interfere with his plan, and—"

"Okay, I understand that," Bishop replied, still not one hundred percent convinced.

Having listened to her seemingly heartfelt words, Bishop felt like he had heard enough though. In fact, he stopped her from telling the rest of her story because she had not mentioned the gift Duke had bought her, which was for Valentine's Day. Duke was excited about that day, and he had bragged about it to Bishop all that week. He was saying how he had taken a page out of his big brother's book, referring to how Bishop captivated his woman with flowers and gifts for special occasions.

Then Bishop asked Sharelle, "Are you sure that was the day?"

Confused by his question, she got quiet for a second while she got her thoughts together. Even though she was still emotional about what had happened to Duke and with him almost dying, Sharelle knew her story was accurate. She then got herself together, apologized for her emotions, and told him, "It was Valentine's Day. He had called me just to start an argument, at least that's how it appeared at first."

She started telling her story again, but this time a slightly different version.

"I remember Duke calling, and he was playing because it was Valentine's Day. I wasn't catching on, because I didn't even remember that it was. We were going back and forth for a while, and I must have said something to make him hang up on me. I called him back and he told me he'd hung up 'cause I wasn't letting him get a word in."

"So, you say, during your conversation, he was already on his way to get you? Is that right?"

"Yes. He was just full of surprises that day. A package had been delivered by FedEx from him right before he got to the house. I was all giddy and blushing, turning fifty shades of red. I was excited, Bishop. Your brother was actually making an effort to show me he was in love with me."

Bishop managed to muster a small smile. He thought about the conversation he had had with Duke and his brother wanting to step-up his game in that department. He had told Duke there was nothing wrong with being in love, but he had also warned him to be careful.

"Bishop, I tell you, it was just an amazing feeling that came over me that day. I finally felt like I was worthy of Duke, worthy of his time and his heart. We were planning on making love the whole night away."

Bishop remembered he had felt a little uneasy about his brother traveling to Pennsylvania by himself. He had simply said to Duke, "Be careful," and he had let Duke know he was going to call his dude who was from out there to let him know his little brother was going to be in town, something Duke did not have a problem with him doing. Bishop knew from Duke that Sharelle stayed in a nice part of town because he called her neighborhood bougie, but he still was going to alert his people up that way and made sure Duke let his crew know his whereabouts. His last words that day to Duke were, "Enjoy yourself." He told Duke to make sure he hollered back once he had arrived.

Bishop sat on the phone, not really listening as Sharelle babbled on. He was thinking that Duke had asked him to use his Aston Martin. He had not let him because he had one of his people coming to town, and they were supposed to hit up New York. Now he wondered, if Duke had been in another car, would that have been a disguise and maybe saved him from the drama? All because he had wanted to take Kara to see *The Lion King*. They had talked briefly about Kara's coming, and Bishop knew Duke was genuinely happy for him. It had been a minute since Bishop had shown any emotion for any chick. Bishop remembered Duke telling him he was going to get dressed and leave.

It had taken him a few hours to get himself together, but after he was done, Duke ensured he was fully equipped and ready to hit the highway. He had jumped in his truck and was looking for his favorite CD before he pulled out of the driveway. He inserted his music in the player, and before he could turn it all the way up and let the subs vibrate the roof, Gooch had hit his phone.

"Yo, what's good?" Gooch asked as Duke was backing out, trying to stay focused on what he was doing,

"Nothing much, my dude. On my way to PA, gotta bounce for a few days. So, make sure you let the crew know and hold down the town 'til I get back."

"I heard. Do you, my nigga. You ain't hard to find. I got this end."

"That's what I wanna hear, my G! One."

"You already know. Peace."

The two disconnected the call after their brief conversation, and Duke proceeded to his destination. Jumping onto the highway, his mind started to reflect on the business and how he was thinking about leaving the streets alone. Right now, he was at peace leaving the streets alone for a few days. Duke was hoping Gooch could handle everything while he was gone, especially since a lot of niggas owed money that needed to be collected. His crew was about their cash.

Duke took his focus off business and focused more on Sharelle and the night he had planned for them, wondering what she was going to be wearing once he arrived. He knew it did not take much for her to look sexy and beautiful, especially since it was normal for her. He could not wait to be that snack they had discussed on the phone. Duke really liked Sharelle. She was a natural beauty who did not need any makeup for enhancement. He knew one thing for certain: no matter how she looked when he picked her up, she would not disappoint. Therefore, tonight would be no different from any other night. Duke felt his manhood rise up, and now, he was growing anxious to see her.

Duke ejected his old Eric B. and Rakim CD and inserted his man Pac. Pac was just that dude who told it to the world like it should have been told. He never took a road trip without bumping Pac.

This be the realist shit I ever wrote / Against all odds ...

Pac was spitting, and Duke bobbed his head to the music echoing out of the surround sound throughout his truck. The mood was set. Listening to

Pac only changed him more into a gangster. Song after song, he listened to, and he knew the words to every Pac song so well that one would have easily thought he had written them. Duke got in highway mode, which was what Pac did to him. He was yelling throughout the truck as if he was signing up for some type of talent show, singing his heart out.

Picture me rollin' in my 500 Benz / I got no love for these niggas, there's no need to be friends / They got me under surveillance, that's what somebody be tellin' / "Know there's dope being sold", but I ain't the one sellin'

As he was singing the Pac lyrics, his phone interrupted his showcase. He noticed it was Sharelle calling him, but before answering his phone, he told Pac, "Gotta get this, Pac. I'ma have to get back with you," as if Pac was actually there in the truck with him. Turning the music down a little bit so he could hear her voice, he answered.

"Hello. What's good, baby?"

"What are you doing, love?"

"Baby, I'm close to your house."

"Don't tell me that!"

"Yeah, baby, "I'm close."

"I'm so excited to see you. I was just over here thinking about you. Another reason why I had to call you. I need to be in your arms. I mean, now!"

"C'mon, babe. I'm driving right now. I can't be driving too excited. What if I get pulled over with a hard dick? How do you think the police would react if they saw this weapon sticking out my pants?"

"Then, baby, I guess he or she is gonna be just as happy as I am," she laughed, and Duke laughed as well.

"That'll be all right, baby, especially if it's a female who pulls you over. I promise she won't be disappointed." The laughter continued from both of them.

"That's what's up, baby. At the same time, I need you too. My shit is rock-hard right now. See how you be having me?"

"Mmm mmm... that sounds so good to me, Duke."

"Oh yeah? You wanna play, huh? You know you're gonna get it!"

"That's what I want. I want to get it! How you say it?"

"Now you're talking my language baby!"

"You have jokes, huh?"

"No, baby, no jokes, for real. I need to touch and kiss all over you. Touching, kissing, sucking, licking—I mean it. All! Things we haven't done in a while!"

"I'm with all that, baby. Damn, you miss the kid that much?"

"Ahhh, baby. Only if you really knew. I miss you so much!"

The sound of a car horn was heard.

"You hear that, right?"

"Wow, already?"

"Yeah. Bring your ass here, girl!"

"Comin' now."

"Yeah. That's how it goes when The Duke wants something or someone badly. Just as badly as you want me!"

"So, you want me badly, huh?"

"As if you really have to ask me that question. My thirst is in overdrive. I WANT YOU!"

Sharelle exited the front door of her building looking like a winner on America's Next Top Model with her tight jeans and Burberry fitted top that hugged her breasts better than he could. She was heading straight for his ride, and being the new man he was, he jumped out to greet her, hugging her and exchanging lip service. They embraced like it had been years since they had seen one another. Their embrace was deep, and he could feel her heartbeat up against his chest.

When she tried to release herself from his hold, he was not ready to let her go, so he held on for a little while longer. He pulled her back against him tightly, as if to say to her, "Where the fuck you going? This my moment." Pulling her close into his body, he kissed her passionately, letting his hands slide down to grip her plump ass cheeks. After a few more seconds of holding her tightly and her savoring the moment, he let her go, just to hear her complain about his loud music. Pac was bumping so loud that the base was shaking her neighbors' windows.

"Boy, my neighbors are going to have so much to say about me. You and your loud music—this music is why you think you're a thug," she playfully said. "Listening to that damn 2Pac all the time—all day, every day! Let's get into the truck, but before we get in, give me another kiss."

Duke complied without argument, kissing her before she got into the truck. Before he got in, he closed her door for her, but before closing her door, he had to let her know something.

"Lil Momma, I fuck with Pac the long way. You know you love his music, not to mention how you love the thug in me!"

"Boy, get outta here with all that mess. Every time you come to my house, you have that music playing. You do know there is other music you can listen to, right?"

"I get it, baby. It's just that—his music, Pac is more realistic to me, for me. You know thug in his dictionary doesn't stand for what people think it stands for. It means The Hate U Give. So, with that being said, shut ya face and give me some more kisses! Fuck all this talking!"

Duke did not like anyone dissing Pac. Falling into place and doing exactly what had been requested of her, she puckered her lips, ready to get on with their evening. They were still in front of her building, and they both knew they had to slow the moment down before things got too out of control. Any other chick would have had to suck his dick right there in public, but Duke chilled out, knowing patience was a virtue. He then closed her door and complimented her on how sexy she was looking.

"Damn baby, you are looking so damn good tonight," he said when he got in on the driver's side.

"Isn't this what you asked of me, baby? To look my best?"

"Yeah, but goddamn! If you continue this type of behavior, I'ma be sticky and messy as hell, and we have yet to get our night started."

"So what? I've waited all day to see you for this. Hell, I've waited weeks for this moment, so let's get messy and sticky together!"

"Trust me, baby, before the night is over, we are definitely gonna get very messy and dirty. But first, let's get this damn night started. Afterward, we can do whatever we wanna do to each other. Oh yeah, before we go anywhere though, I have something for you."

Reaching behind the seat and grabbing his second gift, which was in a Tiffany's bag, he saw she was all smiles.

"Here. This is a little token of my love and appreciation."

Duke handed her a blue Tiffany box. Inside was a diamond-flooded tennis bracelet and matching chain set. She was so excited she almost creamed her Victoria's Secret thongs without being fucked.

"Turn your neck around."

He undid the clasp and put the chain on her. Sharelle was overwhelmed with excitement at her new gift. She wanted to display her gratitude toward Duke because no man had ever given her anything just out of love.

"Oh, baby, are you for real? These diamonds are for me?"

"No, baby, they're for Beyoncé. Of course, they're for you!"

"This is what I mean. You are always spoiling me."

Sharelle grabbed him, pulling him closer to her so she could shower him with more hugs and kisses.

"Yeah, baby, that shit ain't about nothing. I got it like that."

"Duke, I love you so much."

"I love you too, baby."

"It's crazy because after what you have given me right now, what I have for you doesn't come close," she said in a disappointed tone.

"Baby, my gift to you doesn't warrant competition from you. I'm just glad you're sitting right in front of me. You're priceless, queen. You are everything any man could ask for, better than any material gift. You're all I need. Nothing else matters to me. I just wanna enjoy you, especially when I need for nothing but you. Lil Momma, what you must always understand is, since we've been together, my life has been more peaceful and happier than it has been in a long time. You are the best, the best part of me that makes me complete, and I mean that." He paused for a second seeing her eyes water up.

"I live a complicated lifestyle, and so, thank you for you. The fact that you allow me to be me means the world"

"Awww, I am speechless!"

"Ma, certain things don't need to be said, especially when I already know what it is between you and me."

"I love you, Duke."

Duke was never really into the Keith Sweat type shit, but she had him all worked up. He felt like a drink was very necessary for the occasion.

"Ma, we gotta find somewhere to get a few drinks. I need something in my system. You have me all worked up. You just don't know. I've been having these lustful thoughts since you got into my truck looking all good."

"Those are good thoughts, love. Don't calm down on my account. I love you like this, you wanting me as badly as you do!"

"See, I knew you weren't a good girl!" he said, turning a corner and laughing.

"It's you, baby, you who makes me wanna be a bad girl. You and only you!"

Sharelle directed Duke to go to a location she knew that wasn't far from where she lived. They drove up to the spot, parked, and got out. They exited the truck and entered the small establishment. Grabbing themselves a booth in the corner, they sat down close to one another and wasted no time touching and feeling on each other. A few people were staring, and it was obvious to Duke some people seemed to know Sharelle in the small bar. He could tell by how some of them greeted her as she walked in.

Duke had been so engrossed in her that he had forgotten to do something. He told Sharelle he had to call his brother. Bishop had told him to call when he arrived in PA. Letting her know Bishop could be a little overprotective at times, it was best he called him, and she agreed. Duke got up from the table, looking for the men's room, telling her he would be right back.

"Awww, I think that's so cute. The brotherly bond you and Bishop share. I love how close the two of you are, true brotherly love. Don't take too long, baby. Come back to me, okay?"

"Baby, why wouldn't I come back to you? I wouldn't have it any other way. Give me a sec."

As Duke stepped off to call Bishop, he decided he could piss on the side of his truck. As Duke made his way outside the small bar, Sharelle took the initiative to call over a waiter to place an order, thinking he did say order whatever and get him two bottles of Cîroc, which is exactly what she did.

"Talk to me," Bishop answered, noticing it was his little brother.

"Yo, I'm here, all safe and sound."

"All right, that sounds smooth," Bishop replied.

"Me and shorty are good. We just stopped at this lil' bar to grab a few quick drinks before we go on our way. We're gone after we're done here."

"That's what's up. How long are you going to be in PA?"

"Remember, I told you already. I'ma be out here for a couple of days."

Their conversation went on for about five minutes before something caught Duke's attention. Since he'd been outside, he'd kept seeing this four-door, black-on-black Cadillac with light tint circling. He watched as it busted the corner again. It looked familiar, which he thought was just a coincidence, but he didn't believe in coincidences and thought he'd seen the car before. Shaking off the thoughts and simply pushing shit to the side, Duke finished up his conversation with Bishop.

"I heard you, little nigga, a couple of days. Yo, just make sure you holler at me every day while you're out there. Just check in from time to time. That's all I ask of you."

"I heard."

"Plus, I have my baby coming into town from Arizona. She'll be here for a few days herself. So, you know I'ma be catering to her every need, booed up, feel me?"

"Yeah, I gotchu."

"All right then. Again, don't forget to holler at me. My dudes are out there, so you aren't alone. Love you, lil' bruh."

"Love you more. Yo, let me get back inside. It's cold as hell out here. One."

"One," Bishop responded as the call was disconnected.

After Duke got off the phone, he looked around both corners just to be on the safe side, figuring his mind was playing tricks on him. He was looking for the Cadillac, but he didn't see anything in sight. Duke went back into the bar, walking toward the table he was chilling at with his boo, also booed up like Bishop was planning to be.

Duke noticed Sharelle conversing with two guys he had never seen before. He watched the two men as they started walking away from their table when they noticed he was getting closer. When he sat down, he looked directly at his woman, waiting for her to say something. He could tell she was a little agitated about something.

He asked, "What's wrong, baby? What are you looking so mad about?"

Sharelle was reluctant to tell her man what was wrong, only because she knew Duke all too well. She knew he might flip out in the bar and get in trouble. Those were the thoughts running through her mind, and she did not want to ruin their night. So, instead, she tried to avoid it, as if to say, nothing was wrong. However, her face showed a different story. It was obvious to Duke that something was bothering her, and he wanted to know what it was. She again explained nothing to him, trying to convince Duke that nothing was wrong.

"Nothing, really, baby. Let's just enjoy our evening," she said, knowing it was about to become complicated.

"Listen, it is or it isn't. You can't say nothing is wrong, but then say not really. It doesn't add up!"

With Duke being so damn persistent about what was bothering her, he stayed on top of the situation until she finally caved and told him what the issue was.

"Okay, baby, this is what's bothering me. I was talking to those two guys because they felt—or should I say feel—a little sour because I am no longer with their friend, who I dated before you, which was months ago. Baby, he and I broke up over fifteen months ago, around the time you and I met. So, when you left out to call Bishop, the two of them came over here and started asking me all sorts of questions about you. Who are you? Why am I in here with you? And a host of other questions I refused to answer. It was just stupid stuff, baby, and in my eyes, it's none of their damn business."

While she told Duke what had transpired while he was outside, she could see his expression changing. She could tell he was getting upset, and she did not want to see him become angry. She just didn't.

"However, like I already told you, baby, it's nothing," she persisted, trying to calm down a man who was already enraged. She then tried to get them back in the mood they were in before he'd gone to call Bishop.

"Are you good, baby?" she asked, growing concerned for what was possibly to come.

"Yeah, I'm good, baby. It isn't about nothing. I remember you telling me about your ex. He's probably the reason it took you so long to call me back, to call me period, when I first gave you my number. You took hella long to holler at a real nigga, but at the same time, I'm glad you finally did call me. Give me a kiss, baby. Fuck them clowns!" Duke replied, trying to play it off.

Without hesitation, she grabbed his face and planted several very passionate kisses on his soft, juicy lips. She didn't care if the entire bar was watching them. She felt the piercing eyes of the two men and others in the bar staring, but it was her night and she felt like fuck everybody else. Their affection was on full display, and all she wanted was Duke to feel like he was the one. Deep and sensual kisses she continued to bestow on him.

Duke laughed and asked, "Where are our drinks?", feeling like a boss.

"Baby, I was waiting for you to return, but I did order them already."

"Okay, now I'm back! Can we get them or not? I'm ready to turn up."

"Of course, baby. I'm ready too," she responded, pointing Duke to the waiter she had placed her order with.

Duke waved for the waiter, who came to take her order. "Listen, I'ma need two bottles of Cîroc, any flavor."

"Yes, sir, coming right up," the waiter replied hospitably, giving Sharelle a mean look.

The waiter came back with the order, opened the bottle, and started pouring their drinks as he was directed. He was not expecting a tip, because Sharelle had placed an order telling him to wait, but he could see the frustration on Duke's face that his drinks weren't waiting on him. However, Duke still tipped the waiter generously for his service.

Smiling at his woman, Duke moved closer to her, and the two began to cuddle up in their booth. They were smooching and talking about whatever came to mind. Although they were in a crowded place, it felt as though it was just the two of them and they did not care about anything but themselves. They continued through the night as if they were the only two in the bar because no one else mattered.

Then the sudden loud sound of a man's voice interrupted their mood. Out of nowhere, from a distance, one of the guys was heard saying, "Sharelle, you know we don't allow all that shit in our establishment! Take that shit somewhere else!"

Duke was having the time of his life, trying to ignore what had transpired at the table earlier, until the two men started yelling from across the bar. They were jacking hard, like it was illegal to get kissed by your woman in PA. Duke was not originally on any shit; he was just enjoying the night with his woman and trying very hard not to let anything or anyone mess up their flow. Now Duke wished the circumstances were different; he wished his crew were there with him. Duke was trying his best to hold back, thinking, 'If these two guys make any more loud and disrespectful comments, it's on.'

But the two guys did not stop, and their words now had Duke heated. Sharelle could see what was going on, and she tried to calm him down again, but it was too late.

"Baby, those guys are drunk and ignorant. They aren't worth it. Please, please relax. They don't know any better," she said, feeling his right leg starting to shake.

"I'm not feeling any of this shit, baby! Drunk or not, them dudes are being very disrespectful, something I will never tolerate!" he replied, knowing they were cutting it too close.

"Okay then, let's just leave. Let's get our bottle and leave!"

"Baby, just let me go over there and speak to the guys for a second. I promise I will not do anything to fuck up our night. Trust me, I promise. Everything is gonna be okay," he said, smiling at her.

She heard Duke out, but before she could respond to what he had said and tell him no, one of the guys yelled out, "Sharelle, who's the fucking dude you over there with? You have yet to introduce him to us. I know you hear me. Don't make me call Ronny!"

Duke could not take it anymore. "That's it!" he told himself as he got up from the table and quickly walked over to where the two guys were seated.

Now up close and personal, Duke kindly asked the men, "Can I be of some assistance to you fellas? You seem like y'all need some," in a tone that made them fully aware, that if they were to do or say anything stupid, there would be problems and repercussions. He then advised them not to do anything fucked up. Before he could get all the words out, one of the guys side-eyed him.

"Nigga, who the fuck you think you are, coming over here to our table? What the fuck do you think you want over here?" the darker one stated. He looked at his partner and cracked a smile, like they were ready for whatever.

The guy was twirling his sifter full of Hennessey and was becoming very animated with his words. Duke could tell he had not been paying attention when he started speaking to them. So, before doing anything crazy, Duke took a quick look to see if his woman was watching-- and she was. Sharelle was paying very close attention. Duke smiled at her, to let her know everything was okay. He then motioned to her as if to say, "I'm good. You don't have to worry." He blew her a kiss and turned his attention back to the two guys, but the atmosphere in the bar was about to change because he was pissed off!

"See, niggas, I tried to be the bigger man throughout this entire ordeal, but I realize you two niggas only want it one way!" Duke said, barking at the two dudes in front of him.

In one swift motion, he snatched his jacket open and brandished his true companion, his gun, in the presence of the two men who had not known he had it on his person. Sharelle had no idea he had it, even though he never left home without it. Duke had his back turned so Sharelle could not see or hear what he was saying as he continued going in on the guys.

"You bitch ass niggas have me mad as hell right now. You two muthafuckas almost made me make a loud-ass noise in this bitch that would not be good for business. Real talk!"

"Who does this fool think he is?" one of them asked, looking at the other.

"See, my woman begged me not to come over here, but me not listening to her, I came over here anyway! Plus, you niggas kept insisting I come over. I guess an introduction is what the two of you wanted so badly, so here I am—me and my true friend, who doesn't play any games once I let him loose! At the same time, I get it. You niggas saw a new face and thought I was alone as if shit was sweet or something. I'm bugging, right? I know you two niggas wish you could rethink all your decisions now, huh?"

Duke went on with the lesson of the day. He was pointing out to these clowns their mistakes as if he were the teacher and they were his students.

"Now, check it: If this was a different place and time, we wouldn't be having this little chat, because anywhere else, for the slightest disrespect from you niggas, I would have given y'all what y'all was craving. And trust me, you two niggas wouldn't be breathing right now! But since this isn't the time nor the place for any bullshit on my behalf, tonight is y'all's lucky night. It's Valentine's Day... See how good my baby is looking over there?" he said pointing in Sharelle's direction.

Scared to death, the two men looked over at Sharelle with angry expressions plastered on their faces and showed their fear when they looked back at Duke. It was as if they were blaming one another for the other's big mouth, yet they both had been popping shit off at Duke and Sharelle. He spoke so only the two of them could hear; therefore, anything Duke said they just shook their heads or spoke lightly as if to say they understood.

"Yes, she is looking very nice tonight," one man said, and the other replied, "Yes, homeboy, she is looking quite gorgeous tonight."

Duke noticed he had the two men scared out of their minds as he continued with his antics. "Thank you for noticing such a beauty, God's gift to me. Yeah, she belongs to me now!" making it perfectly clear to the men whose woman Sharelle was now. "And just in case the two of you still want to know who I am, Duke is my name."

The name was a name the two men would never forget. Hell, since they had almost fucked his night up, Duke figured he would have a little fun with the lames. He saw no problem with it, so he kept it up.

"Yeah, niggas, as you can clearly see, she is no longer with y'all's friend Ronny. She's with a real nigga now. Y'all understand that, right?"

Their voices shaking, the two men agreed. There was not much more they could do since the nigga named Duke standing in front of them had the upper hand.

"Good. I'm glad we have this understanding. But like I told you niggas a minute ago, do not speak to me in a fucked up manner. It's unacceptable, especially when I'm with my lady. See, my first thought was to take her home, come back, and knock you two niggas' fuckin' heads off. But better yet, I figured I would come over here like a man and put everything into its proper perspective, because we wouldn't want anything like this to happen again. Feel me?"

"Yes, we feel you," one man said, speaking for them both.

Their conversation went on for a few minutes longer, and their only words for the rest of the night were, yes and sorry. They were not trying to make Duke any more upset than he already was. In the midst of everything, being sarcastic, Duke made it his business to compliment his lady once again, showing acknowledgment.

"Honestly speaking, damn, my baby is extra hot tonight! I mean for a real nigga, that is!"

It was his time to shine since the two earlier had had so much to say. He continued, "Yo, I can't even front. My girl is beautiful. I'm bagging the fuck outta her tonight. Yo, Ronny fucked up. Wow! How the fuck did he let something so special like her get away? Stupid ass nigga!"

Duke turned to look in Sharelle's direction and kissed the palm of his hand and blew it at her. Understanding it was time to get back to his night with his woman, Duke finished his business.

"So, now that we've met and we understand one another, I gotta get back to my lady. She's already mad at me for coming over here, fuckin' around with you two clowns."

Never letting go of his true companion, Duke suddenly leaned into the two guys. He stooped down to eye level, staring them both directly in their eyes to instruct the men on how he wanted his night to end. He and Sharelle were planning to leave the bar, and they had ordered their last drinks for the night. Once everything was all said and done, the men slowly got up from their table, and Duke and the men embraced one another as if they were now best friends.

After the embrace, Duke asked, "Which of you are driving?

Shakingly, the darker man replied, "I am."

Duke said, "Hand over the keys. I wouldn't want you getting any quick ideas, ya dig? I'll leave them with the waiter."

The darker man complied and they continued drinking their last drink. Duke was ready to put distance between himself and the guys before he added to PA's unsolved murder cases.

As the two men were making their way toward the exit, Duke said, "By the way, never ever come around here again, because whenever I'm in PA from now on, this is my new hangout spot. If somehow we should cross paths again, you two niggas had better run for the hills. I'm sure I won't be this nice next time around—but I'm hoping there won't be a next time. Do we understand one another?"

"Yes, fully!" the second man answered for the two.

"Good! Now beat it!" Duke said with force.

Without any resistance, the men did exactly what they had been told to do. They got the fuck up out of there!

Watching as they walked toward the door, Duke stood there until they left, trying not to cause any more attention to himself.

Sharelle sat waiting patiently, with an oh-so-calm look on her face, but she was in shock at the same time. She was wondering why the men had had a change of heart so suddenly. What had Duke said to the guys? A question she knew would not be answered. After the two guys apologized to the entire bar for their night and politely said, "Good night, everyone," they left, running for the hills like Duke had said.

Chapter Eight:
Valentine's Day: Part 2

When everything was over, Duke was mentally bugging out, thinking how lucky the dudes had been. 'They were actually very lucky,' he thought. When he had murder on his mind, it usually trumped everything else—especially thinking how he had murdered for less. He hoped both of those niggas were counting their blessings and thanking the Man above that he was on some other shit. Duke remained cool at the moment, being as though he could not move as recklessly as he wanted to, not with Sharelle being at his side and all. Besides, he wanted to show her a good time.

The woman had his heart turning from the dark side to the rays of light, beating now for his future. For the first time in his life, Duke felt a glimpse of love and happiness from a female. Therefore, he knew how important it was to keep her safe and not act like a fool. It was amazing that she had Duke rethinking his miscreant ways. His street life behavior was lethal and dangerous, but she was starting to have an effect on him that he'd never thought possible. He knew Sharelle was the type of woman a nigga would die for, literally. She was going to be the woman he would learn to love unconditionally, which was something he had noticed he was feeling months ago about her love, and he felt she would reciprocate that very same affection.

Thinking with his big head, which was new for him, he walked back over to where Sharelle was still seated, observing him from afar. He was back in her presence, and before she could get one word out, Duke kissed her in the mouth without wasting any more time. She did exactly what he had thought and reciprocated with the same amount of passion he had provided. She did it without asking any questions about what had just transpired between him and the two guys. All they could do was smile at one another, as if to say, everything was okay.

Sharelle was not sure what had taken place between Duke and the two guys, but since her man was back by her side, in her comfort zone, nothing else really mattered to her at the moment.

"This has been one of the most memorable nights of my life," she said.

She was thinking that the most memorable moment had been when the two guys left the bar. Duke had punked them so badly that they had almost run out the door. Their apology was funny too. Right after that, Duke broke into her thought process.

"Babe, you good?" he asked, feeling they were going to be good.

"Yes, babe, I'm good, now that you're back over here where you belong," she replied. "Listen, babe, you can't be doing stuff like that!"

"I know, and I am truly sorry for that bullshit. It won't happen again; I can promise that as long as no one disrespects me or my lady."

"It had better not, 'cause I would go crazy if something happened to you."

"I feel you, girl. However, what you gotta understand is, that was hard for me. People don't talk to me like that, or fuck with anyone who's with me. So, when everything went down, I was caught off guard, ready to get into that mode. It took a lot for me to restrain myself from doing bad things to them lames. At first, I just reacted without thinking, because that's how I was raised. Kill first, worry about it later. But, again, I am truly sorry. So, so sorry babe!" he explained.

Duke wanted Sharelle to understand he wasn't a bitch ass nigga by no means. The only reason them dudes had gotten a chance to see another day was because he was with her and in public.

"I understand, babe, but yes, you weren't thinking and neither were those two guys. However, I am impressed and very proud of how you handled yourself tonight. I think you handled yourself very well. I've got a confession to make, babe," she said with a smile.

"Oh yeah, a confession, huh? So, what's your confession?" he asked.

"Your gangsta really turned me on a little bit," she said, smiling from her remark. "Am I wrong for that?"

"Naw, babe, you aren't wrong at all; you're just keeping it real. You ain't seen my real gangsta yet," Duke replied, feeling a little turned on himself, and smiled a wide grin of his own.

The two of them flirted back and forth, causing things between them to heat up fast. Knowing how turned on she was about his actions, Duke knew it was time to be himself once again.

"Yo, where's the fuckin' waiter in this muthafucka?! It's time to go! Shit... My baby is turned on."

"I'm ready when you are."

"Well, let's get our bottles to go! It seems like I'm still getting my Valentine's Day gift after all, huh? So, I guess all is forgiven?"

"First off, yes, babe, you are forgiven. Second, you definitely are still getting your gift!"

"Good. Plus, I have one more surprise for you tonight. One last gift," he replied, happy she was still in the mood to finish the night.

"See, Duke, I don't know how to take you and all these gifts. Babe, you're so good to me. The way you love me, provide, and protect me—no one has ever been as loving to me as you are. What have I done to deserve you?"

"For one, baby girl, you can stop asking yourself that question. I feel it's me who's the fortunate one. What have I done to deserve you is the real question! And if you were never loved like this before, then you haven't fucked with a nigga who truly deserved you," he said and paused. "Either way, I love and appreciate you more than words can actually express. So, just know that every time I give you any sort of gift, it only compliments me, and I'm compensating you for those lost words and expressions. That is the true story."

After that statement, the two of them were very quiet for a few seconds. Duke smiled inside to himself as he thought about everything the two of them had just expressed to each other. He also smiled to himself for the simple fact that his next surprise was going to blow her away. The thought of the brand new 2020, smoked-grey, four-door Mercedes Benz S63 AMG. The car was sitting in front of her house with a big ass red bow attached to it. It was all hers, paid for and ready for her to drive. He was gloating to himself because he had done something for someone without any ulterior motives.

His only intent was both of their satisfaction. He knew the gift was there, because during his encounter with the two guys, a text message had come over his phone, letting him know Sharelle's gift had arrived, which meant it was time to go.

"Now that we are done playing around here, can we go somewhere and play around with each other?" she asked, still feeling horny. "Tell you the truth, babe, I am eager to get where we are going. I need to feel you inside me—like now!"

"Say no more," Duke replied as he held up his hand and snapped for the waiter. A different server than the first one showed up.

"Check please, and we'll take them two bottles of Cîroc to go. For real!"

Duke helped her put on her North Face, thinking about the next gift he was going to shower her with. Maybe a blue iris mink, something not many women in PA would have. The two got their bottles and hurried out the bar's front door. They both were smiling as they walked out. He had his hands around her waist, wanting to grip her fat ass as he sparked a brief conversation. Duke whispered something in her ear.

"For real, babe," she replied, looking over her shoulder at him.

"Ma, I told you, you was a square!"

"See, Duke, this is the type of talk right here that got me naked the first time," she replied, loving what he'd just whispered to her, and smiled.

"Stop talking like that to me, babe, before you have to do me right here!

"Babe, I'm just playing. Let's get the fuck out of here. I need you for something."

"I need you too and I can't wait to give all of me to you!"

Duke finally let her waist go, getting a quick feel on her plump ass-cheeks as he walked his girl to his truck. Helping her inside, he smacked her on the ass again. Duke strolled around his vehicle to the driver's side so he could get in as he fumbled for the key again. Duke smiled as he thought about a scene from one of his favorite gangsta flicks, A Bronx Tale. Sharelle had leaned over to unlock the driver-side door for her man, just like Sonny from the movie had said a keeper broad should do.

Out of nowhere, Sharelle noticed two figures appear swiftly from the shadows. Dressed in all black, they both had on masks, hiding their faces, and pistols in their hands. The men moved swiftly as they approached Duke, like hungry foxes in a rabbit's den.

Duke saw the scared look on his girl's face, causing his natural instincts to kick in, and he understood something behind him was not right. His second instinct made him remove his heat so he would be prepared. Duke caught a reflection in the window of two masked men raising their weapons and pointing them in his direction.

"Shit, these fools want to fuck in my business," he said, turning around and letting half a clip head in their direction.

He started blasting before a word was said. Chaos erupted quickly in the parking lot as bullets were exchanged. All the people in their cars could hear was gunfire. It went on for about ten seconds, which felt like ten minutes to Duke. One of them even reloaded just as Duke emptied his first clip. That ten seconds had felt like an eternity.

There was a heavy amount of ammunition still being exchanged between Duke and the two men. The killers were adamant about their mission to end Duke's life. Duke being Duke, he was determined not to let them successfully complete the job. Focusing on everything that was taking place before his eyes, he started yelling instructions to Sharelle.

"Lock the doors, babe! Lock the damn doors!" he yelled as he crouched down outside the truck, his guns blazing.

He reloaded and gunfire erupted heavily once again. Sharelle heard him yell to her what to do, but the thought of leaving him out there alone, one against two, scared the shit out of her. That was not what she wanted to do, nor did she have plans of locking him out there with those two killers, not without trying to help him in some type of way. It was unacceptable to leave him to fight the battle alone. He had come all the way to her town to see her, so she was not about to do any of that!

At that moment, fear mixed with her job training forced her instincts to kick into action, and she reached further over into the driver's seat. She shoved the driver's door wide open, just missing Duke's head. All she could hear was the pinging of bullets flying by her head, hitting her windshield. Sharelle paid no attention to the hot lead falling near her but not penetrating the windows.

At that moment, Duke realized what she was doing, backing up so he would be able to situate himself to slide into the truck. The sudden grab of his shirt pulled him backward in her direction and into the truck, and he knew right then that his babe was down with him. He pushed his Timbs backward, scuffing the rubber soles to help the situation out a little more. Sharelle was grabbing and pulling him with everything in her.

"COME ON, BABE! GET THE FUCK IN HERE!" she screamed, tears flowing heavily.

Finally, with one powerful tug, finding strength she didn't know she had, she got him inside. He quickly told Sharelle to get down on the floor. His body was riddled with bullets. He also had blood leaking from both sides of his face or head, and neither one of them knew where it was coming from. His adrenaline was rushing faster than a crackhead who had just found twenty dollars.

Duke got the door closed as they tried to figure out where the blood was coming from. The two masked men were now standing outside the truck, still determined to kill Duke. They fired a few more shots as they attempted to get in the truck. They continued to fire on the vehicle relentlessly, reloading for a third time. The two men fired again and again!

The sounds of the gunfire stopped! It took Duke a minute or two to realize he was still alive. Why wasn't he dead yet was the million-dollar question he wanted answered as he looked at the gunmen who were firing heavily on his truck. 'Nothing is happening,' he thought. The bullets were still bouncing off the vehicle as if they were not hitting it. At first, Duke was wondering if he was in some kind of dream, if this was really happening. Remembering how this truck was a gift from his big brother, Duke smiled. It had taken him a few seconds to finally figure it out.

He said to himself, "Yo, this nigga brought me a bulletproof truck! Only this nigga would do some shit like this without telling me!"

About the same time Duke realized what was going on with the truck, the two gunmen understood it too.

"The truck is bulletproof!" one of the gunmen yelled out.

"Damn!" the other one said as he finally noticed the same thing.

Understanding there was no more they could do, disappointment was plastered on their faces because their unsuccessful mission had come to an end. The two men took off running down the street, disappearing into the dark night. As the two men made their getaway, Duke heard Sharelle crying as he lay back into the seat, adjusting the lumbar control. He was going crazy trying to comfort her and trying to get her to calm down.

"They're gone, babe. We're safe," he said, still not realizing because of his adrenaline rush just how badly he had been hit.

"Babe, you're bleeding, and I don't know where it's coming from!" she cried out to him. She had never been involved in anything this extreme before, and she was scared out of her mind.

"Babe, calm down; I'm good. It's just a little blood. I'm going to need some new clothes," Duke replied.

He was trying to be modest and funny at the same time. Sharelle could not understand how he could have such a sense of humor after two masked men had just tried to kill him and her too.

"There's nothing funny about this situation, Duke!" she said in a terrified tone.

"This man bought a bulletproof truck," he said as if he had heard nothing she was saying to him. Delirious to the point he was unaware of what was going on with his body and mind due to him being shot multiple times, he was not even sure who he was talking to.

"This man? Who is this man, Duke? Who got you a bulletproof truck? Are you talking about Bishop?"

"Yeah, my brother," he replied, smiling and letting his pistol fall to the floor beside the gas pedal. "My brother is smarter than any motherfucker I know," he remarked just before he passed out.

"That's good, babe," she said, holding him tightly.

Confused as to what she should do next, she searched his body to find out where the blood was coming from. Duke was going in and out of consciousness. His eyes opened slightly again and he grabbed her hand, telling her he was good. Sharelle started rubbing her hands over the bulletproof vest that covered his chest. His eyes closed again, then opened again, which she knew could not be good. He was probably losing oxygen to his brain, which she knew would cause him to go into a coma.

He smiled and said to her, "I guess I'm not getting my Valentine's Day gift now, huh?"

"Babe, stop it! You're probably dying right now. Please stop playing around. This is a serious matter and you're bleeding badly."

"Get rid of the gun, babe. We've got to call 9-1-1 or get me to a hospital."

Duke wasn't from there, so he had no idea where he could get the closest medical attention, but he knew them people would show up when they reported a gunshot victim. Sharelle had never held a real gun and didn't have the slightest idea where to hide it. She looked down on the floorboard between his blood Timberlands and saw it lying there. It looked huge, like an army cannon. She did not know how he had hidden it so well from her vision in the first place.

"Babe, hide it where?"

He gave her instructions on how to get into the stash compartment he had built into his truck.

'Thinking of everything,' she thought about her man.

Sirens were heard in the distance and getting closer. He had a quick flashback from his childhood when his father had lain there dead in his parent's bedroom. It sounded to him like the same sirens, and he was wondering if Burcheck was finally going to get his man.

———————————————————

Sharelle told Bishop everything she remembered about that night. Then she told him, "And that's what happened. If there was more to tell you, I would, but that's all I know."

She hesitated before continuing. "Bishop, you do know I love your brother with everything in me, right? I just want him to come back to us."

Bishop could hear her crying through the phone, and it sounded genuine. Bishop now felt guilty for having her go through that again, silently accusing her of being behind what had happened to his brother, which she knew was what he was assuming about her. They both understood the magnitude of the situation. They both wanted to know what had happened to Duke and who was behind it. He also had his emotions, but he figured, *'Fuck them tears!'* He was trying not to be a coldhearted bastard, but he still needed answers and he was determined to get them. When it came to his little brother, Bishop felt like, fuck who didn't understand; that was his attitude.

"Okay. We'll talk again soon. Don't talk about this with anyone else, you hear me?"

"Yes, I hear you."

"I'm dead ass serious," Bishop told her before hanging up the phone.

To Sharelle, he still sounded extremely cold about everything.

Duke had so many enemies. Without any real leads to find those behind Duke's lying in the hospital in a deep coma and knowing how it could be a host of different people involved in this matter, Bishop was at a standstill, causing him to pound his fist on his dashboard.

Chapter Nine:
The Boys...How We Rollin'

Bishop was riding the highway like crazy, driving listlessly as he tore the road up as he reflected on his family life. His mind was racing as fast as the pistons in his engine. He could not slow down any of the memories as he sifted through all his thoughts. He put most of what had happened to his little brother on himself. Leaving Duke for so many years had to have taken a toll on his little brother. They were void of a father, and it was supposed to have been Bishop's job to step-up, but he could not do that from prison.

Thinking about all they had had to go through as children and all the shit Duke was getting into while he was away in prison, Bishop knew it was going to be a serious obstacle to deal with. Now all he could do was reflect on how he had approached life upon coming home, wholeheartedly believing it may have played a part as to why Duke was fighting for his life at this very moment.

Although he had always felt their father was a bitch ass nigga who needed to die a thousand deaths, there was something good that had come from the man. He felt he and Duke had learned certain things from him that had made them men. The man had birthed and raised them, and at times, he had shown them things they would be able to utilize on their journey through life. Their motto was to never back down from a person, no matter how big or small. They were taught to fight until there was no more fight left in them.

The people around the neighborhood knew early that Duke and Bishop were going to be a problem. Together they were viewed as a serious duo to be reckoned with. Growing up, the boys used to have problems with the fact that no matter how many times their mother and father got into it— and it was loud enough for everyone in the entire building to hear—sadly, no one ever tried to help her or come to her rescue. They both knew the feelings they held would be a grudge they would hold against society for a very long time to come.

Black people had lost their sense of duty to the community, especially black men. It was what it was, even though some of the neighbors had had their own opinions about the family and the boys as they were growing up. Most of them had felt Duke was the badass and the black sheep of the two boys. They had figured Duke probably deserved getting his ass kicked from their father on a daily basis. They were nosy neighbors who were oblivious to what Bishop and their mother had to endure from their father's hands.

The community had always felt it should have been Duke who went to jail for killing their father instead of Bishop. They had always thought Duke had done it, and Bishop had taken the wrap. Someone said that the day their father was murdered, gunshots had been heard way before Bishop came home from school. Some people also had said Bishop was downstairs with them when they heard the fatal gunshots that had ended their father's life. However, it just so happened they had not made themselves part of the case, or let their damaging statements get back to Burcheck.

It was a sad and tragic situation for the family, whichever way it had gone. What they did realize was it was best to mind their own business growing up in the hood. No matter how much a person might want to help the next person, people did just that: minded their own shit to prevent any repercussions.

Duke stayed being viewed as a young menace around the way, and it had gotten to the point where people were placing bets on his lifespan—meaning people were betting he would not make it to a certain age. If Vegas was taking odds, they would have quickly placed a wager that he would not live long. Most people picked, that by his eighteenth birthday, he either would be in heaven or hell—but most likely hell, they would wager, would be his new home. With all the shit he was getting into, they suspected Duke would meet a harsh reality that would not end well for him. Some felt it was sad to say that about a child, but that's how people felt, and being he was so goddamn bad, they might have been on to something.

Adults and children alike resented Duke and his wicked ways. His behavior was out of control by far. No one in the hood wanted their children hanging around him, whether it was playing with him or other activities. Duke knew it, but he surely never gave a fuck about what other people wanted or felt. His main priorities were his brother and his mother. The struggles he and Bishop endured growing up had only prepared them for the future. The two feisty little niggas were ready for whatever life was going to throw their way. "Bring it on!" was their slogan, along with a few others they had acquired as they aged.

Bishop, being the calmer one of the two and predominantly the deadlier one, only enhanced his ideas and abilities to become the most feared and respected gangster in the hood. Dying was not supposed to be an option for him or Duke. They both had the chance to become whatever they wanted in life; the choice was theirs. Bishop knew firsthand how coming from the hood and becoming a gangster was a career choice. It was also the goal for a lot of their peers. Almost everyone around them, including their ride-or-dies, craved some form of street life. However, only a select few would get the chance to actually live their story, and then tell about it.

The glamor of street life was their motivation to a better lifestyle. It was about the money, the power, and the fear instilled in those who opposed them. Those were the three elements, that if one possessed them, he would see respect on autopilot. They were going to force respect from people, whether they wanted to respect them or not. That was their mentality, especially Duke's, but working toward any of these goals was going to be harder than they had thought. Whether they were boys or men, they were going to strive. They knew only time would determine their fate, and they were headed straight in the direction of actuality.

The whole gangster mentality the boys craved had begun with their father's abuse. That and watching gangster movies had helped fuel the drive inside them, not to mention how they had seen so much violence on Chadwick and Avon Avenues. People who were from there had to learn how to survive in the darkness of its trenches. Forty-four Chadwick Avenue was known throughout the city as a crack-infested area, or heaven for an addict. But, no matter how dangerous things would become out there, Bishop and Duke had made it one of their earliest stomping grounds. So much money had been made on that block because of the heavy flow of traffic going through it, and children their age were not supposed to know what to do with that much money. While Duke and his friends ran around becoming miscreants, Bishop had had a hand in Chadwick's money pit.

Duke always stayed behind to fuck around with Malik, Gooch, Billy O., and Billy's little brother, Bop. Bop was a bad motherfucker who ended up going to prison years later behind stupidity. When he and his brother ended up going to prison, it brought about changes and new faces. Face Hound and Sheedah were the new additions to Duke's crew. The ironic thing about where they hung out was there was a school and a graveyard a few hundred feet away from each other. It was like somehow the two presented a choice: go to school or end up ten toes up. Nevertheless, it was obvious school had become secondary to them.

Before their time and after, Chadwick Avenue was a known stomping ground for gangsters. First to run through the block was a Jamaican by the name of Kelly, a real ruthless motherfucker who killed as if it was normal behavior—a rude boy you never would want to get caught within a dark alley, especially alone. A vicious killer. A zero-tolerance type of guy. It was always said that his crew moved on his every order—no matter what the issue was, no questions asked. See, back in the Kelly era, Chadwick was located in the South Ward area with Clinton, Hawthorne, Lyons, and Chancellor Avenues, all running parallel to Kelly's madness, it all seemed to be under his control. The length of his power seemed endless.

Kelly and the members of his crew made it apparent their terror stretched far—too far for anyone to be able to hide. He had power and respect, enough of it that a nigga or a bitch could not hide from him even if they had wanted to. Newark, the Brick City, has always been a place where people on the streets thought they were either the toughest of their crew or the most dangerous of all crews. They think they are better than anyone and everyone else who ran those same streets—whether they are a nigga or a bitch, not seeming to know there is always someone tougher and ready to go in full throttle. In Brick City, if you play the game, you had better understand that murder is the prize. You cannot win or be considered a valid contestant if you do not have a body count on your resume. Like DMX said, "Everybody is the man in their own hood." Or they pretend to be. In certain cases, that is true. People are someone in their own hood. Outside of that, they aren't shit!

Duke respected the stories of real gangsters, but at the same time, he felt like, fuck them! They all had had their time. He felt it was his time now; even as a kid growing up, he had felt that way. Duke felt like it was his era now, and no matter what, he was going to make sure his name rang bells throughout the city. His goal was to go beyond the limitations of his block. If he was going to run shit, it was going to be in his hood as well as the hoods of so many others. He was going to ring loudly, and he felt his name was going to ring well beyond his death. That was how he was carrying it, and his actions showed it.

For Duke and Bishop, the mistakes they had seen so many others make before them were not going to be theirs. It had always been told to them growing up, that no matter how much a person beefed or went to war over the streets, no one actually won. They had learned early in their young lives, that either you die a vicious death by your enemy, or live and go to prison for life. Either way, you live by the gun, you die by the gun.

There is never a winner when it comes to the streets, especially when the streets do not belong to you in the first place. The certainty or reality is the streets are going to be around and have been around before anyone claimed them and will be around well after everyone is done warring over them. In real life, you only gain the upper hand when you realize the streets only belong to one of two governments—the state demons or the federal fools—and no one else.

Yet, they had seen life in a different form. They were determined to win and own the streets, despite the stories. They were two young niggas who thought they were smarter than everyone else before them. Losing was not going to be an option. They had had this notion as young as they were because their minds' capacity went outside the box of the average thinker. The brothers possessed experience and knowledge the basic kids would not have at their age. They actually felt the average adolescent would not know what to do with the power of street knowledge that had been bestowed on them. The game was to be sold, not told, and most youngsters were naïve when life lessons were being taught to them. And yet, the fate involving these young guys' lives had the majority of the votes. Meaning, some people believed they would prevail, while most had them failing. In life, the majority ruled.

The stakes of them becoming bigger than their opposition were at an all-time high for them both. Again, only time was to decide the outcome of how they viewed reality. Thus far, it was not looking too promising for the brothers chasing their illustrious street dreams. Problems were just beginning. Bishop went away for seven years. Billy O and Little Bop were also gone for some years—ten for each of them.

Chapter Ten:
Nothing More, Nothing Less

Ironically, it was now a little past Duke's eighteenth birthday. So, whoever made the bet he would not make it, guess what? They had lost their paper because he had fucking made it. Duke was now legally a grown man, and his mind was made the fuck up. He was set on making sure the streets were his playground and making doubly sure the hustlers were going to invest in his goals. Duke was ambitious to rise to the top and make a name for himself, so he made sure the players got their early notices.

Duke was not into doing things for the love of it, especially since he believed love did not exist between two niggas. He was doing what he was doing for survival purposes only. Duke always had been told only the strong survived and that was him all the way. He easily could have done shit for a reputation, but gaining that was imminent once he had put the fear of a nigga's worst nightmare coming to fruition in their domes. That is what fueled him, drove him to be as gangsta as gangster could get. He had silently pledged to himself what he had vowed the outcome was going to be.

With Bishop gone—still doing prison time—life was starting to take a serious toll on Duke, and when things would become too much for him to handle, he would sit back and reflect on he and his brother's relationship. It seemed to ease his mind and bring him peace. The thoughts of certain conversations and advice Bishop had drilled into his mental always put things back into a real perspective for Duke.

It was hard to swallow at times because of the real reason Bishop even was gone. It had left a cold void in his heart. The emptiness that was left when they had sentenced his brother was one filled with ambition, anger, and a whole lot of frustration. Most of his emotions were feelings that haunted him and could not be contained, so he felt the one thing that would help ease him was releasing it all on those in the streets.

There were those individuals who swore they had the streets on lock, like they were in control of not only their own set, but the entire city. Duke was not having that any longer. He thought he knew what his primary focus was until Malik came up with a suggestion. Since they knew people all over town, there weren't too many places they could not go; whether people wanted them there or not was not their concern.

"I think we should go over to the section. My man, Sco, is over there eating. I feel he's a real dude," Malik said.

"He'd better be a real dude," Duke uttered to him.

Hearing what Duke said made Malik bat an eye. "What do you mean, making a statement like that?"

"I'm just saying, this nigga is your man, right? So, that's what the fuck my statement meant. He'd better be just that—yo' man!"

"Yeah, you heard him!" Sheedah interjected her comment now as she sided with Duke like she always did.

"Of course, you're gonna side with Duke. I'm pretty sure everyone else feels the same way too, right?"

Nodding their heads in agreement with Duke, Face and Gooch showed their loyalty as well when Malik questioned them, letting it be known it was Duke or nothing. Duke's squad was as loyal as they come. He felt Malik was loyal as well, but he knew Malik better than anyone.

"It's not unexpected to me to know y'all feel the way y'all do. I'm all for Duke too, but like I said, without anyone doubting my words, Sco is my man and that's what it is. My word is gold; it always has been. Don't ever question that shit. Y'all already know," Malik said.

Malik was feeling the need to give the crew reassurance and clear the air of any skepticism anyone was having about his man Sco. He felt it was necessary to tell them how and what it was. "I said it and I meant it, Sco is good! I would stake my life on it!"

"Yeah, bro, we ain't doubting you at all. It's the niggas we don't know that our trust issues fall into play with. At the same time, my brother, we hear you speaking up for your dude. He's your man, and trust me, we all get it. That's what it is! We were just saying—and I believe I speak for the crew—

he'd better be your man—for your sake. You should already know: your life will be staked on your belief!" Duke made his position, as well as the crew's position, known.

Their conversation continued for a few more seconds before an understanding was reached between all of them, especially Duke and Malik. The crew was always concerned about outsiders coming into their circle, and invading what they already had set, which was another reason why it was hard for everyone to get on the same page at first with Malik's suggestion. They had things in place for reasons and outsiders had to fit in, which not many were capable of doing. It was the codes they lived by that kept them safe and made their crew that much different from everyone else's crew. Duke prided himself on the codes and made sure his crew was a totally different breed from others. He insisted they possess an unbreakable bond that many people would not be able to understand or conform to.

Outside of Malik and Bishop, at first, it had been kind of difficult for Duke to embrace Gooch, Face Hound, and Sheedah. He had trust issues for so many reasons. It was not a secret, and Malik, of all people, knew Duke better than everyone else, which was another reason Duke allowed Malik to express himself as freely as he did. If that had been anyone else exercising their mouth, it would have been, hell to the naw, because plain and simple, that type of outburst would have been considered disrespectful and dealt with accordingly. There would have been a totally different result and would have ended up being rectified differently.

Also, Malik knew beforehand how far he could push Duke. Ultimately, Malik knew if he had kept challenging Duke word for word with his slick ass undertones, it would not have mattered who he was. That would have been unfortunate, but it would not have stopped there. Let's just say Malik understood deep down that he did not stand a chance of winning any altercation with Duke.

Still feeling the need to continue their discussion, thinking he had to make his point, Malik could not seem to bring himself to leave well enough alone. This time, he was adding even more sarcasm to his tone as he spoke.

"Yo, like I was saying before Duke so rudely interrupted me, Sco, that nigga, that's my man. He is over in the section on the small block, Goldsmith. It's a four-corner block where we can see everyone and everything from all angles. There are three small high-rise buildings located on the same corners. The buildings are good for us for so many reasons.

Lookouts can be posted with heat on two of them for sure. It will be our block and no one else's," Malik said.

"I'm looking at it as another block for us to do whatever we desire to do with it," he continued as he rubbed his chin.

After hearing Malik out, their meeting concluded. Exhausted from the back and forth with Malik, Duke felt the need to relax, so he went into one of the empty rooms in the apartment to lay it down. It was because of their friendship that Duke was feeling like Malik was trying to push his buttons, knowing he had no wind, but he had tried him anyway. It was another reason Duke thought it was necessary to relax before the shit got ugly.

Sheedah also saw the frustration sitting on Duke's face, which is why she waited ten minutes before following him into the bedroom. Duke and Sheedah had a complex relationship, but they knew each other's boundaries. Their intimate relationship had been over for years, but they still possessed a bond and chemistry that connected them way beyond your typical male and female relationship. She truly was a ride-or-die chick for him, and he was the same for her. In essence, Duke was her protector.

Both of them understood their history, which they did not allow to become detrimental to the team. That also was the reason their history did not stop them from indulging in a little pleasure from time to time, especially times such as the one she felt Duke needed her for right now. When she walked into the bedroom, the first thing she noticed was him lying on his back, one leg knee bent upward and the other leg flat, foot on the floor. He had his right arm over his eyes, which expressed how tired he was. Without saying a word, Sheedah took the initiative to do what she always did for him and for herself. She lay on top of him, putting her hands down his pants, with Duke not putting up much of a fight. He just lay there, allowing the moment to transpire and take its course.

"Yeah, babe," he said as he realized her hesitation.

They began removing their clothes and easing into what was about to take place between the two of them. The anticipation caused Duke to get a little aggressive, with him grabbing Sheedah tightly along the sides of her hips and pressing his big hands into her thighs. He clutched a chunk of her protruding ass cheeks and pulled her body into his. He needed to get the full effect of the lust boiling inside them both. Wild thoughts were all they could think about, and with his manhood now pressed against her body, he slowly maneuvered its way to her front entrance–knocking. He did not need to send a second request, seeing how wet her fat pussy was already.

He too was excited from all the touching and feeling they were doing. It was time now to do what they did when they longed for each other. It was a special place for him, and once again, it was time to walk through heaven's door. He was instantly engulfed inside her tender tissue. Duke's strokes showed eagerness, but he remained skilled and kept it at a much-controlled pace. Sheedah knew what was to come–whether they fucked, made love, or he pounded. Controlling the pace was Duke's thing. He was the one in control, and she knew it was what made her bust.

Sheedah had first thought the top position was going to be to her advantage. It had now become her greatest challenge and much more challenging than she could handle. It was like the first few hard and aggressive strokes to her vagina showed she had not had sex in a while. The tightness of her fat cat enthralled Duke even more. After a few hard strokes at it, moans erupted, filling the room with seductive tones. The moans only validated and added to his ego and pride of being all the lover she needed, giving him that extra boost he desired to feel worthy of satisfying her.

"Babe, please... don't stop! Please don't stop! Mmmmm..." she insisted as words of pleasure started to escape her sensual lips.

Her manicured nails had begun to dig deep into his chest, penetrating the skin, which did not seem to bother him one bit. Every minute was being enjoyed. Then, suddenly, in the midst of a few hard strokes, Duke lifted Sheedah and threw her on her back. Now, it was he who was on top. He quickened his motions, still maintaining his position inside her. Duke threw her legs on top of his shoulders as he began to long stroke his way into a glorious, gratifying array of movements. Power stroking her, Duke drilled one stroke after another, as if he was in an Olympic swimming tournament, chasing the gold medal. Again, she moaned out loudly as she accepted every inch he had to offer.

"Damn, babe! What's gotten into you?" she asked, more so as a statement than a question. She continued her seductive rants as Duke continued releasing everything that had been pent up inside him. "Damn, this feels sooooo good!" she wailed and instructed him subconsciously to go harder. "Harder, babe. Harder!"

Her moans and facial expressions told her story, letting him know he was hitting all the right spots. Their breathing heavily increased and sweat started to fall from them both. The harder he pounded, the wetter she got. The more physical he became, the harder she threw herself into him. Turning the tables on the man who had once had control and adding a little control of her own, Sheedah lowered her legs from his shoulders, taking his manhood out of her for a quick second.

She was gifted at what she did. Getting on her knees, she grabbed hold of his manhood again. She licked her palm, stroked him, then inserted him back into her pussy, cupping his balls and using her other hand to pull him by the waist into her body. As her ass clapped, her thickness slammed back and forth into his hips. Duke continued to pound away aggressively, feeling as if he was about to cum.

"No, babe!" she said, feeling him swell to his full potential.

"We're almost there! Almost!" were the words that traveled out as she arched her ass high into the air, advising Duke to slow down a little bit. "Not so fast, babe."

"Yeah, yeah, babe... right there," she continued, stretching her body upward, grabbing and pulling on the headboard tightly. Her face and hair were soaked and sweated out.

Duke was approaching that moment, causing him to throw himself into Sheedah's wetness with extreme power. From the workout he was giving, Sheedah's pussy started to clench onto his manhood with a grip that would not loosen up. Duke knew she was thriving from the pleasure of his thunderous pounds. Juices from her pussy started to gush out profusely. Everything seemed to stand still for a second as her legs started trembling from a well-deserved climax.

"Aaahhh, babe... Wow! That was so good!" she said, falling off to the side of him. They both knew it was a well-needed workout.

"Babe, I needed that," Duke admitted. "You never missed a beat," he said, complimenting her on her physical act of affection.

"You weren't bad yourself," she replied, being modest about how hard he had actually gone in on her, not wanting to blow his head up any more than she knew it was already blown up.

Exhausted from fucking so hard, all either of them could do was lie there and reflect on the workout before rolling back-to-back and falling asleep.

Duke and Sheedah had an understanding that extended far beyond their sexual relationship, knowing and understanding that what had just happened between them was strictly about having a good time—nothing more or nothing less to it.

Chapter Eleven:
That's My Nigga

The following day was just like any other day for the crew as they were back on their money hunt. Duke seemed mentally exhausted, and it was noticeable he had a lot on his mind. He never talked about his personal life with anyone, and the crew respected that about him. All they knew was Bishop would be coming home soon, and Duke could not wait for the arrival of his best friend and only brother. Even with that day arriving soon, today was business as usual, but Duke knew it would not be much longer!

With regard to the stories circulating about their father, the streets had their own theory as to what had happened, but Duke never talked about the incident. All everyone knew was Bishop had gone to jail for seven years for supposedly murdering their father. No one had the courage or the guts to ask him what really had happened that day. He was young and everyone knew portions of what they had heard and they had heard it from other people, which meant ghetto rumors. People who usually had no idea what they were talking about were common in the hood for spreading their own thoughts.

Duke lived a very complex life, along with everyone else in the crew. Some of them had it worse than others. It was just that Duke walked around with a big-ass chip on his shoulder that derived from his adolescent years. It was as if the world owed him something, and he was out to collect the debt— sort of like how his father had felt about his life but had never done anything to change his situation, a father neither Duke nor Bishop wanted to be anything like. They had a mission and were determined to see it through. No matter what the odds were against them, their mission was for their lives to be more fruitful than their fathers had been. They were going to be somebody in life and they had pledged to live life on their own terms, by any means necessary.

Those were not words they used to express their agenda about life, not in that sense anyway. However, it was obvious how Duke felt by the way he went about things. A person who interacted with Duke could tell he was not mentally stable. Another reason why when he spoke, everyone listened, a lesson he continued to impress on those in his inner circle. Teaching lessons he had learned from Bishop was something he felt was needed to keep the strong bond in the crew.

It was a dark and chilly night in the section and everything seemed all good, for the most part. The crew jumped into the Benz truck Duke had bought and was ready to get in the wind. It was Friday, which was party night, a reward to themselves for working the way they had. It was Sheedah, Face Hound, Gooch, Malik, and of course, Duke, all packed into the foreign SUV. Duke had gone even a step further and invited Sco to come along, something the crew had not done since they had arrived in Sco's territory. Duke felt it was one of those nights to kick it since everyone was feeling good. Drinks were flowing and money was being made by the barrel. Shit was good and no one out of place was even better, so they shot over to New York—42nd Street—known to the rest of the world as Times Square. There was always something to get into over there because, of course, it was the "City that never slept."

Once they arrived, the crew hit a couple of popular food spots, ate well, and went to a few different clubs until they found the right one. They were enjoying themselves, which was very rare for the crew to do as a unit. New York had some of the flyest clubs you would ever want to visit. It was not unique to see a celebrity or a famous rapper hanging out and drinking top-shelf cognac or champagne. Duke had something on his mind in the works for Sco. He made sure to order plenty of rounds for everybody because he wanted his crew tipsy on the ride back, especially Malik, who he knew would be a little sensitive about what was going to go down.

They stayed in New York until about four a.m. that morning. On their way back to Newark, Duke informed Malik, who was driving, that he had to piss.

"Yo, pull over somewhere. I gotta drain this muthafucka," Duke said, wiggling both knees with urgency.

Malik laughed, but quickly complied with Duke's request, knowing Duke could not wait.

"Good thinking," Face Hound said since he and Duke were on the same page.

Everyone had to use the restroom. They had partied hard and drank so much Hennessy that the whole unit had to piss badly. Malik pulled over somewhere close to Newark International Airport, which he figured was a reasonable place for the guys to take a leak. Duke, Gooch, Face Hound, and Sco jumped out of the truck quick as hell once Malik pulled to a complete stop. As they pissed, flying loudly above them were a few planes that seemed too close for comfort.

After everyone was done, they all jumped back into the truck feeling relieved and refreshed. Duke, Gooch, and Face Hound remarked on how good they felt. Duke nodded his head, signaling to Malik to pull off.

Noticing Sco was not with them, Malik said, "Hold up. We gotta wait for Sco."

Everyone looked around and noticed Sco was not back yet.

"Nah, he's good. Go ahead, pull off!" Duke demanded.

Malik was baffled by what was going on when Duke told him again, but this time with a little more force.

"Nigga, either drive or go with him. Either way, we're out!"

After sitting there a few seconds, Duke's words sank in, making it obvious Sco was not coming back. Instead of putting too much into it, Malik simply drove off. When they were back in Newark, Malik drove everyone to their cars, wondering why everyone had been quiet during the ride. Before getting out, Duke sparked a conversation with Malik.

"I had a good ass time tonight, my nigga. Good lookin'; catch you later, my nigga."

Malik was at a loss for words. He knew when and when not to question Duke, but something was not sitting right with him. He was going to push the issue, but decided to let it play out and see what transpired with Sco and his sudden disappearance.

Days passed and Malik was still lost as to why Sco had not come back to the truck from taking a piss. No one had a clue as to what or why he had not returned. Malik was still upset over the entire situation, and if Duke had a plan for his man, why had they not discussed it prior? It was all Duke's decision, as always, and Malik was getting tired of Duke doing things that way.

It was about seven a.m. as Malik lay in bed, unable to really sleep. He was seriously pondering how a person needed to bring about a better way and a better day. The sudden sound of his phone ringing jogged him from his reverie. Picking up the phone from the floor, he checked the caller display to see who was calling. The first thing he noticed was the call was from Duke. The words were big as hell on the screen the way he had saved it to his contacts, THE DUKE.

Before answering it, which he had thought about not doing at first, he silently said to himself, "Damn, this nigga don't sleep!"

He was really reluctant to take the call, but since he needed to holler at Duke about Sco, he simply pressed the talk button on the phone. In a really calm tone, he said, "What's good, nigga? It's early as hell. Why are you calling me this fuckin' early? We don't have any business today."

Duke, not reading much into Malik's tone, did not respond right away. He heard the frustration in Malik's voice and realized he was probably mourning the death of his man—which he understood, but did not give a fuck.

"I don't know what's gotten into you lately, bro, but you're acting like you don't know how this game goes," Duke said, getting tired of Malik's rebellious attitude.

"What d'you mean, my nigga? All I know is we go out of town to turn up, and we come back light one man," Malik replied, wanting to know what had happened to Sco.

"You know how I get down, nigga. If a piece of the puzzle don't fit, it can't go back in the same box."

Malik now understood Sco had been left somewhere ten toes up, not hearing the planes overhead. A cold chill went through his spine, and he felt Duke was out of order for offing his man in the middle of an observation sight.

"Nigga, when you gonna get over that shit? That nigga's gone! He's playing chess with his Maker right now. Move on! In fact, I've got something to cheer you up," Duke said, like anything he had was supposed to cheer Malik up.

"Turn on the TV, my nigga, and make sure you turn to ABC News, channel 7. There's something I want you to check out."

"Yeah," Malik said in a dry tone.

Malik was furious about how Duke was acting. It was like Duke did not care who was cool with him, and Sco had been. Nonchalantly, Malik did everything Duke had asked him to do.

"I'm there, nigga. Now what am I supposed to be looking at?"

"Patience, my nigga."

"All I see is some news reporter bitch, A.J. Ross. How is she supposed to cheer me up?" he sarcastically questioned.

Duke knew what he was doing. "Nah, nigga. Although she does look like something and she could definitely cheer me up, but nah, that isn't why I told you to turn to the channel 7 news. Dig, look at the bottom where the words are scrolling, the words that tell you what's going on. At the bottom of your TV, nigga!"

The prompter read: **An unidentified male body, with two gunshots to the back of the head, was found by the airport's observation site late this morning.**

"I'm reading the shit. I guess you're feeling yourself for offing my man, huh?" Malik asked.

"Nigga, is you a clown or what?!" Duke spat back.

Just as he did, the gorgeous reporter was interrupted for a news break.

"The unidentified man found looks to be FBI informant, Hakeem Wright, whom they have been searching for over a week. The police say he has been working for them for a while and was working on several different cases, which is probably what led to his death. The chief of police says it looks like a professional hit and they are investigating, but they do not have anyone in custody. Crime Stoppers is offering a reward for anyone with information regarding this crime. Please contact us at..."

Confused by what he was reading and hearing, Malik knew exactly who they were talking about: his man Sco, whose real name was Hakeem. Malik had nothing to say after reading and hearing that. Duke smiled wryly and decided to help him out.

"Nigga, you should be a dead man right now! Your words are gold, huh? Trust you, huh? Nigga, you're lucky as hell I love you as much as I do, because if I didn't... Well, you already know it would be off with ya fuckin' head!" he said, throwing Malik's words back at him.

"What the fuck, my nigga?!" Malik said.

Duke could tell by his response and tone Malik truly had been oblivious to what his man was on.

"Nigga, from now on, you'd better not ever question me!"

Duke's words were followed by silence on the phone, and Malik knew Duke was gone. He had hung up on Malik, and he was not going into it with Malik how he had known Sco was a snitch. In fact, it was something they never would speak about again.

Malik lay back down, throwing his phone on the floor. As long as he and Duke had been friends, there were only a few times he had ever questioned Duke. Most of the time, he did whatever Duke stood on, which would turn out to be the right move for the crew. Malik felt a little envious of Duke because he knew Duke had learned how to shake and move from his big brother. Malik wished he had had someone like Bishop in his life to teach him the ropes. Then he had a revelation, he did have someone—he had Duke! He threw his arm over his eyes, blocking the morning sunlight that was shining through his room window. He made a vow to himself at that very moment...Never question Duke again!

Chapter Twelve:
Underdogs

When things went down that really weighed heavy, there was only one person whom Duke knew he could confide in. He never confided in the crew, because he needed to keep his superior edge over all of them. That was just the way real bosses rolled. The very next day, he went to see Bishop, who had been locked down for almost seven years now. Duke and their mother made it a priority to visit Bishop as much as they could. Sometimes, it was hard for their mother because of her job, but Bishop understood that totally and never held it against her. He knew she was working vigorously toward better times and much better days. Although her work schedule got in the way, they both knew how much she loved them. Her undeniable mother's love for her boys was why Bishop understood life and respected her efforts in doing her best to raise them. Bishop was grateful every time he got to see her face, even as it was becoming rare.

Yardville was a Youth Correctional Facility and home to Bishop for the time being. It was the place where everyone his age and some a little older did their time. Duke waited patiently in the waiting room, looking at a few other brothers who were on a visit with their families or girlfriends. He was looking at one dude kissing his girl like he was trying to eat her lips off her face. There was another white boy sitting with his mom, crying that he wanted to be free, and another big, muscle-bound brother doing crosswords with an older woman who looked like she could be his grandmother.

Jail is not the place for anyone, and Duke could not wait to have his brother home, back on the streets with him. He was much calmer knowing how this should be his last time coming to see his brother since his time as a Yardville inmate was almost complete. Duke watched everyone closely as they entered the visiting hall, visitors and inmates alike. A smile instantly covered his face upon seeing a taller version of himself saunter in. Bishop finally came walking through one of the steel visitation doors that separated him from the real world. Bishop, who seemed to have packed on a few pounds of muscle, was as solid as he had ever been. Not like he had been out

- 102 -

of shape when he was on the bricks, he had just toned up, and it suited him well. As usual, Duke was dressed to impress in his expensive jeans and new retro-throwback North Carolina-colored Jordans. A smile was smeared across both their faces as Duke stood up to greet his big brother with a handshake, then a hug.

"Damn! It's almost unbelievable," Duke said, sizing up his brother more closely now.

"What's that, little bro?"

"This shit is literally weeks from being over, bro," Duke replied happily.

"Yeah, but it's not over until it's over! I'm still doing time. Anything could happen between now and then. Let's just hope life goes as we expect shit to go."

"God willing, nothing happens. Aside from that, thank your man for that information he provided on dude. Shit could have gotten bad without it."

"I figured you'd handled your business, huh?" Bishop asked, not really looking for an answer. He knew his brother and how he got down.

"You know it. Too easy, big bro, too easy. So that means dude owes you one. Correction, dude owe us one," Duke quipped.

"Bro, a lot of these fools owe us one—two, maybe even three. You'll see! Like I said, if shit goes as expected, I'll be home real soon, my dude!"

"Yeah, and I can't fuckin' wait!"

"So dig, you gotta fall back now. You've done entirely too much during the course of my incarceration. I feel we've come too far to see something fucked up happen to either of us, especially you."

Duke listened as his brother spoke, looking around as if he were looking for someone. Bishop raised an eyebrow when he realized his brother was not paying attention to what he was saying.

"Nigga, do you hear me?" he said in a fatherly tone. Bishop could always tell when Duke was channeling his focus elsewhere.

"Yeah. I hear you. Stop talking to me like that; I'm not a kid," Duke spat back.

"I wouldn't have to if you were listening, paying attention. This shit's about to get really real, and you're looking like you're lost in space."

"I am paying attention to you. It's just that I haven't seen my lady friend the last couple of times I've been up here. What's up with her, I wonder," Duke asked, taking another look around despite what Bishop had just said.

Bishop just nodded his head. "I knew something else had your mind all caught up. I heard that broad was on a leave of absence due to some personal shit. Word is she's cool though and still fine as ever."

Bishop smiled and his words quickly put a smile on Duke's face, but he still wished he could see her for himself.

"Nigga, it's been damn near seven years, so if you haven't gotten her yet, ain't nothing happening." Bishop tried letting his little brother down easy with his words, as if Duke did not have a chance with the female he was fond of.

"Yeah, okay, seven years, but every time I'm here, she's smiling at a real nigga. Oh, first chance a young nigga gets, you can believe I'ma get her. Watch what I tell you."

"Yeah, okay, I hear you. More power to you on that note."

After Bishop made his last comment, the two again focused on Bishop's arrival back into society, a society in which he had no idea of how they were going to accept his return. Bishop spent the next five minutes commending Duke on how he had stood strong and firm out there. He let his little brother know he was impressed with the way he had created a circle of loyal goons he could trust.

However, when it came to Bishop, Duke knew things were going to change on his arrival. He also had faith that the changes were going to make them both all right.

"Bro, I'm proud of you for so many reasons. In a minute, all you'll have to do is fall back and relax. Let me handle things from here on out," Bishop remarked.

"I get it, Bish," Duke replied, not knowing if he actually wanted to relinquish his street throne to his big brother.

Their visit was minutes from being over since the facility didn't allow people to come and stay all day. With things coming to an end, Duke and Bishop stood and embraced each other with a brotherly hug.

"See you soon, bro," Bishop said.

Duke stood motionless for a second as he looked at his older brother walking away, heading back to his cell; soon, it would be his last and final time. Duke got into the parking lot and looked back one more time at the hellhole which temporarily held his brother. He looked up and thanked God that this chapter was almost coming to an end. He jumped into his car, noticing he had a few missed calls that needed to be returned. One call was from his mother, whom he knew just wanted to make sure he had gone to see his brother. The other missed calls were from his crew. Gooch, Face Hound, and Sheedah had all hit his line, wanting him to slide through. They each had sent a text letting him know they would be at the clubhouse waiting for him.

While reading his messages and driving back to Newark, Duke reflected on his short visit with his brother, thinking how refreshing it was to him as well as how it was going to be when Bishop touched down. Also, he thought about how he was going to tell his crew he was falling back once Bishop came home. He was still a little reluctant to let his crew know Bishop was going to be taking over the everyday operations. There were some things he would tell them that he knew they would not have any issues with. Plus, they knew Duke always had their best interests in life and in heart.

It was not a secret about the two brothers and their bond. Everything they had been through solidified what they meant to one another. Duke and Bishop's bond had only gotten stronger over the course of time—the same way Duke and his crew's bond had become stronger over the course of time. Over the years, Duke and his crew had gotten closer as they had forced their way into the lives of other people—and not in a good way either.

The crew stayed on the hunt for the bag—whether it was robbing people, home invasions, sticking niggas in the trunk of their cars, or just robbing gambling halls around the city. No matter what it was or who it was who ran the spots they invaded, they were after the money and the money was their only concern. From kidnapping to murders, they had seen it all and done it all without any hesitation. Ballers and gangsters alike had felt the wrath of Duke and his crew. No one was off-limits.

Everyone with the big names around the city got it and knew they had better watch their backs closely. The bigger the name, the more attention they got from the crew. They made it known there was not an untouchable soul in the world when they came for you. They had ultimately struck fear into the hearts of everyone who played the game. Although Newark was a big enough place to spread their wings, chasing the bag was their motto. Never settle for anything less than what you deserve. They wanted their share and the share of many others. It was the new American way.

Fear was not the only part of their reputation; taking over other people's territory was a factor as well. It was part of their madness. It was nothing for them to come over in your area and claim stock in it. No matter who a person thought they were or who anyone seemed to be, that did not matter to them. What did matter was if a person had a problem with how they conducted business, and if that was a problem, then just know they would put in the work and make it count. Once someone reacted wrong to any request or action they displayed, they already knew what was to follow.

It was like a scene from the old gangsta flick, A Bronx Tale. Duke remembered the scene vividly. A motorcycle crew walked into Sonny's joint and got really disrespectful. Sonny asked them to leave, giving them a chance. When they refused the boss' kind offer to get the fuck out, Sonny had one of his goons lock the door. What was so gangsta was when he looked them in the eye and said, "I asked you to leave, now you can't leave." The fear in their eyes was so noticeable that the movie could have ended right there.

Death was on the crew's menu, and it was a dish always served cold, with body bags as the dessert. Literally, the crew stated claims throughout the city, controlling blocks and street corners around town: Goldsmith, Avon Avenue, Clinton Avenue, Irvine Turner Boulevard, Prince Street, High Street, and Spruce Streets, just to name a few. Their list of blocks was endless, and for the record, not everyone hated Duke and his crew. There was some love for them among a few people. In fact, they got love from the underdogs, because Duke and his crew were underdogs themselves, so it was all good.

For Duke, the thing he had to get behind him was that his brother had done seven years of his young life behind bars for something he had done, which was fucked up. It fucked with his head at times and his heart daily, so the whole world was going to feel his pain, even if they were not at fault. He felt like revenge was justice, that his way was only right. The fucked-up remorse he felt bothered him no matter how many times his brother told him to calm down or relax until he got home. Duke could not relax or calm down, the same way Bishop could not with the little time he had left, which was only a few weeks. So, of course, not now—not ever—was Duke going to let up on the streets. He and his crew knew anything could happen to them at any given moment. That was why he felt the need to keep the streets in a chokehold, and they did it constantly.

Chapter Thirteen:
One Last Lick

With the streets talking the way they talked, guys in prison knew shit before people in the free world knew it. Therefore, Bishop recognized the work Duke and his crew were putting in. It was a dangerous game and required any and every player who indulged to be focused. The only thing Bishop could focus on was his family and how important they were to him. He thought about the endless conversations he and his mother had had regarding Duke. Their chats did not have him worried because he had faith in Duke.

But on so many different occasions, Bishop had realized the only way Duke was going to calm down and stay alive was when he got home and exercised his tutelage. He felt Duke was a marked man, especially knowing how hardheaded and stubborn his little brother was. It was starting to take a toll on both of them in many forms—mentally, physically, and emotionally. No one wanted to lose a loved one, and losing Duke was a constant worry.

Countless discussions with Duke, their mother, and those around him had Bishop's head in a whirlwind of thoughts. Duke, on the other hand, did not really acknowledge the tension his lifestyle caused his family. He always had to have some form of relief, thinking he knew what his mother and brother thought about the future. Instead of getting a woman to do what they were good for, then relaxing—which was the normal way of doing things under such circumstances—Duke knew he would rather lay down the law on a few muthafuckas in the streets. Nothing was better than procuring a bag full of money.

Like now—Duke was getting his crew together for one last sting before the return of Bishop. He knew his brother wanted him to lie low since his release date was around the corner, but this last lick was too easy to pass up. Duke and the crew had gotten word there was a private function going on with a few ballers and hustlers at an exclusive social club off Chancellor and Sly Streets. The attitude of Duke and the crew was now on a high altitude.

They felt some type of way that some off-brand niggas were throwing an event and he and his crew had not been invited. He thought it was very rude of them not wanting the presence of some real niggas at their function.

With thoughts circulating of how disrespectful these fools were, he figured he would go play a little dice and a few hands of poker. Duke loved to gamble, assuming the risk was going to be well worth the reward. The crew minus Sheedah, who would still get her fair share of whatever they came off with, got ready to go out on the town and check on that risk. He had a plant in place—a reliable source inside the social club—ahead of time. His mole was how he had known what was going on there. His men were ready and suited-up for business. They had black masks to drape over their faces to conceal their identities, and they were carrying guns the size of cannons.

Duke gave his inside man a phone call once they were situated and in close proximity. He did this to let his lookout know they was only minutes away and it was about to be showtime. His mole answered the call on the first ring.

"Come outside," Duke said, ending the call right away, not waiting for a response.

The timing of the crew's arrival could not have been more perfect. Things were unfolding exactly the way Duke had expected them to. After his inside man received the vacate the premises call, his protege was soon seen exiting the club and getting to safety. The signal was the tipping of the plant's hat before climbing into a Pontiac parked in front. Once Duke saw the signal given, it really was showtime. They were going in like the beginning scene from the movie Belly.

"Okay, y'all know what time it is," Duke said, pulling his mask down over his face.

This was what the crew lived for: the moment of truth and dare. Everyone's life was on the line, so they knew they had to be careful not to deviate from Duke's plan.

"Let's do this," Malik said, moving the vehicle closer to the entrance.

"Paper time," Face Hound added. "Let's get this money, fellas," he continued, cocking his gun and making sure a live round was in the chamber.

Malik slowly eased up to the location, stopping right at the front door. Duke, Gooch, and Face Hound darted out the vehicle like trained assassins. Once inside, they peeped how everyone in the place was busy—some showing off their diamonds and drinking expensive champagne, some showing off their latest tailor-made clothes, and some just talking shit about who had the most paper. For at least ten seconds, Duke and his crew were unnoticeable. Duke thought about how much like some showboating clowns they looked. Before anyone realized what was going on, Face Hound smacked the first man he walked up on in the head with the butt end of his MAC-11.

"Everybody hit the muthafuckin' floor NOW!" Duke shouted.

Then he let a round-off that hit the ceiling and shattered one of the light fixtures. As glass remnants rained down, Duke ordered everyone, including the bitches, to get face down on the floor and lick wood if they had to. The man Face Hound had smacked grabbed his face, in excruciating pain from the blow.

"We can make this quick and easy, or one of you niggas can be an example of what happens to heroes," Duke said, continuing to give out orders like he was ordering food.

"This is a muthafuckin' stick up, but we can easily make it a coroner pick up. If any of you niggas have plans on leaving this muthafucka alive, then I suggest no one tries my patience. I truly mean that shit, and believe me, it is short today."

Without any resistance from the men lying face down on the floor being robbed, Gooch, Face Hound, and Duke did exactly what they had come to do: rob the place. Face Hound was grabbing all the money off the tables and placing it in a New Jersey Nets duffle bag. Gooch was busy removing the men's Rolexes and money clips from their pockets. He noticed a black face Presidential on one of their wrists that was encrusted with too many diamonds to count.

"Take that muthafucka off or lose your whole arm!" Gooch said, standing with the heel of his Timberland in the man's back. His broad was alongside him, crying and screaming she knew she should have stayed home.

"Big man, huh? You niggas are some real big men, coming up in here like this, fuckin' with us," the sharply dressed man said, referring to Gooch.

Gooch had extremely short patience, just like the boss, and applied a little more pressure to the man's back with his boot.

"Oh, this nigga's got an attitude about these little kibble and bits. I think it needs adjusting," Gooch said, raising his boot again, higher this time, and bringing it down full power onto the man's head. Blood gushed from his ear, and his woman cried hysterically, covering her eyes and begging her man to just comply with the robbers and shut the fuck up.

"Check everyone's pockets for money and any other personal items we can keep. Check every bitch's panties for any stash as well," Duke continued.

That type of shit was right up the crew's alley. They got to rub on some wet pussy and get paid for doing it.

"Now, if I find anyone of you muthafuckas is in possession of anything of value, your mommas can start ordering flowers."

After those words left Duke's mouth, within a matter of seconds, there was approximately one hundred thousand in cash staring them in the face, not even counting the jewelry, which appeared to be very expensive. Things were going just fine—until the sound of a gunshot suddenly rang out.

POW!

"What the fuck is you doing?!" Duke asked his partner.

"Damn, man, my bad. The trigger to my gun is way too fuckin' sensitive."

"Sensitive as hell," Duke replied, not wanting to leave a body this close to Bishop coming home.

"I only shot him in the back; he should be okay. Most that should happen is he will be shitting in a bag. His bitch can clean him up. But, if not, then hey... shit happens," Face Hound told him.

"Nigga, you crazy," Duke responded as he smiled at his young trigger-happy homeboy.

Duke felt the need to ease the nerves of the crowd of people lying on the floor, so they would not have to leave more gun smoke in the air. He quickly told everyone to simmer down, assuring his hostages that the shot was an accident.

"But the next one may not be!" he added.

"Y'all got everything?" Duke asked his crew, and they nodded their heads in response.

"WE GOT EVERYTHING IN THIS BITCH!" Gooch screamed out.

"Okay. The police will be here soon. Let's get ready to go," Duke replied, looking at his watch, knowing the response time of the police.

"That's what's up. Let's get the fuck outta here," Gooch replied, happy with the score.

As the men started moving backward, side by side toward the exit, they kept their guns drawn until they were clear. Duke decided to say one more thing before leaving.

"Yo, listen, get that nigga some medical attention because he don't look too good."

With those words, the crew left, running out the club and jumping into the waiting getaway car.

"DRIVE, NIGGA, DRIVE!" Gooch yelled to Malik.

Malik raised his mask and took off when everyone was safely in the car. He mashed the gas pedal to the floor and the only noise heard was the screeching of tires. The dark-colored SUV took off like a thief in the night.

"DAMN! WHAT A FUCKIN' RELIEF!" Face Hound screamed.

"Yeah. Outta sight, outta mind," Duke responded.

'That shit could have gone badly,' Duke thought as they drove off, reflecting on how Face Hound had accidentally shot one of the men. As far as Duke was concerned, this was going to be the crew's last score for now. Duke felt the need to take Bishop's advice and fall back until he was home free, which would be two weeks from the day.

Taking a deep breath into his lungs, Duke exhaled, only to say, "A real nigga is coming home! It's been long enough, but we are here now! Finally!"

Chapter Fourteen:
The Release

For the next two weeks, Duke ducked off in straight chill mode. He was taking Bishop's advice and waited for his brother's homecoming. He wanted nothing more than for them to have a celebration together. The time seemed like it was ticking at a second per day, but that second somehow turned to minutes, then hours, and finally, it was that day. Duke was excited to know the third member of his family was going to reunite them as a whole unit once again. Duke and Momma Evans were very excited to see this day come.

Bishop was now minutes away from becoming a free man. He was filled with so many emotions as he sat patiently in his cell, waiting to hear his name called and his cell bust open. His only thoughts were to embrace his family tightly and never let them go again. He knew it was the same thing the other two were thinking as well.

Duke was not holding back any razzamatazz for his brother's arrival. Momma Evans was much more of a nonchalant type of person. She really did not approve of showing the world your hold card, but she knew her youngest son did not want to hear that.

"You are always trying to show off. Your bother is nervous enough as it is, so why do you always have to take things over the top?" she asked.

"Mom, you're buggin'! My brother deserves nothing but the best the world has to offer him. He's supposed to come home in style. A stretch BMW limo is what's up," Duke told his mother.

"Was this big truck really necessary, Duke? You're such a player," she sarcastically told her son.

Duke laughed at his mother's remark and told her, "Yeah, everything we do is necessary, and a player I am."

Sharing a laugh between them and a little sarcasm back at her, their words went back and forth to shake off the anxiety everyone was feeling; laughter was their best distraction. After a few more moments in the house, they were ready to roll. The two went outside and hopped into the stretch limo awaiting them. They were ready to take the three-hour ride, knowing how this time, instead of a visit, they were going to pick up their other third. That one aspect made this particular ride well worth it. Bishop was coming home!

The ride was silent of conversation, but Pac's Me Against The World disc was playing on repeat. Duke did not blast it too loud because it seemed like his mom was in deep thought about her eldest son's transition back into society. Duke was busy rapping the lyrics once again like he had written another banger for his favorite artist.

Can you picture my prophecy?

Stress in the city, the cops is hot for me

The projects is full of bullets, the bodies is droppin'

There ain't no stoppin' me

Constantly movin' while makin' millions

Witnessin' killings, leaving dead bodies in abandoned buildings

Carries to children 'cause they're illin'

Addicted to killin' and the appeal from the cap peelin'

Without feelin', but will they last or be blasted

Hardheaded bastard.....

Pac was deep with his shit and touched Duke in so many ways. It was like the man was shadowing Duke, singing to the public about his life. That was why he related to Pac more so than anyone else in the rap game. A lot of music made young fools go out and do things they had heard, but it was the other way around for Duke and Pac. He rapped about things Duke and his crew lived, did, and would continue doing not caring if the police were hot for them.

Finally arriving at the facility, both of them were ecstatic, figuring Bishop would already be out front waiting on them—but he was not. The only thing they knew to do was relax and wait patiently for Bishop's release. A few minutes or even a few hours to wait was nothing compared to the seven years they already had waited for him. As they sat there waiting, they saw people coming in and out of the facility, most likely coming and going from visits. Some who worked in the facility and some who were inmates who worked around the facility were in movement as well. But still no Bishop!

The two started to wonder if they had the wrong date about Bishop coming home, or if something had happened to fuck up his chances of coming home. They were beginning to think something must have gone south for Bishop, knowing how his attitude could get him in trouble at times. The thought of him not coming out today crossed their minds.

Suddenly, all that crazy thinking stopped upon hearing a familiar voice saying to Duke, "Yo, lil'nigga! What's up?"

Duke faked like he was offended and happy at the same time, barking back to say, "Who the fuck said that?!" and turning directly around to where the voice he was hearing was coming from.

"Bishop!" he shouted and stepped toward his big brother.

The two of them embraced with a big hug. Their embrace lasted for minutes before they broke apart. Momma Evans stood back until it was her time to hug her son, admiring her sons' brotherly affection for one another and understanding their bond and love. Smiling to herself, she watched the two interact, playing with one another, and play fighting as if they were kids again.

She said to herself, "Damn! My baby has turned into a grown man behind bars."

Sad and happy at the same time, she noticed how he had gained so much weight while locked up. He was no longer that scrawny young man she had raised. His once sinewy frame was void of the thin build and had been replaced with muscles. His hair had grown long in his seven-year stay; on his shoulders was where the dreads now lay. Bishop was physically fit and he was very handsome.

'Yes, he is definitely a man,' she thought as she continued to watch her two sons horseplay around and hearing them talk to each other.

"Nigga, I'm going to knock ya big ass out," Duke said as he threw a few light jabs at his brother.

Bishop smiled as his little brother jumped around, throwing his little jabs, looking at how grown his little brother had become. They pranced around as if he was really ready to get into a cage with an untamed lion. Finally, the shadow boxing ended and Bishop told him, "Come over here and give me another hug, and Mommy, you too. Group hug please!"

The trio embraced one another as requested.

"Yeah, that's what I'm talking about," Bishop told his brother and mother as he looked back over his shoulder at his old address.

They hugged again, and this time the hug lasted a little longer than the first one or two times they had hugged. In the midst of their hug, Duke expressed to his big brother, "Damn, it's been a long time coming, bruh. You already know what comes next for us!"

Bishop cut that part of their conversation short by telling him, "Listen, we'll talk later. You know Mommy worries. Stop talking like that around her. Breathe easy!"

"Son, he acts as if he's the parent and you're the child. You'd better check your brother. He's been very excited to see you," Ms. Evans interjected.

Duke, feeling the need to respond, said, "Yeah, why wouldn't I be excited to see my brother? That's my big brother in every sense of the word. I loved and missed my guy for years during this entire process. Listen, we can be a family now. It's time to catch up. Let's get into the limo and bounce!"

Unknown to Duke or Bishop, while they were embracing each other and engaging in small talk, there was someone lurking in the distance, watching. Sitting on the side of the facility with a pair of military binoculars sat Detective Burcheck. Still not satisfied with how things had gone seven years ago, he was reluctant to let the family breathe. He watched the family as they interacted, licking his lips like his hard on for the truth had not gone down. The family did not have the slightest idea they were being watched, which he had been doing for the years since his encounter with the boys.

"Yeah, seven years and I can finally nail their asses to the wall," were the words uttered from his mouth as he sat watching with anger.

With Bishop not being the flashy type, he noticed how his little brother had shown up in the slick limo and felt he needed to address a few things with Duke right away.

"Bro, a limo, man?"

"You already know, my guy. We have to travel in style," Duke replied.

"I told him it wasn't necessary and you wouldn't approve. However, you know your brother; he doesn't listen to anyone," their mother interjected.

"C'mon, Mom, real dudes do real things. Anything less isn't who we are as brothers," Duke said with a hint of arrogance.

"Mom, the limo is cool. I'm not mad at him, but that's another reason we gotta kick it with each other, just him and me. By the way, good taste on the ride," Bishop said, making sure his little brother felt the gratitude he really had.

Hearing his big brother's approval, Duke felt a sense of satisfaction. Feeling like he had gotten his brother's validation was something that meant a lot to him. He also could tell Bishop realized how he had some big things going on.

Bishop was very impressed with how his little brother had established himself while he was gone, and at the same time, he had implemented what he had had on his mind for years. Ideas on how to get into the mix of things was always the main focus. Bishop knew, in order to make things much more prosperous for them both, they had to be on the same focal points. He had to break it down to his little brother the right way. Duke was going to have to calm down, slow down on the flashy and reckless shit he had been doing.

After seven years of outta sight, outta mind, a lot of things had changed, and he knew the streets were going to be watching from all angles and talking. Therefore, he knew making money was going to take patience and time. Bishop felt he was going to have to be under the radar in order for his new plans to be successful. Sitting and thinking things through for those seven years had made him recognize the challenges that lay ahead. He was ready for the task, especially with the plans he had for being the best version of himself.

Bishop figured his plans were simple. His mission was to make so much money that they would not know what to do with it. He wanted to secure for himself and Duke. A future way beyond the streets by doing something many of those who ran the streets had never had the opportunity to do. Get money and get out the game rich—minus the worries and concerns of their past catching up with them later. His plan was to get money and go legit. His plan was called Longevity! He had thoughts and ideas he wanted to share with Duke, but until the time came, he returned his attention to focus more on Duke's conversation.

Duke was busy informing Bishop of what was in store for him and his coming home. Duke let him know how he had put together a welcome home party for him.

"It's gonna be a chill time for us both. I have the crew coming through too. They're bringing a few chicks just in case you wanna indulge in a little pleasure. Nothing too big though, feel me?"

"That's what's up, little bro. I need to unwind a bit. I'm looking forward to meeting your crew and the females they're bringing." Bishop smiled, letting him know he understood.

"But first, I gotta take you on a small shopping spree. No more prison gear for my main man," Duke continued, letting him know he needed some new, updated garb for this occasion.

Duke threw Bishop a little something for his pockets. It was a stack about two-inches high, nothing but hundreds and fifties. "Here's twenty-five thousand to get you into a few things you might need for a few days. There's much more where that came from, believe that shit," Duke said, boasting a little bit.

Bishop accepted the money and thanked his brother for everything he had shown thus far. The money only added to the plan he had in mind.

Once in the hood after the long ride, Duke decided it was important to have the limo driver drive through the hood so Bishop could get a good look at how much things had changed.

"Damn, shit has changed a lot!" Bishop uttered to himself aloud, watching the bricks from what the city had changed into. No more projects, certain blocks no longer existed, while other blocks had been turned into one-way streets with speed bumps to slow down the traffic. There were gang colors painted on the blocks and streets signs they passed—blue, red—shit was as if he was in a different world. The bricks he had once known no longer existed—something he had heard about, but it was different when he saw it with his own eyes.

"It's crazy out here," he said, sharing part of his thoughts with Duke.

"Nothing we can't handle now that you're home. Let's go party!" Duke said, smiling at those words as they had the driver drop their mom off.

Bishop promised her he would return to talk more in-depth with her. She understood her son wanted to spend time with his brother. She smiled and kissed his face, stepping out the limo at her home.

"You boys be careful," she said, watching the limo ease from the curb as off they went!

Detective Burcheck was a hardheaded son of bitch cop who did not like having a hard-on for so long. Usually, when he got an erection for a perp, he would relieve himself with a conviction. He had gotten a conviction, but he knew, deep in his heart, there was more to these boys' story. Burcheck was going against his superiors' order by still investigating the case. He had been given an order by the captain to let it go. What bothered Burcheck wasn't the fact that he had been given the order and usually he would listen, but he also knew his captain was just gung-ho to get a conviction due to the upcoming elections. It always looked good for the captain and the mayor when the murder conviction rate was dwindling because they had gotten their man, and for that reason alone, Bishop had become their man. No real police work, no detective snooping, none of that was required since they had a full-fledged confession.

Burcheck watched as the boys dropped their mother off and wondered where they were on their way to now. He figured Bishop, being like any other man who had just done seven years, was going to be on the hunt for some wet pussy. He knew, if it was him, that was what he would be doing. He looked in the rearview mirror at the grey hairs now protruding from his chin and knew they were from the long nights of stressing over what had really happened.

He knew it was going to take some time, but he was going to get his man—one way or another.

Chapter Fifteen:
Heart To Heart

Duke had outdone himself with Bishop's welcome home gathering, making the night seem like it would never end. He and his crew had fired up blunt after blunt and had the music in the clubhouse on concert. Bishop was most definitely enjoying everything that had been done for his coming home. He had toned his body and flushed his system during his seven years, so the drinking was cool, in moderation, but he was not smoking. Duke had invited a few dime pieces, making sure his brother had the pick of the cream of the crop.

Gooch and Face Hound were living it up as they played NBA live on the seventy-inch, and Malik stayed busy with a couple of cuties in a corner. Duke had adjoining presidential suites at the Sheraton Downtown, and he was hoping his brother would take a couple of chicks with him. That surely was his plan.

"Yo, lil' bro, I think I'm going to wrap it up and head to the room," Bishop said, looking at his watch.

"Man, you trippin', big bruh? You fresh out and I got all this booty on duty for you, and you wanna go get some rest?" Duke asked, seeing how his big brother had matured even more.

"Man, this ass is going to be there when I go to sleep and it's going to be there when I wake up. I just did seven, bro, and guess what?"

"What's that?"

"There was ass before I left and even more now that I'm home. I got all the time in the world to fuck. I got to get my rest, so I'm fresh in the a.m."

"I feel you, bro," Duke said, calling to Malik to drive Bishop to the room. Duke slid Bishop an extra nine mill he had tucked in his waist band.

"Better to be caught with it than without it, my nigga," Duke said.

"Better to not get caught at all," Bishop replied, accepting the nickel-plated killing machine.

He waited a minute on Malik, who was in the middle of a public blow job. Once Malik wrapped it up, they left, and Bishop headed to the room to get some rest.

After the night was over, the sun rose for the morning to arrive. Bishop hopped out the bed as if he was still locked up, looking around. When he did not hear black steel-toes walking past and someone screaming, "CHOW TIME!", he realized for the first time that he was a free man. He had had a routine when he was down, so he was used to getting up earlier than everyone else. Bishop did not care; he liked getting out of bed, stretching his bones, and preparing for what was ahead. He felt that he did his best thinking in the morning, when it was quiet and void of other voices.

Looking for something to get into, Bishop decided he would check on his brother, whom he had heard come in only a few hours earlier. He went to the connecting door and pushed it open. Without hesitation, he grabbed Duke as he still lay with the two females in bed and shouted, "Get the fuck up, nigga! We've got a lot to talk about!"

"Bishop, get the fuck outta here! I'm tired as hell! You know what the fuck we did last night. Why the fuck are you coming in my room like this? Don't you see these two bitches in my bed?!"

"Lil bro, if it wasn't important, I wouldn't fuck with you. Plus, I don't really think the females would mind if I spent a little time with my brother. They should be able to relate to a brother's love for one another."

"A'ight, man! Damn! Give me about fifteen minutes to get myself together. I'll be right over."

"A'ight, nigga! Don't play with me either. Get the fuck up now. Don't make me come back here to get you!"

"Nigga, damn! I said I'll be there in fifteen minutes. Get the fuck outta here, son!"

"Now that sounds much better; I'm much more convinced now. Fifteen minutes or I'm comin' back. It won't be friendly either."

"Whatever, nigga! Ain't nobody scared of you. You'd better stop thinking I'm still that little nigga you once watched grow up. Fuck with me if you want to. Your stay home can become very short-lived, nigga!" Duke said, joking around. He wanted to show his big brother he was much tougher now than he was before.

"Oh, yeah? You threatening me, huh?"

"Nah, nigga, no threat. I'm just letting you know what it is. I'm glad to see how some shit never changes, especially when it comes to us. You should already know I would never bring you any harm. You're big bro for real!"

"That's good to hear."

"Listen, bro, the bond we share is forever and beyond. Nothing can ever change that! Remember, I am my brother's keeper!"

"As I am yours as well. Listen, once you get fresh and clean, come over so we can chop it up."

"Gotchu. I'll be there in a few," Duke told his brother, looking at the two females.

He wanted to at least fuck them one more time, but he remembered the words Bishop had said to him last night. The pussy was not going nowhere. Duke got up so he could get himself together. After a few seconds in the bathroom, Duke went to Bishop's room on the other half of the presidential suite. It came equipped with its own kitchen, which was where Bishop was waiting for him.

"What was so important you had to come into my room this morning, waking me up?"

"Bro, listen: Before we start going back and forth again, I just wanna let you know I didn't mean to barge into your room like that, especially with you laying up with your shorties, but I have a lot on my mind that I wanna discuss with you."

Cutting Bishop off for a second to let him know, Duke replied, "Bro, it's bros over hoes all day; that's first. Second, you heard what Jay-Z said:

Only life of mine is a life of crime. Yeah, I'm that same nigga. What's on your mind? Talk to me!"

"A very smart man once told me, if I want to make God laugh, tell Him my plans, so here we are. You're a crazy ass nigga. Any who, I would like to start off by expressing my gratitude to you. I appreciate the generosity you've shown me on my arrival back into society. Thank you for that. I appreciate you more than you will ever know and understand. I sincerely mean that shit too, bruh.

"For the next couple of weeks, I'm going to be observing the business closer to find ways to enhance growth and development in the areas where it may be lacking. Therefore, making the business stronger, more efficient, and much more lucrative. My main goal is to improve and start strengthening the strongholds, weaning out any and all weak points. Therefore, I am ready to come in and turn things up," Bishop said, pouring himself a glass of orange juice.

"I give you credit for creating something special and I just wanna add to what's already established in the best way possible. Listen bro, I wanna relieve you from your duties and obligations to the streets, and give you the same support you've given me for the last seven years. The same support and love you continued to provide me and Mommy. I'm going to need to know your obligations and expectations as well as the assistance from members in your crew in order for things to be as successful as we, or I, intend it to become. Duke, you have made some good and bad decisions over the course of me being gone," he continued, pouring a second glass of juice, this time only half-full.

"When it comes to life in general, it's time to make things better, which is why I don't want you to misunderstand anything I'm saying to you. No fault of your own, I get it, because some of the shit you had to do to survive was necessary."

"You're damn right, bro," Duke interjected.

"However, I commend you on everything you've accomplished over the course of time, which is why I'm here now. Dig, I'm your big brother, and as your big brother, I believe it's my duty to make you better on every level there is to the game, make you a well-rounded person, ya dig?"

"I do dig, but what exactly are you saying?"

"You're too reckless, too flashy. Plus, you wear your emotions on your sleeve for those who don't deserve it, and that shit can often times blind you from seeing the snakes and rats in your circle. It's a major recipe for destruction. Bro, on some real shit, you're a ticking time bomb ready to explode, true story!"

Duke was listening to everything his brother was saying. He was getting a few revelations, but he loved his life, loved getting money the way he did. The thrill was not in punching a clock at a factory or dropping fries in some hot grease for some fucking idiot who did not respect you because you worked at a fast-food joint. The thrill was in watching a nigga squirm and beg for his life while you relieved him of all his prize possessions including his cash. That was just the way it was for Duke, but he knew Bishop had some valid points. One thing he was not ready to face was death, and he knew, by listening to his big brother, it was very possible to avoid going that route.

"Listen, my guy, I promised myself, once God granted me my freedom back, that by any means necessary, I would never see the inside of another jail again. You either! And I meant every word too, for the both of us. Give me death or give me life, but I wanna live free, feel me?"

As Bishop spoke, Duke sat there and listened as if he was in class and his teacher was giving him a valuable lesson on life—and a lesson on life is what he was receiving. It was ironic Bishop would say those words right after he had just thought about life or death.

"Lil bro, there is no way in hell my little brother is gonna be thrown into some white man's prison. No way in hell! I can go on for days with this discussion, but I believe you get the bigger picture, right? Talk to me."

"Yeah, I get it, bro. The picture is definitely bigger than what so many can see. But then again, most don't see the picture that's presented to them, especially the way you're putting it to me. I hear you, Bishop, and I respect and love your responsibilities as my big brother. Bruh, there is nothing to really say after the shit you've just expressed to me. I gotchu. I have no problem providing you with the necessary information and resources you need to move our business forward. You're my muthafuckin' big brother, and on that note, I feel like what's mine is yours! It's an honor to be your little brother. I trust you with my life. It's not like we haven't been here before. I won't ever regret putting my life in your hands."

"Not to cut you off, little bro, but check it: I don't want you thinking negative when it comes to the death of our father. Fuck that bastard! He got what he had coming to him. I only regret not killing him sooner myself. The seven years I did, I would do it again for you—I swear in a fuckin' heartbeat—for you and Mommy. Plus, the world is a better place without him. Trust and understand this: You did the world and our family a big service by ridding us of the coward who caused us pain damn near our entire young lives. So, not to encourage you or anything of that nature, but to tell you the truth, bro, it's all good."

"Yeah, I hear you, bro. Thanks for saying that. That shit has been eating away at me for so long, I mean, eating me alive. Been fucking with my conscience for years. I think I needed to hear that from you, for real, no B.S. So, now that we got all that outta our system, where do I sign?" Duke said in response to everything Bishop had expressed to him.

He was ready to move forward and sign on the dotted line in regard to Bishop's moving their business to the next level. They both got to laughing and felt this conversation was long overdue.

"Yo, you're a crazy lil' nigga."

"Big bro, I know your worth. When you were down, I remembered how you would talk about so many ways to be successful, as well as the many different strategies to get to this money. I've been waiting for this day to arrive for a very long time. Let's get it!"

Although Bishop knew their mindsets were totally different, he still felt they were on the same page about everything which connected them on so many levels, and he hoped over the next couple months of grinding it would show.

Chapter Sixteen:
Making Rounds

A Few Months Later...

Since the brothers had made their transition, Bishop was satisfied with the growth and development the business was transitioning into. Duke also felt a sense of relief that he had made the decision to allow Bishop to come and make things right. He truly felt it was one of the best decisions he had ever made. Duke had always wanted to take the crew to the next level, but he had been unable to do so because of the personal issues he was dealing with. He felt they had kept him stagnated. Now, since those issues were no longer a concern, he knew Bishop was going to do his part. At the same time, he knew and felt like there was so much more that needed to be done. Figuring it out was next, because deep down, he was tired of taking his anger out on the streets, and he was pretty sure the drug dealers and gangers were tired of him as well.

Bishop was thinking, *Fuck this small shit! I gotta holla at my brother* and called Duke's phone.

"What's good, big bro?" Duke said on answering.

"Shit, over here thinking about us! I need to get with you, so I decided to call your phone."

"That's crazy because I'm walking through the front door as we speak."

"Good."

The two disconnected the call and met up in the living room to share some brotherly banter, both flopping down on the couch at the same time, like they had when they were shorties. Duke wasted no time wanting to hear what his big brother had to say.

"What's on your mind, bro?" Duke asked curiously.

"Over here bugging and tripping off that heart to heart we had a few months ago."

"Yeah, I remember your ass waking me up all early and shit!"

"Naw, not the actual conversation, but more so what I did afterward."

"What did you do? Man, what the fuck are you talking about?!"

"Calm down, lil' nigga, and shut the fuck up! A grown man is talking."

"A'ight, nigga, run your mouth if you want to!"

"Dig: Once our conversation was over that day, I didn't want to waste any more time, so I went right upstairs to get my ashy, dark colored bag I came home with. You remember me carrying that bag, right?"

"Yeah, I remember."

"Well, anyway, I have all my important contacts in that bag, shit like numbers, addresses, and everything we're going to need to get fuckin' rich!" Bishop said, laughing to himself.

"Okay, so what's the problem?"

"Yo, you should've seen me hauling ass up them fuckin' stairs to get the bag, but since you didn't see what happened, fuck it!"

Duke smiled after Bishop's statement and slick remark.

"Yeah, I wish I could've seen ya big goofy ass running up some fuckin' stairs! I would've been laughing my ass off, but other than that, the trip down memory lane doesn't do it for me. Don't we have some business to discuss?"

"Yeah, nigga. Stop acting like you're extorting me or something. Your money is on deck. I'm not one of those niggas on the streets."

"Bro, I know who the fuck you are!"

"Then act like it!"

"My bad. I got it."

After they were done talking shit and playfully exchanging words, they exchanged cash from big brother's hand to little brother's hands. Duke was holding the money in his hand, eyeing the height of each stack.

"This is the good life," he said, smiling to himself. "Good thing you're home," Duke continued as he placed each bundle in his own bag.

"What's that supposed to mean?" Bishop asked. Now he was the one with a curious look plastered on his face.

"For one, it's good to have my big brother home, period. Second, you have done things within our circle that I haven't been able to do since God knows when. I had a lot to carry on my shoulders that was weighing me down. My pain and guilt toward you going to jail prevented me from reaching my full potential out here, bro," Duke said hesitating, making sure he chose his words precisely. "Which is why I found comfort in the first place in extorting drug dealers, bitch ass gangbangers, and even time to time, doing a little carjacking. Bro, I've done a host of robberies and other shit that was just extra. I got my kicks from applying pressure on them clowns. I did it as if it was normal behavior, but really and truly, all this shit came at a cost! Feel me?"

"I feel you, little bro. I'm glad to be home too. Because if anything had happened to you while I was gone, man! Only God would have been able to judge me. The streets haven't witnessed no real drama before, and hopefully, they'll never have to. Real talk."

Bishop explained to Duke how now was the time to expand the team's goals to bigger and better things. His mind was set on creating other options which would provide them with better capabilities to do greater things. He felt, given new resources they had not known existed before would broaden everyone's horizons. He wanted to be making more currency on a day-to-day basis.

"And I know just what to do. These last six months have been lovely, but now it's time for me to go into my bag of tricks," Bishop said.

He reached into his prison bag and picked through the phone numbers and addresses, hoping to come across just the right people. He picked up the phone to call the first person on his list. This was the type of nigga you called when you were tired of playing with small money and ready to reach for the stars. This dude ran everything up and down the I-95, no matter what direction a person was traveling. He was a big, fat ass nigga, the type of nigga who had given back fifty-five years and taken nothing for granted, charged as a kingpin. He went by the street name of Boss Hog; it fit him very well.

Boss Hog and Bishop had met during their time in the joint. Bishop had put in a little work for him, and that was how they had become cool. After the impressive work displayed by Bishop, for which he had not expected anything in return, the two of them had become the best of friends. Boss Hog had told Bishop, whenever he got home, to make sure he hollered at him. So, being as how he was home, it was time to take the Boss up on his proposition. Bishop proceeded to dial Boss Hog's number and licked his lips, knowing Boss Hog was who he said he was. After a few rings, someone picked up.

"Hello?"

Being a little sarcastic with his tone when he spoke, Bishop replied, "What's good, Mr. Bigs?"

Not recognizing the voice, he responded "Who the hell is this?"

"It's me, Bishop."

"BISHOP!" he screamed the name in a high tone, excited to hear from his friend whom he had not spoken to in years.

"Yeah, the one and only," Bishop replied.

"When did you get home?"

"I've been home for about five or six months now."

"Oh yeah, my dude? And you're just reaching out to me?"

"Yeah, bro. I had to get a few things in order before reaching out to you, or anyone else for that matter. I had to plant my feet firmly into society's ass first. I told you some of the stories of what I endured over the years, along with my reckless ass little brother."

"Yeah, I remember, my dude. Crazy lil'nigga, but hardcore. I like that type, shit!"

"Yeah, bro, he was still reckless as hell. He was all over the place when I got home, but he has calmed down now, and on the real, I'm trying to keep it like that."

"I hear you, bro. So, what can I do for you? How can I be of assistance to my friend?"

"You know me. I can't go to war unless my money is right, so I've got that handled. Now I'm ready for war!"

"Yeah, that's what I wanna hear!" Boss Hog replied, rubbing his chin.

"You know me, a man of a few words."

"Say no more; I got you. Whatever! Whenever! You should already know this!"

"True. I know what our relationship consists of, which is why you are the first one I called before anyone else," Bishop said, knowing he needed to take a trip.

"I'll be out there in a few days to see you. I have a few more people I need to reach out to, so breathe easy until I'm on your end!"

"Word, my dude. You do the same, bro. Handle your business and get at me. PA, baby boy."

"I'm out there. One," Bishop said, bringing their conversation to an end.

"One," Boss Hog responded and ended the call.

With that going just as well as expected, Bishop's next name on the list was a few down south boys he had also encountered during his time in the joint. He called them Country Boys due to their heavy Southern accents. They were straight country too. Bishop had encountered the Country Boys back in the County jail before he had gone up-state. They were three crazy ass, buck wild niggas from Nashville, Tennessee—in the wrong place at the right time for the police. They had gotten caught up on the New Jersey Turnpike for running guns up and down the highway. They had taken a wrong turn down the wrong Jersey street and gotten bumped. Once in the County jail, waiting for their fate to be decided, they had met up with Bishop and become cool.

Bishop had been arrested the same day as the Country Boys were knocked off. He was normally a solo act if it did not include his little brother Duke, and Bishop surely was not looking to make friends with anyone in jail, but he had seen something in them, which reminded him a lot of himself. The pain of the struggle they were enduring brought the four of them together like brothers. They had bonded and had not taken shit from anyone inside. A lot of niggas put on a facade in jail like they were about that life but did not really have the hands to back up their mouths. They had become like the four musketeers, kicking any and everyone's ass who fucked with them. Their motto was one for all and all for one, something they stood by no matter who or what they were up against.

With those thoughts going through his mind, Bishop was excited to talk to them. He dialed their number and the phone rang. A country voice answered without hesitation.

"Hello. Who dis?"

Glad someone had answered, Bishop wasted no time responding. "Damn, brother, you're still one country ass nigga!"

"Who the fuck is dis fuckin' playin' on my phone?!"

"Nigga, shut the fuck up, acting tough. Yeah, nigga, this be that Jersey boy everyone loves to hate!"

Instantly knowing exactly who it was, he said in return, "Bishop!"

"Damn straight, nigga!"

"Aww, man! It's really good to hear from you."

"In ya ear, nigga. What's good, family?"

"Aww, man, when did you get home?"

"A few months ago. I haven't called because I've been chasing dollar bills—which isn't an excuse though. I had to get my family straight before doing anything else, bro. Everything else had to be secondary, feel me?"

"Most def, bro; family first. We understand, if no one else does, and if they don't understand, fuck 'em, bro. I'm just happy to hear from you finally! That's it."

"Yeah, I feel the same on this end, bro. Listen, I miss the hell out y'all country ass niggas!"

"Naw, nigga. It's you and Jersey and dem New York niggas who are country, but at the same time, we miss you too, family."

"Listen, bro, this phone thing ain't my style, as you should already know. So, I'm going to keep things real short and to the point. I'll be down there to visit the family soon, like in a few days."

"Brother, you're always welcome here with us. You only gotta say when and we got you down here, bro, real talk. Come on down!"

"Cool; that's what I needed to hear. I love ya crazy ass. Give my love and respect to your brothers, and let them know I'm on my way down there."

"Will do. I love you too, bro. Get here. Talk to you later, ya heard?"

"No doubt. One."

They disconnected the call, and Bishop felt good about the progress he was making. He was starting to feel a sense of relief and accomplishment after connecting with his guys. Everyone he had called thus far had answered. He had one more person to connect with to make everything complete. This guy he was about to reach out to was the worst of the bunch. 4'2 was his name. Bishop and 4'2 had spent time in County also. They were fighting their cases at the same time. Although 4'2 was in County jail before Bishop, which did not mean anything, they had gotten really cool.

One of two things can happen when stuck in a close, confined atmosphere together: either you become close or you become enemies. In this circumstance, 4'2 became something like Bishop's mentor. County jail is a wild place for a lot of people who thought they could handle it before actually arriving. If you are who you said you are when you were running them streets, you had better be ready to live up to the name you are claiming. County jail and the niggas locked in there are 'bout it, testing your manhood every second of the day. Only the strong ones stand the test of time, and you can trust and believe, the test is not easy to pass.

However, 4'2 was in there because he had been set up by the Feds. He was there for a fifty-kilo purchase that had gone bad: He was serving as an FBI informant. They had gotten to someone who could get close to him because they could never get close enough themselves to catch him committing any crimes. They had tried to catch him in the act of serving, and they had even tried to get warrants to wiretap him, trying to catch him on the phone talking business. But since his accent was so strong and he talked in code, the Feds could not really make out what he was saying.

It was obvious to his legal team they had made shit up as they were going, having never caught him in the act of any crime, but they had put on him what they call "ghost drugs". That is when a person (or persons) is speaking about drugs or guns in the commencement of a drug deal. They charge you with what they believe the amount of drugs cost or sales would have been, and they charge you as if you had really possessed what they say you were trying to sell, which usually stuck to a nigga. It was like a fucked-up conspiracy charge.

In 4'2's case, with a lack of profit and the fact that he had a highly paid attorney, 4'2 had ended up beating all the charges against him, making the Feds really angry, because we all know, no one beats the Feds with their ninety-nine percent conviction rate. However, 4'2 did, but that was after spending a few years in County jail, fighting for his freedom.

Called 4'2 due to his height, he was an older guy, Mexican and Cuban mixed, with some major connects to the underworld. Finding his number, Bishop started dialing. The phone started ringing, then someone picked up. No one spoke for a few seconds, leaving silence on both ends.

"Hello," Bishop stated, since no one had said anything to him upon answering the phone.

Then, in a very low, Mexican accent, "Hello; who dis?" 4'2 said, being cautious as always.

"It's me, 4'2, Bishop," he said, getting straight to it before the line went dead on Bishop.

"My friend, Bishop! Mi amigo! My little soldier."

"Yeah, yeah, it's me, 4'2. What's good?"

"My man... me don't do phones!"

"I know, I know. I'm just glad you picked up. I've been home for five to six months, and I want to come see you, if that's possible."

"Sounds great. When?"

"I don't know; you tell me. I'll jump on a plane now," he said, anxiety in his voice.

4'2 cut Bishop off, saying, "Okay, okay, come my friend. Come now!"

"Say no more. I'm there!"

"Same location."

"Done. I'm leaving tonight!"

"No more talk."

Before Bishop could say anything else, the call was disconnected. Noticing how 4'2 really had not given him a chance to say anything, he thought, 'Fuck it! As long as he answered, it's time to bounce.'

After many thoughts ran through his mind, Bishop called a female friend to take him to the airport, wasting no time booking his flight, which was leaving at six p.m. Knowing he would be leaving soon, Bishop tried to contact Duke to let him know what was going on. However, he was unsuccessful at reaching his little brother, so instead of continuing to blow up Duke's phone, he decided to write him a short note, explaining what and where he was going.

Dear Duke,

I know we haven't been apart from each other since our reconnection and you're probably mad at your big brother for leaving without you suddenly out of nowhere. However, don't be. You know I don't do anything unless it serves a purpose, which is true in this case as well. The purpose for this will be worth everything we've been striving toward, some major business you'll be proud of later.

When I get back, I'll explain everything to you. So, for now, remain on point while I'm gone and look after Mommy. I should be back in two to three weeks. I have to visit a few spots, Pennsylvania, Tennessee, and Arizona. If you get this letter before 5 pm, meet me at the airport, Terminal B. I take off at 6 pm. If not, I'll see you when I get back. I'm going to pick you up a few bottles of Rosy Red on my way back, sort of a peace offering.

Love you, Bro

He left the letter with their mother to give to Duke, who never showed up at the airport. Bishop thought as he boarded the plane about all the relationships he had formed with his people. They had all started off in County jail, where the initial bonding had taken place, then extended throughout their stays in the joint. It was hard to trust criminal minds that thought like he did, but the people he had ended up bonding with had proven themselves to him as he had proven himself to them: Boss Hog, the country click, and even 4'2, whose stay in the joint had not been as long as the rest of his people.

When Bishop watched the power of money and how it worked in the judicial system, he had admired 4'2 for having the ingenuity to hire the right mouthpieces. He dozed off on the plane, thinking about how smoothly his guy 4'2 had beaten the Feds on his appeal. Now, he was about to reunite with him, then the rest of his people. Life was going to change for him and his little brother, and he knew already it would be a change for the better.

Bishop's flight was right on time, and he arrived in Arizona on schedule. Touchdown!

Chapter Seventeen:
Arizona

Arizona was hot! It was like the sun had a death wish it was bestowing on the human race who lived there. Due to the long flight and the increase in temperature, Bishop found himself exhausted. He contemplated putting the meeting with 4'2 off until the morning, as he would be there for five days. He was mentally and physically tired, but he came for business and business came first. He grabbed his phone from his bag and turned it on. Noticing he had a few missed calls from Duke, he called 4'2 a few times but did not get an answer. He dialed Duke and allowed the phone to ring a couple of times, not getting an answer from him either.

He mumbled to himself, "This feels like déjà vu all over again. This nigga never answers his phone."

He called both of them back a few times and still no answer. "What the fuck?!" he muttered, aggravated. "These niggas are making me mad."

Frustrated about Duke and 4'2 not answering their phones, he called 4'2 back for what would be the seventh time. Bishop glanced around the airport to see if 4'2 had sent anyone to pick him up. Some sort of ride, somebody should have been there. After several minutes on the concourse and dealing with hell's heat, he figured no one was coming for him. He was starting to think his trip was a waste of time. While in deep thought, his phone started ringing. It was an unknown number he noticed as he answered.

"Hello? Who the fuck is this?!" he said, agitated.

A female voice with an accent responded, "Buenos días."

Bishop, noticing it was a woman, toned down his attitude and said to the female, "Oh, excuse me if I sounded rude. I apologize for the way I answered the phone. It's just that I was waiting for a call and thought you were them. Trust me, I'm not usually rude; I've just had a long day."

"I understand. Who were you waiting to call you, your girlfriend?" the woman, who had yet to say who she was or what she wanted, questioned Bishop.

"Listen, no disrespect to you, but you're asking too many questions, and I'm not good with answering questions. Not to mention, I don't know who you are or what you want," he replied, looking again at the face of his phone. He remembered the number had shown up as blocked.

"So, let's see how well I already know you. You aren't into answering any questions, which is good to know. You're an angry person for so many reasons, and you are waiting for a phone call. I think that says it all, right? What do you think? Oh, I forgot, you don't answer questions," she said, purposefully being sarcastic.

Bishop, realizing this conversation was not going anywhere and curious to know who the female was and what she wanted, asked, "Listen, Miss, can I assist you with something? You called my phone. Are you sure you're calling the right person?" Bishop was still very agitated.

She still displayed that she was not bothered by Bishop's attitude. "Look who's asking the questions now. No, you can't help me with anything. However, I'm pretty sure I can help you," she replied in a sexier tone now.

"What?!" Bishop yelled into the phone.

"Shorty sent me to pick you up."

Bishop was confused for a minute, not knowing who the fuck the female was referring to when she said Shorty. Then he thought, 'She must be referring to 4'2,' the only Shorty he would know. He found the whole situation a little funny now, being as he had never heard anyone call 4'2 Shorty before.

"Why didn't you just say that from the beginning?" Bishop replied, relaxing a little.

"And ruin the fun? That would have been too easy."

"Oh yeah? This is fun to you?" Bishop replied, liking her better now.

"Listen, you aren't the only person who doesn't answer questions. You didn't see me over here alone, holding up this sign that says 'Bishop' in very bold letters? It is clear as day."

"Where are you?"

"Over here, sweetie."

Bishop was feeling a little embarrassed by the way he had reacted to everything, now knowing the caller was 4'2's people. He looked around as he stepped back inside the concourse and noticed a woman standing to the right side, propped in a corner and holding a sign that read 'Bishop'. There she was with the sign with the bold letters, just like she had said.

Bishop's tone of his voice softened as he said, "Okay, I see you now. Damn, I definitely did not see you standing there."

"What did you just say?"

"Nothing..." he replied, shrugging off her question for good reasons.

"Nothing? I'm hanging up now!"

The call disconnected and the fun was over. Bishop was just relieved that 4'2 had sent someone to pick him up. He had to admit, she had worked his mind; then he did a double take because the chick was drop-dead gorgeous.

Immediately upon their encounter and greetings when they were standing face to face, the flirting began. They embraced with a handshake and quickly commenced to flirtatious conversation. Being two attractive people who found each other very attractive, they continued going back and forth for the entire ride to 4'2's—or the man she called Shorty's—home.

The beautiful woman stood roughly five foot two and was light skinned with a creamy skin tone and long, black silky hair like you only saw on the women on those Telemundo soap operas. Her curves were vivacious and out of this world. She was truly the definition of the Commodore's "Brick House", 36 24 36, and lo and behold, she was mighty, mighty, letting it all hang out. One could tell just by looking at her that she was mixed with a few different nationalities. She was a beautiful woman who was not shy at all.

She drove Bishop to a very elegant home in a secluded part of Arizona, where the houses were set far apart—nothing like the ghettos or projects back home, where you could reach out your bedroom window and shake your neighbor's hand. Once they arrived, 4'2 was standing in front of his palace with his hands in his pockets, smoking on what looked like a Cuban cigar. He had short, wavy hair, with about three solid gold link chains around his neck, and he was flooded with diamonds. The sun was shining endlessly, complimenting the jewelry that adorned him.

When they came to a complete halt, a smile could be seen across the faces of both men. Bishop, wasting no time, hopped out the truck and ran up to 4'2 with a handshake and a hug, uttering to his friend, "Damn, it's good to see you!"

"Yes, yes, my friend, a pleasure to see you," 4'2 replied, holding Bishop by the shoulders and sizing him up. "I see you found my niece, Kara?"

"I sure did!" Bishop replied.

After the moment they had shared, the two walked into 4'2's home, laughing and talking about whatever crossed their minds. Catching up and reflecting on old times, the two of them were extremely happy to finally see each other outside the prison walls. It was like a father and son seeing each other for the first time after many years apart. They walked into a room where anything one could want was set up. All sorts of food, drinks, and other goodies had been laid out in a spread. Bishop rushed over to the table, hungry and amazed at the layout. 4'2 grabbed a glass as he ordered his servant to pour glasses for Bishop and a few of the henchmen who watched his back.

"Pour everyone drinks," 4'2 said, pointing at liquor bottles that sat on the table in plain sight.

Doing as he was told, he passed a glass of liquor to everyone surrounding the table, making sure Bishop got his first. The gesture was given by 4'2 to raise their glasses for a toast, and he said, "To honor and loyalty! Cheers!" Everyone repeated his words, throwing the glass of liquor they had been given down their throats.

Then it was time for another toast, but this time Bishop had a few words to express, taking the lead. "This toast is for freedom, for those who've paved the way before me and the down brothers like me. I'd like to toast to us! My mentor and soul keeper, this is for my past, present, and our future. Drink, my dude! Cheers!"

After they had feasted on an elaborate Mexican spread and had a few more drinks, the two found a quiet spot to talk and catch up on personal stuff.

"I've been waiting seven years for this day to arrive. It was a bittersweet moment when you left me back in the joint. But yet, I understood you had to go. I understood that part of the game, it was just that we had gotten so close to one another... Man! You were one of the first to embrace me, which you already know, I don't play well with others!" Bishop exclaimed as he reminisced on their times together.

"Yeah, yeah, I know, my friend. That's all behind us now. My son is finally with me. You made sure I was good, and now it's my turn to repay the favor," 4'2 responded to Bishop's emotional spiel as he cleaned the long ash off his expensive cigar.

"Listen, you don't owe me anything. Everything I did for you was from the heart. I don't think you understand how grateful I am to be by your side. Other than my own family, you are the closest person to me, something I take very seriously."

"I feel the same way. I love you, my son. That's one of the reasons I sent my niece to pick you up at the airport."

After that last statement by 4'2, the two shared a few more hugs and family stories. Bishop let him know his purpose for the encounter.

"You know my story. My brother killed my father, and I took the rap for it. Those were some difficult times for me, mentally and emotionally. That was until I met you. You helped me learn more about life and how to control my attitude, despite what went on. So, for that, thank you."

"You're welcome, my son. You're welcome. Now, let's party," 4'2 yelled out.

Bishop cracking a smile, said, "Yeah, let's party!"

The next few days were really smooth around Arizona. Bishop was trying to get used to the heat and hanging out in the dessert. He knew he probably would not, but he had to make the most of it since it was a life changing trip. Right in that moment, being so caught up with 4'2 and their reuniting, Bishop had forgotten to try to contact Duke, which he did once he realized he had not spoken to his brother since arriving in Arizona four days ago.

Bishop was telling himself, "I know this nigga is gonna be pissed with me." He reached for his phone and called Duke.

Answering on the first ring in his angry voice, "Hello. Who the fuck is this?!" knowing it was his brother.

"Yeah, yeah, I can tell you miss me, nigga. I get it," Bishop responded, trying to bypass his little brother's anger.

"Whatever, nigga! You leave me behind, and this is the first shit you say to me?"

"Yeah, little nigga. Get out of your emotions. I miss you."

"Whatever, nigga. What the fuck is up? I gotcha letter from Mommy."

"Okay, that's what's up. Like I said in the scribe to you, I love you to the death of me. I do what I do so you don't have to, so be mad all you want. You'd better get over that shit, and I mean quick too!"

"I heard. Listen, I'm not mad. I understand, and understood, all you wrote. Me and Mommy are good. You know how it goes."

"Yeah, I know how it goes, but fuck them. Listen, I might be back earlier than I expected. It's on to the next spot."

"I heard. Where are you?" Duke asked his brother.

Bishop shook off the questions and told him, "That isn't important. All you need to know is we're good. Do what you do until I get back, and never leave home without it!"

"Yeah, I dig you. I'll never leave home without it! Know that, and Rose doesn't have a red!"

Confused about what he was talking about, Bishop says, "What?"

"In your letter, nigga. You said you were gonna bring me back some bottles of Rose Red. Bro, there is no such thing as a Rose Red. Just bring me back some of that Remy VSOP!" Duke said, laughing.

"Nigga, you know what I meant. It may not say red, but it's red," Bishop quipped, feeling the need to tell young Duke, who was laughing into his phone.

"Yeah, I get it, bro. I knew what you meant to say; I'm just fuckin' with you. But, yeah, bring me back some Remy."

"Yeah, I heard. I'm glad you corrected me though. Listen, fuck the bottles. How about some cash instead?"

"Cash? Hell yeah! That sounds so much better. Shit with the liquor; I'll buy my own bottles. At the same time, finish doing you. Be safe out there, ya heard?"

"No doubt. I gotchu and do the same. Kiss Mommy for me. One."

"Gotchu. One."

The ended their conversation, and Bishop was glad Duke was not as mad at him as he had thought he would be.

A day or two later, Bishop felt like his business in Arizona was completed. Everything had gone as well as expected. Knowing it was time to hit his next spot, he let 4'2 know his next steps, getting ready to say his goodbyes.

"Hey, I enjoyed my stay. We have to do this more often. I have a few more stops to make on my tour, before heading back to Jersey. I think my next stop is going to be Nashville, Tennessee. I want to thank you for your assistance and for showing me nothing but love and hospitality. Again, family to the end."

"That's okay. Loved seeing you, my son."

"I get it, but you don't understand. Allowing me to fly to my next stop in your private jet is more than anyone could have done for me. But again, you have always done it big for me; it's no secret." The two laughed as Bishop continued to show his gratitude.

"I definitely understand now why they call it an airport, but you call it a clear port," Bishop said, smiling and thinking he had said something slick by quoting Jay Z.

Smiling back at Bishop, 4'2 responded to his young friend, "I know. You're a good kid. I love you for your honesty and commitment to bring about a better life for you and your family. Me, I respect that, especially with you being as young as you are. Our friendship means everything to me."

"I'm here with you until the death of me, but being you are so much older than I am, you'll probably go first, old head," Bishop responded with a little humor, and 4'2 cracked a smile.

"Also, thank you for allowing your niece Kara to accompany me to my next two destinations. I'll keep her safe."

"No, no, she's a good girl, and I know you'll keep her safe," 4'2 expressed to Bishop.

As they finished up their conversation, Bishop reminded 4'2 not to forget the two packages he had ordered. "Make sure they get there two weeks after I let you know I'm back, okay?"

"No problem, my friend, no problem. You'll like it."

"I'm sure I will."

After Bishop's final remark, he and Kara got themselves ready to leave. For the rest of his last night, everyone chilled.

The next morning, Bishop and Kara embraced 4'2 and headed to the private airfield in Tucson. When they got to the private airport, Bishop was amazed as he passed the hangers and saw how many people in Arizona actually owned their own planes. They made it to 4'2's hanger and quickly boarded the Gulfstream G IV. It was a seven-passenger, luxury plane, equipped with everything a person would want and need. The pilot spoke over the mic once they were aboard, informing them that the flight to Tennessee would take a little over three hours.

"Let's get ready for takeoff. Please take your seats and fasten your seatbelts. Push the service button if you need anything."

The voice faded off, and Bishop felt the plane start to move. They got comfortable and engaged in conversation, trying to understand one another's differences in life. After sharing their likes and dislikes, Bishop asked her for a second or two to himself. He needed to make a phone call. The plane was equipped with a satellite phone, which allowed calls to be made while in the air. Calling the Country Boys, he let them know he would be there soon. When he was done on the phone, he looked over at Kara. Noticing she was sound asleep, he smiled at how beautiful she looked.

"Damn! How the fuck did I get myself into something like this?" he expressed to himself.

Then he closed his eyes and enjoyed the rest of the flight.

Chapter Eighteen:
Back In Jersey

Duke was running around, doing what he did best—creating major problems for everyone who was not part of his circle. He was chilling with the crew and the fellas were wondering where his brother was, since they had not seen Bishop in a few days. It was almost automatic since Bishop had come home that you did not see one without the other, or one a few steps behind the other.

"Yeah, big bruh is crazy. He's on a mission right now," Duke said, not really wanting to go into details.

"What type of mission?" Malik asked.

"He's going from state to state, getting shit right for real niggas. I mean like, yo, this nigga is flying around with this hot ass chick who would make Jennifer Lopez bite her knuckles."

"For real?" Malik said with excitement in his voice.

"For real for real... He just left Arizona. He's now on his way to Tennessee. I just got off the phone with him. You niggas know what it is! Wherever he goes, any moves he makes, he has to check in with lil' bro."

Gooch and Malik shared a laugh or two with Duke as he boasted to his closest friends with a strong choice of words when referring to Bishop. Duke was always acting and trying to sound like he was the big brother, instead of Bishop. He could have received a Grammy for the performance he put on. The trio drove through the hood as they often did, chopping it up and passing a blunt back and forth. While driving, Duke started smelling a stink odor in the air that was not scented by the weed. It was something very funky and foul that played with his nostrils; it almost smelled like they had driven into a pig slaughterhouse. Paying no attention, thinking it must be in the air outside since they did have the windows down a little bit, Duke continued to run his mouth, because he too, just like the crew, was excited.

"Ever since bruh came home, he has been nothing but diligent and strategic about putting shit together. That's my muthafuckin' nigga! Yo, what the fuck is that smell?!" he asked, making a face to show how disgruntled he was becoming.

"How the fuck we know?! I don't smell shit but this weak ass weed we're puffing," Malik replied.

"Damn, Malik! Put the fuckin' window down a little more, nigga, or stop fuckin' talking. Yo, your shit is rockin'!" He had finally realized what the smell was. It was Malik's breath.

Duke and Gooch were both laughing. Duke was serious about the halitosis problem plaguing Malik's mouth.

"No bullshit, nigga! You need to handle that problem, real talk. It's cold as hell out, and we have to ride around with the windows down. Stop at the gas station, so I can buy your ass a case of Double Mint and a bottle of mouthwash!" Duke said.

"Duke, what is your brother up to? He's been OT for a minute," Gooch asked, changing the subject.

He agreed that Malik's funky breath smelled like the elephant cage at Turtle Back, but he did not want to offend his comrade like Duke was doing.

Duke, acting as if he did not hear the question Gooch had asked him, turned in the direction of Malik. The reason he did not answer Gooch's question was the simple fact that he had yet to explain to them he had made a decision to let Bishop take over his day-to-day operations, which included the crew. They had been making moves already, but Duke had not fully explained it was Bishop's expert tutelage that was the new plan maker. He had just felt the need to fall back since Bishop was home and seemed to have everything under control. His changes were something he was going to share at his own discretion. Therefore, trying to skip the subject, he focused on Malik and his funky ass breath.

Duke was still holding his nose as he talked to Malik. He gave him instructions to go over on 16th Avenue and 20th Street. He wanted to hit up the E–ecstasy– spot really quick and check things out. He wanted to do this before they jumped on the highway to Atlantic City. As they approached the E spot, coming to a complete halt and parking near the spot, Duke reached into his pocket and pulled out two hundred dollars for the purchase of pills. He held out his hand with the money, handing it to Gooch.

"Here, go get the pills with this."

Gooch grabbed the money before jumping out the car with a slight attitude. He was mumbling to himself, saying shit under his breath.

Duke heard him say a few words and asked him, "What the fuck you say, nigga?"

Gooch looked back at this friend as if he was going to say something, but instead of causing a confrontation that he was not going to win with Duke, he shrugged his shoulders and said his comment in his head. 'Who the fuck this nigga think I am?'

Waiting patiently for Gooch to come back, Duke and Malik never noticed, that while they were at the E spot, Detective Burcheck was parked a few cars away. He was watching Duke and his crew. He had been on them for quite some time. Gooch returned, jumping back into the car and quickly handing Duke the pills he had just copped. He opened them and passed a few around to Gooch and Malik. They each took their pills in their hand and threw them back with a large bottle of orange juice to wash them down. Not caring who was or was not watching them, they all wanted to get that feeling.

"Yo, throw on that Pac!" Duke said as he slouched back into the seat.

Malik, doing what he was asked to do, put on *Hit 'Em Up* as he jumped on the highway. Floating down I 95 to Atlantic City, the pills started to kick in, and of course, they affected everyone differently. Duke started feeling himself as he spit along with Pac. He started wanting to be Pac. Instead of just listening to his music, he was singing at the top of his lungs.

"Fugees! Fugees and Mobb Deep trying to diss now, huh? Ha ha ha... well, I ain't prejudiced. I don't give a fuck. This is what it sounds like when I ride on our enemies!"

Yeah, Duke was starting to feel himself and yelled to Malik to turn the music up. He continued to sing, "Beyotch! When we ride on our enemies, HEYYYY! Got some static from some niggas on the other side of town.

Lettin' my lil cousin K roll. He's a rider now. What they want from us muthafuckin' thug niggas? Yo, that's what it is!"

"Turn down the music for a minute," Duke asked Malik. "I love you niggas, word up. You dudes are all I got, and now that my brother is home, yeah, it's on! We're great! He's on that shit heavy. That's why I'm falling back from a lot of this shit! He's gonna take over for me, real talk. He'll handle everything."

The E pill was working on Duke's emotions, allowing him to say shit he usually would not say under regular circumstances. But he was high and being high off those E pills brought all types of truths and emotions out of a real nigga—or even a soft nigga. Let's just say the E pill will help the truth come out.

As the E pill took its effect on Duke and Gooch, Malik sat back and listened closely as Duke ran his mouth. He was gone and did not realize he was talking too much. The E pills were starting to get the best of him. He kept talking about Bishop and his plans for the future. The more Duke spoke, the more jealous Gooch was becoming. Duke was drastically off point. He had no idea what he was saying. He was just caught up in the moment.

Duke never peeped the disgusted look on Gooch's face for what he was spitting. The pill blinded him to everything that was going on. He was in a very vulnerable state of mind at the moment, and he continued to run his mouth, because of one thing: Duke felt safe around his own people.

"Yo, my brother is on his job. He's going to make sure y'all is good too, trust me. That nigga is planning to do all types of shit! He's been on it like this since we were kids, from then to now. Yeah, my dude has only gotten sharper, real talk," Duke said, turning his nose toward the cracked window.

"Malik, turn that shit back up, bro! Let's rock Pac's lyrics... I bet all you muthafuckas die when we ride on our enemies!" Duke spat as the pills kept working on him.

"Yo, niggas, I feel lucky tonight. I wanna hit the 40/40 club. Afterward, I wanna drop a few stacks on the table. Blackjack is the game. We'll hit Trump Plaza."

"I'm in," Gooch replied, like he had a choice.

"I wanna gamble, whether it's with my money or my life. Let's get there!"

No one else said anything after that statement. Duke controlled the conversation for the entire ride.

"Malik, turn the music back up. We're here! The lights are fuckin' with my eyes. It's live as hell out here. Yo, I'm feeling nice! No bullshit! I'm fuckin' something nice tonight. Damn, the 40 is packed. Word up!"

"Yo, I heard Maybach Avenue's got these bitches out tonight. You see them chicks right there? Damn, them bitches is nice," Malik commented, saying something for the very first time since chewing the gum they had stopped to pick up.

"Yeah, I see them. I'ma see them bitches inside the 40. I need one of those hoes for something, maybe two. It doesn't matter to me. For real, I wanna fuck!"

After Duke's comment, Gooch and Malik looked at each other and burst out laughing.

"I don't know what the fuck you niggas find so hilarious. Malik, you ain't fuckin' shit 'til you getcha mouth fixed. Dem bitches gonna diss ya ass. We came down here to party and gamble, so if some dude can't control his bitch or his liquor... Yo, y'all already know. Shit is gonna get real dark real quick. No bullshit! The party is gonna be over even faster. That's why I never leave without it."

"We live this shit," they all said at the same time.

The trio had a habit of saying shit at the same time when it counted, especially when Face Hound and Sheedah were not around.

Malik blurted out, "Yo, you niggas know Face Hound and Sheedah are gonna be mad at us for leaving them."

"Shit, I tried calling them before we bounced. I called them and had my homegirl with the clothing store, Ms. Qupid, take clothes to their spots, but no one was around. They'll get over it. Let's ball out!" Duke replied.

All the events seemed to be located on Atlantic Avenue, which is where they were. Malik parked the car at the Grand Hilton, and they reserved the Al

Capone suite. It was surely a room fit for gangsters. At the sight of their suite, Gooch was very impressed with everything. "Duke, yo, this shit is live! This bitch's gotta jacuzzi in the middle of the floor. The whole nine yards is in this bitch!"

"Shit, this is where the party should be! Yo, right here. We don't need to go anywhere. Dig, I'm bringing a few bitches back with me when we leave the club. I wouldn't have it no other way," Malik added. He was chewing the whole pack of gum since Duke had made him conscious of his funky breath.

Duke listened to his friends go crazy over the suite as he admired the suite in a different way, picturing himself in Scarface or The Untouchables. Mimicking some of Al Capone's famous words, he said, "I want that muthafucka dead. I want his family dead. I want 'em to go to sleep with the fish on his head," smiling to himself as if the world had heard him. Duke walked over to check out the view from the window. The pills made him feel a little faint since they were so high up.

"I heard Maybach Ave. is performing Chopper Music tonight. He's killing the state with that song. Yo, everybody who is somebody is down here. So, yeah, it's only right we show our faces. Let's get ready. Time to look like money!" Duke continued as he adjusted his Cartier's to help shield the light.

An hour and a half later, the trio was ready and looking like they were part of the money team, with Duke at the head.

"Damn...." Duke said, looking in the mirror. "My shit's looking tight. I bet my chain could pay a muthafucka's rent and car note for a couple of months, maybe a year! See, this is what blood, sweat, and tears get you, my nigga. My Tuff Luv chain is flooded with hella diamonds."

"Yo, my nigga, I see Robins on 8th over in PA hooked a nigga up," Malik said.

"Fuck local shopping. A nigga's gotta travel to get that good shit. Shit! VVS1's? Nobody in the hood wears shit like this. This shit is hot, right?" Duke continued.

Gooch and Malik nodded their heads in agreement.

"Yo, who the fuck from the hood rocks watches from David Yurman? Niggas and bitches ain't up on this shit. All a muthafucka can do is look at our shine and compliment some real niggas on their shit, for real. Yo, I love these ACG boots too. They should just call me Mr. Exclusive tonight."

Gooch and Malik once again laughed at Duke's outrageous words. Gooch was wondering if the pills still had him on edge because he was not stopping.

"Nah, for real, my nigga. C'mon, niggas, button down fly shit designed by Ms. Qupid from her Tuff Luv collection. Listen, by us wearing her shit, the bitch is gonna get that money. She needs to give a real nigga a cut for this one. She's gonna owe me too. Jeans from Akami by BDK. These designers are up and coming, and we're making them look good. I'ma floss this lifestyle to the fullest. The only way I stop is if God has different plans for me."

Duke posed, crossing him arms. It was obvious he was still high off the E pills. The crew could see the main effect they were having was keeping Duke talkative as hell. He kept bragging and boasting like there was no tomorrow.

"Nigga, you're high as hell, charged up. Nigga, for real for real, your ass hasn't stopped talking since we left the city," Gooch interjected. Duke really was not hearing anything Gooch or Malik had to say.

"Nigga, shut the fuck up! I'm high off life, muthafucka. When the Duke is talkin', either shut the fuck up or say excuse me, nigga. Now let's bounce," Duke demanded after ripping Gooch a new asshole.

Without any words or further backlash, they did as they were told. As they were leaving the hotel, a text came through to Duke's cellphone, a message from Bishop telling him he had just landed in Tennessee. Duke read the text silently.

I should be out here for three days. Then I'm on my way to PA. Last stop. I'll be home soon. One.

Duke typed, replying back to Bishop's message,

I heard my nigga. Love you too bro. Can't wait to see you back home. One.

After the message, Duke, Malik, and Gooch continued on to the 40/40 club and walked straight in past the crowd. Gooch knew the bouncer, so everything was all good. Plus, extending a few dollars never hurt the situation. Slipping the bouncer a couple of hundreds, the three went into the club to see what was cracking. Once inside, Gooch noticed a few familiar faces standing around.

"Yo, you see them birds over there from Avon? Dem bitches be everywhere!"

Duke and Malik did a quick look, then turned back around.

"Yo, DJ Khalid is here tonight. This shit is nice, and it's packed!" Gooch continued, knowing he was going to like the spot.

"Yo, let's walk around for a second. Let's check out some chicks and get a feel for this place," Malik uttered.

"A'ight, bet. Stick together too," Duke replied, not wanting anyone to get lost in the crowd.

The trio walked through the club, mingling with a few freaks and checking out the scenery. Gooch and Malik left Duke to go to the bar while he kicked it with a female he had just met. They had a few Tap That Asses, which is Henny mixed with Alizé, to get their night started. As the two drank, a few jokes followed, attempting to bring a little humor to the scene, especially with the bartender whom they had tipped generously.

Some guy from Newark, whom they had robbed some months back for guns and drugs, appeared out of nowhere. He had seen Duke alone, talking to his female friend, whispering into the shorty's ear. The dude was watching Duke with sneaky eyes that seemed to want trouble. Every move Duke made was made with his eyes glued on Duke's movements. Duke was having such a good time that he did not notice someone was watching him. He was still high and too much into his lady friend to see anything or anyone else.

However, Gooch and Malik were on top of it as soon as they spotted the dude. They watched as the guy watched Duke with a look that could kill in his black, shady looking eyes. As Duke and the female made their way over to the restroom, the guy followed closely on his heels. Duke went into the restroom, and when he walked out, the guy was lurking a short distance away, accompanied by a few of his boys now. They all looked to be packing and they all were watching when Duke came out of the restroom. Malik and Gooch waited to see what they were going to do.

The female had waited for him at the restroom's entrance, and when Duke exited, he put his arm around her and pulled her into his body, pulling her back into the unisex restroom. The pills had him excited and his sexual adrenaline was rushing to his manhood. He was not waiting to make it to a room. Duke started caressing her body, his hands roaming all over her well portioned figure, feeling every curve and sexy hump she had been blessed with. Shorty was what they called "thicker than a Snicker", and he wanted to pack her full of nuts. Duke was moving aggressively and quickly with her. They were not going to make it to the dance floor, let alone a hotel room as they cropped up in the corner of the unisex restroom.

They were fondling the fuck out of each other like they were in their own little world that was void of other patrons. Duke had his hands down her waist high designer jeans, inserting his middle finger in her wet pussy. She was moaning and grinding her hips and kissing his neck at the same time. He was so engrossed in his sexcapade that he didn't notice the nigga he had jacked had walked in the restroom until he heard the voice.

"Yo, nigga! You remember me? What's up now? You had a lot to say the last time we saw each other, when you had that fuckin gun pressed against my head—"

Before the dude could get the rest of the words out his mouth, Duke stole on him with a devastating right hook. His power knocked the dude out cold. Duke was in the mode after that. Seeing the dude he had socked was not alone, he quickly grabbed the closest man to him and slammed his face into the wall. Blood shot from the man's face as he yelled to get Duke up off him. The shorty Duke had been entertaining wasted no time running away from the situation. She was screaming and yelling, "Their fighting!"

Malik saw her running and screaming frantically, and he and Gooch were on top of it. Gooch and Malik got through the crowd and were now in the mix of the things. They grabbed the third guy who was with him and started stomping him. Once the bloody faced dude got himself together, Malik faded him, throwing a flurry of punches nonstop at the guy, who did not know what had hit him for the second time.

The club was packed, and yet, they had made enough room for Duke and his crew to trash the three guys who had opposed them. They beat the living shit out of all three guys, dragging them back into the restroom and leaving them in the corner, piled on top of each other. They were still high as fuck and simply made their way to their VIP box as if nothing had happened.

"Damn, that was fun!" Duke said, wiping a stream of sweat from his forehead. "You niggas good?"

"I'm good. That's what we do," Gooch replied first.

Malik, who had caught a left jab to his top lip, thumbed the trickle of blood and replied as well, "Yo, fuck dem bitch ass niggas."

"I'm with you; it's time to swerve. I have bottles coming, so we can enjoy the rest of our night," Duke said to his two friends.

"Bet," Gooch said, falling back in his lounge seat, letting him know he was down for that.

"This is a good view. We can see everything from up here. Shit, we can peep the entire club," Duke said as he wiped himself down. He was upset he had scuffed up his boots and ripped his shirt pocket. The bottle arrived and Duke grabbed three glasses and started pouring drinks.

"Let's toast to us! Straight thuggin'!"

The trio yelled out at the same time, "Cheers! Straight thuggin for life!"

Without a worry or care in the world, they drank and continued to party the night away. For hours, the boys enjoyed themselves. They had a good ass time despite everything that had transpired that night, which wasn't over yet. Time had flown by, and the DJ was playing Check Out Time by Pac, which was another one of Duke's favorites. It was closing in on four a.m., and neither one of the crew was ready to take it in and lay it down for the night. For them, it was now time to gamble and see if they could get lucky.

"Let's bounce. Trump Plaza is right down the street. I'm ready to go lay some bread on a table and win some of Trump's paper; he can stand it," Duke said.

Gooch and Malik agreed as they started walking behind Duke toward the club's exit. When they got to the outside of the club, it was still hot as hell outside, like it would never cool off. Duke hesitated, catching a glimpse of a familiar face out the corner of his eye.

"Hold up, niggas," Duke said, squinting and making sure it was who he thought it was.

"Yo, what's cracking, bro? Them niggas ain't coming, are they?" Malik asked, thinking he wanted another lick for the bloody lip he had gotten earlier.

"Yo, I think I see something, or better yet, someone, I know," Duke replied, quickly taking off and running after the person he thought he knew, who was already halfway down the street. He was running as if his life depended on it. Duke started yelling out a name.

"YO, SHARELLE! YO, SHARELLE!"

The street was semi packed due to everyone leaving the club. Duke did not give a fuck. He was on a mission to get whomever he was chasing after. The group of females saw Duke from a distance and turned around to see what all the commotion was about. They were anxious to see why this guy was chasing behind them, yelling their friend's name.

"YO, SHARELLE!" he yelled out one last time as he got closer to the females.

They heard him but continued to walk in the direction they were heading. They slowed it down a little bit for Duke to catch up with them, but they all had their hands on the mace spray in their purses. Running out of breath, Duke finally got close enough to be seen clearly.

With a shortness of breath, he said, "Sharelle! Sharelle!" completely exhausted.

All of the women laughed as he became more visible. One of the females said, "Sharelle, who is this mad man running behind us, calling your name like he's crazy?"

"Yeah, girl. Either he's high or insane, or he's just crazy. Whatever his deal, he's buggin'," another one said.

Sharelle, finding a little humor in the situation, said, "Girl, he's probably someone I gave some of this good good to, and he didn't get enough." She laughed.

"Girl, he's close now. Can you tell who he is?" the first female asked.

"I have no idea who he is. Y'all come on before we get robbed out here," Sharelle said, ordering her friends to keep it moving.

Again, the females laughed and finally made their way to their ride. The black-on-black Navigator truck which they had come in was shining and sitting on rims like it belonged to an NBA player. Everyone climbed in, preparing to head back to their hotel or another spot to finish kicking it. Then, out of curiosity, Sharelle turned around one last time before getting in the truck to see if she recognized the crazy man before they pulled off. Quickly, she told her friend Taisha who was driving to hold up. Sharelle realized at that moment, although she did not recall from where, that the face of the crazy man who was calling her name was familiar.

Duke and Sharelle were now face to face, looking at each other—her through slightly intoxicated eyes and him just tired from the grind. He was still winded from all the running he had just done. He looked her up and down, and saw she was just as gorgeous as ever.

"First, I would like to apologize for my unusual behavior, because The Duke don't chase after no woman. I know and understand how hot it is out here, and I appreciate you stopping for me. How have you been?" he asked.

"I'm fine. This is unusual for me as well, but since my curiosity got the best of me, hell, I figured what would be the harm to see who you were. After that marathon you put on, the least I could do was give you the benefit of the doubt and find out how you know me, know my name. Shit, who are you?"

"The Duke, baby," he said with a hint of cockiness.

"Do people really call you that?" she asked the oh so arrogant and handsome man standing there, resting his hands on his knees, still tired after acting like Jessie Owens.

"Yes, people call me that, because Duke is my name. Now, to answer your question as to how I know your name or you for that matter, let's just say I had the opportunity to meet you in person when I used to come see my brother. He was locked up at the prison where you work. I've heard good things about you. Are you still working at that spot?"

"Yes, I am still there. However, now that we've got that out the way, how can I help you?"

"Okay, straight to the point, huh? That's what's up. Like I was saying to you, I saw you a few times when I used to visit my brother, and every time I saw you, I wanted to get at you. However, I didn't think it was appropriate to try to holler at you at your place of work. Plus, your coworkers stayed in my face; those guys stayed on me. It was as if you were one of their girl or something."

"No, that surely wasn't the case. I don't mix bread and head," she said with a smile.

Duke continued on. "But at the same time, I wasn't discouraged behind those guys protecting you. In fact, I promised myself, if I ever saw you anywhere outside of your workplace, I was going to get at you. Tonight was my first opportunity, so I seized the moment. It was me keeping my promise, despite how it may look."

"Persistent and charming. I have to say, you're funny too. Cute also. I guess you were determined, huh?"

"Am I?"

"It's cold out here, and you ran a long way to catch me. Was it worth it?"

"To get a little conversation? Yeah, so far, it's been well worth the run. You're my Kelly Rowland. A little motivation never hurt anyone."

"Kelly Rowland, huh? I like that, although I look so much better than her."

"Yes, you do, so much better," he said, agreeing with her about her beauty.

"So, you mean to tell me, you left your guys to chase after me? Impressive!" she replied, looking past him to see if she could still see his guys in the distance.

"Yeah, they're good. Listen, you keep mentioning my little jog down the street. That wasn't about nothing. You act as if dudes don't chase after you or something."

"They don't."

"Well, they should," Duke said, still being charming.

"So, listen, The Duke, you lied about hearing a lot about me, because, for one, you don't know me. Now, as far as dudes running after me, no guy or guys have ever done what you did tonight. You're the first."

"And, hopefully, the last," Duke told her, and she smiled at his slick comment.

"For one, lil momma, The Duke doesn't lie. Nah, that isn't my style. If tonight is the first time ever a man has run after you, then don't worry, it's my first time too."

"I hear you, and yet, every man lies. I haven't met one who hasn't lied before."

"Okay, I can see where this is going. You must've just gotten out of a really bad relationship, or you've just been fuckin' with some really fucked up dudes! I guess now, me and every other guy who tries to holler at you has gotta pay for the mistakes those lames made, huh? Is that why you believe every man is a liar?"

"No, that isn't it. I'm just a firm believer that every man lies, that's it. I'm not in a relationship and haven't been in one for months, not that it's any of your business."

"Nah, you're right, not any of my business at all. I have to apologize if I crossed the line or offended you in any way. "

"No need for apologies nor did you offend me; trust me, I'm a grown ass woman. I'm just saying, I have to find a man who is worthy enough, boo boo. Sorry."

Sensing the sarcasm in her tone and appreciating a strong black woman and what they possess, Duke responded, "Now you're talking my language. You must have a coat of grease on your tongue because you're talking slick and I like that. So, allow me to introduce myself to you again. Hi; my name is The Duke; however, some people call me or know me as Mr. Worthy!"

"You're crazy, boy," she said with a big ass smile on her face, thinking how he had gotten that one off. "And you say I'm the one with grease on my tongue—whatever. I told you, you're funny and that's a good thing."

"Okay, I'm doing something right. I have you smiling."

"You do."

"That's good to know. That's what I wanna hear, especially coming from you. I'm enjoying our encounter. However, I know your friends are waiting for you. They want you to getcha ass outta this street and into the truck. Don't need you getting swept off your feet."

"So now you're a street sweeper, huh?"

"I wouldn't mind, if what I was getting up was you. We can sweep up each other, sweetie."

"Slow down, cowboy. I only asked a question."

"Now that was funny, and you say I'm the comedian."

"But, in all honesty, why chase after me? I'm pretty sure you could chase after thousands of women. Why me?"

"Why not chase after someone as beautiful as you are? What's going on? Are you into guys? Or do you have some major Jerry Springer secret? Maybe you aren't a chick in real life."

They shared a laugh as Duke looked at her throat, making sure there was no manly lump where it should be smooth.

"Seriously though, Sharelle, you're a very attractive woman who I would love to get the opportunity to understand more. I've felt like this ever since I laid eyes on you. I haven't been able to get you off my mind since the first day I saw your beautiful face sticking out above that uniform. That's how I knew it was you walking with your friends. I would like to think I keep it one hundred ten percent when it comes to life! I would love to get to know you better, which I've already said, as well as me wanting to keep you smiling, but only if you'd allow for me to do that. My life is a never-ending story with so many chapters to it, but that's only until someone special comes into my life and changes all that for me."

"I hear you, and you sound good. You have this chameleon thing going on. It's like you are able to adapt and move swiftly, and there's that crazy part of you. Oh, and for the record, I am five hundred percent woman too, Mr. Funny Man! Can't you tell?"

"Oh yeah, I sure can tell. Aaalll woman, yes, you are!"

"And just to let you know something else, I love men, but for some reason or another, as of lately, I've been attracting little ass

Chapter Nineteen:
Tennessee

The taxi pulled over at the Waldorf Astoria Hotel in downtown Tennessee. It was a luxurious and very upscale hotel, fit for a king and queen. Bishop liked to make sure when he went somewhere outside of his hometown that he stayed in the best places with the best food and customer service. The bellhop met the taxi at the porte cochère at the hotel's entrance, immediately opening the door on Kara's side.

"Welcome to the Waldorf Astoria. Can I please be of service?"

"Yes," Kara replied, seeing the driver had already popped the trunk. "You can take our bags to room 1206 and room 1207."

"Yes, ma'am. The penthouse suite is a great choice." he replied, smiling.

The bellhop had been doing his job long enough to know that customers who stayed on the twelfth floor were good tippers.

"You two can go check in, and I will have these bags placed in your suite by the time you get there."

He smiled again, patting down his black and red skinny suit that all the employees wore. Bishop handed the polite bellhop a hundred-dollar bill and watched as he packed the bags on a metal cart, then rush for the elevator.

Check-in was smooth since Kara had reserved it on her uncle's black card. They were set to see the inside of their suites. Bishop walked slightly behind Kara as she walked to the elevator looking overly exhausted from the flight. He knew she was because he also was a little tired.

The shiny gold door elevator finally arrived on the twelfth floor, and Bishop and Kara stepped out, looking at the wall sign that pointed them in the right direction. The double presidential suite had separate outside doors with connecting doors on the inside middle wall. If one wanted, they could open the doors and the rooms would be one big arena. Kara and Bishop looked around and smiled at each other as they each entered the computerized keys into their slots. Bishop had another reason for smiling, which Kara was about to find out.

Kara entered her room and saw the bellhop was a keeper of his word. Her Gucci luggage was sitting right there, out of the way as he had said. When she looked around her suite, a smile plastered her face from ear to ear.

'Now, when did he have time to do this?' she thought.

There were dozens of flowers spread throughout the entire suite. She had never seen so many flowers in one place, except at her aunt's funeral when she was a little girl. Bishop had taken the liberty to specially order red, white, and yellow roses, and had had them placed on and around her double sized king bed. She found a card and wondered what he had to say. She picked it up and smiled again.

Recently, I met a woman who is everything I have been searching for...

She finished reading the card, looking at all the designer clothes, bags, shoes, and balloons that had been placed around her room. She was still struggling to understand how he had done all this while they were traveling together and he had not left her sight. Kara was blown away as she held up a Pamela Roland dress from Neiman Marcus. She held it to her figure like she was a mannequin.

"Wow," she whispered.

It was perfect, and so were the matching red bottoms she was sure he had chosen to accent the dress. Kara opened her connecting door and knocked on Bishop's door. She banged on the door really hard, ready to confront him in a good way. Her playful side came out as she yelled in a deep voice with her accent, "It's the police! Open up!"

"Who is it?" Bishop asked with authority.

Realizing Bishop was not playing, Kara toned down her voice and simply said, "It's me, Kara."

Bishop opened the door that separated him from his dream girl to get a peek, expecting a big smile since he had already looked at the pictures in his phone of how the people he paid set up her room. It was a one-and-done as Kara did the rest, placing her smooth, manicured hands on his chest and pushing her way into his room. She leaped straight into his arms and started kissing on him nonstop, telling him how great of a man he was and how grateful she was for him. As she tightened her grip around his neck, almost choking him, Kara expressed how she wanted to be with him.

Bishop, calm as ever, simply replied, "This must mean you got my gifts."

"Oh, that's really cute," she said, sliding down out of his arms and feeling the rod that had grown instantly through his jeans.

"You know I received your gifts. Thank you. They are amazing, and the room is beautiful. You have me all mushy inside, but you've got to tell me one thing."

"What's the one thing I've got to tell you? Because I can think of a million things to tell you." He said, getting a whiff of her Tiffany scent.

"How in the hell did you know all my sizes?"

"Ancient Chinese secret," he said, laughing.

"That would work, but you aren't Chinese. I can't believe you've got me feeling like a little girl falling in love for the first time."

"You are a little girl, although you are all woman. It was my pleasure to put a smile on your face. If I had it my way, that's all I'd do for you—make you smile," he replied, letting her words swim around inside his head and heart.

"Awww, that sounds wonderful. You can bet your last dollar that is something I wouldn't mind you doing. Smiling is good, but one more question—well, maybe a few questions," she said, still blushing.

"Cool. I'm here to answer any questions you have. Ask away," Bishop said in an enthusiastic tone.

Kara had him feeling like he had nothing to hide, so he was amped to answer her. A text message interrupted their conversation, streaming across his phone.

"Hold up, baby. Hold that thought for a minute. I have to answer this message," he told her, then responded to the text from Duke.

I heard my nigga. I love you too. Bruh, I miss and love you like no other. Can't wait to see you. One.

Finding his way back, he placed his full attention on Kara, who was still caught up in her moment.

"My bad, baby. I texted my brother earlier, and he was just responding. Now, where were we?"

"Me about to get all up in your business, like real queens do."

"Then come on, get up in my business! I'm going to answer; that is what real kings do," he replied, liking the way they shared banter.

"Okay, so tell me, when did you have time to do all this, especially since I brought my own clothes? I'm glad to know you listen very well, with your slick butt. That's probably why you kept asking me questions about my sizes and other personal things about me."

"Do you wanna know, or don't you, nosy?"

"Yes, I would like to know, okay? Tell me."

"I did everything while you were asleep. The flight here drained you, so I took advantage of that moment. Then I called a few friends and gave them the room number, and they made the rest possible for me—I mean, for you. You deserve that and much more. So, yes, I inquired about your sizes. That was one of many reasons for asking you so many questions, and of course, some for my own personal reasons. I want to know everything about you, everything there is to know about you."

"Oh, one of your many reasons?"

Bishop laughed at her sarcasm.

"Well, I definitely appreciate all you've done for me. To tell you the truth, I am into you, so you don't have to do all this. It's obvious there's strong chemistry between you and me, something neither of us can deny."

"Do you really think I did all this just to impress you? Never that. Baby, read my lips. This thing we share, whatever this is between us, I mean, even I didn't expect this to unfold as it has. But since it is happening, I want both of us to embrace and enjoy the moment, ride this wave together and see where it takes us."

"Yes, baby, that's what I want as well, so please don't take what I said the wrong way. It's just that, in the past, men have tried to buy my attention and affection, so it was an automatic thought when I saw all the stuff in my room. Trying to buy a person is a major turn off for me. But with you, it's different. I have never felt like this before over a guy, especially not in such a short time span. The only man I have ever truly loved was my uncle, who has taken great care of me for years. I feel that this is love at first sight between us. My feelings are so different when it comes to you, Bishop—they are just different, and I'm not scared at all."

"Did you hear yourself?"

"What part of what I said are you asking me about?"

"The part when you said different twice. So that means I am unlike the rest of the men you've encountered throughout your life. What you will learn about me is I don't do things for the sake of buying love or attention. Not from anyone! I get enough love and attention from my brother and mother, who I love to death, and that's something that doesn't cost me one cent. If I have to pay for someone's love, it isn't real. Now, although I never asked for us—you and me—it's God's plan, not mine. That's what makes everything real between us. A beautiful woman such as yourself needs to know real doesn't cost a thing. It doesn't come with a price tag. It's priceless. I spoil mine, and you're mine."

"Oh, just like that, I'm your woman?"

"Out of everything I expressed to you, that's what you got? And yes, you became mine upon our meet and greet the first day we met, the first day we spoke to one another. We are supposed to be together. Your uncle knew it too, that's why he sent you to pick me up at the airport. He knew both of us needed someone special in our lives. That's why, while you were sleep on our flight, I called and asked your uncle for his permission to date his niece, and he gave us his blessings. You know he isn't the type of person you wanna play with, and you also know how much he loves his family, me and you especially," Bishop confided.

"I see someone was very busy while I slept. Wow, you even called my uncle. I can only imagine what the two of you talked about. So, he was in on it too, huh?"

"Of course he was," Bishop replied.

"I'm going to hold you to all these sweet words you're expressing to me. I want you to come by my school and meet some of the children when we're back home. I teach fourth and fifth graders. It would mean a lot to me if you met some of my students. They are the reason I one day want to have a family of my own."

"That's what's up. All we have to do in this world is let life take its course. I'm not going anywhere any time soon. Learn to stop questioning everything, especially when it's real. Give love a chance, at least before running from it. A person of my caliber has to stay busy after losing out on seven years of his life, and I have grown to cherish certain aspects of life that people who haven't been through what I have taken for granted. Not me, not anymore. Time is of the essence, and it's something I don't take for granted, which we all do without meaning to. Time is precious, a gift you can't ever get back."

"You're starting to make me cry, Bishop. Hearing you speak is making me very emotional. I'm sorry you had to sit in prison for all that time, but I do hear and understand you. Time will be what we make it. Time is what we'll give this relationship. I will never take this opportunity from you. I'm not that type of woman," Kara said, letting an emotional teardrop slide down her cheek.

"What is crazy about what you just said is, I know the type of woman you are. The type I could see never turning her back on me, and that's one of the main reasons I fell for you so quickly. Since we are going to be in Tennessee for a few days, we are going to get to learn more about each other," he said.

Kara had the prettiest eyes he had ever seen. They were mesmerizing to the point that he did not even know what color they were.

"Are you ready to go get something to eat?" he asked.

"Yes. I am so hungry right now I could eat a cow! I guess we'll talk more later. Through all this excitement, I've worked up an appetite," Kara said, rubbing her smooth, flat stomach.

"Good, but it's supposed to be so hungry that one could eat a horse," he said, laughing.

"I just wanna eat; give me the whole damn farm," she playfully said, liking everything about Bishop so far.

"That's what I wanna hear, babe. Now, please go finish getting beautiful for me."

"Okay. I'll finish getting beautiful for you, but who do you want me to smell like tonight? Gucci, Beyonce, Chanel, or J Lo?" she asked, referring to her fragrances.

"Baby, I'd rather you smell like Kara. She smells the best to me!"

"Aww, baby... I like that; maybe we can design a scent." She smiled. "Bishop..."

"Yes, babe?"

"You're the best too!" Kara slid back into Bishop's arms, giving him a hug and more lip hugs with her full, sensual lips.

After a few seconds of innocent foreplay, she let him go, knowing the danger zone would be throbbing if she did not. She looked back over her shoulder before entering and closing her door to her room to get dressed. Kara didn't know Bishop had also ordered himself a nice outfit for the evening, so while she dressed, he showered and dressed and got ready for his queen.

They met at the door, and Bishop looked her up and down. The dress he had ordered for her fit her perfectly. It looked like the designer had used her for the pattern, because it fit every curve like she was born in the dress.

"Damn, babe, you look amazing! J Lo and Beyoncé can eat their hearts out," he said, taking her in his arms again.

"Well, Mr. Handsome, you clean up nicely too, I see," she replied, smelling his Dolce.

"We'd better not start, or we won't make it out to eat," he said.

She smiled and agreed before asking him where they were going. Bishop had made reservations at Ruth's Chris, seeing he wanted a nice meal, fit for a king.

"I like that place, and yes, we are dressed to the nines, but I want to do something a little cozier, Bishop. Besides, you've showed me enough glamour for one day," she replied.

Bishop actually liked the idea. When they got downstairs to summon their cab, the same bellhop was still on duty, and when he saw Kara, you could see his jaw hit the floor.

"Excuse me, what's your name? And do you know a good place to get some ribs?" Kara asked.

"My name is Jeffery, and yes, I just happen to know of a great spot. You two might be a little overdressed, but Edley's ribs are so tender, the meat falls off the bone," he said, smiling.

Bishop handed him a second tip, and Jeffery was shocked at his generosity. They thanked him and climbed in the cab, telling the driver to take them to Edley's.

That night was filled with surprise after surprise, and lo and behold, the bellhop was right. The food at Edley's was great. It was like gourmet bar b que, if there is such a thing. After they finished, they hit up a club a block from their hotel for a quick drink. The place was small but elegant, and Bishop had had no idea the music he heard as they entered was a live performance. Kem was on the stage, singing his number one cut, Share My Life. They pulled closely into each other's arms as they danced.

Anxious to get back, Bishop whispered something in Kara's ear and off they went. Instead of catching a cab, they walked the short distance back to the Waldorf, sharing conversation and holding hands. Jeffery saw them coming and gave Bishop a wink that Kara did not see. He also handed Bishop a special key that allowed access to the roof.

Their night ended on the rooftop of the hotel, where Jeffery had taken the liberty to set up a table with a bottle of Moet & Chandon, more fresh roses, and a boom box. Kara looked at Bishop, and once again, she was in awe. He was making her pussy soaking wet without even entering it. She knew he was working his way into her head and her heart, and she loved it.

Kara didn't know the music she heard was live. Bishop excused himself from the dance and disappeared for a spell. upon his return, he was anxious to leave, so he whispered something in her ear, and off they went. Kara was totally unaware of this next surprise Bishop had.

After he filled their glasses, he pressed 'play' on the system to make it seem as if he was turning on music. Then, Kem began singing, Share My Life. They danced for the second time, and this time, even more closely, like their bodies had become one. The music stopped, but the words kept coming. Kara had her face buried in Bishop's chest and wondered why she had never heard the a cappella version of this song. Bishop raised her head, turning her chin toward the way they had entered the rooftop. Kem was walking toward Kara with a microphone, singing the final verse to his song.

She covered her mouth, looking Bishop straight in his eyes, since he had really outdone himself. He looked at her smiling.

"I told you I wanted you to share my world, didn't I."

It was a wrap for Kara. The throbbing in her loins couldn't wait any longer. It had been almost a year and a half since she had been with a man sexually. The men who had tried to shoot their shot had not been worthy of her going the distance, but Bishop was now her new knight in shining armor, and she was ready to bless her knight.

"Can we go inside?" Kara asked.

Bishop still had her wrapped in his arms as they were slow dancing, and he wondered if she was getting cold or something.

"Are you cold, baby?"

"Actually, I'm just the opposite," she replied, kissing the side of his face.

Jeffery was just coming up to check on them. Bishop handed him another hundred-dollar bill, and Jeffery assured him he would clean up after them. Bishop also thanked Kem for coming.

Bishop was inside Kara's room now, standing and admiring her beauty. Her eyes seemed like they had changed to a different color as the lights from the chandelier in the room glistened off them. Kara slid her designer dress off her shoulders, letting it fall to the floor beneath her. She was wearing a burgundy thong, and the print from her pussy made Bishop's manhood rise to its maximum potential. He had never had a woman who affected him the way she did. He walked over to her, and she turned around, giving him instant permission to do the honors of unclasping her matching bra. Kara had the perfect body in Bishop's eyes. She turned to face him, allowing him to admire the butterfly tattoo that lay peacefully on her breast.

They begin passionately kissing, and Kara now had honors of her own to do. She used her hands with her eyes still closed, and their tongues continued their rooftop dance. She was unbuttoning everything on him that had a button. When she came to his suit pants, she felt all of him as she reached for his zipper. He was huge, and she was ready. Her pussy re soaked itself like it had a built-in waterfall. Her moans from just their touching turned Bishop on even more. He was slowly turning into the beast, ready to seduce his beauty. Kara walked closer, making sure neither of them had any personal space. She wrapped herself in his arms again, feeling the print of his hard dick on her stomach, surpassing her belly button.

"All this for me?" she asked.

"Everything I have is for you."

There was a mahogany mantel about two feet from where they stood, and Bishop knew they would not make it to the bed. He ran his thick fingers through her silky black hair, releasing it from the bun she had it in. As each strand fell gracefully past her shoulders, his arousal grew more intense. Turning her abruptly to face the mantel, he reached around her sides, placing her outstretched hands on the mantel. Bishop spread her ass cheeks and slowly guided the tip of his dick inside her wet pussy. Kara moaned with pleasure and used her grip on the mantel to push back into him, making sure her nest covered every inch of what he had said was now hers. Bishop grabbed her around her waist, keeping his balance intact as he enjoyed the ride they were experiencing.

"Damn, Kara, you feel amazing," he said, sweat now making him shut his eyes.

"Fuck me, papi, fuck me. You said this is mine; now fuck me like it's mine."

Bishop had not foreseen that coming from her mouth, but he loved it. He loved her, and it was hers as far as he was concerned. After a few more thrusts, he slowed down to stop the explosion that had manifested its way to the tip of his dick. He stopped and paused for about twenty seconds, ready now to make love to his queen. Bishop scooped Kara off her feet, kissing her as he carried her to the bed and lay her on the king size bed full of different colored rose petals.

Kara spread her legs, exposing the prettiest vagina he had ever seen in his life. Quickly, he crawled between her legs, resting his chin right below her belly button, blowing and kissing his way down until he made it to her pearl tongue. The shivers that made her feel electrified told Bishop she was ready to let out her juices. He continued lapping her pearl tongue until she almost pulled his ears from the side of his head.

"Bishop... I'm cumming..." she cried out in pleasure.

He did not stop. He kept going, almost sending her into a state of shock. Finally, as he was satisfied that she was fully satisfied and not partially happy, he placed the bottoms of her feet on his chest, causing her ass to rise, and angled her pussy toward his shaft. Once she was positioned right, he slowly inserted himself, burrowing deep inside her. Bishop positioned his weight on his forearms so he would be elevated high enough to see every facial expression from his queen. With each powerful thrust, Kara gave him a different reaction. The tightness of her nest was starting to take a toll on his longevity. He would not be able to hold back much longer, and he felt his eruption mounting up.

"Baby, you feel so good; your pussy is doing something to me."

"You like it, papi? You like the way I feel? You said it's all mine, now show me!" Kara demanded as she dug her neatly manicured nails deep in his shoulder blades, causing a small blood trickle. The pain she caused him made more blood flow to his dick. It felt as if he had increased in width almost a whole inch. Now completely feeling like he had filled her to capacity, there was no more holding back for him; it was virtually impossible.

"Baby, your king is about—"

He tried getting the words out, but Kara dug deeper, and he pushed harder, and together they exploded, causing a stickier and sexier mess than he could have imagined.

Chapter Twenty:
Philly

The next morning, Bishop knew he had a little running around to do. He wished like hell this trip was all about him spending time with Kara. She had made the night extremely pleasurable, but he knew he had work to do. The Country Boys showed up at his hotel bright and early, also anxious to see him. They were ready to pick him up and drive him out to their farm. When he came downstairs, he was greeted by Darius.

"Damn, Bishop! You're still the same quiet, observant, dangerous person I remember, the person I have always known you to be. I have always liked that about you. A lot of them big city boys talk fast and move even faster," Darius said, smiling and giving Bishop a hug. He was with one of his brothers, who had also missed the hell out of Bishop.

They climbed into Darius' F-150 that was sitting on twenty-eight-inch rims with a custom interior. He had a lot of chrome on the truck, which reminded Bishop of just how country they were. He smiled at his thought as they traveled I-440 out to the Country Boys' farm. It was a long ride, and Bishop was happy about that. When they arrived, the truck pulled into what looked to be about one hundred acres of land. A simple, but nice ranch-style home sat in the center, with lots of windows and a winding driveway.

"How long y'all been out here on this farm?" Bishop asked as they came to a stop in front of a newly built, six-car garage.

"Shit, at least five years now. It's very peaceful out here. We have over a hundred acres, so there's more than enough space to do what you want, and the law doesn't come about these ways unless they're called—which no one would do. We came out here because it's great for what we do," Darius said, assuring Bishop of its safety.

Once they had come to a complete stop, two of the other brothers greeted Bishop as they opened the barn door and Darius drove into the barn. Bishop was blown away by what he was seeing.

"Ohhh, shiiittt!" Bishop yelled out in amazement.

"I'm sure my brother told you that we had you covered," Jimmy Earl said with a sly grin.

"We have enough of both," Darius said to Bishop, showing him the inventory.

There were three walls, fully lined with semi-automatic weapons and some fully automatic joints. Three see-through glass cabinets were adorned with every handgun you could think of. Smith and Wessons, Rugers, and plenty of ammo to go with whatever a person wanted. The Country Boys had enough firepower to let the U.S. troops stay home while they took on Al Qaeda themselves. The fellas got into their group discussion, only to come to their business agreement. This was something they had talked about with Bishop while in the joint. He knew they were real when they had said they had firepower, but now he really knew they meant business. There was only a handshake between them since they trusted Bishop like he was one of them.

They made plans to start shipping material to Jersey right away. Guns were what they did, so there was no need to waste time. The Country Boys had changed their method of moving their weapons since their last bid. They used cement trucks that were filled with everything except a wet, fast-drying solution that turned to concrete. Bishop was satisfied with his purchase. The youngest brother, who reminded Bishop of Duke, was bending down, wiping mud off his gator boots. When he looked up at Bishop, he looked him right in the eyes and said, "If there ever is a time you need us to pop up out there to Jersey, please, big bruh, do not hesitate to get at us!"

"Yeah, we'll jump on the highway and be coming," Darius said, glad Bishop was home and back making power moves.

"Yeah, I wouldn't mind seeing Biggie Smalls," Jimmy added playfully.

"Bet. I know where our relationship stands. We're family for life!" Bishop replied to all of them, meaning every word he said.

The Country Boys and 4'2 were always going to be his second family outside of Duke and his mother. He would kill for any and all of them, feeling like they would all do the same for him.

"True, family for life!" Darius replied.

After they were done conducting business, the Country Boys escorted Bishop back to his hotel where Kara was waiting. Bishop and Kara gathered their belongings and were taken to the airport by Darius. He had switched rides to his black-on-black extended Excursion. Bishop had told Darius he did not want to inconvenience him by keeping him from handling his business, but Darius had reminded him that they were family and that was what family did for family. Bishop truly understood, because if they were in Jersey, he would have showed him the same hospitality.

The Excursion pulled into the private airfield where 4'2's jet was waiting, and the pilot was set to go. Kara got out the truck, giving the pilot a quick hug and telling him to load their luggage. She figured Bishop wanted to say his goodbyes to his friends.

"I'll be right behind you. Give me a sec," Bishop told his woman, handing her a small carry-on bag.

"Okay, babe," she replied, looking back and waving goodbye to Bishop's friends.

"Damn, Bishop, she's bad as hell!" Darius felt the need to compliment Bishop on the beautiful woman he had traveling with him.

"Thanks, bruh. I truly appreciate everything you guys have done for me. Actions speak louder than words, and y'all's actions have always told y'all's story. So now, it's time to show and prove..."

"I know, Bish... A favor for a favor—that has always been our motto. Remember that."

"Yeah, yeah, bruh. That was nothing when we were in the joint. Real, until our next meet," Bishop said before he and the Country Boys embraced each other one last time.

Bishop walked to the steps of the private jet, and he and Kara wasted no time boarding. This leg of their flight was short, so neither of them slept. They shared a little conversation about their future, and after that, Bishop relaxed, listening on his Beats by Dre, while Kara watched her favorite movie, Selena, starring her favorite actress, J Lo.

The jet arrived at Philadelphia's airport a little earlier than expected, so they had a couple of hours to kill. They decided to check into a hotel, and Kara chose the Hyatt. After putting their luggage away, they chose to do a little bit of shopping and a little sightseeing as well. Bishop planned to keep Kara in Philly for two or three days, then he would send her back to Arizona. He still had to notify Boss Hogg to let his guy know he was in town so they could meet up at the famous steps. Sylvester Stallone had worked out in the Rocky movies on those steps, which is how they had become famous in the first place. Bishop set the meeting up there for the specific purpose of seeing the famous Rocky statue. Boss Hogg agreed and the meet was set.

Bishop and Kara stopped at Geno's in South Philly since it was said the place had the best cheesesteak sandwiches in town. When they got back to their room and finally sat down to eat, Geno's lived up to its reputation. Bishop looked at his watch and saw it was time to head to his meet. He kissed Kara, thinking about what they would do when he returned. She felt the fire in his lips and the kiss instantly wet her pussy like the first kiss on the rooftop had.

"You'd better go, babe, before you miss your meeting," Kara said, wiggling out of his arms, but not by choice. She knew Bishop was a businessman, and she did not want to throw him off his schedule.

"You've got a point," Bishop replied, knowing she was right. He was starting to rise up, and he knew now was not the time.

Bishop had rented a truck, and he arrived on the east side of the art museum where the famous steps and statue were located. He parked the rental right on Benjamin Franklin Parkway and put three dollars in change in the meter. The view was unbelievable as he looked at the seventy-two steps and knew any man would be in fighting shape if they ran up and down those joints once or twice a day.

Boss Hogg pulled up, parking right behind Bishop, driving an exotic Maserati with low-profile tires and rims and an AMG kit that made it look like something from Back to The Future. Bishop emerged from his vehicle with a smile on his face, happy to see his long-time friend.

"Peace, my brother," Bishop said, shaking his friend's hand.

"Bishop, my man! Long time no see," Boss Hogg said in return, with the same love. "You're here now, brother. Let's get business cracking. Tell me what you suggest," Boss Hogg said, getting straight to the point of their meeting.

"A metric ton in weapons!"

"Can you handle that manpower, my guy?" Boss Hogg replied.

"Of course," Bishop said with a modest smile on his face.

"It's done! Hit me when you get back to the bricks. One!" Boss Hogg replied, the same smile on his face.

"Great! Love you for this one, Hogg. One!" Bishop said, wishing they had more time to kick it, but at the moment, Bishop was focused on making life what he had said he was going to make it for him and his little brother.

They kept it short and to the point, the way they both liked it. Now, in Bishop's eyes, all of his business had been taken care of, making it Kara's time. He wanted to spend some time with her, knowing it would soon be time to get back home. He had things that needed to be situated. It was also time to get Kara back to her teaching job.

Bishop sat back, driving listlessly to the hotel. Not only was he thinking about Kara, but he was also contemplating about everyone who was waiting for him to open up his hand. Shit was fucked up, he continued thinking, because soon it would be a bittersweet moment for him and Kara. At the same time, he knew it was time for everything to go back to normal, if there was a such thing as normal.

He parked the rental and rushed into the hotel, stopping at the bar in the lobby and grabbing an expensive bottle of champagne. Unlike Tennessee, this time they had one room, with a king-size bed fit for him, her king. When he walked into the room, his jaw dropped. Kara was standing there in a one-piece, see-through, rose-colored nightie. She had nothing on underneath, but the attributes God had blessed her with. She had the music playing, a tune by Gloria Estefan, Words Get In The Way. It was in Spanish, which Bishop did not speak. Kara started swaying her hips to the beat and translating the words into English as she danced and moved toward Bishop.

"But it's locked deep inside, and if you look in my eyes, we might fall in love again..."

Kara actually sounded good. Bishop smiled as she neared him, smelling like a bed of roses mixed with peaches. It was the new scent she had bought when they had gone shopping earlier. One by one, as she sang the words, she unbuttoned his shirt, exposing the manly physique she had fallen for in Tennessee. Moving her hands slowly down to feel his swollen dick, she undid his belt and the button that held his jeans on him.

"Step out of them, papi!" she demanded, turning around and rubbing her bare ass on his manhood.

That was it! Bishop could not just stand still and become her victim. She wanted control, but she was just too fucking beautiful for him to let that happen.

"Okay, Kara, you asked for this," he said, now totally nude.

Bishop took her hips and turned her to face him. Once he kissed her, he easily lifted her from her feet into the air, telling her to hold on for the ride of her life. Still in top shape from his bid, Kara felt like a feather in his arms. Bishop cupped each of her ass cheeks, helping her momentum as she threw her head back, riding his dick.

"Papi, you're a bull... you're a bull, papi," she moaned with pleasure. Every time she let words come out of her mouth, her accent drove Bishop to a sexual pitch he had never known before.

"Is that all you got? Make me love your rodeo... Come on, papi, fuck my pussy, you bull!"

Bishop, with Kara still in the air, walked her to a wall, where he placed her back against it for support. He was waiting for her to utter one more word, which she did just as the thought crossed his mind.

"That's it, papi... you're going deep... We're fallin' in love again."

Letting the wall support his queen, Bishop reached his hands out on each of her legs, trying to get as close as he could to her ankles. The scene should have been painted by Picasso himself. As each of his back muscles popped out, he merged deeper inside Kara. She cried out now with pleasure as the curve in his dick found every intricate spot, which pleased her. Kara had never in her life felt this way before. Bishop was the ultimate lover, who had shown her what making love was supposed to feel like.

"Kara, I love you," he whispered in her ear as he delivered thrust after thrust after thrust.

Now it was his words that seduced her mind, body, and soul. She knew if he said one more word, she would come all over him.

"Yes, baby," he said, "we are falling in love all over again."

"Come with, honey. I'm about to cum all over you, Bishop," she replied, digging her nails in his back. It felt like she was reopening the wounds she had made in Tennessee.

"Ahhhhh shit, Kara... shit, baby... it's about to be thunder and lightning inside you..."

"PAPI... AHHHHH... OHHHH... THIS DICK!" she screamed as their juices collided with each other.

Bishop and Kara spent the night together while sleeping peacefully in each other's arms.

The next day, Bishop put her on her uncle's jet and promised to keep their relationship going. He had already set up an appointment with her uncle for her to come to Newark in the next couple of weeks. He planned to continue what they had started. They hugged and kissed, looking forward to meeting up later.

"Goodbye, baby," she told him.

"Never goodbye, baby. I'll see you later," he corrected her.

"Okay, see you later," she replied, blowing kissing in the air as she was ready to board.

"I got 'em. I caught every one of 'em," he said, catching her kisses.

She then turned and boarded the jet, with Bishop watching when they taxied off and headed down the runway.

Chapter Twenty-One:
You With Me Or What

A few hours had passed when Bishop arrived back in Newark. He had been gone almost two weeks, and he could not wait to see his little brother and his mother. The good thing for him was he felt the business trip had been very successful. As he rolled back in on I-78, Phillipsburg-Newark Expressway, hitting the New Jersey Turnpike in his Dodge rental car, his view of the city was it looked the same to him. Somehow, he felt different though, almost like everything he had dreamed of was right at his fingertips.

The first thing he needed to do was text Duke to let him know he was back and to meet up at their mom's house. Duke responded right away, telling him his ETA was about ten minutes. That was perfect because he would arrive in about seven minutes. When Duke pulled up, the brothers were excited to see one another. It felt like someone had come home from jail once again. Bishop was glad that was not the case this time.

Once they had seen each other and embraced, they started talking about what was going on in their lives. Bishop told Duke and their Mother how beautiful each state he had visited was and that they had land out of state now, meaning he had bought some land for them while he was out handling business. After hearing the good news, their mother exited the room and Duke started talking about his own good news—his meeting with Sharelle. Bishop thought Duke's story was too close to what he had just experienced—him meeting someone special as well. Although neither of them believed in coincidences, that was what it was—a pure coincidence.

The brothers were happy to have those stories to share with each other. They stayed on the couch for almost an hour, comparing whose woman was the hottest. Both had pages of pictures saved in their cellphones. Just as they figured, neither could decide whose chick was the baddest, not wanting to hurt the other one's feelings. Then the doorbell rang.

Riiiiiing!

"Who the fuck is that?" Bishop asked as Duke got up from the couch to look out the front window with his gun out, down by his leg.

"WHO IS IT?" Duke yelled through the door.

The guy on the other side of the door yelled back. "IT'S A SPECIAL DELIVERY FOR MR. DUKE."

Not sure what the fuck dude was on, Duke yelled back, "WHAT'S UP?!?"

After opening the door, Bishop I to check the shit out.

"I didn't order anything, bruh. I think it's the police trying to set us up. Back up, I'm a push this mothafucka's head back!"

While the delivery man was turning to point toward the gift he had in the driveway, Duke whipped up the gun he was carrying and pointed it directly at the side of the delivery man's head. Bishop interrupted and calmly put his hand over Duke's hand, muffling the hammer of the gun.

He whispered to Duke, telling him, "Fall back. He's good," referring to the delivery guy, who had not noticed the gun to the side of his head.

He then told Duke, "I have a shipment of trucks for Mr. Duke!"

"Maybe he has the wrong house," Bishop said to his little brother.

"No! Hold up! What do you have for Mr. Duke?" Duke asked, becoming curious to know what the delivery man was talking about, while Bishop was in the background laughing.

Duke turned toward Bishop, noticing him laughing behind his back like it was funny. "What the fuck you cracking up for? Strange shit has been happening. Yo, the nigga at the E spot told me five o was following us when I left there about three weeks ago. I don't know if they were on us or not. I was fucked up that night. I'm just trying to be on point about everything around us. Who the fuck is this, big bruh?"

The delivery man told him to sign on his pad. "Sir, your Night XV trucks await you!"

Hesitantly, Duke signed the paperwork, now knowing in his heart that his brother was up to something.

"I'm going to sign because, Bishop, I know your ass has got something to do with this mothafucka being at our door."

"Yo, you know me too well, lil bro. These are our trucks. I had them shipped from Arizona. I knew you would like this state-of-the-art shit!" Bishop said, letting the cat out the bag.

They had not really talked when he was on the road, so Duke did not have a clue what was going on. Shaking off his nerves, he said, "Yeah, you know how I do it!"

Happy now, Duke tipped the delivery man handsomely, showing it was just business, not personal. Once he did that, his excitement for the trucks kicked in.

"Yoooo, these shits are hot! Look at these fuckin' wheels!"

"All handcrafted and fully loaded, bruh. The best for the best, feel me? I love you, nigga!"

Duke, filled with excitement, grabbed his big brother close and told him, "I love you too, bruh."

The brothers then jumped into their new toys and toured the hood. They were riding through the hood, playing chase and acting like little fuckin' kids. Duke had been surprised by Bishop's gift, but felt like he had to let him know. They had had this loving, sibling rivalry type relationship going on since they were knee high. Once they were done riding around acting like kids, the two pulled over to talk.

Duke led the conversation. "Nigga, I love you. I love the trucks too. I'm still surprised, but I'm not one of your chicks."

Bishop laughed at his comment. "Nah, little bruh, I would never confuse the two. You're a crazy ass nigga!"

"Yo, we'd better be the only ones on the East Coast with these trucks!"

"Bruh, these trucks don't even come out until next year, and not too many can afford them. By the time they hit the East Coast, we'll have something new for the following year. I know how you do yours, and I know you don't want anyone having what you have. You're still the same."

"You know It!" Duke said as he jumped back Into his truck. "I'm gonna go get dressed and head to the bricks. What's good with you?"

"Nothing much. I'm about to call 4'2 and make sure everything is all right on his end and to let him know how much you appreciate his gift."

"Yeah, give him my love. Let him know I'm really happy over here!" Duke said, closing the truck door.

He was still smiling like a little ass kid as he headed home to get dressed. After making it home and getting dressed, he decided to drive his new whip out to Newark. He tried to call his crew, Malik and Gooch. Malik was the only one to answer though.

"Yo, I'm comin through to pick you up. Where are you?"

"I'm on Lyons Ave and Alden."

"I'll be through to pick you up in a sec. Where's Gooch? I called him and he didn't answer."

"I haven't seen son in days, ever since we I back from Atlantic City. He's been acting funny as hell lately."

"Why you say that?"

"Bruh, you know we know niggas, and niggas talk like bitches in the hood—"

Duke cut him off. "I'll be there in a sec. Stay where you are!"

"A'ight."

As Duke was riding to pick up Malik, he was trying to process what he had just heard. He could not figure out what he had meant about Gooch feeling some kind of way since they had left Atlantic City. They had had a ball at the club and casino—or so he had thought. Duke became frustrated, not knowing what was up with his man. Coming to an understanding, he said quietly to himself as he pulled up on Lyons Ave, "Fuck that! I'm not letting none of that shit fuck up my day! I'ma see Gooch!"

He pulled up and parked for a few seconds, watching to see how long it was gonna take before Malik noticed him—or anyone else for that matter. While he sat there watching Malik, Duke did not notice Detective Burcheck was on his heels watching him. Detective Burcheck sat in a nearby van with tinted windows near the playground in the middle of the block. After ten minutes had passed, Duke decided he had seen enough and rolled up on Malik, as if he was someone buying drugs, and rolled down his window.

"Yo, you straight?"

Before Malik could answer, he noticed it was Duke, just playing.

"Duke, what up, my nigga?!" Malik said, throwing his hands in the air.

"Getcha ass in the truck! I know they're tired of smelling your breath out here!" Duke replied, demanding his friend get in the truck.

A group of girls walking by heard their conversation and start laughing at Duke's comment.

"Thanks, Duke; he was killing us," the finest chick of the bunch said.

Malik got into the truck and yelled out the window to the girls, "Fuck y'all bitches."

They laughed and watched Duke pull off. Duke still did not notice Detective Burcheck, who was not far behind him. Malik complimented Duke on his new ride.

"Yo, this shit is tight! You're crazy, my guy!"

"If I had a dollar for all the times somebody called me crazy, I'd be RICH, like Jigga, nigga"

"Correction, my nigga! You'd be even RICHER, crazy ass nigga!" Malik said, pumping Duke's head up.

"But, yeah, let me stop frontin'. Bishop had this shipped to the crib today. It's called a Night XV. This shit is fully loaded, and they don't come out until next year!" Duke boasted as they drove around town, stunting on everyone who laid eyes on the new truck.

They noticed how everyone was checking them out. At least the truck was getting plenty of attention. They rode through the city, talking about everything, including Gooch and his antics, and Duke reminded Malik of a few things.

"Yo, remember when we spoke about what transpired when we went to the 40/40 club a few weeks ago?"

"Yeah; what about it?"

"Well, it's happening now. Since Bishop put his plan into action, look at the money that has stacked up. So, instead of y'all playing these weak ass streets, we're gonna step up a level. I'ma play the cut, and if you've got any problems with the decision I'm making, now is the right time to speak up!"

"Duke, when it comes to you, bruh, fuck what anybody has to say. I'ma Duke boy for life. Whatever call you make to better our future, I'm a hundred and ten percent behind you. Yo, I haven't come this far with you to start questioning your decisions now!"

"That's great to hear. Because if you had said anything other than what you said, yo, I would've had to push your shit back."

"Ha ha ha..." The two shared a laugh.

"Nigga, I know you won't do shit to me, but to them other niggas... They're some dead niggas! Not me, though. You know where my loyalty lies. I'm with you, bruh!"

"I already know. That's what's up!"

Duke and Malik continued to ride around and talk about life. As they rode down Clinton Avenue, Malik suddenly cut Duke off.

"Yo, there go that nigga Gooch, over there!"

"Where?" Duke asked, turning his head.

Malik started pointing in the direction of a few guys who were standing in a circle on the corner of Chadwick and Clinton Avenue, where Gooch was seen laughing and joking. Duke saw him and instantly got mad. Gooch was talking to some gangbangers when Duke pulled up on the corner, quickly bringing his new ride to a screeching halt. Some of the bangers started reaching, as if to tell Duke they were packing heat. Duke rolled down the window and noticed the bangers still had their hands on their guns.

"If none of y'all niggas are ready to die tonight, then I'd advise y'all clowns to take y'all's hands off them little ass guns y'all carrying."

The bangers knew Duke was serious about everything he had said to them, so they did what was told of them, moving their hands off their guns. They did it quickly, without another word.

"And the next time niggas act like they wanna pop off on a real nigga, I may not be this humble about shit!"

As Duke gave the bangers his take on things, Gooch interjected, "What's good, my guy?"

"Yo, what the fuck are you doing out here with these fuckin' lames? Especially when you know how we don't fuck with clowns. When I pulled up, it looked like you had something going on. What the fuck is going on? Are you having a meeting without The Duke? That's how you're doing yours?"

"Naw, my nigga. I'm just out here kicking it with these dudes; they know what it is! Nice ride, too. When'd you get this?" Gooch asked, changing the word play.

In the midst of their conversation, Duke's phone started ringing.

"Hold up; let me get this right quick."

"Hello, what's good? Who this?"

"Hey, baby. What are you doing?" Sharelle said.

"Thinking about you. I've been waiting on your call. What's going on? You okay?"

"I'm great now that I'm talking to you."

"Good to hear, but give me a second, baby, okay?"

"Okay."

Putting Sharelle on hold to finish up what he was saying to Gooch, he let him know they were gonna talk more later.

"I might be going to PA tonight, but if not, we'll hook up!"

"A'ight, bruh. We'll talk," Gooch said, not really feeling how Duke had dismissed their conversation.

"Malik, drive! I need to finish this conversation with someone important. Jump on 78 West going to PA," Duke said, changing seats with Malik.

The two switched sides and they drove off, leaving Gooch to finish chopping it up with his friends as Duke got back on the phone. The entire time Duke was having his encounter with Gooch and the bangers, Detective Burcheck had sat in the cut, taking pictures. He then followed Duke and Malik to PA, watching Duke's every move for the rest of the night. He knew he was out of his jurisdiction, but he figured if he was going to make a case, he needed to do whatever he needed to do.

Chapter Twenty-Two:
They Smile In Your Face

The Present...

Bishop's thoughts took him back through his life as if he were reliving the good, the bad, and the ugly all over again. He remembered every conversation he and Duke had had about Duke's encounter with Gooch, the bangers, and when he had gone to pick up Sharelle—as if he had been there with Duke that day in physical form. He was starting to blame himself for all that had happened to his brother, for the simple fact that he had been away for seven years. He felt Duke had had to learn about life on his own, having had to fend for himself and learn proper guidance from the streets.

Bishop's phone vibrated, breaking his thoughts and concentration. Noticing it was Sharelle, he answered.

"Hey, you. What's good?"

"Hello... Bishop?" she asked, not catching his voice.

"Yeah, it's me. What's up?"

"Well, listen... I called you because I have to ask you something."

"Is it about my brother?"

She quickly cut him off. "No, this isn't about your brother. I understand how you feel about everything that has happened—"

"Okay, then why did you call?"

"I would like to know if you know a guy by the name of..." She paused for a second before saying his name. "Gooch? Who is he?" she asked, finally getting it out.

Bishop was baffled at the mention of Gooch's name, being as though she and Gooch had never formally met. Duke had not told Bishop she knew anyone in their crew except for Malik. Therefore, Bishop acted as if he did not know who she was talking about.

"Gooch? What about him?"

"Okay then, listen, let me just tell you. I heard something around the jail while I was at work—"

Bishop quickly cut her off. "Hold up, Sharelle," he said, knowing he needed to switch lines.

"Let me call you back from another phone," he said, ending the call quickly.

Before she could agree and confused by his action, he just disconnected the call. Bishop felt she had something important to tell him, so he wanted to switch phones, protecting him and her. Being as though she worked at a prison and how those inmate niggas knew shit before niggas did on the streets, Bishop felt as though it was only right to talk to her on a more secure and private line.

"Hello?"

"Can I finish now?!" she asked with a small attitude, unsure why he had disconnected the call so quickly.

"Yeah, go ahead." He smiled because he knew she was green as to why he had changed phones on her.

"Okay, like I was saying, today at work at the prison, everyone was talking about some guy named Gooch and something about him and a few gangbangers who'd shot up Duke. Everyone in all the units of the building were partaking in this conversation. They were all talking about Duke and this guy named Gooch. I was baffled because it always seems the prison gets the news before channel 9 even knows."

"Yeah, you are absolutely right about that. What else do I need to know?"

"They said it was done because of you! Gooch was jealous of your relationship with your brother and jealous of you. He felt like he was supposed to be in your position, but instead, Duke let you take control of the business. These dudes in here on my unit say Gooch was trying to get you, but your schedule made things a little too difficult. Everyone was saying Gooch and some other guy—whose name I didn't get—the two of them want you and your brother's power. Something about Duke and you eating too much. I thought they meant they were hungry and wanted something to eat."

'Yeah, she definitely is green to the streets, ' Bishop thought and laughed at her last statement.

Days after Duke, Gooch, and Malik's little trip to Atlantic City, Duke started reflecting back on the life he had experienced with his crew, always wanting the best for them, especially with the decision made as far as Bishop taking over the business. Sheedah and Face Hound were yet to be told about the transition he was making. He had called them both, asking them to meet him at the clubhouse, letting them know he needed to talk. They knew Duke well, and both sensed he had something important to talk to them about. They agreed to meet at 4:30 p.m.

When 4:30 arrived, so did Face Hound, Sheedah, and Duke. They entered the clubhouse, one after the other. Duke come in carrying two backpacks.

Curious to know what was in them, Sheedah asked, "Duke, what's the meeting about, and why are you carrying those two backpacks?"

"Yeah, what's good, big bruh?" Face Hound said, wanting to know as well.

Duke said nothing, as if he had not heard anything they had asked. He stalled for a second or two before saying a word, knowing the minds of two inquisitive people were racing for information he knew they were not going to like. What he was about to tell them was going to be a shocker, which was why his plan was to have a tough love approach, hoping they would come to understand and appreciate him later for making this decision, not just for him but for them also. Life heals all wounds, or so he had been told.

After their questions and Duke's seconds of silence, Duke got straight to why they were there. He first apologized to them for leaving them the night they had gone to Atlantic City. Both of them shook that shit off, saying that wasn't about nothing, especially since they had been doing other shit that night and were not able to go anyway.

Duke and the crew conversed about the gifts he gave them from the trip and a few episodes of their past before he eased into their conversation about how Bishop was going to take over the business. He needed them to understand the sole purpose of this decision was so they would all reach that next level of success, but he felt the next part of their conversation was going to destroy them both. They were all on board with Bishop taking over the business, no argument there.

Duke expressed to them that he had decided the two of them needed to fall back as well. His words instantly brought a frown to both of their faces, confused as to what Duke was telling them, but he knew what he was saying. Duke could see tears starting to form in their eyes. Duke changed the tone of his voice, making it known that his decision was not up for debate. He felt that life was only going to get harder before it got better, and he wanted their options in life to be more than just death or prison, which was inevitable as long as a person remained in the game.

Hearing Duke speak made Sheedah and Face Hound feel as if they were being erased out the storyline. Duke noticed the pain he was causing his friends as well as himself for making them feel the way they were feeling. Not able to take it anymore, he raised up from the couch where he was sitting and handed them each a backpack, letting them know they would be receiving this amount monthly. As long as he was alive and breathing, he made it solid knowledge they were always going to be good. As they noticed what was in the backpacks, Duke told them to make comet count, hoping the "ever'nce was going to ease them a little.

"Making the money means something to you both," Duke said, turning his back and walking out the clubhouse, hoping he would one day see them again. Filled with mixed emotions with tears running down his face, Duke felt like he had made the best decision for the both of them because he felt they would have made it themselves. Now it was back to business.

"Thank you for the information you provided. I'm going to look into everything you've just told me. I'll call you later," Bishop said.

"Okay. Be safe and take care of yourself. If you go see your brother before I do, please let him know I love him," Sharelle replied.

"Okay, gotchu. I'll make sure he gets your message."

When their conversation ended, Bishop finally acknowledged to himself Sharelle's noninvolvement in Duke's assassination attempt. He then started to get mad at his brother for trusting that nigga Gooch, as well as himself for creating more enemies while in PA, as if he did not have enough on his plate as it was.

After a few minutes of thinking, Bishop said fuck it and started putting his murder game into action, especially since Gooch did not have a clue he knew how slimy his ass really was. Gooch had no idea Bishop now knew he was behind trying to kill his little brother, which he knew would work in his favor. Now it was about who got to whom first, and Bishop knew he was gonna need a few treacherous niggas to go on this ride with him, so he called the Country Boys for a little assistance.

Ring-Ring-Ring

"Hello," Darius said, answering the phone without any hesitation, knowing it was Bishop.

"I need you, bruh!" Bishop said as calmly as he could.

"Enough said; I'm on my way," Darius replied without even knowing Bishop's reason—which did not matter anyway. They were family and both of them would kill at the drop of a dime for the other.

After their call, Bishop jumped back on the highway to go see Duke, who was still in a coma in the hospital in PA. He thought, while he was out there, he would drop by to see Sharelle. He felt the need to go see her, for the simple fact that he had been wrong for banning her from the hospital and seeing Duke, among a few other reasons—like blaming her. He wanted to apologize to Sharelle and let her know she was allowed to go see Duke and spend as much time with him as she desired. Plus, he felt the more Sharelle saw Duke and spoke to him, the better his chances were of getting better. The two of them in each other's presence might do them both some justice.

Arriving in PA with no time to spare, Bishop called Sharelle before even going to see Duke, asking her to meet him at the hospital, which she did with no questions asked. Once the two were face to face, Bishop just got to talking.

"I know you're shocked that I called to meet up with you, but don't be. I believe I owe you a *big ass apology* for the way I've treated you, and with everything in me, I am truly sorry! I truly am," Bishop said sincerely.

"For one, Bishop, as a female with two brothers of my own, I understand very well the bond the two of you share. So, with that being said, it isn't a problem at all, because I understand how you felt at the time," she replied, truthfully feeling him.

"Thank you for being so understanding. My brother was right about you—you are a sweetheart. He didn't lie. I didn't tell you, but he come out of the coma for a few seconds and your name was the first thing that come out of his mouth. The doctor told me that, then said he went right back under," Bishop explained, causing Sharelle's heart to thump with momentary excitement.

"You have got to be kidding me?!" she said, her eyes full of tears and voice full of anger.

"No, I'm not kidding at all. I don't really kid around much. I'm going to call the hospital and grant you full access to see him, so you can get up there and see your man. Stay as long you want."

Bishop understood how angry she was with him for keeping her from seeing Duke. She just had not reacted to the anger she felt.

"Thank you for granting me permission to see my baby; that's all I needed to hear. There are some cruel women in this cruel world, Bishop, but I'm not one of them. All women don't come with hidden agendas."

"You're welcome, and you're correct again. I agree wholeheartedly with everything you just said—every woman doesn't come with an agenda. I get it more so now than ever!" Bishop replied, having a quick thought about Kara.

"Also, I am going to do and say whatever I have to, to bring my baby back to us, I promise!"

"Do that for me please, because he needs to hear your voice. I miss the hell out of my little brother..."

"Me too," Sharelle said, ending their conversation on that note.

Wasting no time after Bishop left, Sharelle shot straight up to Duke's room, not knowing Burcheck was not far behind her. He had been watching everyone who come to visit Duke. He had sat patiently in the cut while Duke lay helplessly in his coma. Burcheck did not care if he survived or died.

Either way it went for The Duke, he just wanted both of the brothers' heads on a platter—dead or alive. He knew if Duke passed, he would most likely be going to hell, and in Burcheck's eyes, he wished all guys like him would burn forever and ever.

Chapter Twenty-Three:
Plan In Motion

A Week Later...

After Bishop's visit with Duke, he left and checked in with his people in Newark whom he had keeping tabs on Gooch's movements. He had met with Darius and the Country Boys at the airport days earlier, and he had taken the liberty of setting them up in a really nice, low-key spot in Morristown, New Jersey. Bishop had supplied them with some premium smoke and whatever they wanted to drink. He also had plugged them with a few freaks to keep them busy until he was ready to make his final move.

Everyone in the city knew about Duke being shot, except one person—their mother. Duke had been in the hospital for weeks, and his mother had not the slightest idea he was fighting for his life. She had been calling them both for days, trying to reach out and check on her boys, but no one was answering. She had tried hard not to worry, but she was starting to wonder why she had not heard from her boys, knowing how unusual it was for them not to call her after a certain number of days had passed.

Bishop had totally forgotten to keep his mother in the loop, but with so much going on, he hoped she would charge it to his head and not his heart. Finally, he broke down and headed south to see her face to face. He also knew how tough the news was going to be for her. Any mother in fear of losing a child would be livid and upset, and her losing Duke if he did not pull through was going to have their mother upset at the world. Bishop trusted and believed that.

Bishop arrived at his mother's front door, using his own set of keys to get into the house and walking straight toward her bedroom. He called out to her, "Mom!"

It only took a second for him to realize she was not in there. As he walked through the house, he heard her voice from afar.

"Bishop? I'm back here, son!" she said.

"Mom!" he said, looking in her eyes. Quickly noticing something was wrong in her son's approach and the tone of his voice, she asked, "Bishop, what's wrong, son? Where is your brother?"

"Yes, Ma," was all he could say.

She instantly knew something was wrong with Duke and broke down. "What happened to my baby?!"

"He's been shot up, Mom. Duke's been shot."

"WHAT?! SHOT?! TAKE ME TO MY SON, NOW!" she demanded.

Bishop knew there was not a waiting time to her request; she wanted to see her baby now! They locked up the house and rushed back to PA. When they got to the hospital, she encountered Sharelle, whose name she had heard before, but they were actually meeting for the very first time. It was like they already knew each other after hearing so much about each other. She looked down at Duke, then the machines that were keeping him alive, before walking straight over to her son's bedside, grabbing hold of his hand, and caressing it.

Bishop waited outside so he could use the phone. Momma Evans and Sharelle got into a discussion, trying to console each other.

"Baby, how have you been handling things?" Momma Evans asked her. "This boy talks about you like you're Queen Elizabeth," Momma Evans continued, actually liking her first impression of Sharelle. The fact that she was by her son's side in trying times meant something to Momma Evans.

"Fine for the most part, Momma Evans. It's just tough, the waiting and not knowing, but I prayed all night, and every time I walk in this place, I say another prayer. God is a loving God, isn't He?" Sharelle asked, trying not to break down in front of Duke's mother.

"Yes, honey, the Bible says that He..." Momma Evans paused, pointing upward toward the sky. "God won't put you in a situation you can't handle. Duke is tough and has been through so much, and I'm sure God has His own plan," she explained, also fighting back a tear that was trying to drop.

After Momma Evans spoke her words of faith, the two of them hugged, sharing an embrace as if they had known each other for years. Bringing some light to a very dark situation, Momma Evans asked Sharelle, "So, you're the woman my son said he's going to marry, huh?"

With excitement in her voice, she replied, "He said that?" It was a total surprise to her that Duke felt that strongly about their relationship.

"Yes, he did, and on several occasions. I had asked myself, when I was finally going to meet you."

"Well, I guess I am her, and here I stand," Sharelle replied, hugging Duke's mother again. She was loving her charm and knew now where Duke got his charm from.

"Well, baby, all I know is we have a lot of work to do! It's time to bring my baby out of this coma."

Sharelle agreed. Momma Evans cupped Duke's still hand in her hand and started talking to him. She believed in God and knew He heard every word she was expressing to Duke. She continued rubbing Duke's hands and head, speaking life back into her baby boy. After a few minutes, Duke's fingers started moving. They saw what was happening and called the nurse, pressing the alert button. The nurse rushed in, and when she saw the movement in the patient, she summoned the doctor on duty.

"Yes? Can I help you?" the doctor asked as he looked at the two women in the patient's room.

"My son j j just moved his fingers."

"Which hand was he moving?"

"His right hand."

"That's a good sign. Your voice, smell, etc., could have been the cause of his reaction. You should continue to do that because it can help a person in his condition. That is sometimes what they need to help return," the doctor said as he used his stethoscope, checking Duke's heart rate.

"Okay, I will do that. I'll stick around for a while and help bring my son back. Doctor, I will move heaven and Earth for my boys," Momma Evans said, still looking down at Duke's closed eyes.

"He truly needs you," Sharelle said. Then she offered, that if Momma Evans wanted to stay in town, she had room for her.

"Okay, baby. We have to help my son come back. My faith is strong, and what comes from God, no man can take."

The two most important women in Duke's life stood by his side now. He lay there wishing he could open his eyes, wishing he could tell them he loved them both. He was a fighter and those who knew him knew he was going to fight death for the entire fifteen rounds. Duke's mind was working while he lay comatose, but it was not enough for him. He needed his lips to match the things going on in his head and heart. Soon, he hoped and prayed.

Bishop was outside, calling the Country Boys to see if they had gotten any more information on Gooch and the gangbangers responsible for his brother being in the condition he was in.

"What's good? Any word yet?"

"Nah, bruh. We went through the areas you told us to check out, but no Gooch in sight. We've also been riding through them sets you told us. *Nothing!* But the shit is hot in some spots. Other spots are quiet. However, what we are hearing about it is, there's supposed to be some big party at the Key Club this Friday. Other than that, we're on the job," Darius replied to Bishop's questions.

"Thanks, G. That's what's up. I'm—"

Another call was coming through on Bishop's phone.

"Yo, let me hit you back. This is that nigga Gooch callin' me now," Bishop told Darius.

"Oh yeah? Bet! It's show time! Go ahead and answer it!"

"Right. Out."

Bishop figured the nigga Gooch had to have some nerve, but he figured it was also smart to call, trying to cover his tracks. He hurried up and clicked over before Gooch hung up.

"Hello?"

"Awww, man! Bruh, I just heard about Duke! When are we gonna ride on them niggas who did this shit?! You're my heart, B. I'm ready to put that work in, ASAP!" Gooch said, faking as usual.

Bishop figured he would play right along with his games, keeping him at bay. Keep his friends close and his enemies closer was his motto.

"Yeah, my brother was on some reckless shit! He got into a little beef with some local PA niggas. How did you find out?" he asked, not realizing Gooch had him on speaker and the bangers were listening to every word Bishop spoke.

Bishop knew Gooch was gonna lie about what he knew and had heard, but he still wanted to pick Gooch's brain.

"Yeah, I was callin' Duke's phone for days and was unable to reach him, so I called Malik and he told me everything. I can't find Sheedah or Face Hound; it's like they've fallen off the planet or something. Have you heard from them?"

"Nah, bruh. I'm sure they're good though. But, yeah, you know I'm going to need you on this one. I got these kids covered, so I'm going let you know when it's time to ride," Bishop said, being as fake as Gooch was.

"Bet, it's on, B. We're going to handle these bitch ass niggas," Gooch said, winking at the bangers, who were listening and licking their lips at a chance to finally get Bishop and end him like they had tried to with Duke.

"Aye, Bishop, you hear about the show Friday night?"

Bishop played stupid. "Nah; what show?"

"Friday, at the Key Club. Come out and have a few drinks with ya boy. Bruh, I'm going to need some fly shit to wear. What's that fashion designer chick's name you and Duke be fuckin' with?"

"Her name is Ms. Qupid. She has that Tuff Luv Line. Here's her number," Bishop offered, wondering where Gooch was going with this change of subject.

"Bet; I'ma hit her up."

"Do that. She's gonna take good care of you. I'll meet you down at the club around midnight so we can kick it!" Bishop said, planning Gooch's demise as they spoke.

"Yeah, that's what I'm talkin' about. Fuck with a real nigga, one time..." Gooch replied to Bishop

"Which will be your last time," Gooch mumbled to the bangers, causing them to laugh as he spoke, setting up Bishop—or so he thought.

"Yeah, you already know I'm there! One..."

"A'ight, one!" Gooch said, ending the call.

After hanging up with Gooch, Bishop quickly called Ms. Qupid to give her a little 4 1 1.

Bishop explained to Ms. Qupid what he needed her to do. As he filled her in on his plan to a small extent, she agreed to assist him. Ms. Qupid was a childhood friend Duke and Bishop had known all their lives. The love they had for each other could not be compared to anything they had for the rest of them niggas on the streets. Ms. Qupid and her girlfriends had always thought Bishop and Duke were some of the realest niggas they knew. If there was ever a time when they needed her, she would be there—like now! She was gonna be there for Duke and Bishop.

Part one of Bishop's plan was simple for Ms. Qupid to follow. Since she was the angel of love, Bishop was sure she had some fine-ass chick friends to keep Gooch occupied while he was getting sized up for his fit. Ms. Qupid had just the two ladies in mind, a sexy set of twins from Cali, Tameka and Tina. They had relocated to Jersey after setting up every nigga on the coast.

Seeing how Bishop had explained that Gooch was a big trick, Ms. Qupid was sad she could not get out of character and handle it herself. But she was sure her friends would do a better job, both being high yellow, thick redbones, with naturally long, black silky hair that touched the tip of their fat asses. They were bad enough that Obama would have done a double-take right in front of the First Lady. They also were party animals and did a little blow here and there, but living the life they lived, Ms. Qupid understood that the bitches needed to be under the influence.

Bishop explained that he wanted her people to make sure to get Gooch's cell number and make him confident they would be meeting him at the club to party. Bishop needed the number to make sure, that if Gooch decided to get smart and fall back to a burner, he would still be able to reach him.

"Okay, I gotchu, Bishop. That shit is wrong for the shit he did to Duke!"

"No doubt. That's what I needed to hear. I'm going to take great care of you and your girls. Trust me, this will be worthwhile for everyone. All they have to do is call me when he is in the last stall in the restroom in the club that night..."

"I got this shit! I'll have my girls, like you said, entertaining him like they're remaking the movie, *Players Club*. By the way, how is your brother coming along?"

"I'm up here at the hospital now! I'm about to go in and check on him in a second."

"Okay, let me know something. One."

"I gotchu. One."

Bishop then called the Country Boys to inform them that he needed them to post up a few blocks away from the Key Club. They were ready. Then he told them how he wanted them niggas to be treated like wild bears. On cue, too. Keep it clean. When Bishop disconnected the call, he felt like everything had been set into motion.

He went back into the hospital room to check up on his family, including Sharelle. He had to admit to himself that he had figured her all wrong. Her feelings for his brother were clear as day, and he liked her for that reason alone. Seeing her in her civilian clothes and thinking about how smitten his brother was with her when he was locked up, he was glad Duke had gotten the chance to get at her. He smiled as he rode the elevator up to the coma ward.

When he entered Duke's room, he was surprised to see there were not tear-filled tissues everywhere. The two of them were handling things well, he thought.

"Ma, how is everything going in here? How's my lil brother coming along?"

"Son, he moved his fingers when we first arrived, which is a good sign the nurse and Dr. Burgess said. The nurse also said he had not done that before and expressed to us how we should spend more time with him. It will possibly help bring him out of the coma and back to us! It's important he knows that he has a lot of love around him."

"That sounds great! I have to go back to town and take care of some important business. What do y'all wanna do?" he asked.

"I'm staying at Sharelle's house until he comes out of this."

"Is that okay with you, Sharelle?"

"Of course, it's okay with me. Even if Duke wasn't going through what he's going through, your mother will always be welcome in my home."

"Listen, if the two of you need anything, make sure you call me. I've got someone on deck in this area who will come as needed. I'll call y'all later."

Bishop gave them a hug and left his mother and Sharelle to watch over his brother.

Chapter Twenty-Four:
Death Awaits You

Bishop hit the highway like a bat out of hell, driving at top speed! He had nothing on his mind but to smoke Gooch and his entire crew of wannabes. As soon as he got back to the Bricks, he picked up Malik from his house.

"What's good, man? What's been going on?" Bishop asked.

"Yo, I'm hot, fuckin' with Gooch. Everyone on the streets is saying he just got in with Lil Sha and his homies. They gave him status after the shit with Duke. That's the reason he did what he did to my boy—to show his loyalty and get his own crew. Not to mention, he was jealous due to the relationship you and your brother share."

"Wow! Gooch is finished. Fuckin' backstabber!" Bishop shouted out.

They rode and talked briefly, but Bishop did not fully reveal his plan to Malik. He was not sure who he could trust, so he was not going to be reckless. Once they were done with their brief conversation, Bishop dropped Malik off.

Bishop lurked around town for a few days, checking on this and that, but his main focus was getting prepared for Friday's event. He knew, just as he was planning Gooch's demise, Gooch was doing the exact same thing, planning to kill him. He thought about an old saying: Never bite the hand that feeds you. Then he thought, *'Whoever created that saying, should have finished it with, "If you do, death awaits you."'*

Bishop realized he had not eaten in almost twenty-four hours and decided to stop at BK Lobster to grab some classic lobster rolls and salmon cakes. He grabbed a sweet tea and jumped back on the highway.

"Yeah, tomorrow I'm going to push that nigga's head back! I'm going to do it right in front of the club for everyone to see too! I just need you niggas to play outside by the car, ready! So, when I dump on 'em, we're out, straight up! We're gonna ride straight up Central Avenue and blend in with the traffic, then cross Bergen Street. Are you niggas with me or what? Are y'all ready for this shit?" Gooch said, exercising his new rank.

Sha was the first one to answer. He was the leader of the crew, the one who had put Gooch onto the hood. "Yo, let's kill this nigga! And if Duke comes out of the coma, we're gonna finish the job! Real talk, I'm about that life! I'm going to have a few homies across the street near the park ready!"

He liked Gooch because he knew Gooch was a good addition to their crew. He knew, that coming from under Duke, Gooch was a stone-cold killer, so that was why Sha had given him some rank over his other members. Gooch had the heart to kill his old boss and set up Bishop. Sha was about that fuck boy life, and it was his crew's time to control the streets.

Gooch hit the blunt they were smoking, satisfied with what he was hearing. He was feeling appreciated for the first time, something he felt Duke and Bishop were incapable of. Hitting the blunt one last time, he smiled. "Yeah, you're wide open! Let's bounce!"

They all got up and left the stash house with none other than Detective Burcheck not too far behind.

Friday morning and it was the day of reckoning. Bishop woke up at his crib in Ft. Lee in his king-size bed, reaching out for Kara. He had a mission today to complete, and he was not going to stop at anything until the job was done. The wrong thing anyone could do was fuck with his family, especially his mother or brother; that was a sign of pure disrespect, and he was not the one for it. He called Kara, wanting to hear her voice, which he knew would uplift his spirits and ensure he came home after the mission.

They talked for a while about the next time they would see each other, and Kara talked about her students and how everyone was excelling and progressing under her tutelage. Bishop smiled at every word she said as if he was sitting right next to her, looking in her eyes. While they were deciding the next meeting place, a familiar number appeared on his caller ID screen. Seeing Sharelle's name, he had to take the call. Boss Hogg was on standby in case she or his mother needed anything, from food to protection. Bishop had no need to worry.

"Kara, baby, I've got to take this call. It's Duke's girl or my mother; I'll hit you back."

"Okay, babe – love you," she replied.

Bishop removed the phone from his ear and looked at it. Her words penetrated his heart, and they were easy to respond to because he felt the same way.

Clicking over, he spoke. "Hello, Sharelle. Is everything okay? You or Momma need something?"

With excitement in her voice, Sharelle yelled into her phone, "BISHOP! YOUR BROTHER IS COMIN' OUT OF HIS COMA! ME AND YOUR MOTHER HAVE BEEN PRAYING FOR HIM, RUBBING HIM DOWN WITH OILS, AND TALKING TO HIM ABOUT EVERYTHING WE KNEW HE'D WANT TO HEAR. HE STARTED MOVING HIS TOES ABOUT AN HOUR AGO. YOUR MOTHER WANTED ME TO CALL YOU AND LET YOU KNOW. ALSO, WHEN ARE YOU COMING TO THE HOSPITAL TO SEE HIM?"

He was happy to hear of his brother's improvement, but he still had work to do, work he knew Duke would have handled the same way he was if the shoe was on the other foot.

"Listen, Sis, I'll be there later tonight. Hold the fort down, and tell Momma I'll be there late in the evening."

"Okay, I will let her know, but Bishop..."

"Yeah?"

"Please be safe out there. This lady has been through enough. She loves and needs her boys," Sharelle said, loving the fact that a minute ago he had addressed her as Sis. That meant a lot to her, seeing how she knew Duke had plans for their future. He really had planned on making her Bishop's sister.

"I got this; don't worry about anything. If y'all need anything before I come up, don't hesitate to call."

"I won't, Bro."

After hearing the news about Duke, he hung up, ready to call Kara back. He even had more to share with her now. She picked up on the first ring and could hear the excitement in her man's voice as he told her about Duke moving his fingers and toes. She also was happy to hear that Duke was coming back to his family. They spoke about her students; he loved to hear about anything that made her happy. After they finished talking about when they would see each other again, Bishop looked at his Rolex, knowing he had some important calls to make.

"Babe, I'm going to call you back a little later, okay?" he said. "I've got some important business I need to jump on."

"Okay, baby. Make sure you're careful. I can't wait until we're together again," she said, causing a smile to cross his face.

"I will..."

Once Bishop ended his call with Kara, he called the Country Boys. He told Darius that he and his brothers were to meet him on Clinton Avenue and Chadwick in two hours. He planned to have them take the gangbangers' stash car while everyone was getting ready for tonight's show. Once he was done giving them the plan, he called Ms. Qupid to check up on how things were going on her end. He wanted to make sure everything was in place, knowing how important tonight was going to be and how he could not afford to make any mistakes.

"Everything is good on my end, Bishop. Gooch just spent two stacks with me, and of course, he showed mad love to my bitches. He said he and Sha were at their spot, chilling."

"Good to know," Bishop replied and thanked her, telling her she should be getting something real sweet for her help in a day or two.

Ms. Qupid told Bishop she did not want anything. She knew what he was doing was for Duke, and to her, Bishop and Duke were like her extended family. He thanked her again before ending the call.

Everything was going right on schedule, just like he had hoped. It was eight p.m. when Bishop got a call from the Country Boys.

"What's good, my brothers?" he asked, looking at his watch again.

"Bishop, you aren't going to believe this."

"What going down?" Bishop asked, not liking the tone in Darius' voice.

"I need to see you immediately!!" Darius said with seriousness.

"Okay, not a problem; just meet me at Weequahic Park," Bishop told him.

"Okay!"

When they arrived at the park, Darius got into the truck with Bishop, opening up a duffle bag he was carrying, along with an all-black briefcase. It was filled with all types of information and money: information on informants and pictures of different people he knew and did not know. There were locations and addresses of people's homes, businesses, etc. Bishop could not believe that his and Duke's information and pictures were in the briefcase along with that of informants, high-ranking gangbangers, community leaders, politicians, audio tapes, etc.

"We found all this shit in the gangbangers' stash car," Darius told Bishop, not really understanding what they had found. Bishop was confused as well.

"Yo, half this shit I don't understand. You take the briefcase and duffle bag, and see what you get out all this shit! This shit is crazy!"

"Thanks. I'm going to let you know what's going on with this bag once I find out myself. For now, all I wanna know is, are y'all good for tonight?"

"Yes, sir. Good as we've ever been. We will be set and ready to go with my 30/30 by 11:30."

"I'll be there by eleven. I'm going to be on the side by the NJ PAC, watching everything and everyone, coming and going. Wait for my cue!"

"Gotchu."

Darius had come across a lot of information that looked like the Feds were getting ready to hand out some serious indictments. It appeared to him that someone was doing some major talking, which made him think back to when he was in the joint and the information had come to him that Duke was fucking with a snitch. It seemed to Bishop, that every time you killed one snitch, the police had a way to re-up and find another one to do the job for them. It was obvious that Gooch and his crew were up to playing the game like a group of rats. The best way to catch a rat was to let the cat out the bag. Shit had just got a little more serious for Bishop.

Bishop decided to call Gooch, still playing it cool, and at the same time, he needed to pick his brain to see what was up. He wanted to make sure he was still going to be there at the time he had given him.

"What's up, Bishop?" he answered, knowing who it was due to the caller ID.

"What's really good with you, my guy? It's still on for tonight, right?"

"Hell yeah! Some little nigga stole my fuckin stash car. I had over forty stacks in there. My man, Sha, had a few things in there too, but fuck that! I'm ready to play! I'm going to be there, waiting out front for you. I gotta see my nigga Jim Jones rock live!"

"Bet, nigga! Don't be late. You know it's gonna be crowded."

"Gotchu. One."

"One."

Both of them were playing cat and mouse, trying to figure the other one out, but the one thing Bishop had over Gooch was intelligence. Gooch did not have the slightest clue Bishop was on to him, and now that he had mentioned the stash car being gone, Gooch had just added more bullets to his expiration date.

———————————————

Gooch finished getting dressed, thinking, *'Yeah, I gotchu all right, muthafucka!'* Thinking about the conversation he and Bishop had just had, he called Sha. *'Let me check on shit.'*

"Hello?" Sha answered.

"What the fuck are you doing? Nigga, are you ready?"

"Yeah, I'm ready. I'm going to get a few blunts from the store. The lil homies are already at the club, posted up. I'll meet you at the spot; we can ride together."

"Okay, bet; I'm there!"

"Okay, I heard. One."

"One."

Sha did exactly what he said, but instead of going into the store for the blunts as he had mentioned to Gooch, Sha was handed something that appeared to be a folder full of paperwork from some strange white guy. The white guy had on a cheap suit, and he did not look like he was from the hood. Sha told the white guy what was going on with the party and who all was going to be there. After their brief encounter, the two of them parted ways, going in different directions.

It turned out Sha was an operative for the government. Burcheck had been following Sha since he had left the spot earlier that evening. He had recorded the entire meeting with Sha and the tall white guy, not understanding what was going on. It was plain to see the white guy was some type of law enforcement.

It was showtime!

Chapter Twenty-Five:
Lights Out

The Key Club was almost at capacity before midnight. People were everywhere—inside and outside in front of the building, mingling, and some trying to find parking spaces. Bishop pulled up in a hoopty, dressed in a restaurant uniform purposely. Nobody recognized him sporting his irregular garb. He quickly radioed the Country Boys, checking everyone's position.

Country Boy Darius answered. "We're here and we're ready, bro."

"Are you on them two jokers wearing all red? You see them, right?"

"Roger that. It's a wrap for both of them. Just let me know when!"

"True. I gotchu," Bishop replied.

Bishop had decided to use the Nextel because they could chirp back and forth and have an untraceable conversation. With the paperwork that had been found in Sha's car, he knew he had to be very careful.

Just as Bishop finished checking in with the Country Boys, Sha and Gooch pulled up together in a new Dodge Charger. He had an eye on them as they sat in the car for a second, probably passing a blunt back and forth. They watched how a few of their homies lingered around, blending in with the party goers outside the club. Gooch had them packing guns the size of a person's arm.

Bishop had the drop on them already. It was now 11:50 p.m., and Gooch was starting to feel some type of way. He had yet to see Bishop, thinking he was not going to come. However, instead of seeing Bishop, he saw Ms. Qupid and a few of her homegirls he had met at the shop.

"Damn, them bitches look good!" he said, ready to trick on them some more.

He told Sha to come on as they finally exited the rental. "It's time to party," he continued, still looking for Bishop.

Gooch got straight out and headed over to the small crowd to holla at some females he knew from around the way.

"Yeah, sexy ladies, y'all are lookin' very good tonight!" he said, shooting at the tall, light skinned one who had a Mississippi built body.

"What's good, Gooch? That Tuff Luv is looking really good on you," Ms. Qupid said, walking up from behind. "Are y'all going inside?"

"Only if y'all are. Thanks for the compliment; you hooked a brother up!" Gooch replied, admiring the gear Ms. Qupid had plugged him with.

"Come on, ladies, let's go inside," Ms. Qupid said to her girls. She knew Bishop was somewhere lurking in the shadows, waiting to end the nigga Gooch's life for what he had done to Duke.

"I'm right behind y'all. Drinks are on me too!" Gooch shouted, showing off.

He turned to look at the Mississippi redbone, winking at her, like it's on later. He liked her body, but Ms. Qupid and her girls were not playing either.

"Come on, Sha; it's on!"

"Nah, G, you go on with those freaks. I'm gonna wait on Bishop. I'll hit you when he pops up."

"You see these ladies?! Okay, suit yourself."

"C'mon, Gooch," Ms. Qupid said, still playing her position.

"Okay, hit me when he arrives," Gooch whispered in Sha's ear.

"I heard," Sha replied, giving Gooch dap as they were splitting up for a moment.

As they stood in front of the club talking, Bishop watched as everything was unfolding. He was down the street, patiently waiting for his opportunity to strike. Bishop still had to wait on Ms. Qupid to call and let him know when Gooch went to the restroom. He watched Sha and the two bangers salute each other and start rambling about something. Most of the people who had been standing outside were now inside, getting their groove on. The place was over capacity, and the security was starting to send the latecomers away. It was getting close to time for Bishop and his people to make their move.

Inside, Gooch was in superstar mode, buying out the bar and dancing with two or three females at a time. He was also taking triple E stack pills with nothing to drink. One of the females grabbed his hand, putting it up her dress. She wanted him to feel how wet her pussy was, knowing she was void of panties. Then she told him how she wanted him to slide up in her. She was horny herself from the E pill Gooch had given her. She told Gooch straight up that she was wanting some dick and she wanted him to fuck her now.

"I wanna fuck!" she said with no remorse. These were words Gooch did not mind hearing one bit.

"Come on; come with me," he replied to her advance.

Gooch led her straight to the restroom, just like Bishop had known he would. Gooch was a simple nigga, and for Bishop, simple niggas were so fuckin' predictable. A pretty face and sexy waist would make any nigga think with his little head instead of his big head.

Once in the restroom, Gooch and the female started kissing and feeling on each other's intimate spots, causing Gooch to forget he was supposed to be waiting to merc Bishop. There were doing a lot of touching as the girl, whose name was Kelli, was trying to undo his belt. Kelli told Gooch her mouth was watering, and she needed it filled with some dick. Her comment blew his mind. She led the way, grabbing Gooch aggressively and pulling him toward the last stall.

It only took a second once inside the stall for her to finish undoing his pants. In the process of doing that, she watched Gooch eyes roll back and that gave her the second she needed to hit the 'send' button on her phone. That was Ms. Qupid's signal to let Bishop know it was now his show. Kelli swallowed Gooch little dick, making it disappear down her throat, causing his knees to buckle and him to lose his balance.

"You okay, baby?" she asked as she stood, turning around and allowing him to raise her dress. She knew she would not feel any real excitement, seeing he was not larger than a fifth grader, but it was all in a day's work for her.

"Am I okay? I'm about to bust these guts, bitch," Gooch bragged.

She laughed to herself at his comment, but she was going to play him like he was actually busting some guts. Reaching for her ass, which was fat as hell, he entered her ocean of wetness. Gooch grabbed her around her waist and started cursing like he was putting in that work.

"Yeah, bitch, how you like dat there? That's the good dick," he said.

"Yeah, Gooch, you're touching my heart... fuck me... fuck me..." she responded, causing him to be so distracted that he was not paying attention to the sounds coming from the stall next to them. There was one being put in the chamber that had his name written on it.

Bishop signaled the person in the stall next to the one Gooch and the female were fucking in that it was show time. Once his person received Bishop's signal, he quietly stepped down off the toilet bowl unnoticed. The youngest Country Boy walked out the stall he was in, only to appear right out in front of the stall Gooch was in with the female. With speed and no hesitation, the stall door quickly was opened.

Kelli looked back to see the gunmen, who put his finger to his lips, making sure she did not say a word. She knew it was not about her and she complied with Bishop's people's order. Gooch was none the wiser, still humping away with his eyes closed and sweat pouring down his back, ruining his new outfit. He was enjoying the wetness of his lady friend, thinking he could get use to her pussy. As quickly as she could, she pulled herself forward, causing Gooch to wonder what the fuck was up. He was just about to bust all up in her, even though he had forgotten to put on a rubber.

"What the fuck, bitch? You're messing up my nut!" he cried out, opening his eyes and staring down the barrel of the prettiest automatic weapon he had ever seen.

"You are a fucking nut, bitch ass nigga! This is from The Duke," the youngest Country Boy let him know before chopping his head to go meet his Maker. The bullets from the gun injected into Gooch's skull, spitting blood all over the stall and Kelli's outfit. After shooting Gooch directly in the face five times, he handed Kelli a bag which contained a new outfit for her to go change, so she would be able to slide out the club like she had had nothing to do with it.

Before he left the restroom, Kelli stopped him and said, "If you ever need some pussy, call me."

The youngest Country Boy looked her up and down, not saying a word; instead, he just smiled and left. Gooch lay dead, his bloody head slumped over in the toilet like the piece of shit he was. One was down, and the plan was going just as Bishop knew it would.

Chaos in the club erupted immediately, causing everyone to start running, trying to get to their cars. Bishop saw it was now time to finish what they had come to do. He signaled Darius, knowing they were wholeheartedly waiting for their opportunity to join the fun. The code to act was sent by the two-way Nextel, and the dark windows slid down in the truck Darius was driving. He had Sha and his homies in sight. The Country Boys were all good shots and did not need to use red beams.

Sha and his homies did not know what was happening. All Sha knew, when he saw one of his homies' head explode as he stood right next to him, was his turn was coming. He and his other worker ducked behind a black-on-black CTS, trying to take cover. Darius looked at his middle brother Carl, who was now licking his lips. This was the moment Carl had been waiting for. They had just gotten in some special military brand AK 47's, and a piece of metal was no match for its firepower.

"You got these niggas, baby boy?" Darius asked his brother.

"Is a pig all pork? You know I got these niggas," Carl said, lining up the shot.

Sha was trying to get a call out on his phone. He was supposed to have protection from some people against something like this. He pulled up his federal friend's cell number, ready to push 'send', when his head exploded, sending brain fragments halfway down the block. Bullets riddled the car Sha had thought was his shield. Several bullets entered his and his homies' bodies simultaneously.

Bishop was still wearing his outfit, looking like he worked for the party as a server as he approached the last of Gooch's click.

"Hey, man, they're shooting down there," Bishop said to the two dudes who were smoking a blunt.

"Yeah, well, long as they ain't fucking with our people, we're going to finish this here good-good and get back in there and find some bitches," one of the dudes said.

"Ain't no going back in. I heard they killed some gangbanger in a slick ass Tuff outfit."

The guys looked at each other, remembering what Gooch was wearing. The one with the blunt took one more hit before stomping it out.

"That sounds like our nigga! You got your heat on you?"

"Man, my shit's in the car."

"Mine too! Damn, we gotta get to the car. They shot Gooch."

Bishop was within a foot of them now. He looked them right in their eyes and saw the fear that had come over them.

"Y'all don't have to worry about getting to the car for your heat," Bishop said.

"Nigga, what you talkin' bout?! You'd better go serve some cold shrimp," the tall one said, peeping and hearing sirens wailing in the distance.

"You're right, but it won't be shrimp. I serve dead bodies to the morgue," he replied before letting his 40 Glock rock them to sleep. He grabbed their cellphones as he stood over them and made sure their lights were completely turned out.

"This is what happens when you don't pay your energy bill—lights out..."

———————————————

Gooch and his posse were all dead. The Country Boys packed up and left the city; back home they went. They were trained hunters who were used to killing, especially when it came to big game. This was what they were trained to do. All they had talked about with Bishop in prison was how they had killed shit growing up and who was the best shooter between the three of them, which they were all good shooters. Tonight, proved that. Bishop had pulled it off without a trace of him even being there.

Ms. Qupid and her girls came out of the party with the crowd. Ambulance and police sirens were heard blocks away as people were screaming and crying over the bangers' and Gooch's death. It was chaotic at the spot to change clothes and vehicles; then he jumped on the highway and headed straight to the hospital to see his little brother. Burcheck tagged right along with him. He had watched everything unfold at the club and knew he had Bishop and Duke right where he wanted them, with plans to arrest them both real soon.

Chapter Twenty-Six:
Feds Watching

Bishop took the bag the Country Boys had given him containing all the information with him so he could eventually share it with his little brother. Burcheck followed Bishop, and the agent Sha and Gooch had worked for followed Burcheck. Burcheck had no idea, that while he was watching everything the brothers were doing, he also was being watched. When the agents had been doing their investigation, Burcheck's name had come up as the arresting officer of one of the brothers. When he was supposed to be interviewed, he was unavailable and the Feds had placed a tail on him for his suspicious behavior.

Burcheck was ready to approach with all the evidence he had on them, but at the same time, he was still trying to figure out what was going on as he pulled into the parking lot of the hospital, still hot on Bishop's trail. He knew he was not supposed to be tampering with the family, per strict orders from his boss, so he would have to be careful about how he presented his report once he nailed them.

Bishop's cellphone rang.

"Boy! Where are you?! Your brother just opened his eyes and said your name!" his mother stated.

"Ma, I'm downstairs in the lobby as we speak," Bishop replied, excited for his family.

"Well, you'd better hurry and get up here!"

Bishop ran onto the elevator, pushing the button for the floor Duke was on. He was nervous and happy at the same time as he arrived at the floor. He ran off the elevator and rushed into Duke's room. He immediately greeted his brother, whose eyes were now wide open. Bishop shed tears of joy with a big ass smile on his face.

"Duke, bro, I love you, man!" he said with a hoarseness in his voice.

It was amazing and had to be an act of God. Bishop had talked to the doctor previously without their mother's knowledge, and the doctor had told him it was not looking good. He also had said Duke's brain had been deprived of oxygen, and there was a good chance, that if his little brother did come around, he could be a vegetable. Bishop had been worried ever since he had that conversation, but he had been hopeful for a miracle, and it seemed to him that God had come through.

In a soft but strong tone, Duke replied, "I love you too, bro."

"Revenge is the sweetest joy, next to getting pussy."

The sounds of a mother's prayer and a girlfriend's concerns were heard in the background. After being in and out of consciousness, his eyes were open slightly and he still was drowsy from the medication, but Duke had awakened for good and spoke to everyone.

"What's all that noise? I'm trying to rest over here."

Both women stared, pleased to hear him speak. Excitement turned to tears of joy for them like it had for Bishop.

"Oh my God!" his mom said, her voice strong but weary.

"Babe, we've been *very* worried about you. How are you feeling? Do I need to call the doctors? Do you need me to do something?" Sharelle asked, not giving him a chance to answer the questions.

"Sweetheart, first I'm going to need you to calm down," Duke said, managing a smile. "I haven't seen your pretty face in a while. Look at you, you're all over the place. I just wanna look into the eyes of my angel. Can I get that? Other than a little pain, I'm okay. The real question is, are you doing all right? Where am I?

"Hey, Mom," Duke continued, looking at the walls of the hospital like he had missed so much of his life. Both women spoke at the same time.

"Hey, Son."

"Yes, I'm all right, babe."

"You scared me for a minute, boy. I'm glad to see your eyes open. How are you feeling?" his mother said, releasing a sigh of relief.

"I know I scared you, probably scared all y'all. I'm sorry for that. I'm good though. This medicine has me a little out of touch. Again, where am I?" Duke asked, looking around the hospital suite.

"You're in Philadelphia Emergency Center, babe. You needed medical attention fast and this hospital was the closest one. Plus, your brother thought it would be a good idea if you stayed in Philly."

"Man, you had me worried," Bishop said, wiping a tear from his eye.

"Man, you a pussy now? You scared a few bullets were going to take me out?" Duke said playfully.

"I see them bullets didn't kill your weak ass sense of humor," Bishop replied, managing a laugh.

"Hey, Mom, can you and Sharelle give me a minute with this dude? I need to talk to him in private," Bishop asked.

His mother did not like it, but she agreed to give her sons a moment alone.

"Okay, me and future daughter in law will go get something to drink, but we will be right back, so y'all make it quick," she replied.

Sharelle gave her man a quick peck as she smiled and told him she would be right back. Duke could not help looking at her ass as she walked out with his mother.

"I told you I would get the girl," he said to his brother as he tried to turn on his side, but the pain was too much.

"Yeah, you did that," Bishop replied, "but we've got bigger fish to fry, bro."

"What are you talking about?"

"Well, for starters, your shooters have been dealt with. It was your boy Gooch; he was working with some bangers."

"That bitch ass nigga?! Fuck that nigga! I'm sure he got what he deserved. Just remind me to send flowers to his mother," Duke said, knowing Gooch was now ten toes up.

"That ain't the half of it."

"Fuck you mean? There is more to this story?"

"Gooch and the nigga he was running with were working for them people and our names are on an indictment. I mean, this nigga must have cut a sweet deal. He told them everything, even implicated himself."

"Damn, I just woke up from death, and I'm not trying to go to the joint."

"We ain't going to jail. A dead man can't testify, can he?"

"Oh yeah, I get it. The State doesn't have a case without their snitch."

"Bingo!"

Just as they were finishing their conversation, their mother and Sharelle walked back in the room smiling. She had a couple of bottles of water for Bishop and Duke. Right behind them, a man in a cheap suit with a mustard stain on his tie entered. I Evans was the first to see the man, who she thought she had seen some place before.

"May we help you?" I Evans asked, noticing the man was not a doctor.

Bishop and Duke knew exactly who the man was.

"No, not really Ms. Evans. I'm here to see your sons."

"Okay, since you already know my name, may I ask who you are?"

"Sure, of course. My name is Burcheck, a detective with the Newark Homicide Squad. I'm here on behalf of my department, in regard to a few murders, and I need to ask your sons a few questions."

Seeing Burcheck flooded memories back to Bishop's mind. He remembered seven years ago, being in the interrogation room, and Burcheck sweating him to say he was not really the one who had killed their father. Now, seven years later, his greatest foe was back on the scene and ready to cause more trouble. Bishop did not speak. He let his mother continue cracking at the detective, but he was ready to do Burcheck like the cops had done him. The bad cop/good cop role they had played was going to be reversed. It was going to be good mom/bad son day, and Duke's hospital room was the new interrogation room.

"This is Philadelphia, Detective. You're a long way from home, don't you think?" she asked, curious to why he was so far from home.

"Yes, I am, I–"

"Ms., I'm not married."

"I think he knows that, Mom," Bishop replied.

"Excuse me, *Ms.* Evans, I apologize if I misspoke, but to answer your question, yes, I am very long way from home. However, I am on police business; hopefully, that isn't a problem."

As the brothers listened carefully, Burcheck revealed his intentions for being there. Bishop and Duke glanced back and forth at one another, Bishop gripping his guns tightly. He then broke into their conversation.

"Mom, you and Sharelle go get the car ready. Duke and I will be right behind y'all."

I Evans wanted to say Duke had just come out of a coma and he was not ready to go anywhere. Instead, her motherly bond kicked in. The tension in the room alerted both women to know how serious things was about to become. Sharelle and I Evans moved according to Bishop's request. Duke, now aware of the circumstances, managed to sit up. As the women exited the room, Burcheck watched them leave, taking his eyes off the brothers, only to turn back around, face to face with two large guns.

"Sorry, Officer, but I don't believe your reason for being here, so before a lot of doctors come running in here due to the loud noise, I'd advise you to pass my brother your gun and handcuffs. It isn't that hard. Any wrong moves and I will not hesitate to wallpaper your face."

"I'm a cop! You can't do this! By killing me, do you boys really believe y'all will make it out of this hospital alive? There are cops all in this place. Are you going to kill me like y'all killed my wife?"

Baffled by the "wife" comment, Bishop told Duke to get dressed.

"I'd rather take my chances. Plus, I have enough ammunition on me to get out of any situation. I I fully prepared for events such as this one. As for you being a cop, fire first, ask questions later. Your wife? Listen, neither me nor my brother has any idea who or what you mean regarding your wife. I think you have the wrong two brothers," Bishop said, trying to figure out what the fuck the cop could be talking about.

"Yeah, right. I've been investigating the two of you for years. Killing people is what you two do. My wife was just one of many murders y'all committed— for instance, like tonight at the Key Club."

Duke was lost at the mention of the Key Club. He had not gotten the full rundown of Gooch's demise yet from Bishop, so he had no idea what Burcheck was on.

"The Key Club, huh? As I just told you, Officer, we had nothing to do with your wife—or any murders committed either tonight at the Key Club or elsewhere. But since you insist on believing what it is you believe, let us cut this conversation short.

"Duke, get his gun and handcuffs," Bishop replied, sticking to his story.

"Come on, bro, I waste this pig? Give me the word! I promise you; they'll be in here picking his face up! Off with his head!" Duke said, ready to end the cop's life right there.

"At least he can get medical attention," Duke continued as he put on the fresh change of clothes his mother had brought him in hopes of God hearing her prayers.

"Chill, lil bro, not here. This isn't the time or the place for a cop to lose his life. You heard what he said, the hospital is crawling with cops, not to mention all the innocent people who could get caught in the crossfire. I just wanna get you outta here, not get you shot again! Cuff him."

Bishop had to think of a plan. He knew Burcheck was not going to go downstairs quietly. It took a few minutes, but he figured it out.

"Sit yo' ass down right there," Bishop said, pointing to the right side of Duke's bed.

Burcheck, understanding the situation he was in, sat down as he was told. Bishop took the IV with the morphine that had been in Duke's arm and stuck it in Burcheck's arm. The morphine was fast acting, and Burcheck began to get drowsy within minutes.

"Damn, bro, you're a fucking genius," Duke said, checking out his brother's plan.

Bishop removed Burcheck's suit jacket, putting it on. He also placed Burcheck's badge on his own belt buckle and handed Duke a gun.

"We're the cops now and he is the prisoner. This should get us out of here."

As the brothers were exiting the room, the two agents who were following Burcheck were now getting off the elevator. Now dressed like agents, the brothers and Burcheck were making their way toward the elevator.

"Duke, watch them two dudes getting off the elevator walking toward us."

"Got 'em, bro"

The brothers' and the agents' eyes connected as they passed each other.

"There's Detective Burcheck over there with those two other guys. Who are they?" the dark-skinned agent asked his white comrade.

"I'm not sure, but something's wrong."

The two agents reached for their service weapons, and Duke and Bishop reached for their weapons as well.

"FBI! Let the detective go!"

"You gotta be fuckin kidding me!" Duke yelled out.

Blam! Blam! Blam! Blam!

With gunshots going back and forth for minutes, the agents and the brothers found themselves in an unexpected dilemma. Burcheck dropped to the floor, escaping the brothers' abduction, even though the morphine drip was still kicking in. Grabbing hold of his lil brother, Bishop and Duke made their way to the elevator, pushing any button to get them out of the chaos.

Blam! Blam! Blam! Blam!

"Awww, man, FBI?! Where the fuck did they come from?"

"Bro, I don't fuckin' know. Are you all right?" Bishop asked, knowing Duke had to be in pain.

"Shit, yeah! I'm Gucci, bro. Fuck that! We gotta get the fuck outta here, my G!"

"Yeah, you're right. We gotta make it to the G ride."

The elevator doors opened, allowing them to make their way to the women. Bishop knew the Feds would have to back off while they were in the hospital because they could not risk civilian lives in a shootout. Duke and Bishop noticed the nervousness on the women faces as they saw the two of them heading to the car. Briefly explaining the situation, Bishop told Duke to have Sharelle take them somewhere safe, expressing he had something else to do. Duke, not wanting to split up, gave Bishop a look he knew all too well. He had lost his brother for seven years and did not want to lose him again.

"You heard me. I can't debate with you now about my request, Bro. Just have your girl take you all somewhere safe. I'll catch up with you later," Bishop said, quickly running to his truck to retrieve the duffel bag.

"Here, take this with you."

"What's this?"

"I'll finish filling you in on everything later. I don't have time for this shit, Duke. We're wasting time."

"All right, later," Duke said, still hesitant.

"I love y'all. Wait until you hear from me. I'll be okay, so don't worry.

"Mom, I'm sorry."

"Love you more, baby," she replied.

"Be safe, Bishop! I don't want to lose my brother before he's actually my brother," Sharelle said, worried about the outcome of the situation.

She knew the brothers were going up against highly trained professionals with skills. Bishop watched Sharelle pull off before returning to his truck and leaving skid marks in the hospital parking lot.

Chapter Twenty-Seven:
It's Personal

The agents made sure the coast was clear and there was no additional return fire that could come their way. They saw the coast was clear and found Detective Burcheck under a gurney, gasping for breath. Helping Burcheck to his feet, the taller agent was stumped and wanted to know what the fuck was going on.

"What the fuck just happened? Who the hell are they?" he asked in an angry voice.

"They are two brothers who you wouldn't want to run into in a dark alley—or a crowded hospital, as you can clearly see," Burcheck responded, still groggy.

"That's obvious, Detective, but this is no time for humor. Someone could have been killed behind those guys' recklessness. Wow, I can't believe no one was hurt."

"We were very lucky, Detective, but we need to talk!" his partner said.

"Yes, definitely. I notice you identified yourselves as FBI. Are you really FBI?" Burcheck asked, knowing if the Feds were snooping around, something else major was brewing.

"Yes, Detective. Unfortunate that we had to meet under these circumstances, but yes, I am Agent Collins and this is my partner, Agent Ortez. We are here investigating the death of one of our agents."

"Pleased to meet you, Detective," Ortiz said, extending a hand.

The agents and Burcheck found a place where they could talk while the Philadelphia Police Department was securing the crime scene. Agent Collins explained in more detail to Burcheck the extent of their investigation— Newark's organized crime, including corrupt police, prosecutors, politicians, and heavy gang activity. Collins also disclosed Burcheck's role in their investigation and the loss of their undercover agent.

"Sha Backster was undercover in the field going on ten years. He was collecting intel on various people who were running underground enterprises, like the mafia. Tonight, he was murdered outside the Key Club in the line of duty. We saw you fleeing the scene," Ortez added.

"Our intentions were, after tonight, to finally end our ten-year investigation, but he insisted he wanted to collect additional valuable pieces of evidence he felt were needed to ensure the prosecution. Agent Backster was a real hard ass and part of the reason we maintained a ninety-nine percent conviction rate. He wanted to make sure he retrieved every piece of evidence that had ever existed to put those involved away for the rest of their lives. A very passionate agent, he did his job very well," Collins said, backing up what his partner had said.

"Excuse me, Agent Collins, who were you and Agent Backster investigating?"

"Organized crime perps. We have been investigating and collecting intel on prominent figures within Newark's corrupt communities: police, prosecutors, politicians, gangs, etc. We have enough evidence to charge them with corruption, money laundering, bribery, murders, guns, drug trafficking, etc. Detective, the crimes their people are involved in are quite extensive."

"Okay, Agent Collins, I think I've heard enough. I understand very well. I also know what it feels like to endure a long and draining investigation. And, yes, due to my own intel, I was at the Key Club tonight. A lot of people were murdered tonight; sadly, one of us. I had no idea the Feds were even in Newark, especially undercover. So, how can I help you?" Burcheck wanted to get in where he fit in.

"We have been waiting ten years to take down this corrupt organization, but there's a problem. Our evidence for the last ten years either was misplaced or stolen during the course of this incident," Ortez revealed, looking at his partner and rubbing the twenty-four-hour stubble growing on his chin.

"Like I said, Detective, our plan was to end our investigation tonight. Agent Backster had everything in his car, but unfortunately, prior to his assassination, his car was stolen. So, since you know the city of Newark better than we do and seeing you've conducted your own investigation over a long period of time, I figure, hell, why not join us and kill two birds with one stone. We can share intel and resources that may have the potential to end both of our investigations," Collins said.

"Agent Collins and Agent Ortez, I have no problem with combining intel if that will help take down the bastards who killed your agent. A favor of your agency's magnitude to capture these brothers is just the favor I need. Yes, it would be an honor to assist you guys."

"The Department appreciates you being in agreement, Detective. Catching those responsible for the death of our agent is important. However, as it pertains to your investigation, Detective, I request that our presence in this investigation is kept discreet, due to those involved. We don't know who to trust. Agent Ortez and I will need you to stay in contact with us directly, and only us."

"Of course, Agent; no problem. Trust is definitely a big issue, especially since corruption seems to plague my department as well. I also request the same discretion."

"Absolutely, Detective; no problem. We wouldn't have it any other way," Ortez said.

Collins was listening to everything Burcheck was saying. He did not have a reason not to trust Burcheck since he and his partner had checked his service jacket while following him from Jersey to Philly. He was clean with no record of having dealt with Internal Affairs. They knew for sure he was not on the take, but Collins still had one more thing he needed to know.

"Oh yeah, Detective, may I ask you a question?" Collins asked, dotting his last I, before crossing his last T.

"Of course."

"What is the nature of your investigation?"

"Those two brothers—"

"The ones from tonight, right?"

"Yes. They killed my wife!"

"Sorry to hear that," Collins replied, shaking his head. He was shaking his head for more reasons than one. It was sad the detective's wife had been killed, but it was also sad to see a ranked detective on a personal mission. That could end up bad.

"My condolences go out to you and your family, Detective," Ortez added when he heard the nature of Burcheck's investigation.

"Thanks, but there's no need for that at this point. It's been over ten years since I lost her. The only thing that has even the slightest possibility of giving me some closure is that these brothers pay for what they've done. A lot of people have died by the hands of these guys. No one can seem to build a solid case on these fellas; it's as if they're untouchable! I truly believe tonight's massacre at the Key Club was in retaliation for the assassination attempt on the youngest brother's life three weeks ago. The brothers have a bond between them that can't be compared to or described. I've never seen anything like them! So, if anyone knows what happened tonight and who killed Agent Backster, they do."

He did not It to lose Duke and his brother to the Feds, but if they were in the paperwork that had been stolen, he saw a win/win situation. With his wife's murder and a federal indictment, he knew for sure Duke and Bishop would die in prison—maybe come back reincarnated as ministers or something. He smiled to himself, knowing that was hardly likely since he really did not believe in reincarnation, but he surely believed in karma.

Their discussion about evidence went on for hours, with both departments combining intel. Burcheck was silently ecstatic, with him being local and joining forces with the Feds to take down corrupt people, in addition to taking down the brothers. Just maybe, when all of it was over, he would put in a transfer to become a federal agent.

Bishop's mind was working nonstop. It was unbelievable that the same detective who had put him away seven years ago was still hot on his trail. He knew Burcheck had some notion that he and Duke were responsible for the death of his wife, but Bishop had no idea what the hell Burcheck was talking about. He figured he would try and piece it together later, but for now, he had business to take care of. He picked up his cell and called the Country Boys.

"What's good, B," Darius said, expecting his call.

"Listen, bro, change of plans. I know you and your brothers were scheduled to leave after the party, but something has come up. How far out are you?" Bishop asked.

"Say no more. We're turning around now, bro. Give me a couple of hours and we're there! One."

"Cool. One," Bishop replied and ended the call.

He was glad he had met Darius and his brothers and had become family with them. There were not many men Bishop would ever trust the way he trusted the Country Boys and 4'2. He hurried and got himself situated at the spot, waiting for the return of the Country Boys.

Bishop looked at his watch when he heard the Country Boys pull up. They were the only ones besides Duke who knew about this particular spot, so Bishop felt safe conducting his meet there. When they entered, they all noticed the worried look on Bishop's face and wanted to know what was wrong. Bishop sat them down and they discussed everything that had taken place, including what had transpired between him and his brother with the agents at the hospital. Bishop also briefed them on the contents of what was in the duffel bag that had been procured from Sha's vehicle. As well as what was to come next, they all knew Bishop would devise a plan. That was what Darius had admired about Bishop from day one, the fact that he always had a plan. It did not matter if they were on lockdown or in the free man's world, Bishop always had something up his sleeve.

Chapter Twenty-Eight:
The Meet Up

A few days had passed after the incident between the brothers, Burcheck, and the two agents. Duke had started regaining his strength, and Bishop and Duke had decided it was important that he remained strategically in seclusion, out of sight. They now knew they would always be in the forefront of Burcheck's mind. Bishop had researched Burcheck, the two agents, and the information in the duffel bag, and he had started gathering momentum on what to do next. Word of the locals and the Feds joining forces got back to Bishop, and he sensed that would mean double trouble to deal with. The plot was getting thicker and he had to be ready. He was not going back to the joint, and he was not allowing anyone to take both of his mother's sons from her.

Burcheck lay in his leather recliner, sipping tea until he fell asleep watching reruns of *Miami Vice,* his favorite television show. For years, he had been trying to cope with the reality of that cruel day he had gotten that tap on his shoulder from the bank security guard. He drifted into a nod that became a deep sleep, and eventually, came the haunting dreams that plagued him, preventing him from ever getting his proper rest.

Their kiss had been so passionate and Burcheck had had no idea, that by stepping out of the car and going into the bank on Market Street, it would alter his life forever. He wished it was him who had died that day, instead of his wife.

"Babe, I'll be right back. Let me go in this bank right quick. I have to go deposit a few checks. I'm going to double park right here. I shouldn't be more than ten minutes. Give me another kiss," he said, leaning over to feel her soft lips again.

"Okay, hun; hurry up, all right? I want to get to the mall before rush hour. I do not want to get caught up in all that traffic. So, babe, please hurry it up," his wife replied, batting her long eyelashes at him. He knew that meant it was going to be a good night for him when he got home.

"I'll be as quick as possible, baby. I love you so much. Be right back," he said, skipping along like an adolescent in love for the very first time, not knowing it would be their last kiss—or the last time he would see her alive. The car door closed behind him.

While he was in the bank, three young individuals approached the parked car. They had to be between the ages of fifteen and eighteen years old. As the three boys approached the car, one of them asked Mrs. Burcheck for a little change, claiming to be hungry. As nice and kind as she was, her sympathetic side kicked in, and she grabbed her purse to help the young boys out in their struggle.

"Yes, I have some change for you boys," she said smiling, knowing she was doing a good deed. She had been raised by Christian parents who had taught her it was better to give than to receive.

As she fumbled through her pocketbook, one of the hoodlums noticed more than a little change poking from her little clutch purse. The youngest of the click reached into his pants, pulling out a .44 Bulldog from his waist.

"Bitch! Give me all your fuckin' money. Don't let this muthafucka explode!" he said, causing instant horror to cover her face.

"What's going on, boys? You don't have to do this. You can have all my money. Please don't hurt me!" she cried as she begged them not to hurt her.

"Shut the fuck up, bitch! Stop talking and pass over the cash before I blast ya fuckin head off! Now, bitch! Now! You're moving too slow..." another one of the culprits demanded.

She looked him in his eyes and saw that he was a little older than the first boy. She could see how treacherous his pupils looked.

"Okay, okay. Here, here... just take it! You can have it all. I have a family. PLEEEASE, don't do anything you will regret," she continued, begging and hoping at the same time her husband would come to save her.

The older miscreant felt she was not complying fast enough to their demands. He looked at his younger partner, and in a split second, Pow! Pow! Pow! Pow! Her body slumped over onto the driver's side. The shots could be heard inside the bank.

Still inside the bank, Burcheck heard the thundering roars of a gun coming from a distance. Husbandly instinct kicked in, knowing he had left his beloved wife outside. He turned around and looked out toward the double-parked car. Then he took off at full speed. Fear of his wife being harmed took over his physical and mental existence. Never seeing the third person, he noticed two young boys fleeing from the car.

Gun drawn, he yelled out, "I'm a cop. Freeze! Police! Everyone get down! Get on the ground! Police!

No longer able to see his wife in the passenger seat, his fear increased tremendously. The two figures, who appeared to be two young boys, had now disappeared.

'Where is she?! Where is she?!' Burcheck wondered as the bank security accompanied him outside with his piece drawn. In search of his wife, he finally got to their Buick, which seemed like forever. At that moment, Burcheck's greatest fear became a reality.

"OH MY GOD! WHY HER? GOD, WHY?!" he screamed, snatching open the door and pulling her bloody body tightly to him.

Security was right there, placing a hand on his shoulder. His wife's body lay lifeless in his arms, her body drenched in blood. Bullets had ripped the flesh of her breasts like lunch meat. Small holes in the front where the bullets had entered left holes the size of tennis balls in her back. He attempted to revive life back into her lungs, only to realize she was no longer part of this world. Loud screams erupted from his mouth.

"MY WIFE... MY WIFE... SHE'S GONE! WHY HER, GOD?!"

Throughout the midst of the chaos and his wife no longer being alive, all he could remember was the two boys he had seen running away from the scene. He swore with a vengeance, that by any means necessary, he would find the two responsible for the death of his wife.

———————————————

The phone rang, waking him up from his dream.

"Hello," Burcheck answered in a groggy voice.

"How are you doing, Detective? Sorry I woke you," Bishop said, knowing the detective would not know his voice.

"Who is this?" Burcheck asked, confused.

"No names are necessary. Let's just say, me and my brother are doing very well."

"How did you get my number?" Burcheck asked, waking up fully, and now aware the person calling his phone was one of the brothers.

"See, Detective, it wasn't that hard to figure out who I am. Yes, it is I! I know you have to be surprised."

"What do you want, besides a long vacation in a small cell somewhere?"

"Now, Detective, you don't seem excited to hear from me. That is no way to treat a friend."

"You are no friend of mine," Burcheck responded, gulping down the cold tea left in his glass.

"You are absolutely right, Detective. We are not friends. Not yet, anyway, but I have a feeling we're going to become very close."

"Close my ass! We will never become close, *ever*!" Burcheck said, feeling the caller was antagonizing him now.

"Have it your way, but never say never, Detective. Things change."

"Say whatever you want, but I would like to know why you called me."

"Time and location—I believe I have something of yours—rather, something that belongs to your agent friends."

"Yes, I believe you do. I think you and your brother should turn y'all selves in, bringing the agents' evidence along with you. Sorta like a good gesture."

"Listen, Detective, I don't do good gestures. As for me and my brother turning ourselves in, that's out of the question. We've done nothing wrong," Bishop insisted.

"What about the incident at the hospital? That was nothing to you? The murder of an FBI agent and my wife—you find nothing wrong with that? That's just how your everyday normal life goes? Shooting up hospitals and killing people? What fuckin' planet are you from?"

"The agents pulled their guns first; we were only protecting ourselves. As for whoever killed the FBI agent, it wasn't me or my brother. And, again, we had nothing to do with your wife's death. Now you can continue to believe whatever it is you want, but either way it goes, we aren't turning ourselves in! Forget it! Listen, I have some important information I'm pretty sure you'll find interesting, information only you and I can discuss."

"I'm not sure why me, but I'll bite," Burcheck said, making a coughing noise. "Okay, let's meet. We can talk about whatever, as long as the discussion includes my wife," Burcheck continued, thinking about how he would have Collins and Ortez corner the brothers, and finally, he would get his men. Not only that, he would have built a solid rapport with the Federal Bureau of Investigation. All he could see was a promotion bouncing side to side in his head.

"Thanks for agreeing," Bishop replied, already ten steps ahead of Burcheck's predictable plan. "Text the time and location of our meeting; I can't wait for our date. Oh yeah, *again,* your wife isn't an issue of mine. You have the wrong people with that one. I'm sorry about your loss, but you should go ahead and finish getting your beauty sleep. You need it! One."

"Hello... hello?"

Bishop had ended the call without giving Burcheck the chance to respond. The next day, a text came through Bishop's phone that read:

2:30 P.M. Broad Street in front of City Hall

'He could not have picked a better location,' Bishop thought. Crowded and public, perfect.

Burcheck had informed Agent Collins of the meeting that was to take place. When Bishop received Burcheck's text, he sent the information to

Duke and the Country Boys, telling them to be there a few hours earlier than the time Burcheck had said to be there.

It was about ten o'clock, and Burcheck sat in an undisclosed location with Collins and Ortez, getting ready for the meet.

"If he sees you guys, it can go all bad," Burcheck said. "Listen, these brothers aren't stupid just because they come from the ghetto. They are smarter than you think. Do not underestimate the situation," he continued, explaining his thoughts to the FBI.

"Don't worry, Detective. We have agents all around this location. There is no way he or his brother will escape us. Just make sure he speaks directly into the wire. We need to hear him clearly," Collins said, double checking Burcheck's wire.

"Check one, check one. Can you hear me?" Ortez said.

"Yes. Can you hear me?"

"Yes, perfectly," Ortez replied, throwing Burcheck the thumbs up.

"Agent Collins, just be on top of your game. These brothers are dangerous. I don't see them surrendering peacefully. I doubt they will surrender at all," Burcheck added.

"And we don't expect to take them peacefully either. I have you covered every step of the way. People like these brothers who show a blatant disregard for life never go peacefully. I have profiled many criminals just like them, Detective."

"I hope so. It's getting close to that time. Let me go."

"Oh yeah, Detective, we will be watching closely, so make sure you get the evidence first and foremost," Collins reminded Burcheck.

"I understand, Agent."

Chapter Twenty-Nine:
Red Dot

It was time to put a major plan into action. This was just a minor setback for a major comeback in Bishop's eyes. He hurried to hit up his people, calling the Country Boys first.

"Bishop, everything secure?" Darius asked.

"Everything's Gucci on this end. Stay focused on anyone who looks suspicious. Although I told him to come alone, he's a cop; they never follow directions. Once I give you the word, blast away! Look for my signal," Bishop said, knowing Burcheck was going to be on some bullshit.

"Roger that!" Darius spat back through the Nextel.

"Duke, are you ready?"

"Do you really have to ask me that question? Revenge is the sweetest joy, next to getting pussy. Let's do this shit, bro."

"Okay, little bro, he's here. It's all or nothing," Bishop said, making sure everyone heard that.

The brothers approach Detective Burcheck at 2:37 p.m. outside City Hall. It was very public and enough people, that if Bishop and Duke had to go to war with the law, there would definitely be some civilian casualties, which the law did not want.

"A little late, Detective, but overall, I'm glad to see you made it," Bishop said, a serious look on his face.

"Likewise. Good to see you brought your little brother with you," Burcheck replied.

"Yes, sir; somebody has to have my back. I'm pretty sure you have someone watching your back as well," Bishop replied, giving a little smile.

"Of course I do. It wouldn't be a party if I couldn't invite someone too." Burcheck had a little cockiness to his tone.

"Party, huh? Sounds good, but fuck all the small talk. Let's get down to why we're here," Duke said, keeping his hand close to both his Glock 40's.

"Duke, calm down. I got this."

"Yeah, put a leash on your dog. It's against the law to walk a pit bull without one, you know," Burcheck said, being sarcastic.

"Who the fuck you calling a dog, pig? Don't get it fucked up, Detective. This was my brother's idea, not mine. If I'd had my way, I would've knocked your head off back in the hospital room."

"Good thing you didn't have your way," Burcheck replied, knowing Duke was serious.

He suspected it was most likely Duke who had been the trigger kid who had killed his wife and the real killer of their father. He could not prove it, but he had been a law official for a long time and he had learned gut instincts were usually right.

Darius and his brothers were set up in a prime location to watch. He noticed a couple of suits heading toward Bishop and Duke.

"B, someone's approaching y'all. Do you want me to shoot?" he whispered through the high-tech earpiece Bishop was wearing.

"Nah, not yet," Bishop said.

Burcheck wondered who he was talking to.

"Detective, I asked you not to bring anyone. Your agents from the hospital, right?"

"I I I " Burcheck said, trying to speak, but only stuttering words rambled off.

"No need to say anything, Detective.

"Allow me to introduce myself. Yes, I am the agent from the hospital; I am Agent Collins. I believe you have something that belongs to me."

He really was not concerned with Burcheck's issues at all. He felt a little sorry that his wife had allegedly been murdered, but the federal government's business took precedence over his personal shit. Collins knew on meeting Burcheck that he was the perfect pawn he and Ortez needed to get to the culprits.

"Agent Collins, yeah I think I do, but you need to hear me out," Bishop said.

"Make this quick, kid. You've got a cell on a rock waiting for you."

"For starters, let's say you were mentioned. It's plain to see it's your voice heard throughout a lot of these wiretaps I've been listening to for the last week or so. It's apparent, Mr. Agent guy, that you're just as corrupt as the FBI agent who was murdered. I thought it was crazy at first, the Feds hooking up with the FBI to bring down street-level dealers and low-life politicians," Bishop said.

Burcheck was surprised to hear the exchange of rhetoric, not aware of what was going on or the real contents of the duffle bag, other than what Agent Collins had told him about it being pertinent evidence in a multi-level indictment.

"What is he talking about, Agent?" Burcheck asked, suspecting something really fishy was going down. He looked around for the team of Feds that were supposed to be protecting him and their comrades, but he was not sure who was who.

"That is not your concern, Detective. We're here to retrieve evidence and kill two brothers. I thought that was our plan," Collins said.

"*Kill?* Our plan was to arrest the brothers, not kill anyone," Burcheck stated.

"And if that was the plan, did you really believe it would be that easy, Collins?" Duke asked, putting his hand on the butt of his pistols. "That surely won't be happening today!"

"I think you heard my little brother. If anyone's dying today, it won't be us. So before you do anything you'll regret, I seriously suggest you rethink your master plan, Collins. I would if I were you," Bishop said, almost ready to give his country brothers the signal.

"Is that my evidence you have in your hands?" Collins asked, ignoring Bishop and Duke's premature threats.

"Maybe, maybe not. Are you Indian?" Bishop asked.

Collins didn't understand the line of questioning, but figured he would play the game for a few more seconds.

"No, I'm Caucasian. Why Indian? Do I look Indian?"

"Hell, you could've fooled me. With that *big ass* red dot on your forehead, you sure look Indian to me!" Bishop said, smiling for real now.

"What? What red dot?" Collins said, reaching for his forehead to feel what was there.

"Yes, Agent, there is a red dot on your head!" Burcheck assured him.

"Listen, we have this place surrounded. There's no escape, so even if you do kill me, you will be dead before my body hits the ground."

"Are you sure about that, Agent? By the time your body hits the ground, we'll be long gone, trust me." Duke boasted, knowing his brother always made sure his plans were foolproof.

"All these people out here? You wouldn't dare kill a federal agent," Collins suggested.

"On the contrary, Agent Collins. See that's what makes killing you so much easier—we can blend in with the people," Bishop said.

Burcheck was as confused as he had ever been in his whole career.

"Are y'all really ready to do this to an agent?" Collins asked.

For the first time, Collins felt fear. He had yet to count on the brothers knowing what was on the wiretaps. They were encrypted and needed a special listening device to access.

"You asked are we ready. We're ready as we'll ever be," Duke spoke.

"Too much talking, Agent Collins. Shut up for a second while Detective Burcheck determines what happens next. Again, Detective, we had nothing to do with your wife's death. The agent you seem to have an agreement with seems more corrupt than the rest. I'm pretty sure after he kills me and my brother, you're next. See, Detective, you gotta be more conscious and aware of who you get into bed with," Bishop said, making Burcheck rethink everything he had thought.

"Is that true, Agent?" Burcheck asked, not really expecting an honest answer.

Before Collins could answer the Detective's question, Agent Ortez and other agents commenced firing! Bishop, Duke, and Burcheck took cover. Burcheck was convinced now that the brothers were telling the truth—not just about Collins and his rogue agent friends, but that they had not killed his wife. His mind kept reflecting back to the gun they had retrieved at their father's murder scene and the ballistics revealing it was the same gun that had been used to kill his wife. Now, there was an all-out war and action-packed shootout in front of City Hall, leaving Burcheck to make more decisions on the spot. His head started pounding as he watched agents falling dead, blood exploding out their heads like watermelons. Bystanders were being killed, and from what Burcheck could tell, it was because of the recklessness of the rogue agents, who were supposed to be trained.

"Whoaaaaa! This is what the fuck I'm talking about!" Duke said as he let off a few shots in the direction of the rogue agents.

Blam! Blam! Blam! Blam!

"Duke, come on; we gotta go! Let's stick to the plan," Bishop insisted.

"Come on, bro; I'm just starting to enjoy myself," Duke replied.

"Bro, stick to the fuckin' plan! This is not PlayStation, nigga," he said, reaching for his earpiece.

"Darius, I'm on my way!" Bishop said, alerting his people it was time to extract him and Duke from the scene.

"Come on, brother! I've got your back!" Darius replied, letting Bishop know it was time for the grand finale.

Blam! Blam! Blam! Blam!

Rapid gunfire was sent into the direction of more agents, taking their lives, one by one.

Bishop and Duke made it safely, just as Bishop had designed the plan. Once the shooting stopped, it was clear there were casualties everywhere, which left Agent Collins and Agent Ortez to explain things to the local law enforcement. Deceitful with their explanation, they made it look like it was Detective Burcheck who was the corrupt one, and it was his revenge against the brothers that had taken him rogue, killing all those innocent people and agents. The brothers were also a part of this senseless and deadly circumstance. In the midst of the shootout, Bishop had dropped the duffel bag full of evidence, leaving Agent Collins to believe he had won. Burcheck was in a serious catch 22, left with no other choice but to team up with the brothers.

Newspapers and broadcasts everywhere reported:

Be on the lookout for two brothers, Duke and Bishop Evans. They are accompanied by a highly decorated detective, Dennis Burcheck, who federal agents say has gone rogue. The trio is wanted for murder, corruption, money laundering, extortion, and a host of other charges. They are considered armed and extremely dangerous. There is a five-million-dollar reward for information leading to the capture and conviction of these individuals. Again, they are armed and extremely dangerous. PLEASE do not try to apprehend these suspects yourself. Call your local police department or contact the FBI at 555 777 0707.

The press release was on every news station, even Nancy Grace had picked up the bulletin and given her opinion.

Burcheck had no clue what had happened back there at City Hall. He believed Bishop and the story he had told right in Collins' face. Burcheck knew it was the truth because Collins wanted Bishop and Duke dead, instead of them facing their day in a courtroom. That was not supposed to be the way the law worked. Burcheck never thought he would see the day where he would be forced to work with the people he always had assumed had murdered his wife in cold blood. All because he had to clear their name, and his own, of the bogus charges Agent Collins had brought against them.

Bishop felt the same way, but he vowed to assist Burcheck in finding those responsible for the death of his wife, knowing it would clear him and his brother. He knew he was smart for having made copies of every piece of evidence in the duffel bag, which Agent Collins had no idea existed. The trio put their heads together to take down the most dangerous and corrupt organization Newark, New Jersey, had ever seen. If successful, the brothers had sworn to leave the game and the streets for good.

Chapter Thirty:
4'2 Private Jet

It was time for the second phase of Bishop's plan, which was to get his little brother to safety. There was no way they could be safe in Newark at this time. He made a call to his other brother, and in minutes, his woman was in the air, headed to a discrete location to retrieve him.

"Baby, thanks for coming to get us. My face is plastered in the papers and on news channels everywhere. It was hard to get around," Bishop said, giving Kara a big hug and kiss. His stomach was in knots, but he knew it was not from fear, just the fact that so many innocent people had lost their lives.

"Bishop, I'd do anything for my man. You should know that. Yes, baby, your face is everywhere," she replied. "You've become a very bad boy," she continued in a sexy voice.

He was trying not to be turned on at the moment, but hearing her voice and looking at her sexy legs protruding from under the designer dress she was wearing was hard.

"Stop it. Stop talking to me like that; you know how I get," he said, knowing there was not time to finish what they had started on their first date.

"Exactly, that's definitely how I want and need you to be. I miss you, baby. I miss my bad boy." She smiled.

"Due to the circumstances, I know you've really got my back and you know something, baby? I miss you too," he said, realizing just how much she reminded him of her uncle, 4'2.

"Excuse me, baby. Let me say something to the cop."

"What do you want, Mr. Evans?" Burcheck said in an agitated tone.

"Come on, man. It doesn't have to be like this. I told you we were not responsible for the death of your wife, and for some strange reason, I think you actually believe me."

"Whatever, man. Still, we are not friends. We have an agreement—that's it, that's all. If I had it my way, you'd be locked up somewhere, maybe not for my wife, but for a host of other shit you're involved in," Burcheck replied, looking out at the clouds.

"Good thing you ain't got it your way," Duke said.

"Who asked the pit bull to bark?" Burcheck replied, knowing how to piss Duke off.

"Honestly, nobody. I just thought it would be funny for you to hear your own words. That's it! Continue with your conversation, Detective," Duke said, smirking.

"Duke, you're always starting stuff," Sharelle said.

"Shut up and give me some kisses," Duke playfully said. He was glad she had accompanied him.

"Bishop, you seem to be the brains of this crazy operation, so my question is, with a five-million-dollar bounty on our heads and wanted by a nation, where can we possibly go without anyone recognizing our faces?"

"That's your problem, Detective, you worry too much. I know asking questions is part of your job description; however, with that five-million-dollar bounty on your head, you have been relieved of your public service. What you should be asking, instead of where we're going, is how we're going to get our lives back, vindicating us of these accusations?"

"You seem to have everything all figured out, so okay, how do we get our lives back, vindicating ourselves of these charges against us?"

"Now, that sounds more like the conversation I'd rather have with you. Allow me to educate you," Bishop replied.

Bishop took the opportunity to educate the Country Boys and Burcheck on what he knew about the agents, their investigation, and the murder of Detective Burcheck's wife.

Duke and Sharelle did not need to be part of the conversation, so they excused themselves and headed back to the plane's master suite.

"Duke, I love you soooo much. When you were shot. I thought I was going to lose you forever. I was terrified, babe, a nervous wreck," Sharelle said, breathing heavily.

"I understand, babe. Me getting shot was pretty intense, but it wasn't intentional on my behalf. Others had planned my demise."

"Yes, they did," she replied, hugging him.

"Whoa, be careful, baby; I'm still a little sore."

"My bad, honey, I just love you so much," she said, making Duke close his eyes for a second and think about the future.

"As crazy as things have become over the past couple of months, I never thought Gooch would be a part of a plot to kill me. I expected that to occur with them soft haters, weak niggas who can't get it out the mud."

"I never got the chance to meet Gooch, only heard stories about him from you. In any event, it seems to always be the ones closest to you who try something as grimy as what Gooch attempted. No matter how much you think you know someone, in all actuality, you have no idea who a person is these days. I love you with every piece of me."

"I love—"

Sharelle cut him off before he could finish his sentiment. "Duke, babe, you don't get it. I didn't say I love you only to hear you say it back. I'm saying it so that you fully understand what I mean when it's expressed. Babe, you almost died, and I'm not sure what my life would've been like without you!"

"I know how it would've been... boring," Duke said, always being the jokester he was. "The way it was before me, fuckin' with those lame ass niggas." He was being funny, but he was also serious.

"Duke, that isn't funny. Can you be serious for once in your life? I am trying to express myself to you and you're joking around. Duke, life isn't a game... Leave me alone," Sharelle said as she tried to push away from between Duke's arms.

He stopped her, grabbing her tightly. "Stop acting like that. Where are you going? Okay, okay, I'm sorry, babe. I understand everything you're saying," Duke replied, not wanting her to be out of his sight for another minute. He knew he had gone too far when he saw her tear up and become silent.

"Come on, babe, don't start crying on me. I said I was sorry."

"No, Duke! You act like you don't understand at times. Here's your brother, me, your mother, Kara, everyone who's close to you—all of our lives are on the line, and you're making jokes."

"Hold up, babe. Listen, I get it. Even when I joke, I'm serious. I play around with you like that, I guess, for the simple fact that I don't want or need you worrying—whether it's about me, you, or anyone else, I love dearly."

Sharelle finally turned to face him and heard him out.

"Yeah, okay, I was shot and I almost died, but they fucked up. I'm still alive! I will never underestimate reality again. As your man, you need to know and understand, I gotchu. For real, I'm like, your fuckin' superhero! I'm not checking out no time soon... or later. Us—you and I—we're forever! Again, I apologize for not being serious enough when you needed me to be, or more sensitive. Wipe your eyes and kiss me."

"No one is playing with you, Duke... My superhero, huh? Really, my own personal Superman? Boy, you're crazy," she replied, giving him one hell of a passionate kiss on his lips.

"Why not? I believe I'm faster than a locomotive when I'm in my car. Able to leap tall buildings, especially when I'm flying over the city. And you already know, I'm known to stop a bullet or two, with your assistance of course."

"I have never met anyone like you, Duke. Just like that, as serious as I was, you bring the silliness out of me. You are driving me insane."

"Hopefully, that's a good thing. Babe, listen, I live a lifestyle where there's good and bad, and at any given time, anything can happen. So, as my woman, you must be prepared for the worst, while hoping for the best possible outcome. Hopefully, when this ordeal with these agents and the gangbangers is all said and done, we are the last ones standing! I'm through with the streets, babe. I have enough money for us to live and travel comfortably around the world without any worries, together and forever, real talk."

"Ooohhh, babe! Now I'm really about to cry. You'll give up the streets for me? Is it that simple?"

"Yes, and yes. I'm doing it for us. You're worth me giving my life for, so the streets are nothing. I've seen, came, and conquered! What's left for me to achieve? I was supposed to tell you this the night I was shot, but we both know how that played out. Babe, I don't wanna lose you," he said, leaving her speechless for a minute.

"You won't, babe... You won't lose me *ever*!"

"That's what's up."

"Ooohhh my God. I don't know what to say, Duke."

"Don't say anything. Dig, we came in here for a reason. Valentine's Day... What? You thought I forgot? You owe me."

"I love you, Duke."

"I love you more. Now shut up and show me what I've missed."

A few moments later, the pilot came over the intercom system. "To all my lovely passengers, we are twenty minutes away from landing in Arizona. I ask that everyone to take your seats and fasten your seat belts."

Hearing the pilot make the descending announcement, Duke and Sharelle came stumbling out the restroom, laughing and fixing their clothes. Bishop looked at the silly couple as they headed to their seats.

"*What*?! Why are you looking at me like that, man? I did something wrong?" Duke asked.

"Nah, man... you ain't do nothing wrong at all," Bishop said, smiling. He wanted nothing more in life than for his little brother to be happy.

The plane landed, and when Bishop got off, he knew they had landed somewhere different than the first time he was here. Kara had told him her uncle had a place that was secure enough to keep them safe. She told her man that her uncle really did not like the fact that Burcheck was with them, but he understood Bishop's plan. They all knew now, with all the alphabet cops on their trail, that they had to be very careful. The DEA was one thing, but the FBI was a totally different ball game. They had ways to tap into thousands of devices to do surveillance on someone.

They were picked up from the private airport, and when they were safely at their destination, there driver waited to take Kara and Bishop to meet up with her uncle. The ride was short and hot to a small town called Mesa. The streets were narrow, and some were still unpaved dirt roads. The scene almost looked like a cowboy movie as Bishop peered from behind the tinted bulletproof windows of her uncle's Hummer SUV. The driver drove up a long driveway, only to stop at a small, ranch style home with an old Mexican man and what looked like his wife sitting on the front porch.

Kara told Bishop they were there. She got out the truck and walked toward the couple with Bishop close behind. She kissed them both on the cheek before noticing her Uncle 4'2 making his way outside. The two men greeted each other with a strong embrace.

"What's going on, my friend?" 4'2 asked in his thick Mexican accent. "Difficult times in the big city?"

"Yeah, a little complicated, but I have everything under control. I just needed somewhere to recoup and get my mind right. Plus, I need some advice from my mentor," Bishop replied, knowing 4'2 would have the right answers.

"Bishop, no problem. Me understand very well. You, me, brother, we will get through this. Me show you how!"

"I needed to hear that. Thanks for everything. I promise you, I'm going to make everything better," Bishop said, knowing he was going to do just that.

Nodding his head, 4'2 replied, "Me know, me know. Let's drink."

Tossing a few shots back, 4'2 provided Bishop with every piece of guidance a man in power needed to face his demons. Bishop and 4'2 ended their conversation, and he and Kara headed back to the compound.

The two weeks they were in Arizona, the crew including Burcheck reviewed all the information it had taken Agent Backster ten years to gather—

paperwork, wiretap sessions, and names and addresses. After listening and reading years of intel that dated as far back to when Duke and Bishop were just kids, Burcheck stumbled across the information that was destined for him to hear. Several of the wiretaps were voices he recognized. Others, he only recognized by name.

Suddenly, ten years of pain came crashing down upon him like a sledgehammer. There were voices of the two individuals discussing the vivid details of murdering a woman and finding out the woman they had shot and killed outside the bank in downtown Newark was the wife of Detective Burcheck. The conversation went on for at least two hours. The phone call had been placed to a gang leader by the suspects who had only placed the call due to their concerns of killing a cop's wife.

In disbelief of what he was hearing, Detective Burcheck threw the equipment to the floor, becoming highly emotional. Right then and there, he knew without a doubt, that after years of blaming the two brothers for his wife's death, he had been dead wrong. Reality for everyone involved could not be any clearer.

He thought, 'It was not them! That means, if I just found out all this information about my wife, then Bishop must have known for weeks.'

Disgusted with his findings and being wrong about the brothers, Detective Burcheck realized the only way to make amends with Bishop and Duke was to man up. Burcheck located Bishop and Duke standing in front of a fire in a group discussion out on the patio. He politely interrupted.

"Excuse me, fellas. Can I speak to the both of you for a sec?"

The pain and distraught on the detective's face was obvious to the brothers. Bishop knew he had heard the truth about his wife. His eyes revealed the pain and struggle he was having with the truth. Duke, being Duke, instantly became impolite.

"Nah, Detective. No disrespect or anything, but you and I have nothing to talk about," Duke said, holding in his hand a bottle of Ace of Spades.

"Babe, stop being so mean," Sharelle whispered in his ear.

"Nah, babe; this cop has been a pain in my ass ever since our first encounter."

"Chill out, Duke. Come on, Detective, let's walk and talk," Bishop said.

"I appreciate that, Bishop."

"No problem."

They took a stroll around the guarded compound. The duo stopped in an isolated area, getting straight to their well anticipated discussion.

"I guess you heard the tapes, huh?" Bishop asked, already knowing the answer.

"Just like you knew I would," Burcheck responded, not trying to sound condescending.

"I didn't tell you for many reasons. For one, I didn't trust you."

"Hell, with everything that's been going on around us, I'm not so sure who to trust either. There's been a lot of false activity going on, so I understand your reasons more than you can possibly imagine. For years, I've blamed you and your brother for murdering my wife, and to find out, throughout all this, I was wrong, I feel really bad."

"Feeling bad is an emotion that shouldn't exist right now. Everyone is entitled to make mistakes, which you did for years. But now you know the truth, and that's all that matters."

"Bishop, you're a unique individual who stands alone," Burcheck said, flashing a smile that did not cover the pain he was feeling.

"Thanks for the kind words, Detective."

"However, I have to man up and take responsibility for my misjudgment. The day my wife was murdered... I never saw three people flee from the scene; I only saw two. Plus, the gun that was used in her death is the same gun used in the death of your father, the father you killed, so why not believe the evidence that pointed in the direction of you and your brother? I was only doing my job. It was a little personal, but it still was the job."

"Detective, I get your duties as a cop to protect and uphold the law, your public service and obligations to the community. However, if I can be honest for a second..." Bishop paused to hear his response.

"Sure, I welcome honesty."

"Listen, you had to blame someone; it's human nature," Bishop started off saying. "Your wife was murdered and someone had to pay. Sad to say, you wanted Duke and me to pay for what happened. I get it! Reality sucks! However, I think, while you were on your hot pursuit for answers, you didn't give yourself enough time to grieve over your wife's death. Somehow, I believe, over the last ten years, with all the built-up aggression and emotions you've accumulated, over the course of time, you lost yourself! That resulted in your hunger for vengeance toward the killers becoming that much greater. I believe the anger you possessed took a tremendous toll on you, so much that you lost perspective on reality. Would you agree?"

"Wow!" Burcheck replied, astonished by Bishop's theory of him. "How old are you again? You continue to amaze me. With everything you've just expressed, yes, there's a great possibility you're right. My revenge to catch those behind my wife's murder compromised my humanity, and of course, clouded my judgement, making it hard for me to find closure. That resulted in my behavior and conduct toward you and your brother. Now I'm not sure that any words at this moment are enough to justify my actions. However, for whatever it's worth, I would like to offer you my deepest apology. I was wrong about you and Duke, and I am sorry for that. With time, I hope you boys can somehow forgive me," Burcheck sincerely responded.

"Like I said, Detective, I get it. I accept your apology on behalf of me and my brother. And since we're being honest, until this moment, what you didn't know about the gun that killed your wife and my father is that, coming home from school one day, my brother and I were playing around and we found that gun along with a dead body on Baldwin Ave. You can check police reports to validate my story. There is no doubt in my mind that there's a report that exists of a dead body being found on Baldwin Avenue after you lost your wife."

"A report such as that probably does exist. However, I don't need to see it. I heard all I needed to hear in regard to those involved in her death. The purpose of this discussion, for me, is that I man up."

"You did, gracefully, if I do say so myself. As far as my brother is concerned, Detective, yeah, you and him finding common ground on this subject is gonna be difficult. However, he understands me, so he will understand our conversation. He is a hothead at times, but overall, a great brother. A little overprotective, which we both are, but he means no harm."

"Yes, he's definitely another issue. You guys' relationship is like no other relationship I've ever witnessed between two brothers. Bishop, you are a very smart young man. I'm very impressed with how you've grown up.... well-established, I see."

"Yeah, I've done a'ight for myself."

"A'ight would be an understatement. You've done very well for yourself," Burcheck replied, finally able to issue a true smile.

"That has yet to be decided. But now that you and I understand one another, does this make us friends? Or are we forever enemies?"

"Friends, huh? I think friends would be pushing it a little too far, with you being considered a thug and me still a detective. I'm not sure if us being friends is even possible. Isn't that against the street code?"

"It is, but in this situation, I'm willing to make an exception."

"We'll see. Right now, I'm still trying to digest the information about my wife. Her killers need to be brought to justice, and now that I know the truth, it's time to get back home and clear our names."

"I agree, home is definitely on my agenda, but before we start making preparations to go back, I need to make a few more phone calls. There's still information and people I need to locate before we make any decisions."

"What do you mean?" Burcheck asked.

Before Bishop could explain, a call interrupted them.

"Hold up a sec. I need to answer this call."

"Go right ahead, son; handle your business."

"Hello," Bishop said into his Nextel.

"I got your message," the woman's voice on the other end said.

"Thanks for calling back."

"No, thank you for calling. Listen, I have a little bad news for you and Duke," Ms. Qupid replied.

"What is it?"

"Well, about seven days ago, the police found Malik in his Mercedes dead. He was shot five times execution style."

Bishop's face frowned in disbelief. He knew how the news was going to fuck with his brother because of how close they were.

"How the fuck did that happen?"

"I don't know. I have Coco Mango out right now getting that information for you. She's been fuckin' with that gangbanger Slim, tender dick ass dude. He'll tell on his mother if the pussy's good. You know Mango, her shit is like that magic lasso Wonder Woman carries." She smiled.

"Yeah, I understand. It's just, if I tell Duke that Malik was murdered, he's gonna wanna come back home tonight, and I'm not ready for us to come back yet. I need that info and more time."

"I get it. Well, until Mango finds out everything on Malik, here is that other info you requested."

"Bet! That's what's up. Thank you for the information. It's fucked up about what happened to Malik, but he wasn't a friend of mine. I just hate to have to tell my brother this shit. He's gonna be furious!"

"Wow, Bishop. What happened the other night was pretty cold blooded. I would hate to get on your bad side."

"Nah, ma, it isn't like that. It's just that I don't trust people. You, I trust; you don't have to worry about my bad side. We're good. It's everyone else who needs to worry," he said in a serious voice.

"Good to know. I feel bad for everyone else," she replied laughing, but knowing Bishop meant every word he'd said.

"Yeah, as you should!" he replied. "Listen, make sure you tell Mango, with her sexy, Caribbean ass... tell her I said good lookin'. Also, make sure she continues to work on Slim. I need her to get dude to talk more about the murder of the detective's wife. He knows the three gang bangers I'm looking for, one of 'em I believe died in a shootout years ago, if I'm not mistaken. Either way, I need the location of those clowns."

Bishop knew helping Burcheck solve the murder of his wife would be pertinent in clearing his and Duke's names.

"I'm all over it."

"Okay, babe, now you can give me that info."

Providing the information he had requested was going to make his odds against the agents and gangbangers that much greater. Bishop and Ms. Qupid ended their conversation on that note. After hearing what had happened to Malik, Bishop tried to make sense of the news, thinking more about how his little brother was going to react to Malik's death since they were childhood friends.

Bishop and Burcheck quickly rejoined the group. Bishop was hoping to break the news about Malik to Sharelle first. He actually liked Sharelle and thought she was a good fit for Duke.

"Sharelle, can I speak to you for a sec?"

Duke was standing behind her with his arms wrapped around her, getting his grind on. He did not seem like he wanted to let go anytime soon.

"Damn, nigga, you should be talked out by now!" Duke said. He was getting horny and just thinking about finding a spot where they could continue what they had started.

"It's a full-time job, bro. I need to holla at your woman for a minute, if you don't mind. It's not like I won't return her in one piece," he joked.

"Damn, nigga, your girl is right over there," Duke said, pointing in Kara's direction. "I'm pretty sure she needs some quality time with her man," he continued, still thinking with his little head.

Bishop was not going to raise any suspicions or argue with Duke; instead, he agreed and pulled Kara to him.

"You're right, little bro.

"Kara, let's go inside," he said, leaving it at that for now.

Kara just smiled and followed her man inside the compound.

Chapter Thirty-One:
Two Days Later

It was time to put the final touches on going home. Bishop had gotten the opportunity to tell Duke about Malik. It was tough on him, not remembering the last time he had seen his little brother cry. When Duke heard the bad news about his childhood friend, it instantly activated a downpour of emotions for his loss.

"That was my man, bro! Niggas did him dirty. Five times to the head... that was overkill. Yo, I can't wait to get home! Muthafuckas are going to pay for this shit! I put that on my life!" Duke spat.

"Bro, I understand how you feel, he was your friend. I understand you need to kill a bunch of muthafuckas, but before you allow your emotions to dictate what happens next, think for a sec. You gotta stick to the script. I promise you, the agents and gangbangers will all receive the same treatment—*death!* Weeks of planning, you can't fuck that up now! Feel me?!" Bishop said, knowing it was going to be hard to keep Duke focused now.

"Yeah, I heard, but I'm *mad* as hell right now!" Duke replied, knowing Bishop was right.

"I understand your pain. However, we've come too far to let things go up in smoke. We gotta stay focused. Mango should have the information I need on those involved when we touch down. All I need from you is to calm down and remain patient."

"I'm Gucci for now, but just remember, you promised me, I'm punishing those niggas! You dig?"

"Together we're gonna punish all these muthafuckin' niggas! You dig?"

"You already know, real talk."

"A'ight then, nigga. Wipe your fuckin' face and let's get the fuck outta here!"

Gathering everything for warfare, Bishop told his crew they were leaving in twenty-five minutes. Nervous and excited at the same time, Duke and Bishop reassured their women that everything would work out for the best and them staying behind in Arizona was not up for discussion.

In the days leading up to their departure, 4'2 had provided Bishop with a wild bunch of Mexicans, who were illegal immigrants, whose only mission was to seek and destroy. Trained to go. Straight shooters! Even Boss Hog contributed shooters from PA to help fortify the mission. Bishop and Duke knew the challenge miles away was not going to be an easy task, and they also knew losing was not an option. Going home was gonna be a *blast!*

Prudential Center, Devils Vs. Boston...

Agent Collins loved himself a good hockey game. Tonight, Jaromir Jag was making his Bruins debut. The stadium was packed to capacity and louder than it had ever been in the history of the team. Agent Collins was greeted with a note by a little boy.

"Excuse me, sir. I was told to give you this note," the little boy said.

"Excuse me?" Agent Collins replied, looking around to see who had sent it.

"Yes, sir. I was told by your friend to give you this note."

"My friend?" Collins responded, really puzzled now.

"Yes, sir. He said y'all were friends, and he gave me a five-dollar bill to give this note to you."

Agent Collins was looking around and thinking, *'This kid must have the wrong person.'* Taking the note, he read:

I'M BACK! DID YOU MISS ME?

He still did not have the slightest idea who had sent the note. He also did not find it amusing. He barely heard his phone begin to ring because of the loud crowd noise.

"Hello. Who's this?" Agent Collins said into the phone, still barely audible.

"There's no need to shout, Agent. I can hear you perfectly," Bishop responded.

"Stop playing games. Who the fuck is this?!"

"No, Agent, far from a game. I thought by now you'd recognize my voice. Bishop... Bishop Evans. Surely your ass remembers me from the hospital, from City Hall, and from all your bad dreams," Bishop responded.

"WHAT?! Either you're a very smart man or a very dumb one. Now how did you get my number?"

"I'll take smart for fifty bucks, Alex," Bishop joked.

"I notice you like a good hockey game too," Agent Collins said, as he could hear the announcer through the phone calling the same foul that had just happened.

"Yeah, I like sports, not so much hockey, but the cotton candy is great here, and I really get a kick out of watching white boys beat the hell out of each other."

"For a man with a five-million-dollar bounty on his head, you sure have some big balls being here."

"COME ON, BRODEUR! YOU SHOULD'VE HAD THAT!" he said, screaming at the misplay by the Devils' goalie.

"Sorry, Agent, I get a little excited sometimes, but yeah, the bounty isn't about nothing. I tend to move under the radar regardless of the circumstances. My brother is the flashy type; I'm not really a people person. How about you?"

"What I like is irrelevant. Now that you have my attention, what the hell do you want? Are you ready to turn yourself in?" Collins asked, knowing his question was a stupid one.

"Oh no, Agent, definitely not doing that. However, you and I have some unfinished business to discuss."

"What business do we have that's unfinished?

Bishop played a portion of a recorded conversation between Agent Collins and a corrupt politician through the phone:

"Councilman Roberts, I have yet to receive my payments. I can make life very miserable for you. I need my money and I need my money today. I can't continue to have Deputy Mayor Smith hold this property for you, especially such a valuable piece of property at this price. My cut is forty thousand dollars..."

"Like I said, unfinished business."

Agent Collins was trying to understand how in the hell Bishop had that recording, especially since he thought he had everything in the duffel bag. He had been sure he was dealing with a couple of dumb Negroes who did not know their asses from a hole in the ground.

"I see you made copies."

"Yes, Siiirrr. I could've turned it over to the FBI, but I see no fun in that."

"Again, what do you want from me?" Agent Collins wondered and waited to hear.

"I just wanted to let you know I'm back, and I'm coming for you! I'll be in touch... Oh yeah, Agent, before I go," Bishop said, looking right at Collins, "you mean to tell me, with all the money you've extorted from people, you couldn't afford better seats?"

Collins rose and looked around nervously, thinking, 'If Bishop can see where I'm seated, then he must be sitting high and close by.'

"Corporate box, huh? Pretty expensive, I'm impressed, Bishop. You are welcome to come get me. I'll be waiting."

"Good to know, and twenty racks for a sky box isn't that impressive. I spend that on earrings," Bishop said, ending the call.

A few seconds later, Collins rushed out the stadium.

Ms. Qupid was chilling at home, doing her normal daily chores, when there was a knock at the door. She was not expecting anyone, so she did not have a clue who it was.

"Who is it?" she asked, without checking the peep hole.

"The Duke. I have someone with me."

"One second, I'm coming," she said, throwing on her robe.

When she was comfortable, she opened the door and greeted Duke with a big hug.

"What's good, Ms. Lady?"

"I've been better. How are you doing?" she asked, then greeted Burcheck by his title, "Detective."

"I've also been better," Duke replied.

"How're you doing, Ms. ...?" Burcheck paused.

"Qupid," she added to fill the lost detective in. "Very well, Detective."

Duke was done with the small talk. "Fuck all that shit. What happened to my man? Who killed him?"

"Duke, you're so rude. Is he good to talk around?" she asked, knowing the street code even though she was older.

"He is, but we aren't. Let's find an empty room," Duke insisted.

"Okay, back here. The room to your right."

She pointed toward a room, looking back at Burcheck. Then she called a few of the females into the living room to keep an eye on Burcheck.

"The ladies aren't necessary, Ms. Qupid," Burcheck said, waving his hand.

"Yes, they are. *Do you see* all these beautiful women? What's wrong with you? I know you ain't sniffed some good pussy in years," Duke said, being funny.

"I'm sorry Detective, but I don't wanna leave you in here alone. Actually, I don't leave any man in my home alone!" she said, making it clear it was accepting the company or wait outside.

"I understand, and there isn't anything wrong with me!" he said as he shot Duke a look that said, "FUCK YOU, BUDDY!"

"I think he's gay," Duke whispered to Ms. Qupid. They both laughed and headed toward the back room.

"I can give you my version of what happened to Malik, but Coco knows the story better than I do," she assured her homeboy.

"Let me speak to her then. I would rather hear her version," Duke insisted, leaving Ms. Qupid to call her girl Coco into the room.

Duke had heard that Coco was one bad bitch who had a serious wet shot on her. When she entered the room, he looked her up and down, liking her full-figured body. That was all he was going to do was look, because he was a one-woman man nowadays.

"First off, how you doing, baby girl?" he asked.

"I'm fine. Sorry about your friend Malik; that's some real foul shit," she said.

"Well, I appreciate that, but more so, what happened?"

"Well, from what I gathered from Slim—"

"Slim who?" Duke cut her off.

"The gangbanger Slim."

"Okay, yeah, I know who you're talking about. Go 'head," Duke replied, knowing exactly who Slim was.

Slim was known to be a pussy pillow talker, so he knew Ms. Qupid was behind Coco getting the information. That was one reason he and Bishop loved her: she always proved her worth to them.

"Anyway, Slim told me Malik was killed behind what happened to Sha and Gooch at the Key Club. I think that night, five of them were killed. It was an order from a higher-up."

"I don't know, I was in the hospital, but who ordered the hit?" Duke asked, very inquisitive to find out who had had the balls to order his man's hit.

"I heard it was Frank White, their leader. They said your brother was behind everything in retaliation. The word on the street is, Gooch and Sha tried to kill you. They followed you to PA," Coco shared.

Duke looked as if it was all news to him. "Yeah, Gooch, was my man. He tried to kill me? For what? That was my nigga."

"They said because he wanted to take over y'all's business and bring the gangbangers in. He was jealous of your brother," she said.

"Wow! That nigga Slim told you all that, huh? You must be really good, like they say."

"I guess, but yeah, he also told me the two bangers who killed the detective's wife are the same ones who killed Malik. Slim was bragging to me, talking 'bout they took turns shooting Malik in the head. I felt real bad hearing that shit. I was scared that he was saying too much. I had to suck the skin off that nigga's dick to make sure he went to sleep." Coco smiled.

"Listen, baby girl," Duke said to assure her, "you don't have to worry. I'm not gonna let anything happen to you or anyone else in this house. Thank you for looking out. Is there anything else I need to know?"

"Oh yeah, I'm supposed to be meeting Slim tonight around 7:30. It's fifteen minutes after seven now. We're supposed to go out to eat, then a movie," she said, giggling.

"What's funny?" Duke asked.

"He thinks he's a baller. We're going to this new place called Above Restaurant And Bar on South Orange Avenue. Do you know where that is?"

"Nah, ma, but that's what's up. Slim's good. Go ahead and do you. If I need anything else, I know how to find you. Again, good looking out. Here's a little something for your troubles," Duke replied, handing her a stack of blue faces. She looked at the bundle and knew it had to be five grand or more.

They left the room, heading back into the room where Burcheck was accompanied by more pussy than he had ever been in the same room with at one time before. Duke looked at Ms. Qupid, thanked her, and told her he would be in touch with her as needed.

He and Burcheck rushed out the front door. When they made it inside the truck, Duke shared with Burcheck everything Coco had told him. It was amazing, that ten years later, the same two bangers who had killed Burcheck's wife were responsible for killing Duke's best friend. How ironic could that possibly be? The info on where Slim was going to be he kept to himself. That was something Burcheck did not need to know. As Burcheck took it all in, he wondered why the truck was not moving.

"Why are we still sitting here?" he asked.

It was just minutes before Slim was due to arrive to pick up Coco. Duke knew by her conversation that his trick ass was going to show and be on time.

"Aren't we supposed to meet Bishop?"

"Yeah, I called him right before we left and told him we'll be about forty-five minutes late. I have to stop by Malik's house and pay my respects. I gotta drop a few stacks off for his kids too. You know that's what homies do for each other," he said, looking Burcheck right in his eyes.

Burcheck knew Duke's comment had an underlying meaning. It was probably street protocol, but it was real-life shit too.

"I understand, but we can't be out here like this. Did you forget? We have five-million-dollar bounties on our heads. For that kind of money, we gotta watch old ladies crossing the street," Burcheck reminded Duke.

"Nah, I haven't forgotten; we're good. No one knows it's us in this truck. This is a new ride. Listen, we'll only be a sec," Duke assured the cop.

Burcheck and Duke saw Coco emerging from Ms. Qupid's pad, heading toward a black-on-black S class Benz that had just pulled up.

"Isn't that the woman you were just talking to? Damn, there are some beautiful women in that house!"

"Yeah, that's her. They're a'ight," Duke replied, thinking Coco was fine, but she wasn't a hair bump on Sharelle's ass.

"All right?! Man, you're crazy. They're gorgeous, says the gay man," Burcheck said playfully.

"Oh, you heard me..." Duke laughed.

"Whatever, man. Let's go."

Slim and Coco left and Duke tailed them from a distance, knowing Burcheck was still a detective—a wanted one, but still the law. Duke did not think it would be a good idea to fill him in on what he was about to do. They were good, but he did not quite trust him. He knew exactly where Coco and Slim's destination was, allowing Duke to turn off and cut through a few blocks, taking a shortcut. A block behind the restaurant, Duke pulled up in front of an unknown address, leaving Burcheck in the truck

"Wait here for a sec, I'll be right back. Malik's family isn't too big on strangers coming to their house, especially a cop."

"I'll wait here; just hurry up. Don't have me sitting out here forever."

"Man, stop crying. I'll be right back; won't be but a second."

Duke walked toward the unknown address and headed to the side of the house as if he was going inside, to throw Burcheck off. He dashed quickly to his real destination once he was out of Burcheck's sight. Duke hit two fences like he was an Olympic high jumper, landing directly in the restaurant parking lot and timing things perfectly. Slim and Coco were just minutes behind him as he peeped Slim looking for a parking space.

He watched with wide eyes as Slim and Coco parked and situated themselves. Slim turned off the car and they were taking their time getting out. Duke removed his mask from his back pocket, making sure he was fully dressed for this special occasion. With mask on and gun in hand, he watched as Slim got out of the car. Duke waited patiently as the driver's side door opened. Duke ran from between the cars he was hiding behind with his gun pointed directly at Slim's dome. Fear never had the chance to appear. Before Slim knew what had hit him...

Pow! Pow! Pow!

Coco shouted loudly, playing her part like she did not know who was behind the hit. Her face turned beet red when she looked at her white Versace dress Slim had spent a bankroll on, seeing his facial fragments splattered all over her outfit. Duke then followed the same route which he had come, hitting the same fences. A few minutes later, he calmly strolled from around the side of the house, as if that was where he had been all along. When he got back to Burcheck, he could hear the sirens wailing in the distance and growing closer.

"What's going on? While I was inside, were those gunshots I heard?" Duke asked, an inquisitive look on his face.

"Yeah, I believe so. I heard them too. It was around the corner somewhere. Cops are all over the place. We gotta get out of here. You see Malik's family? Are the kids all right?" Burcheck asked, none the wiser.

"Yeah... Under the circumstances, they're doing better than I'd thought. Everyone seems to be holding up well. Let's go meet Bishop. I'm hungry."

"We finally agree on something," Burcheck replied.

Chapter Thirty-Two:
Misdirection...Kaboom

"Listen, not to cut off our enjoyable discussion, but just to let you know, we have this place surrounded. Your little brother's getting very sloppy with killing people," Agent Collins said.

Bishop, not looking surprised by the agent's rhetoric, looked at Duke as he talked to the agent.

"Yeah, my little brother can sometimes be a little careless and messy, which is why it's my duty to keep an extra eye out and clean up behind him."

"I'm not sure what you mean or why you sound so calm, but yes, we know it was him who killed the gangbanger at the Above Restaurant. Agent Ortez is right outside the door where you and your crew are holed up. I am being nice and giving you all ten minutes to come out with your hands up. Here is your opportunity to surrender," Agent Collins said with a menacing grin on his face. He was happy Ortez had the brothers right where they wanted them.

"Agent, you know that's not gonna happen tonight—nor will it happen any time soon. Surrendering has never been a thought in my mind. However, may I ask you one question?"

"What is it?" Agent Collins asked, deciding to play along.

"How did you know where to find us?" Bishop asked, wondering where Collins had gotten the intel on them.

"It's part of my job description to locate criminals like you. It gets to be fun when they think they're smarter than we are as well. Your little lady friend, Flo—"

"Yeah..." Bishop cut him off, knowing where he was going with it.

"See I had a unit sitting outside her condo. Once you made me aware you were back, I sat a car outside her house again. I knew you or your brother would go through and check up on her. I've been doing my homework, so when your little brother arrived, we followed him. You know, that's what we do," Collins said, now getting cocky.

Bishop let Agent Collins continue boasting about his accomplishments. The more the agent thought he was in control, the less notice he would be paying attention to the sounds in the background. Bishop slipped out through the trap door that had been created for a rainy day. The passage led them blocks away from any harm Collins had planned for them and Bishop decided to split off from the two; in case there was an issue, he would go down alone. Agent Collins had failed to realize again the brothers were far from stupid.

Bishop had had the entire house boobytrapped with C 4 for a second rainy day. In his eyes, it was now pouring. Agent Ortez and the local cops he had with him had no idea what was in store for them. They were waiting patiently outside the door for the word to raid the spot. Collins' orders were to make sure the brothers were not able to talk. He had also noted to his partner, that if Burcheck was with them, he would get no special privileges for an extended life.

Collins had been on the right side of the law for a very long time and was close to being able to retire. It had taken a lot out of him to cross the line, coming from a long family line of law enforcement. He knew his father would be rolling over in his grave if he knew his only son, who had followed in his footsteps, was on the take. But Collins was in no way going to retire with just a measly pension. He felt he had protected and served long enough; now it was his turn to be protected and served. His plan was to buy a boat and retire somewhere far away with the money he and Ortez had been stealing over the last ten years. Actually, they had enough to buy their own small island.

"Time is ticking, Bishop. You and your crew only have seconds left to make a decision. Tick tock, tick tock... The bad boys are coming for you, Mr. Evans."

"I've made my decision already, Agent Collins. Make sure you get everyone flowers—nice ones too," Bishop replied.

Bishop was in the second safe house now, one only he and Duke knew about. He was waiting patiently for Duke and Burcheck to arrive when he heard Duke's truck pull in underground. He was livid that his little brother had compromised their plans, but at the same time, he had known when Duke found out who had hit Malik, the revenge would be a sweeter joy than even pussy. Bishop knew Slim had bitten the bullet from Ms. Qupid, who had had no idea her place was being watched. He also knew right away when she told him who was responsible.

When they all entered the back entrance, Duke knew right away that his brother knew the deal. He gave him a nod, meaning, let's talk in private. Bishop knew his little brother well, and he knew Duke had had to pull it off without Burcheck knowing. Duke followed his brother into a back room, closing the door behind them.

"Nigga, what the fuck are you doing?!" Bishop asked, running his hand across his head in frustration.

"Man, what the fuck are you talking about? I told you I was gonna be a few minutes late," Duke replied, trying to play stupid.

"Stop trying to play with my intelligence, Duke! *I know what the fuck you did!* I just got off the phone with Flo, and she told me Slim had been murdered. Tell me that wasn't you? Go ahead and lie."

"Bro, you know I'd never lie to you. Yeah, I did it. You knew I was gonna kill that nigga, and if I had the opportunity, I would bring him back to life and do it again."

"Yeah, but that wasn't the plan."

"I know, but the opportunity presented itself, so I knocked his head off, the same way I plan to do the rest of them lames."

"Duke, I feel you, but you *are not* being cautious."

"Nigga, you think you're smart. I know why you sent that cop with me. You thought, by me having a babysitter that I wouldn't do anything wrong. Right?"

"Not exactly."

"What the fuck's *not exactly* supposed to mean?"

While Duke and Bishop engaged in their heated conversation, Agents Collins, Ortez, and a few more local cops were set up outside the brothers' safehouse. Duke had not realized he and Burcheck had been followed. Bishop's phone rang, interrupting the brothers' verbal dispute. He held up a finger, letting Duke know they would finish their conversation later.

"I wondered when you would call me back, Agent Collins. I've been expecting you," Bishop said.

"Glad to see I wasn't missed."

"No, not at all."

Before Bishop words could make sense, Collins had given the order for Agent Ortez and the rest to break down the door.

"We want the brothers and the detective alive, but if they resist, kill them all!" Collins said, trying to make it look good for the locals involved in the takedown.

Once inside the empty house, Agent Ortez and his team notice the bodies they had seen from outside the house were nothing more than mannequins, appearing to look like someone was inside. Agent Collins asked for an update.

"What's going on in there? Do you have the suspects in custody or not?" Collins asked, licking his lips in hopes that the shit was about over.

"No, sir. That would be a negative," Ortez replied.

"Negative?! What the fuck is going on in there then?"

"Sir, the only thing in here is a bunch of mannequins, making it appear as if someone is in here. They got away, sir," Ortez said.

Collins blood started to boil as his phone started ringing again.

"HELLO! EVANS IS THIS YOU?" Collins yelled into his phone.

"Make them cheap flowers too!" Bishop said, smiling. Then he ended the call.

"Hello? Hello? Hello?"

Right then, Bishop's words became clear to the agent, and he yelled into his two-way, "ABORT! ABORT! IT'S A TRAP! GET OUT OF THERE!"

It was too late. Before Agent Ortez and the others could process the words that potentially could have saved their lives, there was a large explosion!

KABOOOOOM!

Everyone outside ducked for cover. There was fire everywhere, causing everyone to run around in a panic and become lost in a chaotic state. The house Agent Ortez and team were in had been reduced to rubble. The heat was so intense, Collins had to back up the rest of the men for their safety.

'This fuckin' shit is getting on my last nerve!' Collins thought.

He was fuming and ready to kill someone himself. Collins knew it was time to turn up the pressure before he was the next casualty—or he was spending the rest of his life next to the thousands of criminals he had sent away.

On the other side of town, the process of elimination was in play. The Country Boys remained on watch outside of Kabirah's Massage Parlor. The information Coco had given Duke, Bishop had already known, and he had put the Country Boys on Frank White and his crew. They had been following the gang leader for the last couple of days.

The Country Boys sent a text message to Bishop's phone. It read:

I have at least 9 of these crazy ass Mexicans and PA niggas with us. We are outside Kabirah's. Them marks arrived 20 mins ago. There are about 9 to 10 bangers inside the parlor including White. These niggas ready for some action. What you want us to do?

Inside the massage parlor, Frank White was enjoying his weekly session as always. He usually did not come this deep, but word on the street was there was a bounty on his head.

"Listen," Frank said to his number one soldier, Chico. "I don't wanna be disturbed while I'm getting my fuckin' massage. When Kabirah gets here, let her know I wanna see her."

"I gotchu, boss," Chico replied.

"You niggas all heard Frank! Spread the fuck out somewhere. Make sure nobody disturbs big bro. Real talk," Romero, his second in command, said to the guys.

"Yo, where the fuck is Kabirah?" Chico asked. He was all over the girl at the front desk.

"She said she'll be here in five minutes. Damn, you act like I'm her keeper!" the girl responded.

"Tell her Frank is waiting for her in room five as soon as she walks in this muthafucka," Romero added, who was Chico's baby brother.

"Will do," the pretty front desk girl said as she raised an eyebrow, as if to say she did not know who the fuck they thought they were.

"She'll be here in five minutes, big bro," Chico said, peeping his head into the room where Frank was waiting in a robe and smoking a cigar.

"That's what's up. I'll relax until she gets here."

"A'ight, boss. I'll be right outside the door. If you need anything, just yell."

"Just send ol' girl in when she comes. That's everything I need."

"Here she is now, bro," Romero said as he escorted Frank's requested chick back to where he was.

"How're you fellas doing today?

"And of course, Frank, you're right on time for your appointment as always," Kabirah said, smiling.

She loved the way Frank tipped, and when she did extra, he paid extra— like a Brink's truck.

"I'm always on time, baby," Frank replied. "All black people aren't always late, but yeah, I'll feel a hell of a lot better after you put your hands on my body. I'm a little tense; I need my body beat up." He winked and smiled at her.

"I'm here to do just that. So, lie down, relax, and let me make you feel better. I'll try to be gentle."

"Gentle sounds like a plan. I'm relaxing for you."

The Country Boys were ready to take action and each of them had trigger fingers that were itching to get this mess over with. Nobody fucked with the brothers, and Bishop had become their brother, which made everyone attached to him like family. It was said that this Frank White sucker was responsible for a lot of bullshit where his demise was mandatory. They were keeping a heavily guarded eye on Frank White and his knockout crew as they waited for their other brother to arrive.

Bishop was still talking to Duke about everything that had transpired. On one hand, he was mad that he had killed Slim, but on the other hand, he was not. Slim's head had been on the chopping block, but Bishop had just wanted to move a little more carefully. It was too easy for Agent Collins to link things together, which would fuck up his plans even more.

"Duke, you have to continue to trust and believe in me. I have your best interests in life, bro. I wouldn't tell you anything wrong."

"I do, bro, always have. There has never been another man on earth I trust the way I do you," Duke replied.

"I say that for the simple fact that I know you so well."

"Meaning..."

"I had Coco tell you everything. I'm talking about the whole thing with Slim coming to get her, the restaurant, and them going to the movies afterward."

"What? You played me?" Duke asked.

"Nah, I'd never play you. But when it comes to knowing my brother, nigga, I know you all too well. I knew Agent Collins had surveillance outside

Ms. Qupid's condo. While he had agents watching you, I had the Country Boys watching his agents. So, when Slim picked up Coco, the Country Boys watched the agents follow you. That's when I told them to stay on top of everything. The rest is history. KA BOOOOM! In yo' face, nigga!"

"Nigga, fuck that! You played me, then you're poppin' shit like you're mad at me."

As the brothers were bonding like they always did, Burcheck looked on as if the two had lost their damn minds. Cutting into their conversation, he said, "Excuse me. I'm still a cop over here. Y'all blowing shit up, killing FBI agents as if that shit is all right?"

"Listen, them muthafuckas ain't agents anymore. They're criminals just like me and my brother. Now, if you feel as though we're doing something wrong, then do your fuckin' duty, Detective, and lock us up. If not, then get with the fuckin' program. If them muthafuckas get the opportunity to kill us, they will without any hesitation. What the fuck do you think? Do you really believe they're gonna let us surrender, knowing as much as we know?! HELL NO! Them bastards are going to fuckin' kill us! *All of us! Including you!*" Bishop said with a tinge of anger in his voice.

"You're probably right, Evans; you are probably fuckin' right about that," Burcheck said, repeating himself. He knew Collins was just dirty enough to do exactly that, kill the brothers and him as well.

"Fuck probably right, nigga; I am right! Open your fuckin' eyes before they're closed permanently. Yes, it's like that!"

"You are absolutely right. They broke the law years ago. Evidence after evidence of corruption, bribery, extortion, and the murder of my wife. How can I still act like a cop?" Burcheck replied, questioning the oath he had taken.

"No, hold up. You're still a cop, Detective. Don't misinterpret anything I'm saying to you. It isn't like you aren't doing your job, because you are. You are chasing the bad guys, which just happen to be Agent Collins and his team. Yeah, they are the biggest criminals we have ever encountered, muthafuckas who think they are above the law because they are part of the law. Get it through your head *before you truly get it through your head!*" Bishop said sarcastically. "They had plans to eliminate everyone inside," Bishop continued.

"Make a choice, cop, or I'm going to have to make it for you," Duke said.

"I'm going to have to agree with my brother on this one, Detective. Either you make a choice, or we will make one for you," Bishop seconded.

"You brothers know how to make an offer a person cannot refuse, but I understand very well."

"And I have a surprise for you two," Bishop said.

"Nigga, you know I hate surprises," Duke said.

"Trust me, little bro, you and Burcheck won't be disappointed. Watch!"

Chapter Thirty-Three:
Kabriah's Massage Parlor

The rental they were driving pulled up behind the black tinted van parked blocks away from Kabirah's Massage Parlor. Bishop, Duke, and Burcheck slowly got out of their truck and jumped into the parked van. Once inside, Darius gave Bishop details on what they had observed, letting him know the crazy Mexicans and the PA niggas were ready and close by. Allowing the information to register for a second, Bishop finally gave the word.

"Send them in. Kill everyone except the three bangers; I want them left alive. Also, don't kill the receptionist or Kabirah, they have nothing to do with this. Everyone else is considered a casualty of a street war," he ordered.

Everyone was ready. They started putting their silencers on their weapons and made sure they had a live one ready in the chambers. Bishop was ensuring that everything was going to go as expected. Duke and Burcheck were out of the loop to what was about to go down. Bishop had said it was a surprise, and it was going to be just that. The Country Boys told the crazy Mexicans and PA niggas to follow their lead. Not really understanding English that well, they did understand how to kill. They just nodded their heads in agreement, understanding only one word: KILL!

They all entered Kabirah's through the front door, wearing masks and carrying assault weapons. Some customers saw the trouble coming, and they began running out, in fear for their lives. Frank White's bangers started pulling out their guns, trying to return fire, shooting at whomever and whatever came in their direction.

Blam! Blam! Blam! Blam!

Blam! Blam! Blam! Blam!

With Darius and his brothers leading the way, the bangers had no idea what was transpiring. The Mexicans were right behind them, full throttle letting off round after round and switching clips in seconds like trained killers. Walking behind the manpower, with guns drawn but without firing a single shot, Burcheck was doing his best to get the innocent out before the wrong lives were taken. The sight of bangers lying dead throughout the parlor was gratifying to Duke's eyes. Just then, a loud shout from the back was heard.

"They're back here!" Darius yelled, signaling where the grand finale was to take place.

The banger who had stood outside the door on guard and the second in command were already inside, hoping to protect their leader, Frank White. Darius started to light them up through the door, but stopped because he knew Kabirah was in there with them. Frank White and his two most loyal soldiers were trapped like rats.

Following the Country Boys' voice, they made their way to room 5, where Frank White was held up. Bishop tried turning the knob, found the door was locked, and ordered them to remove the door. One of the Country Boys knew exactly what Bishop meant. He left for a few seconds, only to return with the 30/30.

"Knock the hinges off this muthafucka!" Bishop said, stepping back.

After the door was blown completely apart, Bishop instructed a few of the PA men and Mexicans to go in first, feeling they were expendable. The goons rushed in full speed, and as expected, the bangers fired their guns, hitting and injuring as many as they could. *Click! Click! Click! Click! Click! Click!* was the sound of empty guns. The trio had run out of ammo with no way out, and Bishop, Duke, and Burcheck took over. Burcheck had lost all sense of what he represented, knowing the people responsible for killing his wife in cold blood were on the other side of that doorway.

"SURPRISE, NIGGAS! Do you like y'all's gifts?" Bishop asked. Then he checked to make sure Kabirah was all right.

"Yes, I'm all right," she answered, nervous and scared out of her mind.

"Okay; then go on and get outta here," Bishop told her, knowing things were about to get ugly as fuck in room 5. Before she left, Bishop handed her a stack of bills to cover the damage done to her place.

"Thank you," Kabirah said, hightailing it to safety. She ran out the room and didn't think about looking back.

"What the fuck is this? Do you niggas know who the fuck I am? Y'all are some dead niggas!" Frank White exclaimed, trying to pull rank and instill the fear he was feeling into Bishop and his crew.

"Nigga, shut the fuck up! After tonight, you'll be nothing but a fuckin' memory. Ain't nobody worried about that shit you talking!" Duke replied, knowing he was listening to the tone of a man scared to death.

"Okay, okay... Let's get acquainted with one another. Let me introduce everyone. Burcheck, these two over here... Yeah, these are the two muthafuckas responsible for killing your wife. They also killed my brother's friend, Malik," Bishop revealed.

Duke's face frowned up instantly as Bishop continued.

"Now, Mr. Big Mouth over here, well, he really needs no introduction, but since everyone isn't familiar with this lame, Duke, this is Frank White. Frank White, this is Duke. Frank here happens to be the bangers' leader, the one who gave the order to kill Malik. Now the rest is up to you guys. I'm done playing host."

Bishop knew what was to come. He stepped aside to watch Frank's reality play out. Burcheck and Duke looked at each other, both thinking, *'What a fuckin' surprise!'* Finally, they were face to face with the men who'd killed Burcheck's wife and Duke was staring in the ugly mug of the man who'd given the order to kill Malik. There weren't going to be enough flowers in the world for his funeral.

"Frank White is all mine. He gave the order to kill my man. I get to handle him personally. The other two are all yours, Detective," Duke said.

It was the first time Burcheck had ever felt his trigger finger shake. It wasn't out of fear, but from the malicious onslaught he wanted to carry out. No words left his lips, and he wasted no time. He took his badge off his belt and tossed it on the floor, thinking, *'Ten years ago they killed a cop's wife, but today, they killed a fugitive's wife.'* The two bangers mumbled a few words, thinking when they'd first seen the badge, there was no way a cop would pull the trigger. They now realized it was too late and they had spoken their last words.

Burcheck walked straight up on them, shooting them directly in the head, one in the temple and the other in the forehead. His obligations as a cop were nonexistent as he stood over the bangers' lifeless bodies. As the two bodies lay there motionless, Burcheck stood over them, shedding a tear for his beloved wife; then he emptied his entire clip. Frank White looked on, shaking for dear life.

"Yo, what the fuck are you doing? You're a fuckin' cop, for God's sake. Man, what happened to you?" Frank pleaded, hoping to get his day in court, but it was too late for that. He was going to be judged by more than twelve of his peers.

"They killed my wife! That's what happened to me!" Burcheck spat in anger, looking at Frank White.

"Duke, you'd better kill this motherfucker before I do," Burcheck continued, knowing the initial order had been given by the Frank who sat on the massage bed with only a towel wrapped around his body.

Frank tried to stand and reach for his clothes; he had a Glock tucked in his pants. He knew it wasn't likely he would get to it, and if he did, these niggas he was facing had an army with them and a cop. He could only think at the moment of all the lives he had ordered taken, all the families he had destroyed for his own gain and some just for fun. You lived by the sword, you died by the sword, and no one knew that better than he did.

'Nigga, getcha bitch ass back on the table. I'm a give your ass a real fuckin' massage. I've never liked you gangbanging niggas anyway. This day right here was inevitable. Instead of going after my man and killing him, you niggas should've come at me or my brother, but since you ordered the hit, wrong move! Oh yeah, before you take your last breath, let me share a little something with you. Did you know your boy Sha was FBI? A straight RAT?!" Duke asked smiling, knowing that every dog really did have their day.

Both of Frank White's eyebrows were raised and his flushed skin tone showed disbelief at Duke's words.

"Yeah, it's true, nigga. You probably also gave the order for Gooch to cross a real nigga. Fuck that, I'm tired of talking!"

Pow! Pow! Pow! Pow! Pow!

"That was for my man."

Pow! Pow! Pow! Pow! Pow!

"That was for the fuck of it, bitch nigga!" Duke wanted more. He wanted to sever the nigga's head and take it to Malik's mother, but the sirens were getting closer.

"Yo, y'all did good. Cops will be here soon. Grab the injured and let's bounce," Bishop said, not wanting to leave any of these people behind.

The Country Boys were cock strong, so it was easy throwing the sinewy Mexicans across their shoulders. Darius' younger brother was so strong he carried three amigos at once. He had Darius grab the surveillance tapes, and they were out of there just as fast as they had entered.

Change Of Scenery...

Agent Collins had commandeered a corner office in the newly designed precinct on the corner of Bergen and Clinton Ave. He had just snapped his favorite ink pen in half, causing blue ink to splatter all over his white shirt. He was livid about losing his partner and the Evans boys continuously getting the upper hand on him. He knew this couldn't be a good thing for his future. He called a meeting, knowing he had to regain control of the situation and do it as quickly as he could. He didn't know what the Evans brothers were up to, and from this point on, he was no longer going to underestimate Bishop's wits.

Agent Collins erupted something furious, lashing out at everyone, breaking shit and tossing paperwork in the air, knowing he was going to be the one chosen to tell his partner's wife he wasn't coming home because a bunch of miscreants had made cinnamon toast out of him.

"Excuse my temper, fellow agents and officers. I'm just disgusted with how this case has been going. WHO THE FUCK DO THESE BROTHERS THINK THEY ARE? THEY'RE KILLING COPS AND AGENTS AS IF IT'S NORMAL BEHAVIOR. HOW THE FUCK ARE THESE BASTARDS MOVING AROUND WITHOUT BEING DETECTED? I'M THE FUCKING FBI! THESE BROTHERS ARE MOVING AROUND AS IF THERE ISN'T A FIVE MILLION DOLLAR BOUNTY ON THEIR HEADS," he yelled.

"Raise the fuckin' bounty to twenty-five million. I want their fucking heads on my desk within forty-eight hours, the damn rogue ass detective's too. All of them, and everyone associated with them," he continued.

Collins was so mad that he demanded assistance from everyone in the department, asking them to use every resource available to locate these madmen. For him, desperate times were calling for desperate measures; his career depended on it. As he continued with his agenda, Councilman Roberts and Deputy Mayor Smith entered the meeting unannounced, bringing the meeting to a halt.

"Excuse me for interrupting, ladies and gentlemen, but we are here to speak to Agent Collins in private," the councilman said, sending a ping of fear through Collins.

"I know you all have a busy day ahead, so we'll try not to keep the agent long.

"Agent, can we speak to you for a sec?" the deputy mayor said in a calm voice.

"Sure, Deputy Mayor," Collins replied, looking past the two of them for minute, issuing orders and showing that it was still his show—for now.

"Ladies and gentlemen, get to work. Turn over every rock and talk to every CI on file. I want successful results in the next forty-eight hours. Thanks for your cooperation. Everyone's dismissed," he continued, taking a napkin and wetting it, trying to blot the ink stain.

The group of law enforcement personnel shook hands with both the councilman and deputy mayor as they exited the meeting. The last person out closed the door behind him. The two higher power men stood in the center of Agent Collins' office. The expression of disappointment was visible on both men's faces.

"Look here, Collins, we thought you had everything under control? This was supposed to be a quiet and easy task. Cops and agents dying! Shit blowing up! Who the fuck are these guys?!" the deputy mayor asked in a firm but aggressive tone.

"And what about that rogue detective?" the councilman added.

"I'm not sure what part Detective Burcheck is exactly playing, sir, but I intend to eliminate him right along with the brothers. Yes, a few mishaps, but everything is under control. The brothers and the detective will all be terminated within forty-eight hours...you have my word on it," Collins boasted, not sure he could actually come through.

Collins racked his brains on how two black kids could be so allusive to a bunch of trained professionals with all the technology in the world. They could find Bin Laden in a hole in the desert, but they couldn't find two kids in Jersey?

"They'd better be! There's a lot at stake, Agent. Do you need to be reminded of that?!" Councilman Roberts asked in a manner that let Collins know, any further mishaps and there was going to be trouble for him.

"Trust me, Councilman, I understand very well what's at stake. I understand *very well* what's at stake," he said, repeating himself. "I underestimated the brothers' capabilities, but I am on top of it now like flies on shit," Collins said, almost as a plea for time.

"What the fuck are you saying, Agent? Are these two punks too much for the local police, and now the FBI's involvement? Hell, instead of arresting them, should we hire them to run National security?" the deputy mayor joked.

"Not at all, sir. It isn't like that at all. It's more like, I didn't expect these brothers to be as bright as they are. Like you said, sir, they blew up a fucking house—destroyed it with everyone inside, including my partner. So again, no disrespect to anyone, Deputy Mayor, but I know exactly what's at stake."

'Agent, we have to retrieve that evidence by any means necessary. These guys have to die!" the councilmen said, with the most serious look in his eye. The wrinkles in his forehead told the story of how worried he had become.

"That is exactly the plan, Sir. Capture and kill them, and retrieve the evidence."

"Listen, I don't give a fuck who they think they are, do whatever you have to do to get the job done!" the councilman said, getting frustrated.

"It's kill or be killed!" the deputy mayor added.

Before the deputy mayor's comment had the chance to fade away into an afterthought, an officer burst into Agent Collins' office, putting the men's intense agenda on pause, only to make the statement Mayor Smith had made about the brothers that much more apparent.

"Don't you see me in here with Deputy Mayor Smith and Councilman Roberts?! You'd better have a good reason for bursting into my office!" Collins said, slamming his fist down on his desk.

"Sir, I apologize for my barging in, but it couldn't wait. Calls came into the station about shots being fired at Kabirah's Massage Parlor. We have officers on the scene, and they said it's a bloodbath down there. From the information we've gathered from the officers thus far, there was a shootout between two groups of guys. The result is there are twelve gangbangers dead, several innocent bystanders injured, and one of the fatalities is gang leader Vince "Frank White" Johnson.

"Witnesses at the scene claim to not have seen anything. They heard gunshots and took cover. What do we do, sir? It's your call," the officer said, still apologizing to the councilmen and deputy mayor for entering their meeting without permission.

As the younger officer delivered the horrible news to the powerful authority figures, Collins let the intel soak in. Collins could only place responsibility for this mess on one group. He knew there were only two men in the whole state insane enough to even do something this horrific—*the Evans Brothers!*

"Thank you, Officer, for the intel. I'll take care of the rest. Get my car ready; I'll be going down to the scene," he said, dismissing the officer. Then he looked both of his higher-ups dead in their eyes.

"I guess this is the brothers' work too, right?" the deputy mayor asked.

"As I mentioned at the beginning of our conversation, sir, these brothers are definitely a top priority of mine. I'll handle it! They have become public enemy number one and two," Collins replied.

"Deal with it now!" the deputy mayor responded.

"And don't fuck up!" the councilman and deputy mayor said at the same time.

"I won't," Collins said, ending their conversation and rushing to his vehicle.

Once in the car, the agent could only think about something Detective Burcheck had said to him about the brothers. *These are guys you wouldn't want to run into in a dark alley.* A small chuckle came across his lips in agreement now that he had seen their wrath. "Bishop and Duke Evans, where the fuck are you?" Collins said. He thought he had spoken under his breath, but he actually had spoken aloud.

"Is there something wrong, Agent?" the young officer driving asked.

"Not at all, son... not all."

Chapter Thirty-Four:
Keep Your Friends Close, But Your Enemies Even Closer

Detective Burcheck was still fighting with guilt. He had thought revenge would be the sweetest joy—next to getting pussy, as he'd heard Duke chant—when he busted Frank White's ass. Once again, he found himself stuck between a rock and hard place. Not feeling any closure for what he had done in taking a life himself, Detective Burcheck was struggling with his conscience, wondering what his wife was thinking of him. He knew she was watching him; he could feel it in his bones. He remembered she used to love watching the court shows and would sit in front of the television all day long, chanting, "Two wrongs can never make a right." He had gone and done exactly what she had been against.

Now they were all at another location, probably owned by the brothers, celebrating, like death was worth a reward. Everyone was tipping champagne bottles—except Bishop Evans. He acknowledged that the task was far from over, and therefore, saw no need to celebrate. His little brother Duke threw on 2Pac's *Greatest Hits*, sipping and pouring some of his drink out, telling his friend Malik it was for him. The crew got beyond themselves enjoying the moment. What was so crazy about everything taking place was, even though the Mexicans barely understood the English language, they knew exactly what 2Pac was saying.

"Come with me / Hail Mary quick see / Killer but don't push me..." one of the Mexicans drinking a Corona chanted.

Duke found the Mexican killer to be extremely funny, encouraging him to keep singing and instructing one of the Country Boys to turn up the music.

"Blast that shit, my nigga. Let that nigga sing. Go ahead, nigga! Sing that shit!" Duke said, bouncing his head side to side. The Mexican was smiling at Duke's request and verbally assaulted Pac's lyrics with his accent.

Duke saw that his brother wasn't as cheery, and he watched every move Bishop made from a distance. Burcheck and Bishop headed inside to the back room to chop it up. Once inside the room, Bishop's back was to Burcheck, only to turn around to face Burcheck who had his gun drawn, pointing straight in his face. Bishop wondered what the fuck was wrong with the detective.

"I can't do this shit with you anymore. I'm nothing like you and your brother. I protect people, not kill them. I am placing you under arrest. Hand over your gun, Evans."

"Are you serious? You're locking me up? I don't think so," Bishop said calmly.

"Listen, I'm not fooling around with you. Pass me your gun, or I will shoot you where you stand."

Bishop handed Burcheck his heat, staring straight into his eyes.

"Thank you. I'm sorry for this, but I can't continue to do this your way. Too many people are dying. That's not what I wanted. That would not be what my wife wanted."

"Do you really believe, if you shoot me, you're gonna get out of here alive?" Bishop asked, still as calm as he was a moment ago.

"Yes; I'm walking straight out the front door. I'm not going to shoot you if I don't have to, so don't make me."

"What is it? Is it because you shot and killed those bangers? Your guilt getting the best of you? If so, they deserved it. Remember, they killed your wife. You said you wanted revenge, and you got it."

"Revenge is definitely what I wanted, but to kill them, that isn't what I wanted. They need to pay for their crimes. Arresting them was my intention, locking them up for life, not death by my hands. I'm not God, and neither are you or your brother," Burcheck said, shaking now.

"Listen, who's to say they would've even gone to prison? A trip to hell was more their fate. They were corrupt human beings. Death for the two bangers was their only option. I get it though. You're a detective, a cop—you lock people up. Two less bangers you have to worry about."

"Do you hear yourself talk sometimes? You've lost your mind."

"Nah, Detective, my mind is very much intact. I've just gained a higher perspective on reality. Some things are unavoidable. Everything we've been through up to this point was meant to happen, there was no avoiding this, which is why after everything is all said and done, you'll never see or hear from me or my brother ever again."

"As good as never seeing or hearing from you or your crazy ass brother again may sound, you and your brother have done too much. The both of you have to pay for all the crimes you've committed."

"And by locking us up, does that make you better than us, Detective? Nobody forced you to kill those two bangers. You asked for this! No matter what else takes place between you and me, your conscience will still be dirty. In fact, you need me more than you actually know. I'm the only one who can really give you your life back. Plus, not only do I have evidence on the agent and corrupt political figures, I also have evidence on you killing them two bangers."

"What do you mean by that? What are you talking about?" Burcheck asked, a surprised look on his face.

Noticing the door opening slowly and quietly, and figuring it was Duke, Bishop began to disclose things to Burcheck arrogantly.

"Yeah, you heard me correctly. I have you on camera killing them bangers. You should already know I come prepared, always steps ahead of my adversaries. You've already said we will never be friends, so why wouldn't you expect this from me? Keep your friends close, your enemies even closer," he disclosed, smiling at the detective.

"I was a fool for trusting you. This was your plan all along, huh?"

"Nah, not really. I really was hoping it wouldn't come to this, but this is just how things played out. Your move, Detective. You wanna try and checkmate? You've lost your queen already."

Hearing his brother tell the detective it was his move, Duke knew it was his cue. Standing outside the room ever since the two had gone inside, Duke slightly opened the door, quickly burst inside, and planted his fifty caliber directly to the back of the detective's head. Both brothers were smiling with devilish grins plastered on their faces. Burcheck's gun was drawn on Bishop, and Duke's gun was placed firmly at the back of Burcheck's head, cocked back and ready to fire.

"Muthafucka, you've got a tenth of a second to get that fuckin' gun out of my brother's face before I drop you to the floor!" Duke said, wanting to kill Burcheck even if he did remove the gun.

"Shoot me, I shoot your brother. The choice is yours, Duke Evans," Burcheck said, using his government name.

"See the difference between you and me, Detective, is I'm not afraid of dying. So, if I give my brother the nod to shoot you, he'll do it without hesitation. I'd rather die like a man than live like a coward. And, honestly, I don't think you have it in you to kill me," Bishop stated.

"Okay, since you don't think so, give your brother the nod," Burcheck challenged Bishop.

"Bro, I've been waiting to knock his head off from day one. I can shoot him before he shoots you, and I promise you, I won't miss."

"I know you won't miss, little bro. Just wait a sec. Let's give the good detective time to make a decision.

"So, what's it gonna be, cop?"

Burcheck was now contemplating his odds, knowing the deck was stacked against him. *'And even if I do shoot and kill Bishop, how would I escape?'* he thought.

"Okay, okay. If I do decide to lower my gun, how do I know your crazy ass brother isn't still gonna shoot me?" he asked, knowing Duke wasn't playing with a full deck.

"You don't know. Again, he understands me, so he'll understand what I say next," Bishop assured the detective.

"Okay, I'm lowering my gun," Burcheck said, one hand up and the other lowering his gun.

Duke was disappointed he couldn't kill the detective. Burcheck lowered his gun like he'd said. Bishop grabbed both guns quickly, while Duke still had his gun planted at the back of Burcheck's head, even though his brother was no longer in harm's way. He stalled for a second before removing the gun. Duke then drew his arm back until it couldn't go back any further and let it rip forward with brute force, smacking the detective with the butt of his gun and knocking him unconscious.

"Man, why the fuck did you do that? He wasn't gonna kill me," Bishop said, looking at Duke.

"Damn, nigga, that's the thanks I get for busting this pig upside his head?!"

"Thanks, but we have to think, bro. There is no time for mistakes. We are at the end of this shit and we don't need new shit on our plate," Bishop said, reminding Duke he needed to stick to the plan.

"That's what's up. And so what, nigga? Whether he was gonna kill you or not, fuck that! Never disrespect a man in his own house," Duke replied. "That's the reason I knocked his ass out—let him know what's what and not to do that shit again. Nigga, I'm going back in the living room. Yo, you gotta see the Mexican sing 2Pac. Bro, this nigga is funny as hell," he continued, still making light of the situation like only he could.

"Bro, you're crazy."

Duke smiled as he exited the room. Bishop was going to follow his little brother's lead, but decided against it. He had questions only Burcheck could answer, so he stayed behind, waiting for the good detective to wake up from his nap. It didn't seem like he'd be waking up any time soon. Duke had put a whammy on him. It was such a hard blow that Bishop thought he'd felt it. A few minutes after leaving the good detective asleep and Bishop playing guardian, Duke walked back into the room with a suggestion.

"Bro, I can't party with these dudes all night. This isn't my twist. I need to surround myself around some beautiful women, and I know just the place, Candy Girls!"

"The strip club on Lyons and Irvington, the new spot?" Bishop asked.

"Yes, sir. Nigga, you know, your candy spot!"

"My candy, huh?" Bishop smiled, thinking about the comment.

"Yeah, you heard correctly. Yoouuurrr candy! You did smash, right?"

"Nigga, stop acting like I don't know who you're talkin' about. I heard she's thick as hell now," Bishop said, reminiscing on their old thing.

"I've heard the same shit. Since she's been back and everything has been going on, I haven't seen her yet, which is why I'm trying to hit that spot up. A little flirting never bothered anyone," he said, forgetting about Sharelle for a moment.

"Okay, nigga. Sharelle finds out and somebody is gonna get fucked up." Bishop replied.

He knew his brother was trying to turn over a new leaf in the ladies department, but Candy was a bad bitch. She might have made Obama step out on Michelle.

"I love mine, my G, and I'm not trying to fuck that up for nothing or no one—no matter how good or thick Candy is looking. Just a little fun to get some of this pressure off a nigga," Duke said, licking his lips.

"I hear ya ass, lil bro."

"Listen, I know how you feel about us going out in public, especially since the streets are talking and a five-million-dollar bounty on our heads, but I have it all covered."

"Oh yeah, you have everything covered," Bishop said in a condescending tone.

"Why wouldn't I? You ain't the only one who knows how to plan shit. Seven years gone, nigga! I think I've done well for us."

"Very well, if I say so myself."

"A'ight then. Dig, I called Candy and told her to clear the place out, keep only the bad bitches who were going in. So, bro, she knows all too well not to cross us."

"Nah, lil bro, her crossing us is the furthest thing from my mind. Loyal broad she is. It's just that, I was waiting for this muthafucka to wake up. You hit him kinda hard," Bishop said, looking at Burcheck sleeping like a baby.

"As I should have. He's lucky I didn't *really* hit him! But, yeah, I understand. Bro, dude ain't waking up no time soon. He'll probably be out until tomorrow, at least that's how the shit is looking. Yo, we can leave a few

PA dudes to watch over him in case he does wake up. I was thinking maybe a few Mexicans, but they might kill him," he said, causing both of them to laugh.

"Yeah, they would fuck around and kill this nigga. We don't want that. Okay, your little suggestion sounds like something nice. Beautiful women... Mmmmm hmmm." Bishop nodded in agreement that the Mexicans might off Burcheck.

"That's what the fuck I'm talking about, just like Candy."

"But check it, the only reason I'm coming is so you don't get into any more trouble. We've got to be careful."

"Come on, bro, trouble? There's only gonna be us and a bunch of sexy ass women in that spot," Duke said, laughing at Bishop always being cautious. "Nigga, what kind of trouble could I possibly get into?"

"As long as we understand one another, we can go. No fuckin problems, feel me?"

"Understood. Now, let's go look at some bitches."

"A'ight then, let's ride."

Before they left, they gave the PA dudes clear and strict instructions on what to do and what not to do, in case the good detective woke up from his deep sleep. They let them know of physical restraints if he tried anything.

"Just don't kill him!" Bishop told the one he had put in charge.

Now comfortable with the decision to go to Candy's, Bishop thought about he and Candy's night of passion. He figured going out couldn't hurt. An opportunity for them to be around beautiful women could be a well-deserved treat for the fellas. They would have a chance to release their built-up aggression. He envisioned what he remembered Candy looking like. She stood at five ten and a half, a model type, dark-skinned, a gorgeous face, short hair, nice smile. Since she'd come back to Jersey after moving away for a few years of trying to "play house," her ambition as a rider had been nonstop.

Once petite framed, but now country thick, she'd opened her second well-established business, a strip club in Atlanta and now one in New Jersey, full of nothing but the best of beauties. Candy knew failure for her wasn't an option. Her motto was, Act like a woman and think like a woman, *a woman who knows exactly what she wants!* She had never had a problem going after what she felt she deserved.

The crew got more excited the closer they got to the spot. Bishop reiterated his directives on what not to do while they were out partying. Attentive and clear on everything, everyone was in compliance. The Duke couldn't wait to see Candy. He hadn't seen her in years. When he'd called to make the private accommodation, he thought the sound of her voice was magnetic, reeling him in like it was her game plan. Hearing her voice made his commitment even stronger to convince Bishop to go out—the only one response he was looking for from his brother and he'd gotten it: We're going.

They pulled into the parking lot and headed to the back door of the club. The brothers looked on, impressed at how she'd established herself. Just like Candy, they thought—classy, sophisticated, and much like the rest of her lifestyle, with extravagant taste. Duke carried seventy-five thousand in a briefcase. Instead of making it rain, the brothers intended to make it *snow!* Duke hit her line right away.

"Hello. Is this you, Duke?" she asked in her sexy voice.

"Yeah; we're at the back door," he replied, licking his lips again. He couldn't wait to party.

"Okay, I'll be right there," she said, heading to the back entrance.

A few seconds later, the woman in charge greeted the crew. Both brothers captured a good look at the Amazon beauty and admired how well she had taken care of herself. Not putting too much emphasis on her appearance, they were ready to party.

"How have you fellas been?" she asked as they trailed her through the back hall, both watching her thick ass sashay side to side.

"How're you doing?" the whole crew said in response in unison.

"Fine; thanks for asking.

"What's up with you two? Are you too cool to speak?" she asked, looking at Bishop and Duke.

"Nah, it isn't like that. We were just allowing these fools to speak first. They're lusting right now at the sight of these lovely ladies, including yourself," Duke replied.

She quickly noticed Duke's flirtatious behavior and gave it right back.

"Well, that's good to know, handsome. Anyway, I have twenty-five of my hottest women here, ready to show you boys an amazing time, and they expect healthy tips for their services. Private rooms are available to be used as fit. And we have all the liquor you can buy. I am y'all's hostess for the night. If there is anything you need, *and I do mean anything,* please, fellas, do not hesitate to ask," she said smiling, showing a double row of perfect, white teeth. It was obvious she'd had some dental work done, and it looked good.

When she spoke, she was checking both brothers out, looking them both directly in their eyes, making them aware of her unlimited power to please.

"That is why we came prepared, and of course, we expect everything too. I called and asked you to clear the space out for me and the crew, and you did that without any questions. So, healthy tips are exactly what we intend to provide. Anything less would be beneath us. For now, we'll have a few bottles of Ace of Spades; let's say, twenty-five bottles to start us off."

"You've come fully prepared I see. Three or four Club Candy's sounds good. Is that all you boys want?" she asked, liking the way things were starting off.

"At the moment, yes," Duke said, as he was doing all the talking.

"And what about you, Bishop, Mr. Too Serious To Talk?"

"You know me, doesn't much change as for what I want. This is my brother's show though; I'm just along for the ride," Bishop said, throwing both his hands in the air.

"Still playing the big brother role, huh? Which is what I have always adored about you two. Y'all stick together. Brotherly love is the best way to describe it."

"You described it perfectly, because there is definitely a lot of love between these two brothers," Bishop agreed with her.

"Awww, isn't that sweet."

"We don't do sweet, at least not with one another."

"I like that classic response," Candy replied, showing them to a table in front of a huge stage that was custom built. Candy beckoned a nice-looking waitress to come over to the table.

"This is Bonnie," she said, looking at the brothers.

"Yes, Ms. Candy. What do you need me to do, boss?" Bonnie asked.

Bonnie had the biggest titties and the smallest waistline Bishop had ever seen.

"Bring these guys twenty-five bottles of Ace of Spades ASAP!"

"Yes, Ms. Candy, coming right up."

Bonnie called for two more girls to help her carry the load the brothers had ordered.

"I dig your little setup you've got here," Duke said, scoping the place out. He saw a few chicks standing off to the side.

"Hey, Candy. Isn't that Coco Mango, Shorty, and Fah over there? Ms. Qupid's girls?" Duke asked, looking at the familiar faces.

"Yes, sure is," she replied gingerly.

"They're getting money with you now?" he asked curiously.

"No, it's not like that. Ms. Qupid and I are intertwined in a business venture. She has a nice portion of herself invested in Candy Girls. We came to the conclusion that together would be more beneficial for both of us. That whole 'us competing with one another' thing serves no purpose. You know me, I'm not the selfish type and neither is she. which is what makes us that much better together as a team."

"I like that. I just have to ask, did you and her came up with this idea all on y'all's own?" Bishop asked, letting his inquisitive side get the best of him.

"Still a smart ass I see," Candy said with a sly grin. "Stop trying to play me. You know I have always been a strong, independent, and very intelligent female, which is what attracted you to me—among other qualities, I might add."

"You're probably right, but trust me, being attracted to you had nothing to do with you being smart—although I loved your brain. You might just be the complete package for the right nigga," Bishop added, knowing Candy was heavy on the intelligence side.

"Whatever, Bishop. I'm not going to sit here and engage in your antics. I see you didn't deny being attracted to me."

"Past tense, babe. Sooooo behind me," Bishop said, having a quick flashback of him and Kara in their hotel room.

"You and I know better," she said, pushing the envelope, which was making her pussy wet.

Bishop was acting tough with her and Candy loved it rough. Just as the conversation was getting heated and Candy's pearl tongue was thumping up against her mini skirt, one of her staff approached.

"Excuse me, but here's y'all's order," the pretty chick said. Duke was checking out the waitress, who was a bad redbone with a southern accent that turned him on.

"I can tell you aren't from around here, right? Your country, sexy ass, and you got them legs like a Mississippi vixen," Duke said, slapping her on her ass.

"No, I'm not from around here I'm actually from Detroit."

"Nah, babe, don't ever address me as sir. That shit ain't cool."

"Sorry; what should I call you?" she asked, hoping she hadn't blown her tip.

"Listen, Ms. Seven Mile, I'm The Duke. Yeah, call me The Duke; sir is for an old man with a minivan and a key chain full of unnecessary keys." Duke laughed.

"Well, in that case, I'm pleased to meet you, The Duke."

"And this is my big brother, Bishop."

"How're you doing, Bishop?"

"I'm fine," Bishop said, keeping it short with her.

Duke was remembering that a couple of his guys were from the same place she was.

"Detroit, huh? I brought some of my brothers with me from Detroit," he said, cocking his neck back some to get a better look down her uniform.

"Really? That sounds cool."

"What's your name, little mama?"

"You can call me Bonnie."

"It's a pleasure to meet you, Bonnie."

"The pleasure is all mine, The Duke."

"You're beautiful. Married, boyfriend, what?" Bishop chimed in and asked the Mariah Carey look alike.

"Thanks for the compliment. I'm single. Is there anything else I can get for you guys?" she bashfully replied as she put the last bottle in front of Bishop.

"Only time will tell, babe. For now, we're Gucci," Duke replied, cutting Bishop off before he stole the show.

"Okay, I get it. So, what about you, Bishop?"

"I'm good."

"All right. If you guys need anything else, call me. See you later," she said, winking at the brothers as she strutted and Candy off.

"Gotchu. Later."

"Peace," Bishop spoke at the same time.

As they both admired her beauty, Duke noticed she put a little more emphasis in her walk this time. They were both competitive when it came to times like these. It always added a little fun to things. Duke was watching his crew as they were enjoying popping bottles and doing big things in the company of Candy's stable of beauties.

Candy was grateful and pleased with how generously the men were treating her girls. She stood back in the distance for a second, admiring her establishment and the work she had put in to make it a success. At the same time, she reminisced on the pleasure she and Bishop had once shared. She couldn't help remembering the moments, knowing the sex was some of the best she had ever had, but their history was past tense in real life. Candy had her sights set on a newer delicacy who went by the name of The Duke. He had filled out a little more than the last time she had seen him. He also had a take charge mentality that turned her on heavily. She was not shy about what she wanted. Being shy left closed mouths and dry pussies, and that wasn't her style.

"Excuse me, gentlemen. As much as I think the bonding between brothers is sexy, there are too many fine women in this place for you two to just be over here spending this much time together," Candy said, getting her word game together.

"So, what are you saying, Candy?" Duke asked.

He wasn't seeing what was coming, but Bishop had sensed it from the moment she'd approached.

"So, I'm saying, I'm sorry to have to break up y'all's little whatever this is, but I would like to borrow you, Duke, for a sec. I hope you don't mind."

She called her girl Coco over, and Bishop saw the play she was making. He knew he had some things to discuss with Coco.

"Oh sure, you can borrow my brother. I don't mind at all," he said with his own sly grin now.

"I'm sitting right here. Decisions are being made about me without my approval, as if I don't count or something," Duke said, putting his bottle down for a second.

"Stop it, handsome," Candy said, rubbing Duke's leg. "You very much count, and I'm very sorry if that's how we made you feel. There is no way possible we can sit here and act as if you do not exist. You are very much in existence, babe. Believe me... very much!" she continued, changing her tone to an even sexier alto. She was giving him eye contact, with as much lust as any porn star could have mustered up.

"Yeah, bro, what she said, minus the babe and handsome stuff," Bishop said, causing everyone to laugh.

"A'ight then. Borrow me? What's wrong? One of my dudes acting up or something?"

"Not at all. Everyone is on their best behavior. I just want a little private time with you so we can catch up on the good life, that's all."

"That's a good combination. Let's go talk," Duke replied, grabbing his bottle.

Coco approached the VIP booth at the same time Candy grabbed Duke's hand and escorted him to a more intimate and seductive room in her club. Bishop watched and grinned as his little brother parted ways, hoping he didn't do anything sexually he might regret. When Duke was out of his sight, Bishop returned his attention to talk to Coco about business.

Candy's special room was set up sweet. Duke could tell this particular room was hers and no one else's. She picked up a small remote and dimmed the lights, using the same remote to control the Bose sound system. While H Town's *Knockin' Da Boots* was blaring through the little speakers that sounded twenty times bigger than they were, Candy excused herself for a moment to slip on something a little more enticing to the male eye.

Good lovin', body rockin', knockin' boots all night long, yeah / Makin' love until we tire to the break of dawn...

H Town was sounding good and saying some shit that also was on Duke's mind.

"Thank you for waiting patiently for me," Candy said, now wearing a see-through outfit that exposed nipples a jeweler could use to cut diamonds.

"Don't mention it. Thank you for changing clothes," Duke replied, sipping the last little bit of Ace Of Spades in his bottle.

"I had to slip into something more erotic. I intend on giving you a long and enticing lap dance, something you'll never forget. I came out of retirement for our moment."

"It feels so good to be The Duke, especially if Ms. Candy has come out of retirement for me. You're looking sexy as fuck in that little shit."

"Delicious enough to taste?" she asked, moving in close enough to void any personal space.

"Like *Candy,* babe!"

They both laughed.

"That was cute, but yes... sweet like candy, babe."

"A confident woman, huh? Well, I would hope so. You're beautiful."

"Thank you, and you're handsome. You've grown into a very strong and manly man," Candy said, gripping Dukes biceps.

"That's what's up. It's good to know we're on the same page."

"More than you know, babe. Anyway, I wanted to get you alone so I could actually see for myself how much you've grown up."

"See for yourself, into a grown ass man, babe."

"I see. Plus, I would like to ease your mind. Although it can be good being The Duke, I'm pretty sure it's twice as hard being you also."

"Hard would be an understatement, but I have no complaints; it comes with the territory. My mind could definitely use some soothing. Are you sure you're capable enough to pull off the impossible?" he asked, feeling his manhood ready to rise to the occasion.

"Absolutely, I'm confident enough. It shouldn't be that difficult; this is what I do."

"Oh yeah? I've been told it's very difficult."

"I'm up for the challenge. I understand how you have the weight of the world upon your shoulders, which is why for a few hours, I'm going to do my best to eliminate a little of that pressure—if not all of it."

"If that's your plan, then why are we still talking about it?"

"Funny too. I love a thug with a sense of humor," she replied.

"That I have... love me."

"The talking is so that we, as adults, act as adults. I don't want you getting into any trouble by being in here with me. I wouldn't want your girl cutting you... or me," she said, fishing for information to see what Duke's status was. Candy was wondering if he had a bitch or if he was single.

"Me getting in trouble is the last thing on my mind. Yes, I have a girl, if that's what you wanna know. All that cutting shit though, nah, my chick isn't into violence. She and I have a wonderful understanding, and she knows her position in my life. Plus, she also knows I'm attracted to beautiful women. She has no worries about her position at all, so neither should you." Duke expressed, ready to fuck.

"Yes, you have definitely grown up. You talk like a man is supposed to talk. No worries. I like that."

"Yeah, and you've grown and filled out in all the right places. I remember you being petite, nice, small ass. Now, country thick definitely fits you. Damn, you look sooooo fuckin' tasty! So, without wasting anymore time, like you've done with your ex-boo—"

"Come on now, Duke; you were doing so good. Don't turn me off. We're sooooo close," she replied, taking a small offense to his last comment.

"And we're gonna get even closer. I had to take a little shot at you; it isn't like I'm lying."

"No, you're right, you aren't lying, but still... Now isn't the time to badger a bitch about the past!"

"Listen, tomorrow ain't promised to a real nigga, so we need to enjoy and have fun with this experience, jokes included."

"Shhhhh, Duke. We've done too much talkin'. People are probably missing us. Put me on my back, so we can get back! And you can have one of the best nights of your life!"

Duke knew she was right. He pulled her into him and grabbed her hair, wrapping it in his hand. He pulled her neck back and kissed her, working his way down to her breasts. Candy was moaning and liking the roughness of a young nigga.

"That is what the fuck I'm talking about. Now I can call you The Duke for real," she said, feeling for his zipper. She felt the hardest dick she had felt in a long time, and it made her mouth water.

"You're The Duchess now, so please The Duke," he said, pushing her head down with force.

Candy opened her eyes as she released him, kissing the tip of his dick.

"Rub it in my face, in my hair, all over me!" she begged.

Duke was thinking, *'Damn, this bitch is a freak.'* He liked it, giving her exactly what she wanted.

"Duke, my pussy feels like Niagara Falls, babe."

"I've got that yacht you need. Time to do a little sailing," he said as he lifted her to her feet, not wanting to explode in her warm mouth.

Candy came from nowhere with a rubber and slipped in on him, rolling it down to the base of his dick. Duke lifted her off her feet as she straddled both legs in the crevices of his biceps.

"You got a ticket, babe?" he asked.

"A ticket for what?"

"This roller coaster you're about to ride," he responded as he eased her down on his dick with her still suspended in midair. Duke used his strength to bounce her up and down, while she ripped the skin off his shoulders each time he thrust her downward.

"Damn, your shit's big, babe. You're fuckin' me good!" she cried out.

That was all she was—a fuck. He wasn't going to make love to her, just fuck her and work off all the stress, like she'd said she would allow him to do. Duke turned her around, bending her over a little marble table that looked like it cost a fortune. Candy gripped the sides of the table as Duke entered her ass by mistake.

"BABE, YOU'RE TOO BIG FOR THAT!" she screamed.

Duke ignored her—not intentionally, but now his head was thinking about all he had gone through. The killing, being on the run, the streets talking and saying him and Bishop were worth twenty-five million dead to the FBI, Burcheck back at the house with his shit cracked opened, and the last thought, pulling the trigger to send his own father to meet his maker. He gripped her waist and busted her ass wide open. Candy screamed as her muscles loosened, allowing him to dig deeper.

"Oooohhhh shit... oh, muthafucka, this is it!" she said, with Duke not paying her any mind. Her fingernails were all white as she gripped the table, wishing she was strong enough to crush marble.

"Baby, you feel good. The Duke loves heaven... Oooohhhh shit... this dick's busting."

Duke finally collapsed on the leather couch next to the table. Candy was shaking, trying to regain her composure from what had just happened to her insides. She had fucked a lot of people in her lifetime, but no one had ever traveled to her inside destination like Duke had just done. She had come three times during his penetration. She made it to the couch next to Duke, rolling off the rubber.

"The Duke deserves a little bonus for that," she said, taking his dick in her mouth before it went soft.

She held his balls at the base of his dick, making his manhood rise back to attention. She deep throating it, until his ice cream slid down her cone-shaped throat.

When they had finished, he joined the rest of the crew, ignoring the fact that he had sweated his shirt out so badly. Duke knew she was putting on a show for what was in the briefcase; he didn't mind giving that poker change to a bitch with a royal flush. He'd played hard and it had worked. He'd felt relief for a few moments for the first time since he'd had popped his own father.

It was back to business for the brothers as soon as they left Candy's joint. The wolves had cleared and cleaned themselves of frustration and aggression, only to find their hunger for murder that much more intense. Bishop was thinking hard now. He knew, after tonight's experience, that he wanted more nights like that. He wanted his life back, and he felt it was time to put an end to the whole cat and mouse chase. Bishop was ready to get home to Kara, get Duke back to Sharelle, and leave New Jersey in his rearview. But to complete the last task of business, the first thing he had to do was make sure Burcheck was either with them or against them, knowing if he decided against them, his life would end very quickly.

Chapter Thirty-Five:
Tomorrow...Day Of Reckoning

Finally waking up, Burcheck felt a serious pounding and excruciating thunder flowing between his temples. His head felt like it was about to explode, making him wonder what Duke had clocked him with. Burcheck had a weak bladder and could feel his pants were wet in the front, letting him know he had been out longer than twenty-four hours. He was at a loss for time and didn't know it actually had been two days since he had been knocked out smooth.

Not knowing what to expect from the brothers since the last episode, he was wondering his fate with Bishop and Duke Evans. He had not encountered them since waking from his long sleep, but all that was about to change. Bishop kindly opened the door, playing and fumbling with his gun as he walked into the room. Burcheck wasn't sure, due to the stunt he had pulled, if Bishop was coming in peace or coming to unite the good detective with his wife. Whichever way it went, he was ready to face his consequences.

"Good midday, Detective. You've been sleep for a long time. How are you feeling? I'm quite sure you have a serious headache."

"Yes, my head is killing me, no pun intended," Burcheck replied.

"None taken."

"Okay, Bishop, whatever you're going to do, let's get this over with. I'm tired, if you know what I mean."

"Man, stop acting paranoid. Nobody really wants to hurt you," Bishop stated, knowing his little brother might feel differently.

"So, why are coming in here with your gun all out? Putting bullets in it like I'm a target at the gun range?" Burcheck asked, thinking it was his final moment.

"I was just making sure my shit was clean. I just picked it up," Bishop replied, easing Burcheck's mind for a second.

"Listen, it's time for you and me to get something straight, because I'm ready for all this bullshit to be over. I was serious when I said you would never see me and my brother again. I want you to get your life back and vice versa. But that's only if you don't have plans of locking me and Duke up in a cell. Now think very hard before responding. A lot is riding on what comes out your mouth next."

Burcheck understood that Bishop meant every word he'd spoke. He never really showed any facial expressions, but Burcheck had been around him long enough now to realize he didn't play, which made Bishop much more dangerous in his eyes. Burcheck knew from previous observations and experiences dealing with the brothers that his life truly depended on his response.

"Yes, with everything we've gone through the last few months or so, getting my life back and you and Duke leaving, I'm in absolute agreement with that idea. The question I have is like I said: With our circumstances, which include the deaths of multiple people, including an FBI agent, I'm just curious how do you expect to get around all that?" Burcheck questioned. He still was rubbing the knot on his head.

"Let me worry about that. All I need you to do is call this number I have, Agent Collins on speed dial. Just tell him what I tell you to tell him and arrange the meeting. Plus, since there's a twenty-five-million-dollar bounty on our heads, we aim to collect that reward. The evidence we hold now has a twenty-five-million-dollar price tag attached to it."

In the midst of strategizing his next move, Duke entered the room as Bishop spoke the last few words.

"A twenty-five-million-dollar price tag? That sounds like Mayweather money," Duke said, catching the tail end of the conversation. "Bro, what are we buying?" he asked, wondering what they were discussing.

"We aren't buying anything. It's more like what we're selling." Bishop smiled.

"Okay, what are we selling then?"

"The evidence. But hold up while me and the detective finish talking," Bishop asked of his little brother.

"So, what do you think, Detective?"

"Twenty-five million is a lot to ask for, Bishop. I'm not sure they would be able to account for that disbursement."

"Come on now, Detective, that's pocket change. These are government agents we're talking about. Do you hear yourself? And are you forgetting we have twenty-five million on our heads? Somebody got clearance for that disbursement."

"Again, you're right, but you still haven't told me how we're supposed to pull off this diabolical plan of yours." Burcheck was making motions like he was pulling a rabbit out of a hat.

"For starters, I'm going to give you Agent Collins' number. You are going to call him and arrange a meet, just him and you. Then, you are going to convince him to make an exchange, money for evidence. It's that simple," Bishop explained.

"And if he isn't onboard, then what?"

"Like I said, you're going to convince him. I think this deal is in the best interest of you both. If not, I will be forced to turn everything over to the mayor, media, and the Feds, including the footage of you killing the two bangers. See, Detective, the money isn't an issue. Me and my brother have enough cash to last us for the rest of our lives. After going through everything we've gone through, someone has to pay us. And you ain't got the money, do you?" Bishop sarcastically asked.

Bishop had stuck the dagger through Burcheck's heart when he mentioned the footage of him killing the bangers. He really didn't have a choice but to do what Bishop was asking. If he didn't, there was only one or two other choices in front of him: death by the Evans brothers or a life sentence in Rikers, where he'd put over one hundred criminals who would love to be his cellmate. His mind drifted back to him killing the bangers and the look he remembered that was on his face when he'd pulled the trigger. It was nothing but revenge and satisfaction. Burcheck really didn't have a choice.

"Okay, I will give it my best shot, Evans."

"Your best shot is your only shot, Detective."

"I understand. I'll convince him of everything you said," Burcheck replied, knowing people like Collins didn't play by the rules, even when their nuts were in a vice.

"And trust me, Detective, if anything happens to me or my brother, the plan will still go as planned."

"I'm nothing like you, Bishop. I just want my life back. I don't care about all that extra shit! The money, Agent Collins, all of this—I want no part of it. So, if I do this, do I get the footage?"

"You're just like me. That's why you want the footage. But, of course, I would say you've earned it." Bishop laughed.

"Okay then, let's get this over with," Burcheck said.

"We understand each other. Now, once you convince Agent Collins, give him this information: We are to meet at this place, at this time, and Detective, not one minute late."

Burcheck looked at the note Bishop handed him to give to Collins.

Tomorrow night, 7 o'clock

The Robert Treat Center, PH Suite 7930

He knew exactly where the location was and knew why Bishop had chosen that particular spot. Bishop asked Burcheck to excuse him and Duke for a moment. The two of them had to have a private conversation so Bishop could fill Duke in on the whole talk he'd had with the detective. While the two of them stepped out the room, one of the PA dudes entered, handing Burcheck a burner phone to use. They were practically untraceable, but to make sure, the PA dude had strict instructions to break the phone after Burcheck's call.

Ring-Ring-Ring

A strange, unknown number appeared on Collins' display screen. He had a pretty good idea who it was.

"Bishop, it's about time you called. I was beginning to think you'd forgotten about me," Collins playfully said.

"Good to know, but I'm not Bishop. Sorry to bust your bubble, Agent," Burcheck replied.

"Is this my friend, the good Detective Burcheck, who went rogue?"

"We are not and will never be considered friends, Agent."

"Awww, that breaks my heart. Not friends? So sad, Detective. I was hoping to find common ground between you and me somewhere, especially after everything is all said and done. Very disappointing."

"Listen, I'm not calling to play little games, Agent. Us going back and forth, talking slick to one another, is out. Too much blood has been shed. It's time to put an end to all this bullshit!"

"Awww, the detective no longer wants to play games with me. Now I'm really sad. I thought we'd go to the park, push each other on the swing set, and catch up on old times," Collins said, being an asshole.

"You're a son of a bitch, Collins. See, this is what the fuck I'm talking about. I'm not here for all this. We need to talk face to face. You, me, and no one else. I have something you want, but I assure you, if you don't follow the plan, you'll never get it."

"Okay, Detective, you've got my undivided attention. What do you suggest?"

"Adara, 77 Walnut Street, Montclair. Do you know where that is?" Burcheck asked, spitting out the location for the meeting.

"Of course; they have the best lamb chops in town. What time should I place our orders, Detective?"

"Let's say a half hour from now, and not a minute late! I suggest you take this seriously, as I think you know both of our lives depend on it."

"All right, but you're leaving the tip." Collins laughed.

"And again, Agent, come alone."

"I heard you the first time, Detective," Collins replied, and ended their call.

Bishop and Duke were right there, listening. Burcheck had done well so far. Bishop needed to stress the importance again to Burcheck on getting the agent to go for his plan. He knew it was the only way.

"It's in the best interests of everyone, especially you, Detective," Bishop repeated his words from earlier.

Duke was still a little uncertain about Burcheck, but he was rolling with his big brother's intuition, knowing it was what had gotten them this far. Everyone seemed as if their nerves were on edge, knowing their futures depended on the two cops making a deal. Bishop decided to send Darius along with Burcheck, telling him to stay close enough to detect any foul play. He trusted Burcheck slightly, but Collins was a different ball game. Bishop wanted everyone to get a good night's rest because tomorrow was going to be the day of reckoning.

While his whole crew slept, including Duke, sleep for Bishop was something he didn't have time for. He sat outside the safehouse, smoking a cigar he had gotten from 4'2 when he had first gone to see him. 4'2 knew he wasn't a real smoker, but when he'd told Bishop that particular cigar was his lucky victory cigar, Bishop had kindly accepted it. He blew a thick cloud of smoke in the air as he dialed the pilot's number, alerting him that they would be departing tomorrow. He couldn't wait to get the fuck out of there and back to Kara and his new life.

He made a cross with his finger from his forehead through his chest. He hoped it would be the last time he had to pray about this situation. The pilot told him any and everybody leaving with him had to be at the set-up location by 8:30.

––––––––––––––––––

Burcheck dressed for the day's occasion, with his service weapon in his holster and his throwaway piece strapped to his ankle. Duke tossed him another 40 Glock for his waistband.

"Never know, cop, you might need some extra firepower," Duke said.

"You're right, Evans, you just never know," Burcheck replied, glad it seemed the younger Evans brother had his best interests in mind.

"Be safe, and let's get this done," Bishop said, shaking the detective's hand and looking him straight in the eyes.

It was the first time since everything had been going on that Bishop didn't see fear in the good detective's eyes. He always figured Burcheck to be a good man, but even good men can seek revenge. That had been Bishop's whole angle in the first place.

Burcheck took a black Impala that was sitting out front, staying low-key. Darius was on his heels, making sure the good detective stayed on point. Burcheck was going to stick to Bishop's plan because he too wanted this whole ordeal to be over with. He was lost between retiring after this or staying on to complete his last four years before full retirement. He thought heavily about his wife and hoped like hell she was busy in heaven and didn't have time to look down on what he was doing today.

The thought of Agent Collins came to the front of his mind now. So far everything about Collins seemed shady, and Burcheck believed Collins would have killed him as well as the brothers. He prayed today was not the day for Collins to play hero. Burcheck couldn't help but hope Agent Collins didn't make the power of persuasion too difficult.

Arriving at the meeting spot, Detective Burcheck parked the Impala and headed into the restaurant. Five minutes later, Darius entered the restaurant wearing a straw hat and sunglasses to conceal his identity. He headed straight to the bar, in eyesight of Burcheck, while the detective grabbed a table. Noticing Agent Collins hadn't arrived yet, Burcheck felt the sweat building in the palms of his hands. The pair waited patiently, Burcheck not knowing Darius was there. Country Boy Darius ordered a few Jack and Cokes to ease his nerves while he waited for Collins.

Collins had never been good at following instructions, especially not from the criminals he was chasing. He stuck by the motto that the United States doesn't negotiate with terrorists, and to him, that was just what the Evans brothers were. He showed up ten minutes late and didn't care what Bishop or Burcheck had to say. He had to regain control, and following their directions to the letter would make it seem to his higher ups that he wasn't in control.

He strolled past Darius at the bar, none the wiser who he was, heading straight for Burcheck's corner table. Collins was a good-looking white man, with sandy brown hair, deep blue eyes, and Tom Cruise features. He was accompanied by the young officer who had burst in his office during the meeting. He also had not followed the order to come alone, but he had brought along someone who was expendable, in case things got out of order.

Scene Inside Adara...

"Damn, man! How did you ever climb the ladder in the bureau? You don't listen to directions. I guess this is why people keep dying around you, us. You insist on doing shit your way. I told you to come alone!" Burcheck said with an attitude.

"Man, shut the fuck up! I don't take orders, especially not from a low-ranking ass detective such as yourself," Collins replied, shocking the shit out of Burcheck.

"You talk that shit, you crooked son of a bitch, but if the circumstances were different and you spoke to me in that tone, I would've knocked you the fuck out!"

"I feel the same way, Detective. Only if the circumstances were different, you wouldn't have even made this meeting today," Collins assured him.

"Anyway, enough with the petty threats. I'm here to make sure you get your evidence back, but yet, you continue to play fuckin' games."

"Chump, dig this, you're fucking around in the big boy leagues, and neither of you have the slightest idea who you're fucking with."

"Well, Agent, you sound like Victor Maitland, which we know you aren't, and I damn sure ain't Axle Foley," Burcheck replied, wishing he could pop a cap in Collins' ass himself. "So, whatever you're on, fuck that! Let's get down to why we're here. It's about getting your evidence back."

"That is why I'm here, Detective," Collins said sarcastically.

"It's like this, Collins: The brothers want to bring this war to an end. Everyone, including me, wants to get back to their lives—you know, live normal lives again?"

"After all they've done, how the fuck do they expect to go back to their lives?" Collins asked, wanting to hear this for himself.

"I'm pretty sure we can figure this all out. You want your evidence back, right?"

"Absolutely! You're fucking finally saying something worth listening to, Detective."

"Okay then. These guys are talking about handing the evidence over to the media, Secret Service, and some very important people who aren't heard on these wiretaps. Honestly, I don't believe you want that to happen. No one on them wants that."

"Definitely not. That would mess everything up for everyone involved, including myself."

"You especially, since you seem to be the ringleader of all this bullshit."

"They sent you to speak on their behalf, huh, Detective? I take it these two miscreants have something on you as well."

"I have no idea what you're talking about, Agent; these boys have nothing on me," Burcheck lied. He wasn't going to expose his hand to a crooked Fed.

"Yeah, two bangers were killed in last week's slaughter at Kabirah's Massage Parlor. From the information I've gathered, the two bangers who were killed were the same two bangers who killed your wife. Now, that could be just a coincidence, but I don't believe in those," Collins said, watching Burcheck's face for any signs of guilt.

"Well, you guys need more reliable CI's. It's you they have everything on. Now we can go back and forth with assuming why I'm speaking on their behalf, but that way, I don't see the convo going anywhere. My only concern is trying to find a solution to the madness, so I can get back to my life. You know, I might even take a desk job after all of this." Burcheck cracked a smile.

"All right, Detective, let's just say, I believe what you're saying. How do I know I can trust them again? They made copies once before; how do I know they'll give me everything this time?" Collins asked, not willing to be played twice.

"I'm not really sure how to answer that question. The oldest brother hasn't really revealed that part to me yet. However, from what I did pick up off him, he does want to get back to his family, without looking over his shoulder, him or his brother. We will just have to trust that they mean what they're saying this time."

"Okay, I'm game; let's play ball by their rules. What else do the brothers propose?"

"See, it wasn't that hard! Now let's talk..."

The two lawmen went back and forth for over an hour, bickering over Bishop's demands. Collins thought Bishop had to be straight from the nut house, but he was left with no choice in the end. It wasn't his money anyway, and too many important people's careers and lives were at stake for him not to agree to the demands. He knew he couldn't go to jail for the rest of his life, and he also knew he wouldn't get a deal. Accepting the note Bishop had given Burcheck to give him, it was obviously the final quarter. He had his hockey stick ready to bust one last time at the goalie. He pictured Bishop in the goalie box, trying to stop him from scoring. Collins laughed out loud and Burcheck thought the man sitting across from him was a motherfucking fool.

"Collins, I don't know what you find so funny, but once again, try to follow instructions this time. Come alone. These boys aren't to be fucked with, trust me," Burcheck said, rubbing the knot on his head from where Duke had let him have it.

"I'll try, Detective. I can't really promise you anything," he replied, finding Burcheck's statement a little humorous.

Collins wiped his mouth after taking his last bite of the famous lamb chops. He stood and gave Burcheck a look that said, I'll see you soon. Everyone wanted their lives back, even Collins, but trust between the parties had a liability attached to it that was highly likely to go bad.

"I shall be seeing you soon, Detective."

"Hope not," Burcheck replied, watching Collins walk out, leaving him with the bill.

Burcheck knew if the Evans boys had their way, they would kill Collins in a heartbeat. Burcheck also knew Collins had a mutual feeling flowing through his crooked heart. He sat there for a second, wondering just how many dirty cops had taken the oath. He was unsure of that answer, but he knew one for sure: Agent Collins. He wished he could lock them all up for the rest of their natural lives. Burcheck would have liked nothing more than to see Collins and Bishop playing chess on the yard of some prison. He thought about the money and wondered if Collins was going to produce it. He also wondered if things would have been easier had Bishop not requested the money.

'What the fuck are you up to Evans?' Burcheck thought as he paid the waitress for the meal, not tipping her.

Burcheck headed to the Impala to call Bishop, walking right past Darius, who gulped his last drink down and left a hundred-dollar bill on the bar.

"So, how good did you do at convincing the corrupt agent to agree to my proposal, Detective?" Bishop asked when he answered.

"He's onboard. Everyone involved seems to all want the same thing— their lives back," Burcheck replied, crossing his fingers and hoping Collins really was onboard.

"How about the money?"

"Money included. His only issue was, how does he know you won't make copies again?"

"He doesn't. A leap of faith is what both of you are taking. I never wanted these problems from the beginning. When the bag was delivered to me, I didn't know what it contained. Just so happened, it had my brother's and my freedom inside it," Bishop explained.

"Delivered to you by whom?" Burcheck asked, curious as to how Evans had come across such important evidence that could send away so many very important people.

"Who delivered the bag doesn't matter. This isn't the time to be playing cop. What does matter is this bag has brought me nothing but aggravation. The only reason I've kept hold of it for so long was because it was my only leverage. I'm ready to rid myself of this bad luck."

"Well, I hope so. Because the agent seems to want it badly, especially if he's willing to exchange twenty-five million for it. It was like you said, he's a government official. The money is nothing for him to obtain. He must not be the only one who wants this evidence so badly."

"As I told you before, Detective, you're correct; he isn't the only one," Bishop said, turning to his brother.

"Bro, you can't go with us to make this exchange," Bishop said.

"What?! You're crazy as hell! I'm not letting you go alone!" Duke replied, mad that Bishop would even contemplate going on a mission of such high importance without him.

"Dig, I won't be alone. I'll have the good detective, a few Mexicans, and the PA dudes coming along with me."

"Nigga, fuck that! I'm going!"

"I *said*, you aren't going. Now, you can try to fight me on this if you want, but I see no win in sight for you."

"Whatever, nigga; we'll see!"

"Yes, we will see."

"Okay, say no more!" Duke angrily replied.

"Listen, bro, I'm not trying to leave things this way. It's important that you wait on the jet, make sure things are ready once I'm done with the exchange. Fuel, the pilot is on point, and all the necessary arrangements need to be in proper order. I need you to handle that part."

"Nigga, who the fuck do you think I am? You can have one of these other niggas do that shit! I'm not ya fuckin' errand boy. We'll see in a few hours if I'm going or not."

"That's what's up," Bishop said, knowing it was going to be like chewing a well-done steak with no teeth.

Duke was down for action, especially if the action could claim the life of his brother. He stormed out the room, using all the bad language he had in his vocabulary and tossing shit around. Burcheck was listening and decided to put in his two cents.

"You need your brother by your side. Why would you leave him behind all of sudden?" Burcheck wondered. He knew Duke was a straight up killer and a ride or die when it came to his only brother.

"This isn't any of your business, Detective. But if you must know, yeah, it may seem sudden, but it isn't. You and I both know how reckless he is, and I'm trying to be done with all this shit. Bringing him along would only make things worse than what they are. I don't want anything to go wrong. But, if in any event, things don't go as planned, then I have dudes coming with me, including you, to watch my back."

"Still, that's your brother and you know how he is over you. He wants to be there when everything transpires."

"Again, Detective, it isn't any of your business. I don't owe you or anyone else an explanation. That's my muthafuckin brother and *I am* his fuckin'keeper," Bishop replied.

Burcheck had grown up an only child and had never had love like this before. He tried to understand both sides, but Bishop was right, it really was none of his business.

"I understand, Bishop. I'm done with the matter. I would have wanted to see Duke by your side to the end, that's all."

"And you can bet your pension, if you get one, Detective, he will be by my side to the end. *The end!*"

As both groups geared up for battle, they were expecting everything to go off without anyone getting killed, which was totally a stretch from the truth. Agent Collins had arranged to get the money to exchange for the evidence. While Bishop, on the other hand, was preparing for him and Duke to unite with their family in Arizona—that was if the brothers survived what lay ahead. Burcheck was sitting back, reflecting on the past few months of his life, nervously excited to get away from the crazy brothers. He also looked forward to uniting with whatever family he had.

Ordering his seven-man crew to pack up the truck so they could roll out, Bishop was ready. It was getting close to show time and the show must go on. Four PA shooters and three crazy ass Mexicans—no Duke, no Country Boys, but Burcheck was riding along for the extra manpower. Bishop figured this should be a walk in the park, as everybody involved wanted solutions instead of death.

Chapter Thirty-Six:
The Big Showdown

Bishop had used the Country Boys' bulletproof Excursion for the last and final showdown. He rode in the second row of seats behind Burcheck, who sat in the front. The rest of his people were in another bulletproof car right behind them.

"Text Agent Collins with different instructions. Let him know the meeting spot is still in the Robert Treat, but no longer in Suite 7390. Tell him to meet us in the ballroom on the third floor," Bishop said to the detective.

"Why are we changing the meeting spot?" Burcheck asked.

"Because we wanna be able to see everything and everyone coming and going. The suite doesn't have that luxury. There's only one way out, and I don't trust that agent. I thought you were a cop." Bishop smiled.

"I understand very well. Very smart thinking. Good thing we left your brother behind. Who knows what might happen if he had come with us."

"I know, Detective; that's why someone has to always be the thinker."

"Definitely. and the text is sent," Burcheck said, looking at his phone.

The green dot told him Collins had looked at the text message. Everyone in the truck was cleaning their guns, making sure they were in perfect firing mode. Small talk continued until they reached their destination, just a few blocks away. Bishop could see there was a little event going on in the Center, which they observed for a few minutes for precautionary purposes. He had reserved the ballroom under a bogus name, so he was sure they would at least have that spot all to themselves. They pulled close to the front door, allowing a few of his guys to get out first. They checked around the area to make sure things were safe before signaling the coast was clear.

Bishop exited the vehicle with the wind blowing his jacket, making it look like he was playing the lead role in an action movie. In one hand, he carried a duffel bag containing the evidence; his other hand gripped his piece. Burcheck was right beside him, gripping his piece and keeping a watchful eye for anything or anyone suspicious. They all strolled into the Center as if they were part of the festivities.

Inside The Robert Treat Ballroom...

Setting up directly in front of the stage, which was located further to the back, Agent Collins entered the ballroom followed by eight-to-ten gangbangers, two local cops, and an arrogant smile minutes after their arrival—a smile that said, I told you, Detective, I couldn't promise you anything. Guns were instantly drawn by everyone. The last two bangers closed the ballroom doors behind them. Bishop noticed Agent Collins had brought the money and calmed everyone down, who were all talking and screaming at once.

"Hold up! Hold up! We aren't here for this. You-niggas need to lower y'all's guns," Bishop said.

"Mr. Evans, you're still giving orders, I see," Collins said.

"Listen, nigga! You aren't running shit around here. We're looking for the muthafuckas responsible for killing our homie," the new leader of the bangers interjected.

"Dig, we can deal with this one of two ways, and the second way, everyone is dying. One is optional," Bishop replied as he surveyed the room. Every man in there had a gun drawn down on someone.

"Now we can handle the business we came to handle and deal with the shit with your homies at a later time and date. It's y'all's choice. However, you see it, I'm definitely the muthafucka responsible for killing your homies," Bishop admitted to Collins' surprise.

"Hold up, not yet. He and I have some urgent matters we have to deal with before anyone dies. I believe this matter pertains to y'all too. One reason I brought you bangers along is we're going to kill two birds with one stone," Collins replied.

Bishop had hoped he would keep business on the level, but he had known it was going to be hard to trust a sheisty cop.

"I knew I shouldn't have trusted your corrupt ass, Collins! I'd thought we would be able to conduct business and everyone go their own way, and I thought that was what you actually wanted."

"I did, but you killed too many of my men, not to mention a lot of their guys, Bishop. Shit like that doesn't sit well with me. Allowing you to walk away is a hard pill to swallow. Now as far as the rest of you guys go, feel free to leave with y'all's lives. And, Detective, you can also leave with your life."

"Listen, I'm not sure what book you read before coming here that said Ms. Evans' son was dying tonight, but you've got me fucked up, partna," Bishop spat.

As the two went on with what was going to happen next, everyone looked on expecting the unexpected. Agent Collins was carrying a duffel bag filled with the money that was supposed to be for the exchange.

"Here I thought, we would be exchanging this fifty million dollars for the evidence," Collins said, adding an extra twenty-five million to the equation.

Bishop looked at the detective then back at Collins, wondering what type of shit he was trying to pull.

"Fifty million dollars? I thought it was supposed to be twenty-five million."

"Oh, someone wasn't being honest? Tell me it ain't so, Detective?" Collins said, knowing now Burcheck had tampered with the note.

"Hey, what the hell!" Burcheck said, turning his gun on Bishop. "What the fuck! I figured since everyone else was taking a piece of the pie, why not get my own cake? I believe for everything I've been through, including losing my wife, fifty million was reasonable."

"So, you had plans to take all the money, huh?" Bishop asked.

"Come on, Bishop, you're supposed to be the smart one, remember? I believe you're the one who's always ten steps ahead of everyone else. Isn't that your motto?" Burcheck said smiling, thinking he had finally gotten the Evans boys where he wanted them.

"Yeah, you got me on this one, Detective," Bishop said, smiling sarcastically.

"That was the reason I tried talking you into allowing your brother to come along for the ride. I wanted to put a bullet right between his fucking eyes. But noooo, you had to play big brother. You know what? All that being my brother's keeper shit can get very old fast," Burcheck said, knowing Duke still had to be dealt with. He knew the little brother wouldn't rest if Bishop was killed.

"So, I wasn't wrong about you, Detective? Money seems to change a person. I mean, it is human nature, look at Trump, the Kardashians—hell, one of them even had a sex change. Money is the root to all evil, Detective. Welcome to the dark side," Collins commented.

"Say whatever you want, Agent, but I need to retire comfortably. You may call it the dark side, but it's more like the force is with me. I can buy myself a boat, retire, move to Pittsburgh, and fish the rest of my life away," Burcheck said, sounding as if he had his plan all worked out.

"You muthafuckas ain't shit. I knew I should've let my brother kill your bitch ass," Bishop said.

"You should have, but all that is behind us. Let's start this transaction. I have a life to get to," Burcheck announced.

"Now you're talking, Detective. Pass that bag over here if you don't mind," Collins said, asking the detective to take the bag containing the evidence from Bishop.

"It ain't that type of party. You pass your bag first in my direction," Burcheck replied.

Bishop and his seven-man crew had their guns drawn, thinking the odds were against them. The more everyone spoke, the more intense the shit got. One shot had the potential to erupt into something disastrous. The detective looked over at Bishop, shaking his head.

"I was just starting to like you, Bishop. It's your crazy ass brother I can't stand. I wish he was here now. I would love to have shot him and had you watch him bleed out."

"Detective, be careful what you ask for. I thought you knew me better than this. I always stay ten steps ahead of you, babe," Bishop replied, winking his right eye at the rogue detective who was now showing his true colors.

Right on cue, Duke and the Country Boys darted out from the direction of the stage where they had been all along, watching the whole scenario and awaiting the green light to go. Bishop's cue was the winking of his right eye. Guns started firing from every angle of the ballroom, catching the bangers and agents off guard. Bullets were flying everywhere into the chest of the bangers, opening them up like smashed cantaloupe. Bullets hit both of the cops with Agent Collins and they died on impact. Some of Bishop's crew members also were hit as the bullets ripped their bodies apart as well. Bishop saw Collins and Burcheck trying to make a run for it and yelled out to Duke.

"I'VE GOT THE AGENT! THE DETECTIVE IS ALL YOURS, BRO."

"SAY LESS; I GOT HIM!" Duke replied, licking his lips.

In his heart, he had known they could never trust Burcheck as far as they could see him. Something about the cop had never sat right with Duke, even when he had murdered the bangers in the massage parlor. He just had a look in his eye like he was a double crossing muthafucka, and this day had told the story and would also seal Burcheck's fate. He was going to be with his wife, if Duke had any say so about it.

It was a bloodbath in the ballroom as Bishop could hear fewer shots. He saw one of the Country Boys had taken a bullet, but he wasn't dead. He yelled to Darius to grab the bag. The bag he wanted was the one Agent Collins was trying to escape with.

"GRAB THE BAG! GRAB THE BAG!" he yelled.

"I'M GOING AFTER THE AGENT! HE STILL HAS THE MONEY," Bishop continued as Darius signaled back.

Darius had just let off two shots that had landed in the middle of two bangers' foreheads, sending them buckling over backwards. His younger brother was closest to the evidence bag. Hearing the exchange between Bishop and Darius, he was right on top of things.

"I GOT IT, BRO," he said, holding up the bag just as a bullet ripped through his right arm, blowing half of it across the room.

Darius saw the banger who had taken the shot and sent half a clip in his direction, riddling him full of hot lead and sending him to his death instantly. He rushed over and helped his little brother to safety, grabbing both him and the bag.

The chase continued for several minutes, running through room after room throughout the Robert Treat. They ended up in a much-different ballroom, which was dark, quiet, and with no way out other than through Bishop.

"There's no way out, Agent. Give me the money and I'll think about letting you live," Bishop said, knowing the agent was stuck.

"That's funny, Evans. I was just thinking the same thing," he replied, hiding behind a fixture and looking to see if he could get a shot off.

The two stopped talking and the hunt for each other's soul became strategic, making both of them fair game. Moving through the dark, both men were breathing heavily, leaving Bishop to think the first thing he needed to do when he made it to Arizona was get back in the gym.

Agent Collins saw Bishop's shadow from a nightlight in a socket and got off a shot, hitting him in the shoulder. Bishop fell, tossing his second gun on the floor purposely. Agent Collins smiled when he called out Bishop's name and heard no response. Thinking he had finished the brother off, he looked at Bishop lying motionless, face down on the ballroom floor. He didn't see the bag with the evidence, but that was neither here nor there. Walking slowly over to make sure Bishop was dead, he checked his clip and his gun still had two shots to fire. He was going to put them in Evans head for good measure. Collins kicked the back of Bishop's foot knowing it was finally over for the man who had thought he was smarter than the law.

"Damn you, Evans, you made my fuckin' job harder than it should be," Collins said, expecting he was talking to a dead man. He then turned the motionless body over, wanting to look into the face of Evans when he put his last two in his head.

"You're a dumb kid, Evans, probably the dumbest I've ever encountered," Collins said.

He thought about it and didn't want to explain to IA the extra bullets he was thinking about putting in Evans, so he holstered his gun. In a split second, he noticed Bishop was still alive and reached to retrieve his pistol. Bishop fired a barrage of bullets, every single one striking Agent Collins directly in the face. He was dead before his body hit the floor.

"I'm not that dumb!" Bishop said, getting to his feet.

Bishop was grabbing parts of his body where he had been struck, snatching off the bulletproof vest. The heat was a little much for his skin. He then quickly picked up the bag of money. Bishop had to go find his little brother. They had a plane to catch and a lot of money to spend.

Duke was hot on Burcheck's trail. It surprised him the old man could move as swiftly as he did. They ran through the lobby, out the back through the garbage area, and finally ended up behind the Center in an alley.

"I thought this is what you wanted, Detective. Mr. Crazy is here! I'm here, muthafucka. Come out and get yourself some," Duke said, letting the detective know he had heard the threat he'd made moments ago.

"In due time, in due time!" Burcheck's reply echoed off the building, not giving his exact whereabouts.

Burcheck let off a shot and Duke fired in the area his shots had come from. Shots went back and forth for two clips, but no one was hit. Death between the two would be determined by who got the drop on whom first. Duke heard footsteps splash in a puddle of stinking garbage water. Burcheck had made his move, running through the alley, dipping and dodging obstacles. Duke was firing in his direction, hearing his bullets deflecting off things, but not hitting his target yet.

"Come on, Detective. It shouldn't be that hard to hit me. I'm just a nigga from the hood, and you're a cop, for God's sake," Duke said as Burcheck tried to return fire over his shoulder.

"You know what, you're right," Burcheck said, sending five quick shots. Two of the five struck Duke in the stomach and shoulder. He returned fire, hitting Burcheck in the right leg and stomach. Duke was losing blood, and just like the last time he had been hit, he was slipping out of consciousness.

"Come on, you're The Duke! You can take this muthafucka," Duke said silently to himself.

He had dropped his gun and so had Burcheck as the two were fighting to breathe. Both men were in a dark, wet alley, crawling and reaching for their guns in hopes of killing the other. Burcheck was an arm's length away from his service revolver. Just as he was about to grab it and end the life of the man, he deemed a low-life ghetto punk, his gun seemed to have come to life and skittered across the alley, too far for him to reach. He rolled over and looked up into the face of Bishop Evans.

Not able to really move from the pain, Bishop knew Burcheck wasn't going anywhere. Bishop quickly stuffed a rag in his mouth to keep him quiet while he lay there wincing so he could go over and check how bad Duke's injuries were:

"How bad are you hit?" Bishop asked, hearing Duke hiss from the pain.

"Nigga, I'm Gucci. This shit ain't about nothing. I'm going to live, just a few flesh wounds. We played him, didn't we?" Duke said, reaching out to his big brother.

"Yeah, bro. Arguing with one another in front of him sold the plan. He really believed, that at the most important moment of our lives, I wouldn't have my brother riding with me? Yeah, right! They think we're stupid!" Bishop laughed.

"I know, right?! Help me to my feet so I can finish this nigga," Duke said, taking Bishop's hand in his. "Good lookin', my G," Duke said as he wrapped his arm around Bishop's shoulder.

Bishop helped him hobble over to Burcheck, who was lying on his back, looking into the dark sky between the buildings. He was whispering something neither Duke nor Bishop could make out.

"Take me over there to that muthafucka. Time to put his lights out for good, dirty muthafucka," Duke said.

"I guess I am, Detective..." Bishop said, not being clear what he meant.

"You guess you're what, Bishop?" Burcheck asked, holding his stomach. Blood was seeping between his fingers and his eyes were almost closed.

"I guess I am the smart one."

"And I'm the crazy one!" Duke said, reloading his gun.

"Detective, let me say this: I am sorry you lost your wife, but you picked the wrong two niggas to try to pin it on. Now I'm going to do this favor, and it's for her. You'll be able to kiss that bitch in a few minutes...unless the devil comes for you."

Bang! Bang! Bang! Bang! Bang! Bang!

Duke emptied his clip into the body of the detective, leaving blood now spewing from his mouth and nostrils. The brothers hugged and smiled at each other.

"It's over, bro."

"Yeah, over. Now, don't we have a jet to catch?"

"Damn right! Now let's go home," Bishop replied.

Epilogue

A Couple of Months Later...

4"2' and Bishop were out on his fishing boat, smoking cigars and drinking tequila. The bobber on 4'2's line went all the way under the water, and he realized there was something big on his line.

"Bishop, I got something," he said, almost slipping in his sandals.

Bishop grabbed the line, and together they reeled in the largest bass any of them had ever seen. Duke and Sharelle were in the lower bunk area having sex. When his wounds had healed up enough, they'd fucked nonstop two or three times a day.

Bishop's phone started ringing, and he checked the number to see it was Darius. He answered before it went to voicemail.

"What it do, brother?" Bishop asked.

"Maaaaan, you tell me. We're down here on the farm, just checking out the new shipment of weapons. I was just calling to check on you," Darius replied.

"I'm good. We're out on the blue ocean, doing a little fishing," Bishop replied.

"Well, did you ask your man yet?" Darius asked.

"Not yet, but today is the day."

"One! Brother, I miss you man, but we will be out there soon. Little bro's got a new arm, and he's doing good. Nigga's mad because he now has to learn to shoot with his left, but other than that, we're all good."

"Glad to hear things are good. I will keep you posted, bro. Let me get back to this task." Bishop laughed.

They ended the call, and Bishop went and stood next to 4"2', who was looking at the first fish he'd ever caught.

"I've got a question for you?" Bishop said, passing 4"2' a lighter to relight his cigar.

"Listen, Bishop, you don't need my permission to marry Kara. Go for it!" 4'2 replied, with Bishop not knowing how the hell he'd known what he was going to say.

"How do you always know what's on my mind before I say it?" Bishop asked curiously.

"You don't make it this far in the game if you aren't a wise man," 4'2 replied.

Just then Duke came from the lower area, wearing only a pair of shorts and sweating like he'd just run a mile.

"HEY FELLAS, GUESS WHAT!?" he shouted, getting their attention.

Bishop and 4'2 looked in Duke's direction as if to ask, *What?*

"THERE'S GOING TO BE A WEDDING!" Duke replied, tilting a bottle of Ace of Spades to his lips.

"TELL US SOMETHING WE DON'T KNOW!" Bishop yelled back at his little brother, smiling from ear to ear.

Two Years Later...

It had been over two years since the vicious war between Bishop, Duke, the gang bangers, local police, and FBI agents. Thing is, no one actually knew what the war was about other than the select few who had roles to play. The brother's survival became a myth in the hood. Whatever happened to them, no one really knew. The only thing everyone acknowledged, was that the brothers left behind a slew of bodies everywhere.

Whether or not the streets knew, or cared, about what prompted the war between the brothers and Newark's corrupted figures, it didn't matter. All society knew was that their behaviors and actions were justified and it resulted in a greater door of opportunities opening for the next ballers, pimps – or the next group of corrupt political figures with false agendas. They always seemed to have plans benefiting off of what the brothers set forth.

Therefore, it was time for a different, elite group of individuals to take their place among Newark's history...

www.ingramcontent.com/pod-product-compliance
Lightning Source LLC
Chambersburg PA
CBHW060944030726
47503CB00003B/719